G000256835

IRISH GHOST STORIES

IRISH
GHOST STORIES

Selected and introduced by
DAVID STUART DAVIES

MACMILLAN COLLECTOR'S LIBRARY

This edition first published by Collector's Library 2010

Reissued by Macmillan Collector's Library 2016
an imprint of Pan Macmillan
20 New Wharf Road, London N1 9RR
Associated companies throughout the world
www.panmacmillan.com

ISBN 978-1-5098-2661-2

5 7 9 8 6

A CIP catalogue record for this book is available from the British Library.

Casing design and endpaper pattern by Andrew Davidson
Typeset by Antony Gray
Printed and bound in China by Imago

INTRODUCTION

The Irish writer is ideally suited to creating stories of strange ghostly happenings. At his best the Irish writer has a wild and fantastical imagination causing him to view life though a wonderfully strange distorting mirror. There is something dream-like and unfettered about the Irish creative force which enables these storytellers to travel down different roads from those of other authors; roads which are bizarre, challenging and eccentric in nature, allowing the Irish scribe to conjure up unexpected and often fantastic scenarios. This flavour can be found in the works of such Irish literary giants as Oscar Wilde, W. B. Yeats, George Bernard Shaw, Samuel Beckett, James Joyce, Spike Milligan, Sheridan Le Fanu and Bram Stoker. Not all wrote ghost stories, of course, but all created fictional works which challenged the imagination and took it to stranger places than it was normally allowed to go – the defining ability of a good ghost-story writer.

This is a collection of some of the best ghost tales created by writers who were not only born in Ireland but also inherited that wild and fantastical imagination I referred to earlier. This volume is like a treatise in the art of raising goose pimples.

Let us consider some of the contributors to this heady brew. It is appropriate to begin with Sheridan Le Fanu, whose stories fill half this volume. His work was held in great esteem by that doyen of the macabre narrative Montague Rhodes James. He wrote of Le Fanu:

> He stands absolutely in the first rank as a writer of ghost stories . . . Nobody sets the scene better than he, nobody touches in the effective detail more deftly.

SHERIDAN LE FANU (1814–73) was born in 1814 into a middle-class Dublin family of Huguenot descent. He was educated at Trinity College, Dublin, and though he was later called to the bar he never practised law; instead he turned his attention towards journalism and later fiction. In 1869 he became editor and proprietor of the *Dublin University Magazine*, which in time became a rich repository for horror fiction and ghost stories, many written by himself and often uncredited. The sudden death of his wife in 1858 turned him into an eccentric recluse who wrote his ghost stories in bed. He died of a heart attack in 1873. While he was a popular author for more than twenty years, producing such successful novels as *The House by the Churchyard* and *Uncle Silas*, after his death his work was neglected, especially his supernatural fiction. It was not until 1923 when M. R. James, whose literary style and subject matter were heavily influenced by Le Fanu, was responsible for promoting his stories by editing and providing an astute and illuminating introduction to a collection entitled *Madam Crowl's Ghost and Other Stories* that Le Fanu's work was appreciated more widely. It is now regarded as a landmark publication. In it, James, through meticulous research, was able to present many of Le Fanu's obscure and originally unsigned narratives to the reading public. The collection's title story along with five other tales, 'Squire Toby's Will', 'The Child that went with the Fairies', 'An Account of Some Strange Disturbances in Aungier Street', 'Ghost Stories of Chapelizod' and 'The Vision of Tom Chuff', are presented in these pages.

These tales were written when the ghost story as a genre was slowly developing into a more literary style of fiction. Many of the early examples of the form had used ghosts as a means of preaching a moral or effecting a change in the mortal who had encountered the spirit from the grave. Dickens was a great exponent of this approach. His *A Christmas Carol* is a fine example, but not the author's only one, of this use of spirits as a chastising force rather than as an entity to frighten for its own sake or to fulfil an even more sinister purpose. However, shortly before his death Dickens did pen a ghost story, 'The Signalman', which was dark and chilling without any moralistic or Gothic trappings. It was frightening in itself, involving a haunting which was created to chill the reader as well as the characters within the tale. However, Le Fanu was already practising this approach and, in fact, in a quiet fashion he developed and refined it. Le Fanu insisted above all else on unity of mood and economy of means in telling his ghostly yarns – a very modern approach for a Victorian writer. His stories are chilling because they draw you into the narrative in an insidious fashion by initiating and then escalating an atmosphere of unease.

E. F. BENSON (1867–1940), another great ghost-story writer, observed rather flamboyantly that Le Fanu's tales 'begin quietly enough, the tentacles of terror are applied so softly that the reader hardly notices them till they are sucking the courage from his blood. A darkness gathers, like dusk gently falling, and then something obscurely stirs in it.'

Part of Le Fanu's success is due to his ability to desist from using the usual props of the traditional ghost story, the Gothic paraphernalia: the haunted castle, the moonlit ruin, the saturnine villain and the distressed lady alone in some Godforsaken spot. He tended to set his tales in surroundings that would be familiar to the average middle-class reader, thus giving the narratives an uncomfortable immediacy.

The autobiographical style of 'Madam Crowl's Ghost', in which the author adopts not only the persona of an old woman remembering a strange incident from her past, but also her quaint peasant Irish tongue in which to tell it, is a clear example of Le Fanu using realism to sharpen the supernatural edge to the narrative. The domestic detail early on, especially when the young child is teased and patronised by the adults, and the general tone of an oral history, make the whole narrative more believable, gracing it with an air of verisimilitude. The plot is a simple one, but it is wrought with such cunning and care that the climactic scenes – the appearance of the ghost and the discovery of Madam Crowl's secret – are genuinely frightening because in some strange way one can accept them as true.

It is interesting to contrast this story and the telling of it with the next in the collection, 'Squire Toby's Will', which is related in elegant and sophisticated prose, interposed with realistic dialogue. Using his own knowledge of the law, Le Fanu creates a tale of sibling rivalry tinged with a blossoming strangeness which slowly through the course of the story grows into a chilling account of filial retribution from beyond the grave. It is typical of Le Fanu's slow-burn technique that the reader is almost surprised to discover that he has become unnerved by events related in the narrative.

The stories present a blatant acceptance of the unexplained – the supernatural, if you like. There are no pat excuses or explanations to tidy up the events. They all involve instances where the unknown is an accepted fact. But Le Fanu's cleverness lies in his ability to blur the distinction between reality and the supernatural, making both equally real by presenting his ghost scenes as so psychologically convincing that the materiality or immateriality of the invading presence becomes irrelevant.

Perhaps the clearest statement, if the most paranoid, that we get concerning the reality of the supernatural is in one of his most famous tales, 'An Account of Some Strange Disturbances in Aungier Street'. The title reads like that of a learned thesis and yet the account involves an infernal presence in a house which appears as a 'monstrous grey rat'. The narrator submits to the 'materialism of medicine' and takes a tonic to dispel his 'infernal illusion'. This works for a while, suggesting that perhaps this gruesome vision was conjured simply by an overwrought imagination and a fevered brain. However, by subliminal means, Le Fanu has already convinced the reader that the apparition is 'real' and so we realise before the narrator that medicine will not fend off this reality for long. And sure enough, the rat returns! Le Fanu's narrator assures us that even during the calm period 'the fiend was just as energetic, just as malignant, though I saw him not'.

WILLIAM BUTLER YEATS (1865–1939) not only wrote supernatural fiction but he was a believer in the 'other world'. Along with ghost-story writers Algernon Blackwood and Arthur Machen, he was a member of the Hermetic Order of Golden Dawn, a secret occult society which according to some accounts practised alchemy and magic. His fascination with the supernatural led him to conduct a long series of experiments into automatic writing with his wife, who he believed was in touch with the spirit world.

However, it was during his friendship with Oscar Wilde in the 1890s that Yeats wrote most of the supernatural fiction which James Joyce regarded as tales of 'fantastic terror' and 'the beauty that is beyond the grave'. There are two examples of these works presented in this volume. 'Hanrahan's Vision' and 'The Curse of the Fires of the Shadows' are both atmospheric pieces, the ghosts having historical relevance to the history of Ireland. In 'Vision' we encounter the shades of Dervongilla and Diarmuid, whose sin we are told 'brought the Norman into Ireland' in 1169, thus laying the foundations for eight centuries of Anglo-Irish conflict. 'The Curse' retells the legend surrounding the burning of Sligo Abbey in 1642 by Puritan soldiers and the curse placed upon them by the abbot of the White Friars before dying.

The two other most celebrated authors in this collection are BRAM STOKER (1847–1912) and OSCAR WILDE (1854–1900). Stoker, of course, was the author of the ground-breaking vampire classic *Dracula*, but he also penned several highly effective short tales in the supernatural genre. Perhaps the more chilling of the two tales selected for this edition is 'The Judge's

House'. The notion of a revenging judge represented by the figure of a rat and a strange hanging is similar to that found in Le Fanu's story, 'An Account of Some Strange Disturbances in Aungier Street'. However, while the Le Fanu piece has the charm and the gentle chill of the Victorian ghost story, 'The Judge's House' has a more direct visceral force and a modern theatricality which takes it into the realm of horror fiction. Stoker's tale has a gruesome and fascinating inevitability about it which makes it a gripping read. We can see that in the recounting of the events which take place in the haunted chamber in 'The Judge's House' Stoker's dramatic style looks forward to the kind of supernatural fiction created by the twentieth-century masters rather than harking back to his earlier literary influences.

The second of Stoker's stories, 'The Secret of Growing Gold', may well have been inspired by the exhumation of the poet Dante Gabriel Rossetti's wife, Elizabeth Siddal. On her death Rossetti had buried the only copies of his unpublished poems in the coffin with his beloved wife. Seven years later, in 1869, Rossetti ordered an exhumation to recover the notebook. When the coffin was opened it is said that her hair was still golden and growing. A friend of Stoker was shown some of the hair which was recovered from the perfectly preserved body. It was fine and lustrous as though it had been cut from a living head. This macabre account prompted Stoker to create his story of haunting and revenge from beyond the grave.

At first glance Wilde's 'The Canterville Ghost' is a frivolous light-hearted piece concerning a hapless spirit's attempts to haunt a stately home. Particularly in the early stages of the story the style is very modern,

filled with Wilde's native Irish whimsy and peppered
with witticisms. However the story grows darker and
more serious towards its climax and it is ultimately
a tale of morality, extolling the virtues of Love. In
typical Wildean fashion, Beauty and Fidelity triumph
over the darker forces.

CHARLOTTE RIDDELL (1832–1906), who wrote as
Mrs J. H. Riddell, is not an author well known to the
modern reader, but contemporary reviewers placed
her on the same level as Sheridan Le Fanu. Why she
is now forgotten by all but those familiar with the
ghost-story genre is a mystery in itself. It is certainly
not because she wrote so little. She was the author of
well over forty novels and numerous short stories.
The two tales chosen for this volume demonstrate
effectively that she was a fine exponent of the art of
chilling the reader.

Riddell was adept at creating a sense of place,
especially when involving an old building which in
essence becomes one of the characters in the story.
For example, in 'The Old House in Vauxhall Walk'
the titular property is described thus:

'It's a fine house,' answered William, raking the
embers together as he spoke and throwing some
wood upon them; 'but, like many a good family, it
has come down in the world.'

Of course, the house, which is so beautifully and
expertly described in its neglect and decay, harbours
ghostly secrets and horrors.

Again, in 'A Strange Christmas Game' – a wonderfully conceived and executed short ghost story – a
crumbling old house is the scene of a strange and

revelatory haunting which provides the new tenant of the Martingdale Estate with the explanation as to why the previous owner, a distant relative of his, disappeared without trace on a Christmas Eve many years before. The surprising twist at the end adds extra pleasure and polish to this satisfying story.

No doubt FITZ-JAMES O'BRIEN (1828–1862) would be more well known had he not died at such an early age fighting in the American Civil War. He was born Michael O'Brien in County Cork. After his time at Dublin University, where he showed an aptitude for writing verse, he moved to London to pursue a career in journalism. This eventually took him to America, where he changed his name to the more distinguished Fitz-James O'Brien. His stories showed great imaginative flair and he is regarded as one of the early writers who fostered the genre we would now call 'science fiction'. Two examples of his forays into the ghost-story field are presented here. 'What Was It' is one of the earliest known examples of the use of invisibility in fiction, while 'A Pot of Tulips' is a traditional ghost story, one of the best from the Victorian era.

ROSA MULHOLLAND (1841–1921) is another writer who sadly is little read today. She was born in Belfast and in her youth was determined to become a painter but Charles Dickens was so impressed with her writing that he persuaded her to concentrate on putting pen to paper. The stories included in this collection clearly reveal not only the influence of Dickens on her fiction but also the work of Sheridan Le Fanu. 'The Ghost of Rath' and 'The Haunted Organist of Hurly Burly' have all the pleasing features one delights in and expects from a ghost story, including unexplained noises at night in an old house, strange dreams, spectral visions and, in the latter tale, the nocturnal wailing and moaning of an organ.

THOMAS CROFTON CROKER (1798–1854) was born in Cork and for some years held a position in the Admiralty. Croker devoted himself largely to the collection of ancient Irish poetry and folklore. 'The Haunted Cellar' is told in anecdotal fashion; whether this is because there is an element of truth in the yarn or the author wishes to create that impression one cannot say.

JEREMIAH CURTIN (1835–1906) is the odd author out in this collection in the sense that he was not Irish. He was an American writer but he specialised in folklore and he was the author of two classic books in the genre, *Myths and Folklore of Ireland* and *Tales of the Fairies and of the Ghost World, Collected from Oral Tradition in South-West Munster*. From this latter volume comes 'St Martin's Eve'. The story is told in a very matter-of-fact manner with no attempt to add dramatic dressing. It is a chilling story, simply told and somehow all the more chilling for that.

Although there is a fine variety of ghostly experiences awaiting you in this volume, I believe there is a common thread that links these tales. It is perhaps most noticeable in the Le Fanu narratives, but it can be sensed in the other stories, too. It is that stoical unquestioning Irish acceptance of the belief that we are not alone, that we may be visited by spirits from beyond the grave, and while the experience will be fearful, we should not be too surprised. In some ways, this makes these Irish ghost stories all the more unnerving.

FURTHER READING

Bleiler, E. F. (ed.), *A Guide to Supernatural Fiction*, Kent State University Press, 1983

Le Fanu, Sheridan, *The House by the Churchyard*, Wordsworth Editions, 2007

Morse, Donald E. and Bertha, Csilla (eds), *More Real Than Reality: The Fantastic in Irish Literature and the Arts*, Greenwood Press, 1991

Riddell, J. H., *Night Shivers: The Ghost Stories of J. H. Riddell*, Wordsworth Editions, 2008

Seymour, St John D. and Neligan, Harry L., *True Irish Ghost Stories*, Dover Publications, 2005

Sullivan, Jack, *Elegant Nightmares: The English Ghost Story from Le Fanu to Blackwood*, Ohio University Press, 1978

Walton, James, *The Fictions of J. S. Le Fanu*, Dublin University College and Dufour Editions, 2007

BIOGRAPHY

David Stuart Davies is an author, playwright and editor. His wartime detective series featuring the one-eyed sleuth Johnny Hawke reached its fourth instalment, *Requiem for a Dummy*, in 2009. He is a member of the Crime Writers' Association and edits their monthly publication, *Red Herrings*.

David is regarded as an authority on Sherlock Holmes and has written the Afterwords for all the Collector's Library Holmes volumes as well as for other titles. He is also the author of two Holmes plays, *Sherlock Holmes: The Last Act* and *Sherlock Holmes: The Death and Life*, which at the time of publication are touring and available on audio CD.

David is also the General Editor for Wordsworth Editions' series Tales of Mystery & the Supernatural.

www.davidstuartdavies.com.

CONTENTS

SHERIDAN LE FANU

The Room in Le Dragon Volant

PROLOGUE

The curious case which I am about to place before
you is referred to, very pointedly and more than once,
in the extraordinary essay upon the drugs of the dark
and middle ages from the pen of Dr Hesselius.

This essay he entitles '*Mortis Imago*', and he, there-
in, discusses the *Vinum Letiferum*, the *Beatifica*, the
Somnus Angelorum, the *Hypnus Segarum*, the *Aqua
Thessalliae*, and about twenty other infusions and dis-
tillations well known to the sages of eight hundred
years ago; two of these are still, he alleges, known to
the fraternity of thieves, and, among them, as police-
office enquiries sometimes disclose to this day, in
practical use.

The essay, '*Mortis Imago*', will occupy, as nearly as
I can at present calculate, two volumes, the ninth and
tenth, of the collected papers of Dr Martin Hesselius.

This essay, I may remark, in conclusion, is very
curiously enriched by citations, in great abundance,
from medieval verse and prose romance, some of the
most valuable of which, strange to say, are Egyptian.

I have selected this particular statement from among
many cases equally striking, but hardly, I think, so

effective as mere narratives in this irregular form of publication; it is simply as a story that I present it.

I

On the Road

In the eventful year 1815, I was exactly three-and-twenty, and had just succeeded to a very large sum in consols and other securities. The first fall of Napoleon had thrown the continent open to English excursionists, anxious, let us suppose, to improve their minds by foreign travel; and I – the slight check of the 'hundred days' removed by the genius of Wellington on the field of Waterloo – was now added to the philosophic throng.

I was posting up to Paris from Brussels, following, I presume, the route that the allied army had pursued but a few weeks before – more carriages than you could believe were pursuing the same line. You could not look back or forward without seeing into far perspective the clouds of dust which marked the line of the long series of vehicles. We were perpetually passing relays of return-horses on their way, jaded and dusty, to the inns from which they had been taken. They were arduous times for those patient public servants. The whole world seemed posting up to Paris.

I ought to have noted it more particularly, but my head was so full of Paris and the future that I passed the intervening scenery with little patience and less attention; I think, however, that it was about four miles to the frontier side of a rather picturesque little town, the name of which, as of many more important places through which I posted in my hurried journey, I forget, and about two hours before sunset that we came up with a carriage in distress.

It was not quite an upset. But the two leaders were lying flat. The booted postilions had got down, and two servants, who seemed very much at sea in such matters, were by way of assisting them. A pretty little bonnet and head were popped out of the window of the carriage in distress. Its *tournure*, and that of the shoulders that also appeared for a moment, was captivating.

Resolving to play the part of a good Samaritan, I stopped my chaise, jumped out, and with my servant lent a very willing hand in the emergency. Alas! the lady with the pretty bonnet wore a very thick, black veil. I could see nothing but the pattern of the Brussels lace as she drew back.

A lean old gentleman, almost at the same time, stuck his head out of the window. An invalid he seemed, for although the day was hot, he wore a black muffler which came up to his ears and nose, quite covering the lower part of his face, an arrangement which he disturbed by pulling it down for a moment to pour forth a torrent of French thanks, uncovering his black wig as he gesticulated with grateful animation.

One of my very few accomplishments, besides boxing, which was cultivated by all Englishmen at that time, was French; and I replied, I hope and believe, grammatically. Many bows being exchanged the old gentleman's head went in again and the demure, pretty little bonnet once more appeared.

The lady must have heard me speak to my servant,

for she framed her little speech in such pretty, broken English, and in a voice so sweet, that I more than ever cursed the black veil that baulked my romantic curiosity.

The arms that were emblazoned on the panel were peculiar; I remember especially one device – it was the figure of a stork, painted in carmine, upon what the heralds call a 'field or'. The bird was standing upon one leg, and in the other claw held a stone. This is, I believe, the emblem of vigilance. Its oddity struck me, and remained impressed upon my memory. There were supporters besides, but I forget what they were. The courtly manners of these people, the style of their servants, the elegance of their travelling carriage and the supporters to their arms satisfied me that they were noble.

The lady, you may be sure, was not the less interesting on that account. What a fascination a title exercises upon the imagination! I do not mean on that of snobs or moral flunkies. Superiority of rank is a powerful and genuine influence in love. The idea of superior refinement is associated with it. The careless notice of the squire tells more upon the heart of the pretty milkmaid than years of honest Dobbin's manly devotion, and so on and up. It is an unjust world!

But in this case there was something more. I was conscious of being good-looking. I really believe I was; and there could be no mistake about my being nearly six feet high. Why need this lady have thanked me? Had not her husband, for such I assumed him to be, thanked me quite enough and for both? I was instinctively aware that the lady was looking on me with no unwilling eyes; and, through her veil, I felt the power of her gaze.

She was now rolling away, with a train of dust behind her wheels in the golden sunlight, and a wise young gentleman followed her with ardent eyes, and sighed profoundly as the distance increased.

I told the positions on no account to pass the carriage, but to keep it steadily in view, and to pull up at whatever posting-house it should stop at. We were soon in the little town, and the carriage we followed drew up at the Belle Etoile, a comfortable old inn. They got out of the carriage and entered the house.

At a leisurely pace we followed. I got down, and mounted the steps listlessly, like a man quite apathetic and careless.

Audacious as I was, I did not care to enquire in what room I should find them. I peeped into the apartment to my right, and then into that on my left. My people were not there.

I ascended the stairs. A drawing-room door stood open. I entered with the most innocent air in the world. It was a spacious room, and, beside myself, contained but one living figure – a very pretty and ladylike one. There was the very bonnet with which I had fallen in love. The lady stood with her back towards me. I could not tell whether the envious veil was raised; she was reading a letter.

I stood for a minute in fixed attention, gazing upon her, in the vague hope that she might turn about and give me an opportunity of seeing her features. She did not; but with a step or two she placed herself before a little cabriole-table which stood against the wall and from which rose a tall mirror in a tarnished frame.

I might, indeed, have mistaken it for a picture, for

23

it now reflected a half-length portrait of a singularly beautiful woman.

She was looking down upon a letter which she held in her slender fingers, and in which she seemed absorbed.

The face was oval, melancholy, sweet. It had in it, nevertheless, a faint and indefinably sensual quality also. Nothing could exceed the delicacy of its features, or the brilliancy of its tints. The eyes, indeed, were lowered, so that I could not see their colour; nothing but their long lashes, and delicate eyebrows. She continued reading. She must have been deeply interested; I never saw a living form so motionless – I gazed on a tinted statue.

Being at that time blessed with long and keen vision, I saw this beautiful face with perfect distinctness. I saw even the blue veins that traced their wanderings on the whiteness of her full throat.

I ought to have retreated as noiselessly as I came in, before my presence was detected. But I was too much interested to move from the spot for a few moments longer; and while they were passing, she raised her eyes. Those eyes were large, and of that hue which modern poets term 'violet'.

These splendid melancholy eyes were turned upon me from the glass with a haughty stare, and hastily the lady lowered her black veil and turned about.

I fancied that she hoped I had not seen her. I was watching every look and movement, the minutest, with an attention as intense as if an ordeal involving my life depended on them.

2

The Inn-yard of the Belle Etoile

The face was, indeed, one to fall in love with at first sight. Those sentiments that take such sudden possession of young men were now dominating my curiosity. My audacity faltered before her; and I felt that my presence in this room was probably an impertinence. This point she quickly settled, for the same very sweet voice I had heard before now said coldly, and this time in French, 'Monsieur cannot be aware that this apartment is not public.'

I bowed very low, faltered some apologies, and backed to the door.

I suppose I looked penitent and embarrassed – I certainly felt so – for the lady said, by way it seemed of softening matters, 'I am happy, however, to have an opportunity of again thanking monsieur for the assistance, so prompt and effectual, which he had the goodness to render us today.'

It was more the altered tone in which it was spoken, than the speech itself, that encouraged me. It was also true that she need not have recognised me; and if she had, she certainly was not obliged to thank me over again.

All this was indescribably flattering, and all the more so that it followed so quickly on her slight reproof.

The tone in which she spoke had become low and timid, and I observed that she turned her head quickly towards a second door of the room. I fancied that the gentleman in the black wig, a jealous husband, perhaps, might reappear through it. Almost at the same moment, a voice, at once reedy and nasal, was heard snarling some directions to a servant, and evidently approaching. It was the voice that had thanked me so profusely, from the carriage windows, about an hour before.

'Monsieur will have the goodness to retire,' said the lady, in a tone that resembled entreaty, at the same time gently waving her hand towards the door through which I had entered. Bowing again very low, I stepped back, and closed the door.

I ran down the stairs, very much elated. I saw the host of the Belle Etoile which, as I said, was the sign and designation of my inn.

I described the apartment I had just quitted, said I liked it, and asked whether I could have it. He was extremely troubled, but that apartment and the two adjoining rooms were engaged.

'By whom?'

'People of distinction.'

'But who are they? They must have names, or titles.'

'Undoubtedly, monsieur, but such a stream is rolling into Paris that we have ceased to enquire the names or titles of our guests – we designate them simply by the rooms they occupy.'

'What stay do they make?'

'Even that, monsieur, I cannot answer. It does not interest us. Our rooms, while this continues, can never be, for a moment, disengaged.'

'I should have liked those rooms so much! Is one of them a sleeping apartment?'

'Yes, sir, and monsieur will observe that people do

26

not usually engage bedrooms, unless they mean to stay the night.'

'Well, I can, I suppose, have some rooms, any, I don't care in what part of the house?'

'Certainly, monsieur can have two apartments. They are the last at present disengaged.'

I took them instantly.

It was plain these people meant to make a stay here; at least they would not go till morning. I began to feel that I was all but engaged in an adventure.

I took possession of my rooms, and looked out of the window, which I found commanded the inn-yard. Many horses were being liberated from the traces, hot and weary, and others, fresh from the stables, being put to. A great many vehicles – some private carriages, others, like mine, of that public class which is equivalent to our old English post-chaise – were standing on the pavement, waiting their turn for relays. Fussy servants were to-ing and fro-ing, and idle ones lounging or laughing, and the scene, on the whole, was animated and amusing.

Among these objects I thought I recognised the travelling carriage and one of the servants of the 'persons of distinction' about whom I was, just then, so profoundly interested.

I therefore ran down the stairs, made my way to the back door; and so, behold me, in a moment, upon the uneven pavement, among all these sights and sounds which in such a place attend upon a period of extraordinary crush and traffic.

By this time the sun was near its setting, and threw its golden beams on the red-brick chimneys of the offices, and made the two barrels, that figured as pigeon-houses, on the tops of poles, look as if they

were on fire. Everything in this light becomes picturesque; and things interest us which in the sober grey
of morning are dull enough.

After a little search, I lighted upon the very carriage
of which I was in quest. A servant was locking one of
the doors, for it was made with the security of lock and
key. I paused near, looking at the panel of the door.

'A very pretty device that red stork!' I observed,
pointing to the shield on the door, 'and no doubt
indicates a distinguished family?'

The servant looked at me for a moment as he
placed the little key in his pocket, and said with a
slightly sarcastic bow and smile, 'Monsieur is at liberty
to conjecture.'

Nothing daunted, I forthwith administered that
laxative which, on occasion, acts so happily upon the
tongue – I mean a 'tip'.

The servant looked at the Napoleon in his hand,
and then in my face, with a sincere expression of
surprise.

'Monsieur is very generous!'

'Not worth mentioning – who are the lady and
gentleman who came here, in this carriage, and whom,
you may remember, I and my servant assisted today
in an emergency, when their horses had come to the
ground?'

'We call him the count, and the young lady we call
the countess – but I know not, she may be his
daughter.'

'Can you tell me where they live?'

'Upon my honour, monsieur, I am unable – I know
not.'

'Not know where your master lives! Surely you
know something about him?'

'Nothing worth relating, monsieur; in fact, I was hired in Brussels on the very day they started. Monsieur Picard, my fellow-servant, Monsieur the Comte's gentleman, he has been years in his service, and knows everything; but he never speaks except to communicate an order. From him I have learned nothing. We are going to Paris, however, and there I shall speedily pick up all about them. At present I am as ignorant of all that as monsieur himself.'

'And where is Monsieur Picard?'

'He has gone to the cutler's to get his razors set. But I do not think he will tell anything.'

This was a poor harvest for my golden sowing. The man, I think, spoke the truth, and would honestly have betrayed the secrets of the family if he had possessed any. I took my leave politely; and mounting the stairs, I found myself once more in my room.

Forthwith I summoned my servant. Though I had brought him with me from England, he was a native of France – a useful fellow, sharp, bustling and, of course, quite familiar with the ways and tricks of his countrymen.

'St Clair, shut the door; come here. I can't rest till I have made out something about those people of rank who have got the apartments under mine. Here are fifteen francs; make out the servants we assisted today; have them to a *petit souper*, and come back and tell me their entire history. I have, this moment, seen one of them who knows nothing, and has communicated it. The other, whose name I forget, is the unknown nobleman's valet, and knows everything. Him you must pump. It is, of course, the venerable peer, and not the young lady who accompanies him, that interests me – you understand? Begone! fly! and return with all the details I sigh for, and every circumstance that can possibly interest me.'

It was a commission which admirably suited the tastes and spirits of my worthy St Clair, to whom, you will have observed, I had accustomed myself to talk with the peculiar familiarity which the old French comedy establishes between master and valet.

I am sure he laughed at me in secret; but to my face no one could be more polite and deferential.

With several wise looks, nods and shrugs, he withdrew; and looking down from my window, I saw him, with incredible quickness, enter the yard where I soon lost sight of him among the carriages.

3

Death and Love Together Mated

When the day drags, when a man is solitary, and in a fever of impatience and suspense; when the minute hand of his watch travels as slowly as the hour hand used to do, and the hour hand has lost all appreciable motion; when he yawns, and beats the devil's tattoo, and flattens his handsome nose against the window, and whistles tunes he hates, and, in short, does not know what to do with himself, it is deeply to be regretted that he cannot make a solemn dinner of three courses more than once in a day. The laws of matter, to which we are slaves, deny us that resource.

But in the times I speak of, supper was still a substantial meal, and its hour was approaching. This was consolatory. Three-quarters of an hour, however, still interposed. How was I to dispose of that interval?

I had two or three idle books, it is true, as travelling-companions; but there are many moods in which one cannot read. My novel lay with my rug and walking-stick on the sofa, and I did not care if the heroine and the hero were both drowned together in the water barrel that I saw in the inn-yard under my window.

I took a turn or two up and down my room, and sighed, looking at myself in the glass, adjusted my great white 'choker', folded and tied after Brummel, the immortal 'Beau', put on a buff waistcoat and my blue swallow-tailed coat with gilt buttons; I deluged my pocket-handkerchief with eau-de-Cologne (we had not then the variety of bouquets with which the genius of perfumery has since blessed us); I arranged my hair, on which I piqued myself, and which I loved to groom in those days. That dark-brown *chevelure*, with its natural curl, is now represented by a few dozen perfectly white hairs, and its place – a smooth, bald, pink head – knows it no more. But let us forget these mortifications. It was then rich, thick and dark-brown. I was making a very careful toilet. I took my unexceptionable hat from its case, and placed it lightly on my wise head, as nearly as memory and practice enabled me to do so, at that very slight inclination which the immortal person I have mentioned was wont to give to his. A pair of light French gloves and a rather club-like knotted walking-stick, such as just then had come into vogue for a year or two again in England, in the phraseology of Sir Walter Scott's romances, 'completed my equipment'.

All this attention to effect, preparatory to a mere lounge in the yard or on the steps of the Belle Etoile, was a simple act of devotion to the wonderful eyes which I had that evening beheld for the first time, and never, never could forget. In plain terms, it was all done in the vague, very vague hope that those eyes might behold the unexceptionable get-up of a melancholy slave, and retain the image, not altogether without secret approbation.

As I completed my preparations the light failed me; the last level streak of sunlight disappeared, and a fading twilight only remained. I sighed in unison with the pensive hour, and threw open the window, intending to look out for a moment before going downstairs. I perceived instantly that the window underneath mine was also open, for I heard two voices in conversation, although I could not distinguish what they were saying.

The male voice was peculiar; it was, as I told you, reedy and nasal. I knew it, of course, instantly. The answering voice spoke in those sweet tones which I recognised only too easily. The dialogue was only for a minute; the repulsive male voice laughed, I fancied, with a kind of devilish satire, and retired from the window, so that I almost ceased to hear it.

The other voice remained nearer the window, but not so near as at first.

It was not an altercation; there was evidently nothing the least exciting in the colloquy. What would I not have given that it had been a quarrel – a violent one – and I the redresser of wrongs, and the defender of insulted beauty! Alas, so far as I could pronounce upon the character of the tones I heard, they might be as tranquil a pair as any in existence. In a moment more the lady began to sing an odd little chanson. I need not remind you how much farther the voice is heard singing than speaking. I could distinguish the words. The voice was of that exquisitely sweet kind

which is called, I believe, a semi-contralto; it had
something pathetic, and something, I fancied, a little
mocking in its tones. I venture a clumsy, but adequate
translation of the words:

> Death and Love, together mated,
>> Watch and wait in ambuscade;
> At early morn, or else belated,
>> They meet and mark the man or maid.
> Burning sigh, or breath that freezes,
>> Numbs or maddens man or maid;
> Death or Love the victim seizes,
>> Breathing from their ambuscade.

'Enough, madame!' said the old voice, with sudden
severity. 'We do not desire, I believe, to amuse the
grooms and hostlers in the yard with our music.'

The lady's voice laughed gaily.

'You desire to quarrel, madame?' And the old man,
I presume, shut down the window. Down it went, at
all events, with a rattle that might easily have broken
the glass.

Of all thin partitions, glass is the most effectual
excluder of sound. I heard no more, not even the
subdued hum of the colloquy.

What a charming voice this countess had! How it
melted, swelled and trembled! How it moved and
even agitated me! What a pity that a hoarse old jack-
daw should have power to crow down such a
Philomel! 'Alas! what a life it is!' I moralised, wisely.
'That beautiful countess, with the patience of an angel
and the beauty of a Venus and the accomplishments
of all the Muses, a slave! She knows perfectly who
occupies the apartments over hers; she heard me raise
my window. One may conjecture pretty well for

whom that music was intended – aye, old gentleman, and for whom you suspected it to be intended.'

In a very agreeable flutter I left my room, and descending the stairs, passed the count's door very much at my leisure. There was just a chance that the beautiful songstress might emerge. I dropped my stick on the lobby, near their door, and you may be sure it took me some little time to pick it up! Fortune, nevertheless, did not favour me. I could not stay on the lobby all night picking up my stick, so I went down to the hall.

I consulted the clock, and found that there remained but a quarter of an hour to the moment of supper.

Everyone was roughing it now, every inn in confusion; people might do at such a juncture what they never did before. Was it just possible that, for once, the count and countess would take their chairs at the table-d'hôte?

4

Monsieur Droqville

Full of this exciting hope, I sauntered out upon the steps of the Belle Etoile. It was now night, and a pleasant moonlight over everything. I had entered more into my romance since my arrival, and this poetic light heightened the sentiment. What a drama if she turned out to be the count's daughter, and in love with me! What a delightful *tragedy* if she turned out to be the count's wife!

In this luxurious mood, I was accosted by a tall and very elegantly made gentleman, who appeared to be about fifty. His air was courtly and graceful, and there was in his whole manner and appearance something so distinguished that it was impossible not to suspect him of being a person of rank.

He had been standing upon the steps, looking out, like me, upon the moonlight effects that transformed, as it were, the objects and buildings in the little street. He accosted me, as I say, with the politeness, at once easy and lofty, of a French nobleman of the old school. He asked me if I were not Mr Beckett? I assented; and he immediately introduced himself as the Marquis d'Harmonville (this information he gave me in a low tone), and asked leave to present me with a letter from Lord Rivers, who knew my father slightly, and had once done me, also, a trifling kindness.

This English peer, I may mention, stood very high in the political world, and was named as the most probable successor to the distinguished post of English minister at Paris.

I received it with a low bow, and read:

MY DEAR BECKETT – I beg to introduce my very dear friend, the Marquis d'Harmonville, who will explain to you the nature of the services it may be in your power to render him and us.

He went on to speak of the marquis as a man whose great wealth, whose intimate relations with the old families and whose legitimate influence with the court rendered him the fittest possible person for those friendly offices which, at the desire of his own sovereign and of our government, he had so obligingly undertaken.

It added a great deal to my perplexity, when I read, further –

By the by, Walton was here yesterday, and told me that your seat was likely to be attacked; something, he says, is unquestionably going on at Domwell. You know there is an awkwardness in my meddling ever so cautiously. But I advise, if it is not very officious, your making Haxton look after it, and report immediately. I fear it is serious. I ought to have mentioned that, for reasons that you will see when you have talked with him for five minutes, the marquis – with the concurrence of all our friends – drops his title, for a few weeks, and is at present plain Monsieur Droqville.

I am this moment going to town, and can say no more.

Yours faithfully,

RIVERS

I was utterly puzzled. I could scarcely boast of Lord Rivers' acquaintance. I knew no one named Haxton, and, except my hatter, no one called Walton; and this peer wrote as if we were intimate friends! I looked at the back of the letter, and the mystery was solved. To my consternation – for I was plain Richard Beckett – I read: 'To George Stanhope Beckett Esq., MP.'

I looked with consternation in the face of the marquis.

'What apology can I offer to Monsieur the Mar – to Monsieur Droqville? It is true my name is Beckett – it is true I am known, though very slightly, to Lord Rivers; but the letter was not intended for me. My name is Richard Beckett – this is to Mr Stanhope Beckett, the member for Shillingsworth. What can I say, or do, in this unfortunate situation? I can only give you my honour as a gentleman that for me the

letter, which I now return, shall remain as unviolated
a secret as before I opened it. I am so shocked and
grieved that such a mistake should have occurred!'

I dare say my honest vexation and good faith were
pretty legibly written in my countenance; for the look
of gloomy embarrassment which had for a moment
settled on the face of the marquis brightened; he
smiled, kindly, and extended his hand.

'I have not the least doubt that Monsieur Beckett
will respect my little secret. As a mistake was destined
to occur, I have reason to thank my good stars that
it should have been with a gentleman of honour.
Monsieur Beckett will permit me, I hope, to place his
name among those of my friends?'

I thanked the marquis very much for his kind
expressions.

He went on to say: 'If, monsieur, I can persuade
you to visit me at Clironville in Normandy, where I
hope to see on the 15th of August a great many friends
whose acquaintance it might interest you to make, I
shall be too happy.'

I thanked him, of course, very gratefully for his
hospitality.

He continued: 'I cannot for the present see my
friends, for reasons which you may surmise, at my
house in Paris. But monsieur will be so good as to let
me know the hotel he means to stay at in Paris; and
he will find that, although the Marquis d'Harmonville
is not in town, Monsieur Droqville will not lose sight
of him.'

With many acknowledgements I gave him the information he desired.

'And in the meantime,' he continued, 'if you think
of any way in which Monsieur Droqville can be of use

37

to you, our communication shall not be interrupted,
and I shall so manage matters that you can easily let
me know.'

I was very much flattered. The marquis had, as we
say, taken a fancy to me. Such likings at first sight
often ripen into lasting friendships. To be sure it was
just possible that the marquis might think it prudent
to keep the involuntary depositary of a political secret,
even so vague a one, in good humour.

Very graciously the marquis took his leave, going
up the stairs of the Belle Etoile.

I remained upon the steps, for a minute lost in
speculation upon this new theme of interest. But
the wonderful eyes, the thrilling voice, the exquisite
figure of the beautiful lady who had taken possession
of my imagination, quickly reasserted their influence.
I was again gazing at the sympathetic moon, and,
descending the steps, I loitered along the pavements
among strange objects, and houses that were antique
and picturesque, in a dreamy state, thinking.

In a little while, I turned into the inn-yard again.
There had come a lull. Instead of the noisy place it
was an hour or two before, the yard was perfectly still
and empty, except for the carriages that stood here
and there. Perhaps there was a servants' table-d'hôte
just then. I was rather pleased to find solitude; and
undisturbed I found out my lady-love's carriage, in
the moonlight. I mused, I walked round it; I was as
utterly foolish and maudlin as very young men in my
situation usually are. The blinds were down, the doors,
I suppose, locked. The brilliant moonlight revealed
everything, and cast sharp, black shadows of wheel,
and bar, and spring, on the pavement. I stood before
the escutcheon painted on the door, which I had

examined in the daylight. I wondered how often
her eyes had rested on the same object. I pondered
in a charming dream. A harsh, loud voice, over my
shoulder, said suddenly – 'A red stork – good! The
stork is a bird of prey; it is vigilant, greedy, and
catches gudgeons. Red, too! – blood red! Ha! ha! the
symbol is appropriate.'

I had turned about, and beheld the palest face I
ever saw. It was broad, ugly and malignant. The figure
was that of a French officer, in undress, and was six
feet high. Across the nose and eyebrow there was a
deep scar, which made the repulsive face grimmer.

He turned with an angry whisk on his heel, and
swaggered with long strides out of the gate.

5

Supper at the Belle Etoile

The French army were in a rather savage temper, just then. The English, especially, had but scant courtesy to expect at their hands. It was plain, however, that the cadaverous gentleman who had just apostrophised the heraldry of the count's carriage, with such mysterious acrimony, had not intended any of his malevolence for me. He was stung by some old recollection, and had marched off, seething with fury.

I had received one of those unacknowledged shocks which startle us when, fancying ourselves perfectly alone, we discover on a sudden that our antics have been watched by a spectator, almost at our elbow. In this case, the effect was enhanced by the extreme repulsiveness of the face, and, I may add, its proximity, for, as I think, it almost touched mine. The enigmatical harangue of this person, so full of hatred and implied denunciation, was still in my ears. Here at all events was new matter for the industrious fancy of a lover to work upon.

It was time now to go to the table-d'hôte. Who could tell what lights the gossip of the supper-table might throw upon the subject that interested me so powerfully!

I stepped into the room, my eyes searching the little assembly, about thirty people, for the persons who specially interested me.

It was not easy to induce people so hurried and overworked as those of the Belle Etoile just now to

40

send meals up to one's private apartments in the midst of this unparalleled confusion; and, therefore, many people who did not like it, might find themselves reduced to the alternative of supping at the table-d'hôte or starving.

The count was not there, nor his beautiful companion; but the Marquis d'Harmonville, whom I hardly expected to see in so public a place, signed, with a significant smile, to a vacant chair beside himself. I secured it, and he seemed pleased, and almost immediately entered into conversation with me.

'This is probably your first visit to France?' he said.

I told him it was, and he said: 'You must not think me very curious and impertinent; but Paris is about the most dangerous capital a high-spirited and generous young gentleman could visit without a mentor. If you have not an experienced friend as a companion during your visit – ' He paused.

I told him I was not so provided, but that I had my wits about me; that I had seen a good deal of life in England, and that I fancied human nature was pretty much the same in all parts of the world. The marquis shook his head, smiling.

'You will find very marked differences, notwithstanding,' he said. 'Peculiarities of intellect and peculiarities of character, undoubtedly, do pervade different nations; and this results, among the criminal classes, in a style of villainy no less peculiar. In Paris, the class who live by their wits is three or four times as great as in London; and they live much better; some of them even splendidly. They are more ingenious than the London rogues; they have more animation, and invention, and the dramatic faculty,

in which your countrymen are deficient, is everywhere. These invaluable attributes place them upon a
totally different level. They can affect the manners
and enjoy the luxuries of people of distinction. They
live, many of them, by play.'

'So do many of our London rogues.'

'Yes, but in a totally different way. They are the
habitués of certain gaming-tables, billiard-rooms and
other places, including your races, where high play
goes on; and by superior knowledge of chances, by
masking their play, by means of confederates, by
means of bribery and other artifices, varying with the
subject of their imposture, they rob the unwary. But
here it is more elaborately done, and with a really
exquisite *finesse*. There are people whose manners,
style, conversation, are unexceptionable, living
in handsome houses in the best situations, with
everything about them in the most refined taste, and
exquisitely luxurious, who impose even upon the
Parisian bourgeois, who believe them to be, in good
faith, people of rank and fashion, because their habits
are expensive and refined, and their houses are fre-
quented by foreigners of distinction, and, to a degree,
by foolish young Frenchmen of rank. At all these
houses play goes on. The ostensible host and hostess
seldom join in it; they provide it simply to plunder
their guests, by means of their accomplices, and thus
wealthy strangers are inveigled and robbed.'

'But I have heard of a young Englishman, a son of
Lord Rooksbury, who broke two Parisian gaming-
tables only last year.'

'I see,' he said, laughing, 'you are come here to do
likewise. I, myself, at about your age, undertook the
same spirited enterprise. I raised no less a sum than

five hundred thousand francs to begin with; I expected to carry all before me by the simple expedient of going on doubling my stakes. I had heard of it, and I fancied that the sharpers, who kept the table, knew nothing of the matter. I found, however, that they not only knew all about it, but had provided against the possibility of any such experiments; and I was pulled up before I had well begun by a rule which forbids the doubling of an original stake more than four times consecutively.'

'And is that rule in force still?' I enquired, chap-fallen.

He laughed and shrugged, 'Of course it is, my young friend. People who live by an art, always understand it better than an amateur. I see you had formed the same plan, and no doubt came provided.'

I confessed I had prepared for conquest upon a still grander scale. I had arrived with a purse of thirty thousand pounds sterling.

'Any acquaintance of my very dear friend Lord Rivers interests me; and, besides my regard for him, I am charmed with you; so you will pardon all my perhaps too officious questions and advice.'

I thanked him most earnestly for his valuable counsel, and begged that he would have the goodness to give me all the advice in his power.

'Then if you take my advice,' said he, 'you will leave your money in the bank where it lies. Never risk a Napoleon in a gaming house. The night I went to break the bank, I lost between seven and eight thousand pounds sterling of your English money; and for my next adventure, I had obtained an introduction to one of those elegant gaming-houses which affect to be the private mansions of persons of distinction, and was saved from ruin by a gentleman whom, ever since, I have regarded with increasing respect and friendship. It oddly happens he is in this house at this moment. I recognised his servant, and made him a visit in his apartments here, and found him the same brave, kind, honourable man I always knew him. But that he is living so entirely out of the world, now, I should have made a point of introducing you. Fifteen years ago he would have been the man of all others to consult. The gentleman I speak of is the Comte de St Alyre. He represents a very old family. He is the very soul of honour, and the most sensible man in the world, except in one particular.'

'And that particular?' I hesitated. I was now deeply interested.

'Is that he has married a charming creature, at least five-and-forty years younger than himself, and is, of course, although I believe absolutely without cause, horribly jealous.'

'And the lady?'

'The countess is, I believe, in every way worthy of so good a man,' he answered, a little drily.

'I think I heard her sing this evening.'

'Yes, I dare say; she is very accomplished.' After a few moments' silence he continued: 'I must not lose sight of you, for I should be sorry, when next you meet my friend Lord Rivers, that you had to tell him you had been pigeoned in Paris. A rich Englishman as you are, with so large a sum at your Paris bankers, young, gay, generous, a thousand ghouls and harpies will be contending who shall be the first to seize and devour you.'

At this moment I received something like a jerk

from the elbow of the gentleman at my right. It was an accidental jog as he turned in his seat.

'On the honour of a soldier, there is no man's flesh in this company heals so fast as mine.'

The tone in which this was spoken was harsh and stentorian, and almost made me bounce. I looked round and recognised the officer whose large white face had half scared me in the inn-yard. Wiping his mouth furiously, and then with a gulp of Maçon, he went on – '*No* man's! It's not blood; it is ichor! it's miraculous! Set aside stature, thew, bone and muscle, set aside courage – and by all the angels of death, I'd fight a lion naked, and dash his teeth down his jaws with my fist, and flog him to death with his own tail! Set aside, I say, all those attributes, which I am allowed to possess, and I am worth six men in any campaign for that one quality of healing as I do – rip me up; punch me through, tear me to tatters with bombshells, and nature has me whole again while your tailor would fine-draw an old coat. *Parbleu!* gentlemen, if you saw me naked, you would laugh! Look at my hand, a sabre-cut across the palm, to the bone, to save my head, taken up with three stitches, and five days afterwards I was playing ball with an English general, a prisoner in Madrid, against the wall of the convent of the Santa Maria de la Castita! At Arcola, by the great devil himself that was an action. Every man there, gentlemen, swallowed as much smoke in five minutes as would smother you all in this room! I received, at the same moment, two musket balls in the thighs, a grape shot through the calf of my leg, a lance through my left shoulder, a piece of shrapnel in the left deltoid, a bayonet through the cartilage of my right ribs, a sabre-cut that carried

45

away a pound of flesh from my chest, and the better part of a congreve rocket on my forehead. Pretty well, ha, ha! and all while you'd say *bah!* and in eight days and a half I was making a forced march, without shoes, and only one gaiter, the life and soul of my company, and as sound as a roach!'

'Bravo! Bravissimo! Per Bacco! un gallant uomo!' exclaimed, in a martial ecstasy, a fat little Italian, who manufactured toothpicks and wicker cradles on the island of Notre Dame; 'your exploits should resound through Europe and the history of those wars should be written in your blood!'

'Never mind! a trifle!' exclaimed the soldier. 'At Ligny, the other day, where we smashed the Prussians into ten hundred thousand milliards of atoms, a bit of a shell cut me across the leg and opened an artery. It was spouting as high as the chimney, and in half a minute I had lost enough to fill a pitcher. I must have expired in another minute if I had not whipped off my sash like a flash of lightning, tied it round my leg above the wound, snatched a bayonet out of the back of a dead Prussian and, passing it under, made a tourniquet of it with a couple of twists and so stayed the haemorrhage and saved my life. But, *sacré bleu!* gentlemen, I lost so much blood, I have been as pale as the bottom of a plate ever since. No matter. A trifle. Blood well spent, gentlemen.' He applied himself now to his bottle of *vin ordinaire*.

The marquis had closed his eyes, and looked resigned and disgusted while all this was going on.

'Garçon,' said the officer, speaking in a low tone over the back of his chair to the waiter; 'who came in that travelling carriage, dark yellow and black, that stands in the middle of the yard, with arms and supporters emblazoned on the door, and a red stork, as red as my facings?'

The waiter could not say.

The eye of the eccentric officer, who had suddenly grown grim and serious, and seemed to have abandoned the general conversation to other people, lighted, as it were, accidentally, on me.

'Pardon me, monsieur,' he said. 'Did I not see you examining the panel of that carriage at the same time that I did so, this evening? Can you tell me who arrived in it?'

'I rather think the Count and Countess de St Alyre.'

'And are they here, in the Belle Etoile?' he asked.

'They have got apartments upstairs,' I answered.

He started up, and half pushed his chair from the table. He quickly sat down again, and I could hear him *sacré*-ing and muttering to himself, and grinning and scowling. I could not tell whether he was alarmed or furious.

I turned to say a word or two to the marquis, but he was gone. Several other people had dropped out also, and the supper party soon broke up.

Two or three substantial pieces of wood smouldered on the hearth, for the night had turned out chilly. I sat down by the fire in a great armchair of carved oak, with a marvellously high back, that looked as old as the days of Henry IV.

'Garçon,' said I, 'do you happen to know who that officer is?'

'That is Colonel Gaillarde, monsieur.'

'Has he been often here?'

'Once before, monsieur, for a week; it is a year since.'

'He is the palest man I ever saw.'

47

'That is true, monsieur; he has been often taken for a *revenant*.'

'Can you give me a bottle of really good Burgundy?'

'The best in France, monsieur.'

'Place it and a glass by my side, on this table, if you please. I may sit here for half an hour?'

'Certainly, monsieur.'

I was very comfortable, the wine excellent, and my thoughts glowing and serene. 'Beautiful countess! Beautiful countess! shall we ever be better acquainted.'

6

The Naked Sword

A man who has been posting all day long, and changing the air he breathes every half-hour, who is well pleased with himself, and has nothing on earth to trouble him, and who sits alone by a fire in a comfortable chair after having eaten a hearty supper, may be pardoned if he takes an accidental nap.

I had filled my fourth glass when I fell asleep. My head, I dare say, hung uncomfortably; and it is admitted, that a variety of French dishes is not the most favourable precursor to pleasant dreams.

I had a dream as I took mine ease in mine inn on this occasion. I fancied myself in a huge cathedral, without light except from four tapers that stood at the corners of a raised platform hung with black on which lay, draped also in black, what seemed to me the dead body of the Countess de St Alyre. The place seemed empty, it was cold, and I could see only (in the halo of the candles) a little way round.

48

The little I saw bore the character of Gothic gloom, and helped my fancy to shape and furnish the black void that yawned all round me. I heard a sound like the slow tread of two persons walking up the flagged aisle. A faint echo told of the vastness of the place. An awful sense of expectation was upon me, and I was horribly frightened when the body that lay on the catafalque said (without stirring), in a whisper that froze me, 'They come to place me in the grave alive; save me.'

I found that I could neither speak nor move. I was horribly frightened.

The two people who approached now emerged from the darkness. One, the Count de St Alyre, glided to the head of the figure and placed his long thin hands under it. The white-faced colonel, with the scar across his face, and a look of infernal triumph, placed his hands under her feet, and they began to raise her.

With an indescribable effort I broke the spell that bound me, and started to my feet with a gasp.

I was wide awake, but the broad, wicked face of Colonel Gaillarde was staring, white as death, at me, from the other side of the hearth. 'Where is she?' I shuddered.

'That depends on who she is, monsieur,' replied the colonel, curtly.

'Good heavens!' I gasped, looking about me.

The colonel, who was eyeing me sarcastically, had had his *demi-tasse* of *café noir*, and now drank his *tasse*, diffusing a pleasant perfume of brandy.

'I fell asleep and was dreaming,' I said, lest any strong language, founded on the role he played in my dream, should have escaped me. 'I did not know for some moments where I was.'

49

'You are the young gentleman who has the apartments over the Count and Countess de St Alyre?' he said, winking one eye closed in meditation and glaring at me with the other.

'I believe so – yes,' I answered.

'Well, younker, take care you have not worse dreams than that some night,' he said, enigmatically, and wagged his head with a chuckle. 'Worse dreams,' he repeated.

'What does Monsieur the Colonel mean?' I enquired.

'I am trying to find that out myself,' said the colonel; 'and I think I shall. When I get the first inch of the thread fast between my finger and thumb, it goes hard but I follow it up, bit by bit, little by little, tracing it this way and that, and up and down, and round about, until the whole clue is wound up on my thumb, and the end, and its secret, fast in my fingers. Ingenious! Crafty as five foxes! wide awake as a weazel! *Parbleu!* if I had descended to that occupation I should have made my fortune as a spy. Good wine here?' he glanced interrogatively at my bottle.

'Very good,' said I. 'Will Monsieur the Colonel try a glass?'

He took the largest he could find, and filled it, raised it with a bow, and drank it slowly. 'Ah! ah! Bah! That is not it,' he exclaimed, with some disgust, filling it again. 'You ought to have told me to order your Burgundy, and they would not have brought you that stuff.'

I got away from this man as soon as I civilly could, and, putting on my hat, I walked out with no other company than my sturdy walking-stick. I visited the inn-yard, and looked up to the windows of the countess's apartments. They were closed, however, and I had not even the insubstantial consolation of contemplating the light in which that beautiful lady was at that moment writing, or reading, or sitting and thinking of – anyone you please.

I bore this serious privation as well as I could, and took a little saunter through the town. I shan't bore you with moonlight effects, nor with the maunderings of a man who has fallen in love at first sight with a beautiful face. My ramble, it is enough to say, occupied about half an hour, and, returning by a slight *détour*, I found myself in a little square, with about two high-gabled houses on each side, and a rude stone statue, worn by centuries of rain, on a pedestal in the centre of the pavement. Looking at this statue was a slight and rather tall man, whom I instantly recognised as the Marquis d'Harmonville: he knew me almost as quickly. He walked a step towards me, shrugged and laughed: 'You are surprised to find Monsieur Droqville staring at that old stone figure by moonlight. Anything to pass the time. You, I see, suffer from *ennui* as I do. These little provincial towns! Heavens! what an effort it is to live in them! If I could regret having formed in early life a friendship that does me honour, I think its condemning me to a sojourn in such a place would make me do so. You go on towards Paris, I suppose, in the morning?'

'I have ordered horses.'

'As for me I await a letter, or an arrival, either would emancipate me; but I can't say how soon either event will happen.'

'Can I be of any use in this matter?' I began.

'None, monsieur, I thank you a thousand times.

51

No, this is a piece in which every role is already cast. I am but an amateur, and induced, solely by friend- ship, to take a part.'

So he talked on, for a time, as we walked slowly towards the Belle Etoile, and then came a silence, which I broke by asking him if he knew anything of Colonel Gaillarde.

'Oh! yes, to be sure. He is a little mad; he has had some bad injuries of the head. He used to plague the people in the War Office to death. He has always some delusion. They contrived some employment for him – not regimental, of course – but in this last campaign Napoleon, who could spare nobody, placed him in command of a regiment. He was always a desperate fighter, and such men were more than ever needed.'

There is, or was, a second inn, in this town, called l'Ecu de France. At its door the marquis stopped, bade me a mysterious good-night, and disappeared.

As I walked slowly towards my inn, I met, in the shadow of a row of poplars, the *garçon* who had brought me my Burgundy a little time ago. I was thinking of Colonel Gaillarde, and I stopped the little waiter as he passed me.

'You said, I think, that Colonel Gaillarde was at the Belle Etoile for a week at one time.'

'Yes, monsieur.'

'Is he perfectly in his right mind?'

The waiter stared. 'Perfectly, monsieur.'

'Has he been suspected at any time of being out of his mind?'

'Never, monsieur; he is a little noisy, but a very shrewd man.'

'What is a fellow to think?' I muttered, as I walked.

I was soon within sight of the lights of the Belle

Etoile. A carriage, with four horses, stood in the moonlight at the door, and a furious altercation was going on in the hall, in which the yell of Colonel Gaillarde out-topped all other sounds.

Most young men like, at least, to witness a row. But, intuitively, I felt that this would interest me in a very special manner. I had only fifty yards to run before I found myself in the hall of the old inn. The principal actor in this strange drama was, indeed, the colonel, who stood facing the old Count de St Alyre, who, in his travelling costume, with his black muffler covering the lower part of his face, confronted him; he had evidently been intercepted in an endeavour to reach his carriage. A little in the rear of the count stood the countess, also in travelling costume, with her thick black veil down, and holding in her delicate fingers a white rose. You can't conceive a more diabolical effigy of hate and fury than the colonel; the knotted veins stood out on his forehead, his eyes were leaping from their sockets, he was grinding his teeth and froth was on his lips. His sword was drawn, in his hand, and he accompanied his yelling denunciations with stamps upon the floor and flourishes of his weapon in the air.

The host of the Belle Etoile was talking to the colonel in soothing terms utterly thrown away. Two waiters, pale with fear, stared uselessly from behind. The colonel screamed and thundered, and whirled his sword. 'I was not sure of your red birds of prey; I could not believe you would have the audacity to travel on high roads, and to stop at honest inns, and lie under the same roof with honest men. You! *you!* both – vampires, wolves, ghouls. Summon the gendarmes, I say. By St Peter and all the devils, if either of you tries to get out of that door I'll take your head off.'

For a moment I had stood aghast. Here was a situation! I walked up to the lady; she laid her hand wildly upon my arm. 'Oh! Monsieur,' she whispered, in great agitation, 'that dreadful madman! What are we to do? He won't let us pass; he will kill my husband.'

'Fear nothing, madame,' I answered with romantic devotion, stepping between the count and Gaillarde as he shrieked his invective. 'Hold your tongue, and clear the way, you ruffian, you bully, you coward!' I roared.

A faint cry escaped the lady, which more than repaid the risk I ran as the sword of the frantic soldier, after a moment's astonished pause, flashed in the air to cut me down.

7

The White Rose

I was too quick for Colonel Gaillarde. As he raised his sword, reckless of all consequences but my condign punishment, and quite resolved to cleave me to the teeth, I struck him across the side of his head with my heavy stick; and while he staggered back, I struck him another blow, nearly in the same place, that felled him to the floor, where he lay as if dead.

I did not care one of his own regimental buttons whether he was dead or not; I was, at that moment, carried away by such a tumult of delightful and diabolical emotions!

54

I broke his sword under my foot, and flung the pieces across the street. The old Count de St Alyre skipped nimbly without looking to the right or left, or thanking anybody, over the floor, out of the door, down the steps and into his carriage. Instantly I was at the side of the beautiful countess, thus left to shift for herself; I offered her my arm, which she took, and I led her to the carriage. She entered, and I shut the door. All this without a word.

I was about to ask if there were any commands with which she would honour me – my hand was laid upon the lower edge of the window, which was open.

The lady's hand was laid upon mine timidly and excitedly. Her lips almost touched my cheek as she whispered hurriedly, 'I may never see you more, and, oh! that I could forget you. Go – farewell – for God's sake, go!'

I pressed her hand for a moment. She withdrew it but tremblingly pressed into mine the rose which she had held in her fingers during the agitating scene she had just passed through.

All this took place while the count was commanding, entreating, cursing his servants, tipsy, and out of the way during the crisis, my conscience afterwards insinuated, by my clever contrivance. They now mounted to their places with the agility of alarm. The postilions' whips cracked, the horses scrambled into a trot, and away rolled the carriage, with its precious freightage, along the quaint main street, in the moonlight, towards Paris.

I stood on the pavement till it was quite lost to eye and ear in the distance.

With a deep sigh, I then turned, my white rose folded in my handkerchief – the little parting *gage*, the

55

'favour secret, sweet and precious', which no mortal eye but hers and mine had seen conveyed to me.

The care of the host of the Belle Etoile, and his assistants, had raised the wounded hero of a hundred fights partly against the wall, and propped him at each side with portmanteaus and pillows, and poured a glass of brandy, which was duly placed to his account, into his big mouth, where such a Godsend for the first time remained unswallowed.

A bald-headed little military surgeon of sixty, with spectacles, who had cut off eighty-seven legs and arms to his own share after the Battle of Eylau, having retired with his sword and his saw, his laurels and his sticking-plaster to this, his native town, was called in, and rather thought the gallant colonel's skull was fractured; at all events, there was concussion of the seat of thought, and quite enough work for his remarkable self-healing powers to occupy him for a fortnight.

I began to grow a little uneasy. A disagreeable surprise if my excursion, in which I was to break banks and hearts, and, as you see, heads, should end upon the gallows or the guillotine. I was not clear, in those times of political oscillation, which was the established apparatus.

The colonel was conveyed, snorting apoplectically to his room.

I saw my host in the apartment in which we had supped. Wherever you employ a force of any sort to carry a point of real importance, reject all nice calculations of economy. Better to be a thousand per cent over the mark, than the smallest fraction of a unit under it. I instinctively felt this.

I ordered a bottle of my landlord's very best wine;

made him partake with me, in the proportion of two glasses to one; and then told him that he must not decline a trifling souvenir from a guest who had been so charmed with all he had seen of the renowned Belle Etoile. Thus saying, I placed five-and-thirty Napoleons in his hand. At touch of which his countenance, by no means encouraging before, grew sunny, his manners thawed, and it was plain, as he dropped the coins hastily into his pocket, that benevolent relations had been established between us.

I immediately placed the colonel's broken head upon the *tapis*. We both agreed that if I had not given him that rather smart tap of my walking-cane, he would have beheaded half the inmates of the Belle Etoile. There was not a waiter in the house who would not verify that statement on oath.

The reader may suppose that I had other motives, beside the desire to escape the tedious inquisition of the law, for desiring to recommence my journey to Paris with the least possible delay. Judge what was my horror then to learn that for love or money horses were nowhere to be had that night. The last pair in the town had been obtained from the Ecu de France by a gentleman who had dined and supped at the Belle Etoile and was obliged to proceed to Paris that night.

Who was the gentleman? Had he actually gone? Could he possibly be induced to wait till morning?

The gentleman was now upstairs getting his things together, and his name was Monsieur Droqville.

I ran upstairs. I found my servant St Clair in my room. At sight of him, for a moment, my thoughts were turned into a different channel.

'Well, St Clair, tell me this moment who the lady is?' I demanded.

'The lady is the daughter or wife, it matters not which, of the Count de St Alyre – the old gentleman who was so near being sliced like a cucumber tonight, I am informed, by the sword of the general whom monsieur, by a turn of fortune, has put to bed of an apoplexy.'

'Hold your tongue, fool! The man's beastly drunk – he's sulking – he could talk if he liked – who cares? Pack up my things. Which are Monsieur Droqville's apartments?'

He knew, of course; he always knew everything.

Half an hour later Monsieur Droqville and I were travelling towards Paris, in my carriage, and with his horses. I ventured to ask the Marquis d'Harmonville, in a little while, whether the lady who accompanied the count was certainly the countess. 'Has he not a daughter?'

'Yes; I believe a very beautiful and charming young lady. I cannot say – it may have been she, his daughter by an earlier marriage. I saw only the count himself today.'

The marquis was growing a little sleepy, and, in a little while, he actually fell asleep in his corner. I dozed and nodded; but the marquis slept like a top. He awoke at the next posting-house, where he had fortunately secured horses by sending on his man, he told me.

'You will excuse my being so dull a companion,' he said, 'but till tonight I have had but two hours' sleep in more than sixty hours. I shall have a cup of coffee here; I have had my nap. Permit me to recommend you to do likewise. Their coffee is really excellent.' He ordered two cups of *café noir*, and waited, with his head out of the window. 'We will keep the cups,' he

58

said, as he received them from the waiter, 'and the tray. Thank you.'

There was a little delay as he paid for these things; and then he took in the little tray, and handed me a cup of coffee.

I declined the tray; so he placed it on his own knees, to act as a miniature table.

'I can't endure being waited for and hurried,' he said. 'I like to sip my coffee at leisure.'

I agreed. It really *was* the very perfection of coffee.

'I, like Monsieur le Marquis, have slept very little for the last two or three nights; and find it difficult to keep awake. This coffee will do wonders for me; it refreshes one so.'

Before we had half done, the carriage was again in motion.

For a time our coffee made us chatty, and our conversation was animated.

The marquis was extremely good-natured, as well as clever, and gave me a brilliant and amusing account of Parisian life, schemes and dangers, all put so as to furnish me with practical warnings of the most valuable kind.

In spite of the amusing and curious stories which the marquis related, with so much point and colour, I felt myself again becoming gradually drowsy and dreamy.

Perceiving this, no doubt, the marquis good-naturedly suffered our conversation to subside into silence. The window next him was open. He threw his cup out of it and did the same kind office for mine, and finally the little tray flew after, and I heard it clank on the road; a valuable waif, no doubt, for some early wayfarer in wooden shoes.

I leaned back in my corner; I had my beloved *gage* – my white rose – close to my heart, folded now in white paper. It inspired all manner of romantic dreams. I began to grow more and more sleepy. But actual slumber did not come. I was still viewing, with my half-closed eyes, from my corner, diagonally, the interior of the carriage.

I wished for sleep; but the barrier between waking and sleeping seemed absolutely insurmountable; and, instead, I entered into a state of novel and indescribable indolence.

The marquis lifted his dispatch-box from the floor, placed it on his knees, unlocked it and took out what proved to be a lamp, which he hung by two hooks attached to it to the window opposite to him. He lighted it with a match, put on his spectacles, and taking out a bundle of letters, began to read them carefully.

We were making way very slowly. My impatience had hitherto employed four horses from stage to stage. We were, in this emergency, only too happy to have secured two. But the difference in pace was depressing.

I grew tired of the monotony of seeing the spectacled marquis reading, folding and docketing letter after letter. I wished to shut out the image which wearied me, but something prevented my being able to shut my eyes. I tried again and again; but, positively, I had lost the power of closing them.

I would have rubbed my eyes, but I could not stir my hand, my will no longer acted on my body – I found that I could not move one joint, or muscle, no more than I could, by an effort of my will, have turned the carriage about.

Up to this I had experienced no sense of horror.

Whatever it was, simple nightmare was not the cause. I was awfully frightened. Was I in a fit?

It was horrible to see my good-natured companion pursue his occupation so serenely when he might have dissipated my horrors by a single shake.

I made a stupendous exertion to call out, but in vain; I repeated the effort again and again, with no result.

My companion now tied up his letters, and looked out of the window, humming an air from an opera. He drew back his head, and said, turning to me – 'Yes, I see the lights; we shall be there in two or three minutes.'

He looked more closely at me, and with a kind smile, and a little shrug, he said, 'Poor child, how fatigued he must have been – how profoundly he sleeps; when the carriage stops he will waken.'

He then replaced his letters in the dispatch-box, locked it, put his spectacles in his pocket, and again looked out of the window.

We had entered a little town. I suppose it was past two o'clock by this time. The carriage drew up; I saw an inn-door open, and a light issuing from it.

'Here we are!' said my companion, turning gaily to me. But I did not awake. 'Yes, how tired he must have been!' he exclaimed, after he had waited for an answer.

My servant was at the carriage door, and opened it.

'Your master sleeps soundly, he is so fatigued! It would be cruel to disturb him. You and I will go in, while they change the horses, and take some refreshment, and choose something that Monsieur Beckett will like to take in the carriage; for when he awakes by and by, he will, I am sure, be hungry.'

He trimmed his lamp, poured in some oil; and taking care not to disturb me, with another kind smile, and another word of caution to my servant, he got out, and I heard him talking to St Clair, as they entered the inn-door, and I was left in my corner, in the carriage, in the same state.

8

A Three Minutes' Visit

I have suffered extreme and protracted bodily pain at different periods of my life, but anything like that misery, thank God, I never endured before or since. I earnestly hope it may not resemble any type of death to which we are liable. I was, indeed, a spirit in prison; and unspeakable was my dumb and unmoving agony.

The power of thought remained clear and active. Dull terror filled my mind. How would this end? Was it actual death?

You will understand that my faculty of observing was unimpaired. I could hear and see anything as distinctly as ever I did in my life. It was simply that my will had, as it were, lost its hold of my body.

I told you that the Marquis d'Harmonville had not extinguished his carriage lamp on going into this village inn. I was listening intently, longing for his return, which might result, by some lucky accident, in awaking me from my catalepsy.

Without any sound of steps approaching to announce an arrival, the carriage-door suddenly opened, and a total stranger got in silently and shut the door.

The lamp gave about as strong a light as a wax-candle, so I could see the intruder perfectly. He was a young man, with a dark grey loose surtout, made with a sort of hood, which was pulled over his head. I thought, as he moved, that I saw the gold band of a military undress cap under it; and I certainly saw the lace and buttons of a uniform on the cuffs of the coat that were visible under the wide sleeves of his outside wrapper.

This young man had thick moustaches, and an imperial, and I observed that he had a red scar running upward from his lip across his cheek.

He entered, shut the door softly, and sat down beside me. It was all done in a moment; leaning towards me, and shading his eyes with his gloved hand, he examined my face closely, for a few seconds.

This man had come as noiselessly as a ghost; and everything he did was accomplished with the rapidity and decision that indicated a well-defined and pre-arranged plan. His designs were evidently sinister. I thought he was going to rob, and, perhaps, murder me. I lay, nevertheless, like a corpse under his hands. He inserted his hand in my breast pocket, from which he took my precious white rose and all the letters it contained, among which was a paper of some consequence to me.

My letters he glanced at. They were plainly not what he wanted. My precious rose, too, he laid aside with them. It was evidently with the paper I have mentioned that he was concerned, for the moment he opened it, he began with a pencil, in a small pocket-book, to make rapid note of its contents.

This man seemed to glide through his work with the noiseless and cool celerity which argued, I thought, the training of the police department.

He rearranged the papers, possibly in the very order in which he had found them, replaced them in my breast-pocket, and was gone.

His visit, I think, did not quite last three minutes. Very soon after his disappearance, I heard the voice of the marquis once more. He got in, and I saw him look at me, and smile, half-envying me, I fancied, my sound repose. If he had but known all!

He resumed his reading and docketing by the light of the little lamp which had just subserved the purposes of a spy.

We were now out of the town, pursuing our journey at the same moderate pace. We had left the scene of my police visit, as I should have termed it, now two leagues behind us, when I suddenly felt a strange throbbing in one ear, and a sensation as if air passed through it into my throat. It seemed as if a bubble of air, formed deep in my ear, swelled and burst there. The indescribable tension of my brain seemed all at once to give way; there was an odd humming in my head, and a sort of vibration through every nerve of my body, such as I have experienced in a limb that has been, in popular phraseology, asleep. I uttered a cry and half rose from my seat, and then fell back trembling and with a sense of mortal faintness.

The marquis stared at me, took my hand, and earnestly asked if I was ill. I could answer only with a deep groan.

Gradually the process of restoration was completed; and I was able, though very faintly, to tell him how very ill I had been; and then to describe the violation of my letters during the time of his absence from the carriage.

'Good heaven!' he exclaimed, 'the miscreant did not get at my dispatch-box?'

64

I satisfied him, so far as I had observed, on that point. He placed the box on the seat beside him and opened and examined its contents very minutely.

'Yes, undisturbed; all safe, thank heaven!' he murmured. 'There are half a dozen letters here that I would not have some people read for a great deal.'

He now asked with a very kind anxiety all about the illness I complained of. When he had heard me, he said – 'A friend of mine once had an attack as like yours as possible. It was on board ship, and followed a state of high excitement. He was a brave man like you; and was called on to exert both his strength and his courage suddenly. An hour or two after, fatigue overpowered him, and he appeared to fall into a sound sleep. He really sank into a state which he afterwards described in such a way that I think it must have been precisely the same affection as yours.'

'I am happy to think that my attack was not unique. Did he ever experience a return of it?'

'I knew him for years after and never heard of any such thing. What strikes me is a parallel in the predisposing causes of each attack. Your unexpected and gallant hand-to-hand encounter, at such desperate odds, with an experienced swordsman like that insane colonel of dragoons, your fatigue, and, finally, your composing yourself, as my other friend did, to sleep.'

I was further reassured.

'I wish,' he resumed, 'one could make out who that *coquin* was who examined your letters. It is not worth turning back, however, because we should learn nothing. Those people always manage so adroitly. I am satisfied, however; that he must have been an agent of the police. A rogue of any other kind would have robbed you.'

I talked very little, being ill and exhausted, but the marquis talked on agreeably.

'We grow so intimate,' said he, at last, 'that I must remind you that I am not, for the present, the Marquis d'Harmonville, but only Monsieur Droqville; nevertheless, when we get to Paris, although I cannot see you often I may be of use. I shall ask you to name to me the hotel at which you mean to put up; because the marquis being, as you are aware, on his travels, the Hotel d'Harmonville is, for the present, tenanted only by two or three old servants, who must not even see Monsieur Droqville. That gentleman will, nevertheless, contrive to get you access to the box of Monsieur le Marquis, at the Opera, as well, possibly, as to other places more difficult; and so soon as the diplomatic office of the Marquis d'Harmonville is ended, and he is at liberty to declare himself, he will not excuse his friend, Monsieur Beckett, from fulfilling his promise to visit him this autumn at the Château d'Harmonville.'

You may be sure I thanked the marquis.

The nearer we got to Paris, the more I valued his protection. The countenance of a great man on the spot, just then, taking so kind an interest in the stranger whom he had, as it were, blundered upon, might make my visit ever so many degrees more delightful than I had anticipated.

Nothing could be more gracious than the manner and looks of the marquis; and, as I still thanked him, the carriage suddenly stopped in front of the place where a relay of horses awaited us, and where, as it turned out, we were to part.

9

Gossip and Counsel

My eventful journey was over, at last. I sat in my
hotel window looking out upon brilliant Paris, which
had, in a moment, recovered all its gaiety, and more
than its accustomed bustle. Everyone has read of
the kind of excitement that followed the catastrophe
of Napoleon, and the second restoration of the Bour-
bons. I need not, therefore, even if, at this distance,
I could, recall and describe my experiences and
impressions of the peculiar aspect of Paris in those
strange times. It was, to be sure, my first visit. But
often as I have seen it since, I don't think I ever saw
that delightful capital in a state so pleasurably excited
and exciting.

I had been two days in Paris, and had seen all sorts
of sights, and experienced none of that rudeness
and insolence of which others complained from the
exasperated officers of the defeated French army.

I must say this, also. My romance had taken complete possession of me; and the chance of seeing the
object of my dream gave a secret and delightful
interest to my rambles and drives in the streets and
environs and my visits to the galleries and other
sights of the metropolis.

I had neither seen nor heard of the count or
countess, nor had the Marquis d'Harmonville made
any sign. I had quite recovered from the strange
indisposition under which I had suffered during my
night journey.

It was now evening, and I was beginning to fear that my patrician acquaintance had quite forgotten me, when the waiter presented to me the card of 'Monsieur Droqville'; and, with no small elation and hurry, I desired him to show the gentleman up.

In came the Marquis d'Harmonville, kind and gracious as ever.

'I am a night-bird at present,' said he, as soon as we had exchanged the little speeches which are usual. 'I keep in the shade during the daytime, and even now I hardly ventured to come in a closed carriage. The friends for whom I have undertaken a rather critical service have so ordained it. They think all is lost if I am known to be in Paris. First, let me present you with these orders for my box. I am so vexed that I cannot command it oftener during the next fortnight; during my absence, I had directed my secretary to give it for any night to the first of my friends who might apply, and the result is that I find next to nothing left at my disposal.'

I thanked him very much.

'And now, a word, in my office of mentor. You have not come here, of course, without introductions?'

I produced half a dozen letters, the addresses of which he looked at.

'Don't mind these letters,' he said. 'I will introduce you. I will take you myself from house to house. One friend at your side is worth many letters. Make no intimacies, no acquaintances, until then. You young men like best to exhaust the public amusements of a great city, before embarrassing yourselves with the engagements of society. Go to all these. It will occupy you, day and night, for at least three weeks. When this is over, I shall be at liberty, and will myself introduce you to the brilliant but comparatively quiet routine of society. Place yourself in my hands; and in Paris remember, when once in society, you are always there.'

I thanked him very much, and promised to follow his counsels implicitly.

He seemed pleased, and said – 'I shall now tell you some of the places you ought to go to. Take your map, and write letters or numbers upon the points I will indicate, and we will make out a little list. All the places that I shall mention to you are worth seeing.'

In this methodical way, and with a great deal of amusing and scandalous anecdote, he furnished me with a catalogue and a guide, which, to a seeker of novelty and pleasure, was invaluable.

'In a fortnight, perhaps in a week,' he said, 'I shall be at leisure to be of real use to you. In the meantime, be on your guard. You must not play; you will be robbed if you do. Remember, you are surrounded here by plausible swindlers and villains of all kinds, who subsist by devouring strangers. Trust no one but those you know.'

I thanked him again, and promised to profit by his advice. But my heart was too full of the beautiful lady of the Belle Etoile to allow our interview to close without an effort to learn something about her. I therefore asked for the Count and Countess de St Alyre, whom I had had the good fortune to extricate from an extremely unpleasant row in the hall of the inn.

Alas, he had not seen them since. He did not know where they were staying. They had a fine old house only a few leagues from Paris; but he thought it probable that they would remain, for a few days at least, in the city, as preparations would, no doubt, be necessary, after so long an absence, for their reception at home.

'How long have they been away?'

'About eight months, I think.'

'They are poor, I think you said?'

'What you would consider poor. But, monsieur, the count has an income which affords them the comforts, and even the elegancies of life, living as they do in a very quiet and retired way in this cheap country.'

'Then they are very happy?'

'One would say they *ought* to be happy.'

'And what prevents it?'

'He is jealous.'

'But his wife – she gives him no cause?'

'I am afraid she does.'

'How, monsieur?'

'I always thought she was a little too – a *great deal* too –'

'Too *what*, monsieur?'

'Too handsome. But although she has remarkably fine eyes, exquisite features and the most delicate complexion in the world, I believe that she is a woman of probity. You have never seen her?'

'There was a lady, muffled up in a cloak, with a very thick veil on, the other night, in the hall of the Belle Etoile, when I broke that fellow's head who was bullying the old count. But her veil was so thick I could not see a feature through it.' My answer was diplomatic, you observe. 'She may have been the count's daughter. Do they quarrel?'

'Who, he and his wife?'

'Yes.'

'A little.'

'Oh! and what do they quarrel about?'

'It is a long story; about the lady's diamonds. They are valuable – they are worth, La Perelleuse says, about a million francs. The count wishes them sold and turned into revenue, which he offers to settle as she pleases. The countess, whose they are, resists, and for a reason which, I rather think, she can't disclose to him.'

'And pray what is that?' I asked, my curiosity a good deal piqued.

'She is thinking, I conjecture, how well she will look in them when she marries her second husband.'

'Oh? – yes, to be sure. But the Count de St Alyre is a good man?'

'Admirable, and extremely intelligent.'

'I should wish so much to be presented to the count: you tell me he's so – '

'So agreeably married. But they are living quite out of the world. He takes her now and then to the Opera, or to a public entertainment; but that is all.'

'And he must remember so much of the old *régime*, and so many of the scenes of the revolution!'

'Yes, the very man for a philosopher, like you. And he falls asleep after dinner; and his wife don't, But, seriously, he has retired from the gay and the great world and has grown apathetic; and so has his wife; and nothing seems to interest her now, not even – her husband!'

The marquis stood up to take his leave.

'Don't risk your money,' said he. 'You will soon have an opportunity of laying out some of it to great advantage. Several collections of really good pictures, belonging to persons who have mixed themselves up

71

in this Bonapartist restoration, must come within a few weeks to the hammer. You can do wonders when these sales commence. There will be startling bargains! Reserve yourself for them. I shall let you know all about it. By the by,' he said, stopping short as he approached the door, 'I was so near forgetting. There is to be the very thing you would enjoy so much, because you see so little of it in England – I mean a *bal masqué*, conducted, it is said, with more than usual splendour. It takes place at Versailles – all the world will be there; there is such a rush for cards! But I think I may promise you one. Good-night!'

10

The Black Veil

Speaking the language fluently, and with unlimited money, there was nothing to prevent my enjoying all that was enjoyable in the French capital. You may easily suppose how two days were passed. At the end of that time, and at about the same hour, Monsieur Droqville called again.

Courtly, good-natured, gay as usual, he told me that the masquerade ball was fixed for the next day, and that he had applied for a card for me.

How awfully unlucky. I was so afraid I should not be able to go.

He stared at me for a moment with a suspicious and menacing look, which I did not understand, in silence, and then enquired rather sharply, 'And will Monsieur Beckett be good enough to say why not?'

I was a little surprised, but answered the simple

truth: I had made an engagement for that evening with two or three English friends, and did not see how I could.

'Just so! You English, wherever you are, always look out for your English boors, your beer and *"bifstek"*; and when you come here, instead of trying to learn something of the people you visit and pretend to study, you are guzzling and swearing and smoking with one another, and no wiser or more polished at the end of your travels than if you had been all the time carousing in a booth at Greenwich.'

He laughed sarcastically, and looked as if he could have poisoned me.

'There it is,' said he, throwing the card on the table. 'Take it or leave it, just as you please. I suppose I shall have no thanks for my pains; but it is not usual when a man, such as I, takes trouble, asks a favour and secures a privilege for an acquaintance, for him to be treated so.'

This was astonishingly impertinent.

I was shocked, offended, penitent. I had possibly committed unwittingly a breach of good breeding, according to French ideas, which almost justified the brusque severity of the marquis's undignified rebuke.

In a confusion, therefore, of many feelings, I hastened to make my apologies, and to propitiate the chance friend who had showed me so much disinterested kindness.

I told him that I would, at any cost, break through the engagement in which I had unluckily entangled myself; that I had spoken with too little reflection, and that I certainly had not thanked him at all in proportion to his kindness, and to my real estimate of it.

'Pray say not a word more; my vexation was entirely

73

on your account; and I expressed it, I am only too conscious, in terms a great deal too strong, which I am sure your good nature will pardon. Those who know me a little better are aware that I sometimes say a good deal more than I intend; and am always sorry when I do. Monsieur Beckett will forget that his old friend Monsieur Droqville has lost his temper in his cause, for a moment, and – we are as good friends as before.'

He smiled like the Monsieur Droqville of the Belle Etoile, and extended his hand, which I took very respectfully and cordially.

Our momentary quarrel had left us only better friends.

The marquis then told me I had better secure a bed in some hotel at Versailles as a rush would be made to take them; and advised my going down next morning for the purpose.

I ordered horses accordingly for eleven o'clock; and, after a little more conversation, the Marquis d'Harmonville bade me good-night, and ran down the stairs with his handkerchief to his mouth and nose and, as I saw from my window, jumped into his closed carriage again and drove away.

Next day I was at Versailles. As I approached the door of the Hôtel de France, it was plain that I was not a moment too soon, if, indeed, I were not already too late,

A crowd of carriages were drawn up about the entrance, so that I had no chance of approaching except by dismounting and pushing my way among the horses. The hall was full of servants and gentlemen screaming to the proprietor, who in a state of polite distraction, was assuring them, one and all,

74

that there was not a room or a closet disengaged in his entire house.

I slipped out again, leaving the hall to those who were shouting, expostulating and wheedling, in the delusion that the host might, if he pleased, manage something for them. I jumped into my carriage and drove, at my horses' best pace, to the Hôtel du Reservoir. The blockade about this door was as complete as the other. The result was the same. It was very provoking, but what was to be done? My postilion had, a little officiously, while I was in the hall talking with the hotel authorities, got his horses bit by bit as other carriages moved away to the very steps of the inn door.

This arrangement was very convenient so far as getting in again was concerned. But, this accomplished, how were we to get out? There were carriages in front, and carriages behind, and no less than four rows of carriages, of all sorts, to the side of us.

I had at this time remarkably long and clear sight, and if I had been impatient before, guess what my feelings were when I saw an open carriage pass along the narrow strip of roadway left open at the other side, a barouche in which I was certain I recognised the veiled countess and her husband. This carriage had been brought to a walk by a cart which occupied the whole breadth of the narrow way, and was moving with the customary tardiness of such vehicles.

I should have done more wisely if I had jumped down on the *trottoir*, and run round the block of carriages in front of the barouche. But, unfortunately, I was more of a Murat than a Moltke, and preferred a direct charge upon my object to relying on *tactique*. I dashed across the back seat of a carriage which was next mine, I don't know how; tumbled through a sort of gig, in which an old gentleman and a dog were dozing; stepped with an incoherent apology over the side of an open carriage in which were four gentlemen engaged in a hot dispute; tripped at the far side in getting out, and fell flat across the backs of a pair of horses, who instantly began plunging and threw me head foremost in the dust.

To those who observed my reckless charge, without being in the secret of my object, I must appeared demented. Fortunately, the interesting barouche had passed before the catastrophe, and covered as I was with dust, and my hat blocked, you may be sure I did not care to present myself before the object of my Quixotic devotion.

I stood for a while amid a storm of *sacré*-ing, tempered disagreeably with laughter; and in the midst of these, while endeavouring to beat the dust from my clothes with my handkerchief, I heard a voice with which I was acquainted call, 'Monsieur Beckett.'

I looked and saw the marquis peeping from a carriage-window. It was a welcome sight. In a moment I was at his carriage side.

'You may as well leave Versailles,' he said; 'you have learned, no doubt, that there is not a bed to hire in either of the hotels; and I can add that there is not a room to let in the whole town. But I have managed something for you that will answer just as well. Tell your servant to follow us, and get in here and sit beside me.'

Fortunately an suitable opening in the closely-packed carriages had just occurred, and mine was approaching.

I directed the servant to follow us; and the marquis

having said a word to his driver, we were immediately in motion.

'I will bring you to a comfortable place, the very existence of which is known to but few Parisians, where, knowing how things were here, I secured a room for you. It is only a mile away, and an old comfortable inn, called Le Dragon Volant. It was fortunate for you that my tiresome business called me to this place so early.'

I think we had driven about a mile and a half to the farther side of the palace when we found ourselves upon a narrow old road, with the woods of Versailles on one side, and much older trees, of a size seldom seen in France, on the other.

We pulled up before an antique and solid inn, built of Caen stone in a fashion richer and more florid than was ever usual in such houses, and which indicated that it was originally designed for the private mansion of some person of wealth, and probably, as the wall bore many carved shields and supporters, of distinction also. A kind of porch, less ancient than the rest, projected hospitably with a wide and florid arch, over which, cut in high relief in stone, and painted and gilded, was the sign of the inn. This was the Flying Dragon, with wings of brilliant red and gold, expanded, and its tail, pale green and gold, twisted and knotted into ever so many rings, and ending in a burnished point barbed like the dart of death.

'I shan't go in – but you will find it a comfortable place; at all events better than nothing. I would go in with you, but my incognito forbids. You will, I dare say, be all the better pleased to learn that the inn is haunted – I should have been, in my young days, I know. But don't allude to that awful fact in hearing of

77

your host, for I believe it is a sore subject. Au revoir.
If you want to enjoy yourself at the ball take my
advice, and go in a domino. I think I shall look in;
and certainly, if I do, in the same costume. How shall
we recognise one another? Let me see, something
held in the fingers – a flower won't do, so many
people will have flowers. Suppose you get a red cross
a couple of inches long – you're an Englishman –
stitched or pinned on the breast of your domino, and
I a white one? Yes, that will do very well; and whatever
room you go into keep near the door till we meet. I
shall look for you at all the doors I pass, and you, in
the same way, look for me; and we *must* find each
other soon. So that is understood. I can't enjoy a
thing of that kind with any but a young person, a man
of my age requires the contagion of young spirits and
the companionship of someone who enjoys everything
spontaneously. Farewell; we meet tonight.'

By this time I was standing on the road; I shut the
carriage-door; bade him goodbye; and away he drove.

II

Le Dragon Volant

I took one look about me. The building was picturesque; the trees made it more so. The antique
and sequestered character of the scene contrasted
strangely with the glare and bustle of the Parisian life
to which my eye and ear had become accustomed.

Then I examined the gorgeous old sign for a minute
or two. Next I surveyed the exterior of the house more
carefully. It was large and solid, and squared more

with my ideas of an ancient English hostelry, such as the Canterbury Pilgrims might have put up at, than a French house of entertainment. Except, indeed, for a round turret that rose at the left flank of the house and terminated in the extinguisher-shaped roof that suggests a French château.

I entered and announced myself as Monsieur Beckett, for whom a room had been taken. I was received with all the consideration due to an English milord, with, of course, an unfathomable purse.

My host conducted me to my apartment. It was a large room, a little sombre, panelled with dark wainscoting, and furnished in a stately and sombre style, long out of date. There was a wide hearth, and a heavy mantelpiece, carved with shields, in which I might, had I been curious enough, have discovered a correspondence with the heraldry on the outer walls. There was something interesting, melancholy, and even depressing in all this. I went to the stone-shafted window, and looked out upon a small park, with a thick wood, forming the background of a château, which presented a cluster of such conical-topped turrets as I have just now mentioned.

The wood and château were melancholy objects. They showed signs of neglect, and almost of decay; and the gloom of fallen grandeur and a certain air of desertion hung oppressively over the scene.

I asked my host the name of the château.

'That, monsieur, is the Château de la Carque,' he answered.

'It is a pity it is so neglected,' I observed. 'I should say, perhaps, a pity that its proprietor is not more wealthy?'

'Perhaps so, monsieur.'

79

'*Perhaps?*' – I repeated, and looked at him. 'Then I suppose he is not very popular.'

'Neither one thing nor the other, monsieur,' he answered; 'I meant only that we could not tell what use he might make of riches.'

'And who is he?' I enquired.

'The Count de St Alyre.'

'Oh! The count! You are quite sure?' I asked, very eagerly.

It was now the innkeeper's turn to look at me.

'*Quite* sure, monsieur, the Count de St Alyre.'

'Do you see much of him in this part of the world?'

'Not a great deal, monsieur; he is often absent for a considerable time.'

'And is he poor?' I enquired.

'I pay rent to him for this house. It is not much; but I find he cannot wait long for it,' he replied, smiling satirically.

'From what I have heard, however, I should think he cannot be very poor?' I continued.

'They say, monsieur, he plays. I know not. He certainly is not rich. About seven months ago, a relation of his died in a distant place. His body was sent to the count's house here, and by him buried in Père Lachaise, as the poor gentleman had desired. The count was in profound affliction; although he got a handsome legacy, they say, by that death. But money never seems to do him good for any time.'

'He is old, I believe?'

'Old? We call him the "Wandering Jew", except, indeed, that he has not always the five sous in his pocket. Yet, monsieur, his courage does not fail him. He has taken a young and handsome wife.'

'And she?' I urged.

'Is the Countess de St Alyre.'

'Yes; but I fancy we may say something more? She has attributes?'

'Three, monsieur, three, at least, most amiable.'

'Ah! And what are they?'

'Youth, beauty, and – diamonds.'

I laughed. The sly old gentleman was compounding my curiosity.

'I see, my friend,' said I, 'you are reluctant – '

'To quarrel with the count,' he concluded. 'True. You see, monsieur, he could vex me in two or three ways, so could I him. But, on the whole, it is better each to mind his business, and to maintain peaceful relations; you understand.'

It was, therefore, no use pressing him further, at least for the present. Perhaps he had nothing to relate. Should I think differently, by and by, I could try the effect of a few Napoleons. Possibly he meant to extract them.

The host of Le Dragon Volant was an elderly man, thin, bronzed, intelligent, and with an air of decision, perfectly military. I learned afterwards that he had served under Napoleon in his early Italian campaigns.

'One question I think you may answer,' I said, 'without risking a quarrel. Is the count at home?'

'He has many homes, I conjecture,' said the host evasively. 'But – but I think I may say, monsieur, that he is, I believe, at present staying at the Château de la Carque.'

I looked out of the window, more interested than ever, across the undulating grounds to the château, with its gloomy background of foliage.

'I saw him today, in his carriage at Versailles,' I said.

'Very natural.'

'Then his carriage, and horses, and servants, are at the château?'

'The carriage he puts up here, monsieur, and the servants are hired for the occasion. There is but one who sleeps at the château. Such a life must be terrifying for Madame the Countess,' he replied.

'The old screw!' I thought. 'By this torture, he hopes to extract her diamonds. What a life! What fiends to contend with – jealousy and extortion!'

The knight, having made this speech to himself, cast his eyes once more upon the enchanter's castle, and heaved a gentle sigh – a sigh of longing, of resolution and of love.

What a fool I was! and yet, in the sight of angels, are we any wiser as we grow older? It seems to me only that our illusions change as we go on; but, still, we are madmen all the same.

'Well, St Clair,' said I, as my servant entered and began to arrange my things. 'You have got a bed?'

'In the cock-loft, monsieur, among the spiders, and, *par ma foi!* the cats and the owls. But we agree very well. *Vive la bagatelle!*'

'I had no idea it was so full.'

'Chiefly the servants, monsieur, of those persons who were fortunate enough to get apartments at Versailles.'

'And what do you think of Le Dragon Volant?'

'Le Dragon Volant, Monsieur? the old fiery dragon? The devil himself, if all is true! On the faith of a Christian, monsieur, they say that diabolical miracles have taken place in this house.'

'What do you mean? *Revenants?*'

'Not at all, sir; I wish it was no worse. *Revenants?*

No! People who have never returned – who vanished, before the eyes of half a dozen men all looking at them.'

'What do you mean, St Clair? Let us hear the story, or miracle, or whatever it is.'

'It is only this, monsieur, that an ex-master-of-the-horse of the late king who lost his head – monsieur will have the goodness to recollect, in the revolution – being permitted by the emperor to return to France, lived here in this hotel, for a month, and at the end of that time vanished, visibly, as I told you, before the faces of half a dozen credible witnesses! The other was a Russian nobleman, six feet high and upwards, who, standing in the centre of the room downstairs, describing to seven gentlemen of unquestionable veracity the last moments of Peter the Great, and having a glass of *eau de vie* in his left hand and his *tasse de café*, nearly finished, in his right, in like manner vanished. His boots were found on the floor where he had been standing; and the gentleman at his right found, to his astonishment, his cup of coffee in his fingers, and the gentleman at his left, his glass of *eau de vie* –'

'Which he swallowed in his confusion,' I suggested.

'Which was preserved for three years among the curious articles of this house, and was broken by the *curé* while conversing with Mademoiselle Fidone in the housekeeper's room; but of the Russian nobleman himself, nothing more was ever seen or heard. *Parbleu!* when *we* go out of Le Dragon Volant, I hope it may be by the door. I heard all this, monsieur, from the postilion who drove us.'

'Then it *must* be true!' said I, jocularly: but I was beginning to feel the gloom of the view, and of the chamber in which I stood; there had stolen over me, I know not how, a presentiment of evil; and my joke was with an effort, and my spirit flagged.

12

The Magician

No more brilliant spectacle than this masked ball could be imagined. Among other *salons* and galleries thrown open was the enormous perspective of the Grande Galerie des Glaces, lighted up for the occasion with no less than four thousand wax candles, reflected and repeated by all the mirrors, so that the effect was almost dazzling. The grand suite of salons was thronged with masquers in every conceivable costume. There was not a single room deserted. Every place was animated with music, voices, brilliant colours, flashing jewels, the hilarity of extemporised comedy, and all the spirited incidents of a cleverly sustained masquerade. I had never seen before anything in the least comparable to this magnificent fête. I moved along, indolently, in my domino and mask, loitering, now and then, to enjoy a clever dialogue, a farcical song or an amusing monologue, but, at the same time, keeping my eyes about me, lest my friend in the black domino, with the little white cross on his breast, should pass me by.

I had delayed and looked about me, specially at every door I passed, as the marquis and I had agreed; but he had not yet appeared.

While I was thus employed in the very luxury of lazy amusement, I saw a gilded sedan chair, or, rather, a

Chinese palanquin, exhibiting the fantastic exuberance of 'celestial' decoration, borne forward on gilded poles by four richly dressed Chinese; one with a wand in his hand marched in front, and another behind; and a slight and solemn man, with a long black beard and a tall fez, such as a dervish is represented as wearing, walked close to its side. A strangely-embroidered robe fell over his shoulders, covered with hieroglyphic symbols; the embroidery was in black and gold upon a variegated ground of brilliant colours. The robe was bound about his waist with a broad belt of gold, with cabbalistic devices traced on it in dark red and black; red stockings, and shoes embroidered with gold, and pointed and curved upward at the toes, in Oriental fashion, appeared below the skirt of the robe. The man's face was dark, fixed and solemn, his eyebrows black and enormously heavy, and he carried a singular-looking book under one arm, a wand of polished black wood in his other hand and walked with his chin sunk on his breast and his eyes fixed upon the floor. The man in front waved his wand right and left to clear the way for the advancing palanquin, the curtains of which were closed; and there was something so singular, strange and solemn about the whole thing that I felt at once interested.

I was very well pleased when I saw the bearers set down their burden within a few yards of the spot on which I stood.

The bearers and the men with the gilded wands forthwith clapped their hands, and in silence danced round the palanquin a curious and half-frantic dance, which was yet, as to figures and postures, perfectly methodical. This was soon accompanied by a clapping of hands and a ha-ha-ing, rhythmically delivered.

While the dance was going on a hand was lightly laid on my arm, and, looking round, I saw that a black domino with a white cross stood beside me.

'I am so glad I have found you,' said the marquis; 'and at this moment. This is the best group in the rooms. You must speak to the wizard. About an hour ago I lighted upon them, in another salon, and consulted the oracle by putting questions. I never was more amazed. Although his answers were a little disguised it was soon perfectly plain that he knew every detail about the business, which no one on earth had heard of but myself and two or three other men, about the most cautious persons in France. I shall never forget that shock. I saw other people who consulted him, evidently as much surprised, and more frightened than I. I came with the Count de St Alyre and the countess.'

He nodded toward a thin figure, also in a domino. It was the count.

'Come,' he said to me, 'I'll introduce you.'

I followed, you may suppose, readily enough.

The marquis presented me, with a very prettily-turned allusion to my fortunate intervention in his favour at the Belle Etoile; and the count overwhelmed me with polite speeches, and ended by saying what pleased me better still: 'The countess is near us, in the next salon but one, chatting with her old friend the Duchesse d'Argensaque; I shall go for her in a few minutes; and when I bring her here, she shall make your acquaintance; and thank you, also, for your assistance, rendered with so much courage when we were so very disagreeably interrupted.'

'You must, positively, speak with the magician,' said the marquis to the Count de St Alyre, 'you will be so much amused. I did so; and, I assure you, I could not have anticipated such answers! I don't know what to believe.'

'Really! Then, by all means, let us try,' he replied.

We three approached, together, the side of the palanquin at which the black-bearded magician stood.

A young man, in a Spanish dress, who, with a friend at his side, had just conferred with the conjuror, was saying, as he passed us by: 'Ingenious mystification! Who is that in the palanquin? He seems to know everybody!'

The count, in his mask and domino, moved along stiffly with us towards the palanquin. A clear circle was maintained by the Chinese attendants, and the spectators crowded round in a ring. One of these men – he who with a gilded wand had preceded the procession – advanced, extending his empty hand, palm upward.

'Money?' enquired the count.

'Gold,' replied the usher.

The count placed a piece of money in his hand; and I and the marquis were each called on in turn to do likewise as we entered the circle. We paid accordingly.

The conjuror stood beside the palanquin, its silk curtain in his hand; his chin sunk, with its long, jet-black beard, on his chest; the outer hand grasping the black wand, on which he leaned; his eyes were lowered, as before, to the ground; his face looked absolutely lifeless. Indeed, I never saw face or figure so moveless, except in death.

The first question the count put was – 'Am I married, or unmarried?'

The conjuror drew back the curtain quickly, placed

his ear towards a richly dressed Chinese who sat in the litter, withdrew his head and closed the curtain again; then he answered – 'Yes.'

The same preliminary was observed each time, so that the man with the black wand presented himself, not as a prophet, but as a medium; and answered, as it seemed, in the words of a greater than himself.

Two or three questions followed, the answers to which seemed to amuse the marquis very much; but the point of which I could not see, for I knew next to nothing of the count's peculiarities and adventures.

'Does my wife love me?' asked he, playfully.

'As well as you deserve.'

'Whom do I love best in the world?'

'Self.'

'Oh! That I fancy is pretty much the case with everyone. But, putting myself out of the question, do I love anything on earth better than my wife?'

'Her diamonds.'

'Oh!' said the count.

The marquis, I could see, laughed.

'Is it true,' said the count, changing the conversation peremptorily, 'that there has been a battle in Naples?'

'No; in France.'

'Indeed,' said the count, satirically, with a glance round. 'And may I enquire between what powers, and on what particular quarrel?'

'Between the Count and Countess de St Alyre, and about a document they subscribed on the 25th July 1811.

The marquis afterwards told me that this was the date of their marriage settlement.

The count stood stock-still for a minute or so; and

one could fancy that they saw his face flushing through his mask.

Nobody, but we two, knew that the enquirer was the Count de St Alyre.

I thought he was puzzled to find a subject for his next question, and perhaps repented having entangled himself in such a colloquy. If so, he was relieved; for the marquis, touching his arm, whispered, 'Look to your right, and see who is coming.'

I looked in the direction indicated by the marquis, and I saw a gaunt figure stalking towards us. It wore no mask. The face was broad, scarred and white. In a word, it was the ugly face of Colonel Gaillarde, who, in the costume of a corporal of the Imperial Guard, had his left arm so adjusted as to look like a stump, leaving the lower part of the coat-sleeve empty and pinned up to the breast. There were strips of very real sticking-plaster across his eyebrow and temple, where my stick had left its mark, to score, hereafter, among the more honourable scars of war.

13

The Oracle Tells Me Wonders

I forgot for a moment how impervious my mask and domino were to the hard stare of the old campaigner and was preparing for an animated scuffle. It was only for a moment, of course; but the count cautiously drew a little back as the Gasconading corporal, in blue uniform, white vest and white gaiters – for my friend Gaillarde was as loud and swaggering in his assumed character as in his real one of a colonel of

dragoons – drew near. He had already twice all
but got himself turned out of doors for vaunting
the exploits of Napoleon le Grand in terrific mock-
heroics, and had very nearly come to hand-grips
with a Prussian hussar. In fact, he would have been
involved in several sanguinary rows already had not
his discretion reminded him that the object of his
coming there at all, namely, to arrange a meeting
with an affluent widow, on whom he believed he
had made a tender impression, would not have been
promoted by his premature removal from the festive
scene, of which he was an ornament, in charge of a
couple of gendarmes.

'Money! Gold! Bah! What money can a wounded
soldier like your humble servant have amassed with
but his sword-hand left, which, being necessarily
occupied, places not a finger at his command with
which to scrape together the spoils of a routed
enemy?'

'No gold from him,' said the magician. 'His scars
frank him.'

'Bravo, Monsieur le Prophète! Bravissimo! Here I
am. Shall I begin, *mon sorcier*, without further loss of
time, to question you?'

Without waiting for an answer, he commenced, in
stentorian tones.

After half a dozen questions and answers, he asked
– 'Whom do I pursue at present?'

'Two persons.'

'Ha! Two? Well, who are they?'

'An Englishman, whom, if you catch, he will kill
you; and a French widow, whom, if you find, she will
spit in your face.'

'Monsieur le Magicien calls a spade a spade, and

knows that his cloth protects him. No matter! Why do I pursue them?'

'The widow has inflicted a wound on your heart, and the Englishman a wound on your head. They are each separately too strong for you; take care your pursuit does not unite them.'

'Bah! How could that be?'

'The Englishman protects ladies. He has got that fact into your head. The widow, if she sees him, will marry him. It takes some time, she will reflect, to become a colonel, and the Englishman is unquestionably young.'

'I will cut his cock's-comb for him,' he ejaculated with an oath and a grin; and in a softer tone he asked, 'Where is she?'

'Near enough to be offended if you fail.'

'So she ought, by my faith. You are right, Monsieur le Prophète! A hundred thousand thanks! Farewell!' And staring about him, and stretching his lank neck as high as he could, he strode away with his scars and white waistcoat and gaiters, and his bearskin shako.

I had been trying to see the person who sat in the palanquin. I had only once an opportunity of a tolerably steady peep. What I saw was singular. The oracle was dressed, as I have said, very richly, in the Chinese fashion. He was a figure altogether on a larger scale than the interpreter who stood outside. The features seemed to me large and heavy, and the head was carried with a downward inclination; the eyes were closed, and the chin rested on the breast of his embroidered pelisse. The face seemed fixed, and the very image of apathy. Its character and pose seemed an exaggerated repetition of the immobility of the figure who communicated with the noisy outer world. This face looked blood-red; but that was caused, I concluded, by the light entering through the red silk curtains. All this struck me almost at a glance; I had not many seconds in which to make my observation. The ground was now clear, and the marquis said, 'Go forward, my friend.'

I did so. When I reached the magician, as we called the man with the black wand, I glanced over my shoulder to see whether the count was near.

No, he was some yards behind; and he and the marquis, whose curiosity seemed to be by this time satisfied, were now conversing generally upon some subject of course quite different.

I was relieved, for the sage seemed to blurt out secrets in an unexpected way; and some of mine might not have amused the count.

I thought for a moment. I wished to test the prophet. A Church of England man was a *rara avis* in Paris.

'What is my religion?' I asked.

'A beautiful heresy,' answered the oracle instantly.

'A heresy? – and pray how is it named?'

'Love.'

'Oh! Then I suppose I am a polytheist, and love a great many?'

'One.'

'But, seriously,' I asked, intending to turn the course of our colloquy a little out of an embarrassing channel, 'have I ever learned any words of devotion by heart?'

'Yes.'

'Can you repeat them?'

'Approach.'

I did, and lowered my ear.

The man with the black wand closed the curtains,

and whispered, slowly and distinctly, these words which, I need scarcely tell you, I instantly recognised: '*I may never see you more; and, oh! that I could forget you! go – farewell – for God's sake, go!*'

I started as I heard them. They were, you know, the last words whispered to me by the countess.

Good heavens! How miraculous! Words heard most assuredly by no ear on earth but my own and the lady's who uttered them, till now!

I looked at the impassive face of the spokesman with the wand. There was no trace of meaning, or even of a consciousness that the words he had uttered could possible interest me.

'What do I most long for?' I asked, scarcely knowing what I said.

'Paradise.'

'And what prevents my reaching it?'

'A black veil.'

Stronger and stronger! The answers seemed to me to indicate the minutest acquaintance with every detail of my little romance, of which not even the marquis knew anything! And I, the questioner, masked and robed so that my own brother could not have known me!

'You said I loved someone. Am I loved in return?' I asked.

'Try.'

I was speaking lower than before, and stood near the dark man with the beard, to prevent the necessity of his speaking in a loud key.

'Does anyone love me?' I repeated.

'Secretly,' was the answer.

'Much or little?' I enquired.

'Too well.'

93

'How long will that love last?'

'Till the rose casts its leaves.'

'The rose – another allusion!'

'Then – darkness!' I sighed. 'But till then I live in light.'

'The light of violet eyes.'

Love, if not a religion, as the oracle had just pronounced it, is at least a superstition. How it exalts the imagination! How it enervates the reason! How credulous it makes us!

All this which, in the case of another, I should have laughed at, most powerfully affected me in my own. It inflamed my ardour, and half crazed my brain, and even influenced my conduct.

The spokesman of this wonderful trick – if trick it were – now waved me backward with his wand, and I withdrew, my eyes still fixed upon the group, by this time encircled with an aura of mystery in my fancy; backing towards the ring of spectators, I saw him raise his hand suddenly, with a gesture of command, as a signal to the usher who carried the golden wand in front.

The usher struck his wand on the ground, and, in a shrill voice, proclaimed: 'The great Confu is silent for an hour.'

Instantly the bearers pulled down a sort of blind of bamboo, which descended with a sharp clatter, and secured it at the bottom; and then the man in the tall fez, with the black beard and wand, began a sort of dervish dance. In this the men with the gold wands joined, and finally, in an outer ring, the bearers, the palanquin being the centre of the circles described by these solemn dancers, whose pace, little by little, quickened, whose gestures grew sudden, strange, frantic, as the motion became swifter and swifter, until at length the whirl became so rapid that the dancers seemed to fly by with the speed of a mill-wheel, and amid a general clapping of hands, and universal wonder, these strange performers mingled with the crowd, and the exhibition, for the time at least, ended.

The Marquis d'Harmonville was standing not far away, looking on the ground, as one could judge by his attitude and musing. I approached, and he said: 'The count has just gone away to look for his wife. It is a pity she was not here to consult the prophet; it would have been amusing, I dare say, to see how the count bore it. Suppose we follow him. I have asked him to introduce you.'

With a beating heart, I accompanied the Marquis d'Harmonville.

14

Mademoiselle de la Vallière

We wandered through the *salons*, the marquis and I. It was no easy matter to find a friend in rooms so crowded.

'Stay here,' said the Marquis, 'I have thought of a way of finding him. Besides, his jealousy may have warned him that there is no particular advantage to be gained by presenting you to his wife. I had better go and reason with him as you seem to wish an introduction so very much.'

This occurred in the room that is now called the Salon d'Apollon. The paintings remain in my memory,

and my adventure of that evening was destined to
occur there.

I sat down upon a sofa and looked about me. Three
or four persons beside myself were seated on this
roomy piece of gilded furniture. They were chatting all
very gaily; all – except the person who sat next me, and
she was a lady. Hardly two feet interposed between us.
The lady sat apparently in a reverie. Nothing could be
more graceful. She wore the costume perpetuated in
Collignan's full-length portrait of Mademoiselle de la
Vallière. It is, as you know, not only rich, but elegant.
Her hair was powdered, but one could perceive that it
was naturally a dark brown. One pretty little foot
appeared, and could anything be more exquisite than
her hand?

It was extremely provoking that this lady wore her
mask, and did not, as many did, hold it for a time in
her hand.

I was convinced that she was pretty. Availing myself
of the privilege of a masquerade, a microcosm in
which it is impossible, except by voice and allusion,
to distinguish friend from foe, I spoke. 'It is not easy,
mademoiselle, to deceive me,' I began.

'So much the better for monsieur,' answered the
masquer, quietly.

'I mean,' I said, determined to tell my fib, 'that
beauty is a gift more difficult to conceal than
mademoiselle supposes.'

'Yet monsieur has succeeded very well,' she said in
the same sweet and careless tones.

'I see the costume of this, the beautiful Mademoiselle de la Vallière, upon a form that surpasses her
own; I raise my eyes, and I behold a mask, and yet I
recognise the lady; beauty is like that precious stone

in *The Arabian Nights*, which emits, no matter how concealed, a light that betrays it.'

'I know the story,' said the young lady. 'The light betrayed it, not in the sun, but in darkness. Is there so little light in these rooms, monsieur, that a poor glowworm can show so brightly. I thought we were in a luminous atmosphere, wherever a certain countess moved?'

Here was an awkward speech! How was I to answer? This lady might be, as they say some ladies are, a lover of mischief, or an intimate of the Countess de St Alyre. Cautiously, therefore, I enquired, 'What countess?'

'If you know me, you must know that she is my dearest friend. Is she not beautiful?'

'How can I answer, there are so many countesses.'

'Everyone who knows me, knows who my best beloved friend is. You don't know me.'

'That is cruel. I can scarcely believe I am mistaken.'

'With whom were you walking, just now?' she asked.

'A gentleman, a friend,' I answered,

'I saw him, of course; a friend; but I think I know him, and should like to be certain. Is he not a certain marquis?'

Here was another question that was extremely awkward.

'There are so many people here, and one may walk at one time with one, and at another with a different one, that – '

'That an unscrupulous person has no difficulty in evading a simple question like mine. Know then, once for all, that nothing disgusts a person of spirit so much as suspicion. You, monsieur, are a gentleman of discretion. I shall respect you accordingly.'

'Mademoiselle would despise me, were I to violate a confidence.'

'But you don't deceive me. You imitate your friend's diplomacy. I hate diplomacy. It means fraud and cowardice. Don't you think I know him. The gentleman with the cross of white ribbon on his breast. I know the Marquis d'Harmonville perfectly. You see to what good purpose your ingenuity has been expended.'

'To that conjecture I can answer neither yes nor no.'

'You need not. But what was your motive in mortifying a lady?'

'It is the last thing on earth I should do.'

'You affected to know me, and you don't; through caprice, or listlessness, or curiosity, you wished to converse, not with a lady, but with a costume. You admired, and you pretend to mistake me for another. But who is quite perfect? Is truth any longer to be found on earth?'

'Mademoiselle has formed a mistaken opinion of me.'

'And you also of me; you find me less foolish than you supposed. I know perfectly whom you intend amusing with compliments and melancholy declamation, and whom, with that amiable purpose, you have been seeking.'

'Tell me whom you mean,' I entreated.

'Upon one condition.'

'What is that?'

'That you will confess if I name the lady.'

'You describe my object unfairly,' I objected. 'I can't admit that I proposed speaking to any lady in the tone you describe.'

'Well, I shan't insist on that; only if I name the lady, you will promise to admit that I am right.'

'*Must* I promise?'

'Certainly not, there is no compulsion; but your promise is the only condition on which I will speak to you again.'

I hesitated for a moment; but how could she possibly tell? The countess would scarcely have admitted this little romance to anyone; and the masquer in the La Vallière costume could not possibly know who the masked domino beside her was. 'I consent,' I said, 'I promise.'

'You must promise on the honour of a gentleman.'

'Well, I do; on the honour of a gentleman.'

'Then this lady is the Countess de St Alyre.'

I was unspeakably surprised; I was disconcerted; but I remembered my promise, and said, 'The Countess de St Alyre *is*, unquestionably, the lady to whom I hoped for an introduction tonight; but I beg to assure you also, on the honour of a gentleman, that she has not the faintest imaginable suspicion that I was seeking such an honour, nor, in all probability, does she remember that such a person as I exists. I had the honour to render her and the count a trifling service, too trifling, I fear, to have earned more than an hour's recollection.'

'The world is not so ungrateful as you suppose; or if it be, there are, nevertheless, a few hearts that redeem it. I can answer for the Countess de St Alyre, she never forgets a kindness. She does not show all she feels; for she is unhappy, and cannot.'

'Unhappy! I feared, indeed, that might be. But for all the rest that you are good enough to suppose, it is but a flattering dream.'

'I told you that I am the countess's friend, and being so I must know something of her character; also, there are confidences between us, and I may know more than you think of those trifling services of which you suppose the recollection is so transitory.'

I was becoming more and more interested. I was as wicked as other young men, and the heinousness of such a pursuit was as nothing now that self-love and all the passions that mingle in such a romance were roused. The image of the beautiful countess had now again quite superseded the pretty counterpart of La Vallière, who was before me. I would have given a great deal to hear, in solemn earnest, that she did remember the champion who, for her sake, had thrown himself before the sabre of an enraged dragoon, with only a cudgel in his hand, and conquered.

'You say the countess is unhappy,' said I. 'What causes her unhappiness?'

'Many things. Her husband is old, jealous and tyrannical. Is not that enough? Even when relieved from his society, she is lonely.'

'But you are her friend?' I suggested.

'And you think one friend enough?' she answered; 'she has one alone, to whom she can open her heart.'

'Is there room for another friend?'

'Try.'

'How can I find a way?'

'She will aid you.'

'How?'

She answered by a question. 'Have you secured rooms in either of the hotels of Versailles?'

'No, I could not. I am lodged in Le Dragon Volant, which stands at the verge of the grounds of the Château de la Carque.'

'That is better still. I need not ask if you have courage for an adventure. I need not ask if you are a man of honour. A lady may trust herself to you, and fear nothing. There are few men to whom the interview, such as I shall arrange, could be granted with safety. You shall meet her at two o'clock this morning in the park of the Château de la Carque. What room do you occupy in Le Dragon Volant?'

I was amazed at the audacity and decision of this girl. Was she, as we say in England, hoaxing me?

'I can describe that accurately,' said I. 'As I look from the rear of the house in which my apartment is, I am at the extreme right, next the angle; and one pair of stairs up from the hall.'

'Very well; you must have observed, if you looked into the park, two or three clumps of chestnut and lime trees, growing so close together as to form a small grove. You must return to your hotel, change your dress and, preserving a scrupulous secrecy as to why or where you go, leave Le Dragon Volant and climb the park wall unseen; you will easily recognise the grove I have mentioned; there you will meet the countess, who will grant you an audience of a few minutes, who will expect the most scrupulous reserve on your part, and who will explain to you, in a few words, a great deal which I could not so well tell you here.'

I cannot describe the feeling with which I heard these words. I was astounded. Doubt succeeded. I could not believe these agitating words.

'Mademoiselle will believe that if I only dared assure myself that so great a happiness and honour were really intended for me my gratitude would be as lasting as my life. But how dare I believe that mademoiselle does not speak rather from her own sympathy or goodness than from a certainty that the Countess de St Alyre would concede so great an honour?'

'Monsieur believes either that I am not, as I pretend to be, in the secret which he hitherto supposed to be shared by no one but the countess and himself, or else that I am cruelly mystifying him. That I am in her confidence, I swear by all that is dear in a whispered farewell. By the last companion of this flower!' and she took for a moment in her fingers the nodding head of a white rosebud that was nestled in her bouquet. 'By my own good star, and hers – or shall I call it our "*belle étoile*"? Have I said enough?'

'Enough?' I repeated; 'more than enough – a thousand thanks.'

'And being thus in her confidence, I am clearly her friend; and being a friend would it be friendly to use her dear name so; and all for sake of practising a vulgar trick upon you – a stranger?'

'Mademoiselle will forgive me. Remember how very precious is the hope of seeing and speaking to the countess. Is it wonderful, then, that I should falter in my belief? You have convinced me, however, and will forgive my hesitation.'

'You will be at the place I have described, then, at two o'clock?'

'Assuredly,' I answered.

'And monsieur, I know, will not fail through fear. No, he need not assure me; his courage is already proved.'

'No danger, in such a case, will be unwelcome to me.'

'Had you not better go now, monsieur, and rejoin your friend.'

'I promised to wait here for my friend's return. The Count de St Alyre said that he intended to introduce me to the countess.'

'And monsieur is so simple as to believe him?'

'Why should I not?'

'Because he is jealous and cunning. You will see. He will never introduce you to his wife. He will come here and say he cannot find her, and promise another time.'

'I think I see him approaching, with my friend. No – there is no lady with him.'

'I told you so. You will wait a long time for that happiness if it is never to reach you except through his hands. In the meantime, you had better not let him see you so near me. He will suspect that we have been talking of his wife; and that will whet his jealousy and his vigilance.'

I thanked my unknown friend in the mask, and withdrawing a few steps, came by a little *circumbendibus* upon the flank of the count.

I smiled under my mask as he assured me that the Duchess de la Roquème had changed her place and taken the countess with her; but he hoped, at some very early time, to have an opportunity of enabling her to make my acquaintance.

I avoided the Marquis d'Harmonville, who was following the count. I was afraid he might propose accompanying me home, and had no wish to be forced to make an explanation.

I lost myself quickly, therefore, in the crowd, and moved, as rapidly as it would allow, toward the Galerie des Glaces, which lay in the direction opposite to that in which I saw the count and my friend the marquis moving.

15

Strange Story of Le Dragon Volant

These fêtes were earlier in those days, and in France, than our modern balls are in London. I consulted my watch. It was a little past twelve.

It was a still and sultry night; the magnificent suite of rooms, vast as some of them were, could not be kept at a temperature less than oppressive, especially to people with masks on. In some places the crowd was inconvenient, and the profusion of lights added to the heat. I removed my mask, therefore, as I saw some other people do, who were as careless of mystery as I. I had hardly done so, and begun to breathe more comfortably, when I heard a friendly English voice call me by my name. It was Tom Whistlewick, of the 8th Dragoons. He had unmasked, with a very flushed face, as I did. He was one of those Waterloo heroes, new from the mint of glory, whom, as a body, all the world, except France, revered; and the only thing I knew against him was a habit of allaying his thirst, which was excessive, at balls, fêtes, musical parties and all gatherings where it was to be had, with champagne; and, as he introduced me to his friend, Monsieur Carmaignac, I observed that he spoke a little thick. Monsieur Carmaignac was little, lean and as straight as a ramrod. He was bald, took snuff and wore spectacles; and, as I soon learned, held an official position.

Tom was facetious, sly, and rather difficult to under-stand in his present pleasant mood. He was elevating his eyebrows and screwing his lips oddly, and fanning himself vaguely with his mask.

After some agreeable conversation, I was glad to observe that he preferred silence, and was satisfied with the role of listener, as I and Monsieur Carmaignac chatted; and he seated himself, with extraordinary caution and indecision, upon a bench beside us, and seemed very soon to find a difficulty in keeping his eyes open.

'I heard you mention,' said the French gentleman, 'that you had engaged an apartment at Le Dragon Volant, about half a league from this. When I was in a different police department, about four years ago, two very strange cases were connected with that house. One was of a wealthy *émigré*, permitted to return to France, by the Em – by Napoleon. He vanished. The other – equally strange – was the case of a Russian of rank and wealth. He disappeared just as mysteriously.'

'My servant,' I said, 'gave me a confused account of some occurrences, and, as well as I recollect he described the same persons – I mean a returned French nobleman and a Russian gentleman. But he made the whole story so marvellous – I mean in the supernatural sense – that, I confess, I did not believe a word of it.'

'No, there was nothing supernatural; but a great deal inexplicable,' said the French gentleman. 'Of course, there may be theories; but the thing was never explained, nor, so far as I know, was a ray of light ever thrown upon it.'

'Pray let me hear the story,' I said. 'I think I have a claim, as it affects my quarters. You don't suspect the people of the house?'

'Oh! it has changed hands since then. But there seemed to be a fatality about a particular room.'

'Could you describe that room?'

'Certainly. It is a spacious, panelled bedroom, up one pair of stairs, in the back of the house, and at the extreme right, as you look from its windows.'

'Ho! Really? Why, then, I have got the very room!' I said, beginning to be more interested – perhaps the least bit in the world disagreeably. 'Did the people die, or were they actually spirited away?'

'No, they did not die – they disappeared very oddly. I'll tell you the particulars – I happen to know them exactly, because I made an official visit, on the first occasion, to the house, to collect evidence; and although I did not go down there upon the second, the papers came before me, and I dictated the official letter dispatched to the relations of the people who had disappeared; they had applied to the government to investigate the affair. We had letters from the same relations more than two years later, from which we learned that the missing men had never turned up.'

He took a pinch of snuff, and looked steadily at me.

'Never! I shall relate all that happened, so far as we could discover. The French noble, who was the Chevalier Château Blassemare, unlike most *émigrés* had taken the matter in time, sold a large portion of his property before the revolution had proceeded so far as to render that next to impossible, and retired with a large sum. He brought with him about half a million francs, the greater part of which he invested in French funds; a much larger sum remained in Austrian land and securities. You will observe then that this gentleman was rich, and there was no allegation of his having lost money, or being, in any way, embarrassed. You see?'

I assented.

'This gentleman's habits were not expensive in proportion to his means. He had suitable lodgings in Paris; and for a time, society, the theatres and other reasonable amusements engrossed him. He did not play. He was a middle-aged man, affecting youth, with the vanities which are usual in such persons; but, for the rest, he was a gentle and polite person, who disturbed nobody – a person, you see, not likely to provoke an enmity.'

'Certainly not,' I agreed.

'Early in the summer of 1811, he got an order permitting him to copy a picture in one of these *salons*, and came down here, to Versailles, for the purpose. His work was getting on slowly. After a time he left his hotel, here, and went, by way of change, to Le Dragon Volant; there he took, by special choice, the bedroom which has fallen to you by chance. From this time, it appeared, he painted little; and seldom visited his apartments in Paris. One night he saw the host of Le Dragon Volant, and told him that he was going into Paris, to remain for a day or two, on very particular business; that his servant would accompany him, but that he would retain his apartments at Le Dragon Volant, and return in a few days. He left some clothes there, but packed a portmanteau, took his dressing case, and the rest, and, with his servant behind his carriage, drove into Paris. You observe all this, monsieur?'

'Most attentively,' I answered.

'Well, monsieur, as soon as they were approaching his lodgings, he stopped the carriage on a sudden, told his servant that he had changed his mind; that he would sleep elsewhere that night, that he had very particular business in the north of France, not far from Rouen, that he would set out before daylight on his journey, and return in a fortnight. He called a *fiacre*, took in his hand a leather bag which, the servant said, was just large enough to hold a few shirts and a coat, but that it was enormously heavy, as he could testify, for he held it in his hand, while his master took out his purse to count thirty-six Napoleons, for which the servant was to account when he should return. He then sent him on, in the carriage; and he, with the bag I have mentioned, got into the *fiacre*. Up to that, you see, the narrative is quite clear.'

'Perfectly,' I agreed.

'Now comes the mystery,' said Monsieur Carmaignac. 'After that, the Count Château Blassemare was never more seen, so far as we can make out, by acquaintance or friend. We learned that the day before the count's stockbroker had, by his direction, sold all his stock in the French funds, and handed him the cash it realised. The reason he gave him for this measure tallied with what he said to his servant He told him that he was going to the north of France to settle some claims, and did not know exactly how much might be required. The bag, which had puzzled the servant by its weight, contained, no doubt, a large sum in gold. Will Monsieur try my snuff?'

He politely tendered his open snuffbox, of which I partook, experimentally.

'A reward was offered,' he continued, 'when the enquiry was instituted, for any information tending to throw a light upon the mystery which might be afforded by the driver of the *fiacre*, "employed on the night of" (so and so), "at about the hour of half-past ten, by a gentleman with a black-leather travelling-bag in his hand, who descended from a private carriage, and gave his servant some money, which he counted twice over". About a hundred and fifty drivers applied, but not one of them was the right man. We did, however, elicit a curious and unexpected piece of evidence in quite another quarter. What a racket that plaguey harlequin makes with his sword!'

'Intolerable!' I chimed in.

The harlequin was soon gone, and he resumed,

'The evidence I speak of came from a boy, about twelve years old, who knew the appearance of the count perfectly, having been often employed by him as a messenger. He stated that about half-past twelve o'clock on the same night – upon which you are to observe, there was a brilliant moon – he was sent (his mother having been suddenly taken ill) for the sage *femme* who lived within a stone's throw of Le Dragon Volant. His father's house, from which he started, was a mile away, or more, from that inn, in order to reach which he had to pass round the park of the Château de la Carque, at the site most remote from the point to which he was going. It passes the old churchyard of St Aubin, which is separated from the road only by a very low fence, and two or three enormous old trees. The boy was a little nervous as he approached this ancient cemetery; and, under the bright moonlight, he saw a man whom he distinctly recognised as the count, whom they designated by a sobriquet which means "the man of smiles". He was looking rueful enough now, and was seated on the side of a tombstone on which he had laid a pistol, while he was ramming home the charge of another.

'The boy got cautiously by, on tiptoe, with his eyes all the time on the Count Château Blassemare, or the man he mistook for him: his dress was not what he usually wore, but the witness swore that he could not be mistaken as to his identity. He said his face looked grave and stern; but though he did not smile, it was the same face he knew so well. Nothing would make him swerve from that. If that were he, it was the last time he was seen. He has never been heard of since. Nothing could be heard of him in the neighbourhood of Rouen. There has been no evidence of his death; and there is no sign that he is living.'

'That certainly is a most singular case,' I replied, and was about to ask a question or two, when Tom Whistlewick who, without my observing it, had been taking a ramble, returned, a great deal more awake and a great deal less tipsy.

'I say, Carmaignac, it is getting late, and I must go; I really must, for the reason I told you – and, Beckett, we must soon meet again.'

'I regret very much, monsieur, my not being able at present to relate to you the other case, that of another tenant of the very same room – a case more mysterious and sinister than the last – and which occurred in the autumn of the same year.'

'Will you both do a very good-natured thing, and come and dine with me at Le Dragon Volant tomorrow?'

So, as we pursued our way along the Galerie des Glaces, I extracted their promise.

'By Jove!' said Whistlewick, when this was done; 'look at that pagoda, or sedan chair, or whatever it is, just where those fellows set it down, and not one of them near it! I can't imagine how they tell fortunes so devilish well. Jack Nuffles – I met him here tonight – says they are gypsies. Where are they, I wonder? I'll go over and have a peep at the prophet.'

I saw him plucking at the blinds, which were constructed something on the principle of Venetian blinds; the red curtains were inside; but they did not yield, and he could only peep under one that did not come quite down.

When he rejoined us, he related: 'I could scarcely see the old fellow, it's so dark. He is covered with gold and red, and has an embroidered hat on like a mandarin's; he's fast asleep; and, by Jove, he smells like a polecat! It's worth going over only to have it to say. Fiew! pooh! oh! It *is* a perfume. Faugh!'

Not caring to accept this tempting invitation, we got along slowly toward the door. I bade them good-night, reminding them of their promise. And so I found my way at last to my carriage, and was soon rolling slowly towards Le Dragon Volant, on the loneliest of roads, under old trees, and in the soft moonlight.

What a number of things had happened within the last two hours! what a variety of strange and vivid pictures were crowded together in that brief space! What an adventure was before me!

The silent, moonlighted, solitary road, how it contrasted with the many-eddied whirl of pleasure from whose roar and music, lights, diamonds and colours, I had just extricated myself!

The sight of lonely nature at such an hour acts like a sudden sedative. The madness and guilt of my pursuit struck me with a momentary compunction and horror. I wished I had never entered the labyrinth which was leading me, I knew not whither. It was too late to think of that now; but the bitter was already stealing into my cup; and vague anticipations lay, for a few minutes, heavy on my heart. It would not have taken much to make me disclose my unmanly state of mind to my lively friend, Alfred Ogle, nor even to the milder ridicule of the agreeable Tom Whistlewick.

16

The Park of the Château de la Carque

There was no danger of Le Dragon Volant's closing its doors on that occasion till three or four in the morning. There were quartered there many servants of great people, whose masters would not leave the ball till the last moment and who could not return to their corners in Le Dragon Volant till their last services had been rendered.

I knew, therefore, I should have ample time for my mysterious excursion without exciting curiosity by being shut out.

And now we pulled up under the canopy of boughs before the sign of Le Dragon Volant and the light that shone from its hall-door.

I dismissed my carriage, ran up the broad staircase, mask in hand, with my domino fluttering about me, and entered the large bedroom. The black wains-coting and stately furniture, with the dark curtains of the very tall bed, made the night there more sombre.

An oblique patch of moonlight was thrown upon the floor from the window to which I hastened. I looked out upon the landscape slumbering in those silvery beams. There stood the outline of the Château de la Carque, its chimneys and many turrets with their extinguisher-shaped roofs black against the soft grey sky. There, also, more in the foreground, about midway between the window where I stood and the château but a little to the left, I traced the tufted masses of the grove which the lady in the mask had appointed as the trysting-place where I and the beautiful countess were to meet that night.

I took 'the bearings' of this gloomy bit of wood, whose foliage glimmered softly at top in the light of the moon.

You may guess with what a strange interest and swelling of the heart I gazed on the unknown scene of my coming adventure.

But time was flying, and the hour already near. I threw my robe upon a sofa and groped out a pair of boots, which I substituted for those thin heel-less shoes, in those days called 'pumps', without which a gentleman could not attend an evening party. I put on my hat, and lastly I took a pair of loaded pistols, which I had been advised were satisfactory companions in the then unsettled state of French society; swarms of disbanded soldiers, some of them alleged to be desperate characters, being everywhere to be met with. These preparations made, I confess I took a looking-glass to the window to see how I looked in the moonlight; and being satisfied, I replaced it, and ran downstairs.

In the hall I called for my servant.

'St Clair,' said I, 'I mean to take a little moonlight ramble, only ten minutes or so. You must not go to bed until I return. If the night is very beautiful, I may possibly extend my ramble a little.'

So down the steps I lounged, looking first over my right and then over my left shoulder, like a man uncertain which direction to take, and I sauntered up the road, gazing now at the moon and now at the thin white clouds in the opposite direction, whistling, all the time, an air which I had picked up at one of the theatres.

When I had got a couple of hundred yards away from Le Dragon Volant, my minstrelsy totally ceased; and I turned about and glanced sharply down the road, that looked as white as hoar-frost under the moon, and saw the gable of the old inn, and a window, partly concealed by the foliage, with a dusky light shining from it.

No sound of footstep was stirring; no sign of human figure in sight. I consulted my watch, which the light was sufficiently strong to enable me to do. It now wanted but eight minutes of the appointed hour. A thick mantle of ivy at this point covered the wall and rose in a clustering head at the top. It afforded me facilities for scaling the wall, and a partial screen for my operations, if any eye should chance to be looking that way. And now it was done. I was in the park of the Château de la Carque, as nefarious a poacher as ever trespassed on the grounds of unsuspicious lord!

Before me rose the appointed grove, which looked as black as a clump of gigantic hearse plumes. It seemed to tower higher and higher at every step and cast a broader and blacker shadow towards my feet. On I marched, and was glad when I plunged into the shadow, which concealed me. Now I was among the grand old lime and chestnut trees – my heart beat fast with expectation.

This grove opened, a little, near the middle; and in the space thus cleared, there stood, with a surrounding flight of steps, a small Greek temple or shrine, with a statue in the centre. It was built of white marble with fluted Corinthian columns, and the crevices were tufted with grass; moss had shown itself on pedestal and cornice, and signs of long neglect and decay were apparent in its discoloured and weather-worn marble. A few feet in front of the steps a fountain, fed from the great ponds at the other side of the château, was making a constant tinkle and plashing in a wide marble basin, and the jet of water glimmered like a shower of diamonds in the broken moonlight. The very neglect and half-ruinous state of all this made it only the prettier, as well as sadder. I was too intently watching for the arrival of the lady, in the direction of the château, to study these things; but the half-noted effect of them was romantic, and suggested somehow the grotto and the fountain and the apparition of Egeria.

As I watched a voice spoke to me, a little behind my left shoulder. I turned, almost with a start, and the masquer in the costume of Mademoiselle de la Vallière stood there.

'The countess will be here presently,' she said. The lady stood upon the open space, and the moonlight fell unbroken upon her. Nothing could be more becoming; her figure looked more graceful and elegant than ever. 'In the meantime I shall tell you some peculiarities of her situation. She is unhappy; miserable in an ill-assorted marriage, with a jealous tyrant who now would constrain her to sell her diamonds, which are – '

'Worth thirty thousand pounds sterling. I heard all that from a friend. Can I aid the countess in her unequal struggle? Say but how, and the greater the danger or the sacrifice, the happier will it make me. Can I aid her?'

'If you despise a danger – which, yet, is not a danger; if you despise, as she does, the tyrannical canons of the world; and, if you are chivalrous enough to devote yourself to a lady's cause, with no reward but her poor gratitude; if you can do these things you can aid her, and earn a foremost place, not in her gratitude only, but in her friendship.'

At those words the lady in the mask turned away and seemed to weep.

I vowed myself the willing slave of the countess. 'But,' I added, 'you told me she would soon be here.'

'That is, if nothing unforeseen should happen; but with the eye of the Count de St Alyre in the house, and open, it is seldom safe to stir.'

'Does she wish to see me?' I asked, with a tender hesitation.

'First, say have you really thought of her, more than once, since the adventure of the Belle Etoile?'

'She never leaves my thoughts; day and night her beautiful eyes haunt me; her sweet voice is always in my ear.'

'Mine is said to resemble hers,' said the masquer.

'So it does,' I answered. 'But it is only a resemblance.'

'Oh! then mine is better?'

'Pardon me, mademoiselle, I did not say that. Yours is a sweet voice, but I fancy a little higher.'

'A little shriller, you would say,' answered the de la Vallière, I fancied a good deal vexed.

'No, not shriller: your voice is not shrill, it is beautifully sweet; but not so pathetically sweet as hers.'

'That is prejudice, monsieur; it is not true.'

I bowed; I could not contradict a lady.

'I see, monsieur, you laugh at me; you think me vain, because I claim in some points to be equal to the Countess de St Alyre. I challenge you to say my hand, at least, is less beautiful than hers.' As she thus spoke, she drew her glove off and extended her hand, back upward, in the moonlight.

The lady seemed really nettled. It was undignified and irritating; for in this uninteresting competition the precious moments were flying, and my interview leading apparently to nothing.

'You will admit, then, that my hand is as beautiful as hers?'

'I cannot admit it, mademoiselle,' said I, with the honesty of irritation. 'I will not enter into comparisons, but the Countess de St Alyre is, in all respects, the most beautiful lady I ever beheld.'

The masquer laughed coldly, and then, more and more softly, said, with a sigh, 'I will prove all I say.' And as she spoke she removed the mask and the Countess de St Alyre, smiling, confused, bashful, more beautiful than ever, stood before me!

'Good heavens!' I exclaimed. 'How monstrously stupid I have been. And it was to Madame la Comtesse that I spoke for so long in the *salon*!' I gazed on her in silence. And with a low sweet laugh of good nature she extended her hand. I took it, and carried it to my lips.

'No, you must not do that,' she said, quietly, 'we are not old enough friends yet. I find, although you were mistaken, that you do remember the Countess of the Belle Etoile, and that you are a champion true and fearless. Had you yielded to the claims just now pressed upon you by the rivalry of Mademoiselle de la Vallière, in her mask, the Countess de St Alyre should never have trusted or seen you more. I now am sure that you are true, as well as brave. You now know that I have not forgotten you; and, also, that if you would risk your life for me, I, too, would brave some danger, rather than lose my friend for ever. I have but a few moments more. Will you come here again tomorrow night, at a quarter past eleven? I will be here at that moment; you must exercise the most scrupulous care to prevent suspicion that you have come here, monsieur. *You owe that to me.*'

She spoke these last words with the most solemn entreaty.

I vowed again and again that I would die rather than permit the least rashness to endanger the secret which made all the interest and value of my life.

She was looking, I thought, more and more beautiful every moment. My enthusiasm expanded in proportion.

'You must come tomorrow night by a different route,' she said; 'and if you come again, we can change it once more. At the other side of the château there is a little churchyard with a ruined chapel. The neighbours are afraid to pass it by night. The road is deserted there, and a stile opens a way into these grounds. Cross it and you can find a covert of thickets to within fifty steps of this spot.'

I promised, of course, to observe her instructions implicitly.

'I have lived for more than a year in an agony of irresolution. I have decided at last. I have lived a melancholy life; a lonelier life than is passed in the cloister. I have had no one to confide in; no one to advise me; no one to save me from the horrors of my existence. I have found a brave and prompt friend at last. Shall I ever forget the heroic tableau of the hall of

the Belle Etoile? Have you – have you really kept the
rose I gave you, as we parted? Yes – you swear it.
You need not; I trust you. Richard, how often have I
in solitude repeated your name, learned from my
servant. Richard, my hero! Oh! Richard! Oh, my
king! I love you!'

I would have folded her to my heart – thrown
myself at her feet. But this beautiful and – shall I say
it – inconsistent woman constrained me.

'No, we must not waste our moments in extravagances. Understand my case. There is no such thing
as indifference in the married state. Not to love one's
husband,' she continued, 'is to hate him. The count,
ridiculous in all else, is formidable in his jealousy. In
mercy, then, to me, observe caution. Affect to all you
speak to the most complete ignorance of all the
people in the Château de la Carque; and, if anyone
in your presence mentions the Count or Countess
de St Alyre, be sure you say you never saw either. I
shall have more to say to you tomorrow night. I have
reasons that I cannot now explain for all I do and all
I postpone. Farewell. Go! Leave me.'

She waved me back, peremptorily. I echoed her
'farewell', and obeyed.

This interview had not lasted, I think, more than
ten minutes. I scaled the park wall again, and reached
Le Dragon Volant before its doors were closed.

I lay awake in my bed, in a fever of elation. I saw,
till the dawn broke and chased the vision, the beautiful
Countess de St Alyre, always in the dark, before me.

17

The Tenant of the Palanquin

The marquis called on me next day. My late breakfast was still upon the table.

He had come, he said, to ask a favour. An accident had happened to his carriage in the crowd on leaving the ball, and he begged, if I were going into Paris, a seat in mine. I was going in, and was extremely glad of his company. He came with me to my hotel; we went up to my rooms. I was surprised to see a man seated in an easy chair, with his back towards us, reading a newspaper. He rose. It was the Count de St Alyre, his gold spectacles on his nose; his black wig, in oily curls, lying close to his narrow head and looking like carved ebony over a repulsive visage of boxwood. His black muffler had been pulled down. His right arm was in a sling. I don't know whether there was anything unusual in his countenance that day or whether it was but the effect of prejudice arising from all I had heard in my mysterious interview in his park, but I thought his countenance was more strikingly forbidding than I had seen it before.

I was not callous enough in the ways of sin to meet this man, injured at least in intent, thus suddenly without a momentary disturbance.

He smiled.

'I called, Monsieur Beckett, in the hope of finding you here,' he croaked, 'and I meditated, I fear, taking a great liberty, but my friend the Marquis d'Harmonville, on whom I have perhaps some claim, will perhaps give me the assistance I require so much.'

'With great pleasure,' said the marquis, 'but not till after six o'clock. I must go this moment to a meeting of three or four people, whom I cannot disappoint, and I know, perfectly, we cannot break up earlier.'

'What am I to do?' exclaimed the count, 'an hour would have done it all. Was ever *contretemps* so unlucky?'

'I'll give you an hour, with pleasure,' said I.

'How very good of you, monsieur, I hardly dare to hope it. The business, for so gay and charming a man as Monsieur Beckett, is a little *funeste*. Pray read this note which reached me this morning.'

It certainly was not cheerful. It was a note stating that the body of the count's cousin, Monsieur de St Amand, who had died at his house, the Château Clery, had been, in accordance with his written directions, sent for burial at Père Lachaise, and, with the permission of the Count de St Alyre, would reach his house (the Château de la Carque) at about ten o'clock on the night following, to be conveyed thence in a hearse, with any member of the family who might wish to attend the obsequies.

'I did not see the poor gentleman twice in my life,' said the count, 'but this office, as he has no other kinsman, disagreeable as it is, I could scarcely decline, and so I want to attend at the cemetery to have the book signed, and the order entered. But here is another misery. By ill luck, I have sprained my thumb, and can't sign my name for a week to come. However, one name answers as well as another. Yours as well as mine. And as you are so good as to come with me, all will go right.'

Away we drove. The count gave me a memorandum

of the Christian and surnames of the deceased, his age, the complaint he died of, and the usual particulars; also a note of the exact position in which a grave, the dimensions of which were described, of the ordinary simple kind, was to be dug, between two vaults belonging to the family of St Amand. The funeral, it was stated, would arrive at half-past one o'clock a.m. (the next night but one); and he handed me the money, with extra fees for a burial by night. It was a good deal; and I asked him, as he entrusted the whole affair to me, in whose name I should take the receipt.

'Not in mine, my good friend. They wanted me to become an executor, which I, yesterday, wrote to decline; and I am informed that if the receipt were in my name it would constitute me an executor in the eye of the law, and fix me in that position. Take it, pray, if you have no objection, in your own name.'

This, accordingly, I did.

You will see, by and by, why I am obliged to mention all these particulars.

The count, meanwhile, was leaning back in the carriage, with his black silk muffler up to his nose, and his hat shading his eyes, while he dozed in his corner; in which state I found him on my return.

Paris had lost its charm for me. I hurried through the little business I had to do, longing once more for my quiet room in Le Dragon Volant, the melancholy woods of the Château de la Carque and the tumultuous and thrilling influence of proximity to the object of my wild but wicked romance.

I was delayed for some time by my stockbroker. I had a very large sum, as I told you, at my banker's, uninvested. I cared very little for a few days' interest –

very little for the entire sum, compared with the image that occupied my thoughts and beckoned me with a white arm through the dark towards the spreading lime trees and chestnuts of the Château de la Carque. But I had fixed this day to meet him, and was relieved when he told me that I had better let it lie in my banker's hands for a few days longer as the funds would certainly fall immediately. This accident, too, was not without its immediate bearing on my subsequent adventures.

When I reached Le Dragon Volant, I found in my sitting-room, a good deal to my chagrin, my two guests, whom I had quite forgotten. I inwardly cursed my own stupidity for having embarrassed myself with their agreeable society. It could not be helped now, however, and a word to the waiters put all things in train for dinner.

Tom Whistlewick was in great force; and he commenced almost immediately with a very odd story.

He told me that not only Versailles, but all Paris, was in a ferment, in consequence of a revolting, and all but sacrilegious, practical joke, played off on the night before.

The pagoda, as he persisted in calling the palanquin, had been left standing on the spot where we last saw it. Neither conjuror, nor usher, nor bearers had ever returned. When the ball closed, and the company at length retired, the servants who attended to put out the lights and secure the doors found it still there.

It was determined, however, to let it stand where it was until next morning, by which time, it was conjectured, its owners would send messengers to remove it.

None arrived. The servants were then ordered to

take it away; and its extraordinary weight, for the first time, reminded them of its forgotten human occupant. Its door was forced; and judge what was their disgust when they discovered not a living man but a corpse! Three or four days must have passed since the death of the burly man in the Chinese tunic and painted cap. Some people thought it was a trick designed to insult the allies, in whose honour the ball was got up. Others were of opinion that it was nothing worse than a daring and cynical jocularity which, shocking as it was, might yet be forgiven as arising from the high spirits and irrepressible buffoonery of youth. Others, again, fewer in number, and mystically given, insisted that the corpse was *bona fide* necessary to the exhibition, and that the disclosures and allusions which had astonished so many people were distinctly due to necromancy.

'The matter, however, is now in the hands of the police,' observed Monsieur Carmaignac, 'and we are not the force we were two or three months ago if the offenders against propriety and public feeling are not traced and convicted, unless, indeed, they have been a great deal more cunning than such fools generally are.'

I was thinking within myself how utterly inexplicable was my colloquy with the conjuror, so cavalierly dismissed by Monsieur Carmaignac as a 'fool'; and the more I thought the more marvellous it seemed.

'It certainly was an original joke, though not a very clear one,' said Whistlewick.

'Not even original,' said Carmaignac. 'Very nearly the same thing was done, a hundred years ago or more, at a state ball in Paris; and the rascals who played the trick were never found out.'

In this Monsieur Carmaignac, as I afterwards discovered, spoke truly; for, among my books of

French anecdote and memoir, the very incident is marked, by my own hand.

While we were thus talking, the waiter told us that dinner was served; and we withdrew accordingly; my guests more than making amends for my comparative taciturnity.

18

The Churchyard

Our dinner was really good, so were the wines; better, perhaps, at this out-of-the-way inn than at some of the more pretentious hotels in Paris. The moral effect of a really good dinner is immense – we all felt it. The serenity and good nature that follow are more solid and comfortable than the tumultuous benevolences of Bacchus.

My friends were happy, therefore, and very chatty; which latter relieved me of the trouble of talking, and prompted them to entertain me and one another incessantly with agreeable stories and conversation, of which, until suddenly a subject emerged which interested me powerfully, I confess, so much were my thoughts engaged elsewhere, I heard next to nothing.

'Yes,' said Carmaignac, continuing a conversation which had escaped me, 'there was another case, beside that Russian nobleman, odder still. I remembered it this morning, but cannot recall the name. He was a tenant of the very same room. By the by, monsieur, might it not be as well,' he added, turning to me, with a laugh, half joke whole earnest, as they say, 'if you were to get into another apartment now that the house is no longer crowded? that is, if you mean to make any stay here.'

'A thousand thanks, no. I'm thinking of changing my hotel; and I can run into town so easily at night; and though I stay here, for this night, at least, I don't expect to vanish like those others. But you say there is another adventure, of the same kind, connected with the same room. Do let us hear it. But take some wine first.'

The story he told was curious.

'It happened,' said Carmaignac, 'as well as I recollect, before either of the other cases. A French gentleman – I wish I could remember his name – the son of a merchant, came to this inn (Le Dragon Volant), and was put by the landlord into the same room of which we have been speaking. Your apartment, monsieur. He was by no means young – past forty – and very far from good-looking. The people here said that he was the ugliest man, and the most good-natured, that ever lived. He played on the fiddle, sang and wrote poetry. His habits were odd and desultory. He would sometimes sit all day in his room writing, singing and fiddling, and go out at night for a walk. An eccentric man! He was by no means a millionaire, but he had a *modicum bonum*, you understand – a trifle more than half a million francs. He consulted his stockbroker about investing this money in foreign stocks, and drew the entire sum from his banker. You now have the situation of affairs when the catastrophe occurred.'

'Pray fill your glass,' I said.

'Dutch courage, monsieur, to face the catastrophe!' said Whistlewick, filling his own.

'Now, that was the last that ever was heard of his

money,' resumed Carmaignac. 'You shall hear about events. The night after this financial operation, he was seized with a poetic frenzy: he sent for the then landlord of this house, and told him that he had long meditated an epic, and meant to commence that night, and that he was on no account to be disturbed until nine o'clock in the morning. He had two pairs of wax candles, a little cold supper on a side table, his desk open, paper enough upon it to contain the entire *Henriade*, and a proportionate store of pens and ink.

'Seated at this desk he was seen by the waiter who brought him a cup of coffee at nine o'clock, at which time the intruder said he was writing fast enough to set fire to the paper – that was his phrase; he did not look up, he appeared too much engrossed. But when the waiter came back, half an hour afterwards, the door was locked; and the poet, from within, answered that he must not be disturbed.

'Away went the *garçon*. Next morning at nine o'clock he knocked at the door, and receiving no answer, looked through the keyhole; the lights were still burning, the window-shutters were closed as he had left them; he renewed his knocking, knocked louder, no answer came. He reported this continued and alarming silence to the innkeeper, who, finding that his guest had not left his key in the lock, succeeded in finding another that opened it. The candles were just giving up the ghost in their sockets, but there was light enough to ascertain that the tenant of the room was gone! The bed had not been disturbed; the window-shutter was barred. He must have let himself out, and locking the door on the outside, put the key in his pocket, and so made his way out of the house. Here, however, was another difficulty: Le

Dragon Volant shut its doors and made all fast at twelve o'clock; after that hour no one could leave the house, except by obtaining the key and letting himself out, and of necessity leaving the door unsecured, unless he had the collusion and aid of some person in the house.

'Now it happened that some time after the doors were secured, at half-past twelve, a servant who had not been apprised of his order to be left undisturbed, seeing a light shine through the keyhole, knocked at the door to enquire whether the poet wanted anything. He was very little obliged to his disturber, and dismissed him with a renewed charge that he was not to be interrupted again during the night. This incident established the fact that he was in the house after the doors had been locked and barred. The innkeeper himself kept the keys, and swore that he found them hung on the wall above his head over his bed, in their usual place, in the morning; and that nobody could have taken them away without awakening him. That was all we could discover. The Count de St Alyre, to whom this house belongs, was very active and very much chagrined. But nothing was discovered.'

'And nothing heard since of the epic poet?' I asked.

'Nothing – not the slightest clue – he never turned up again. I suppose he is dead; if he is not, he must have got into some devilish bad scrape, of which we have heard nothing, that compelled him to abscond with all the secrecy and expedition in his power. All that we know for certain is that, having occupied the room in which you sleep, he vanished, nobody ever knew how, and never was heard of since.'

'You have now mentioned three cases,' I said, 'and all from the same room.'

'Three. Yes, all equally unintelligible. When men are murdered, the great and immediate difficulty the assassins encounter is how to conceal the body. It is very hard to believe that three persons should have been consecutively murdered, in the same room, and their bodies so effectually disposed of that no trace of them was ever discovered.'

From this we passed to other topics, and the grave Monsieur Carmaignac amused us with a perfectly prodigious collection of scandalous anecdotes, which his opportunities in the police department had enabled him to accumulate.

My guests happily had engagements in Paris, and left me about ten.

I went up to my room, and looked out upon the grounds of the Château de la Carque. The moonlight was broken by clouds, and the view of the park in this desultory light acquired a melancholy and fantastic character.

The strange anecdotes, recounted of the room in which I stood by Monsieur Carmaignac, returned vaguely upon my mind, drowning in sudden shadows the gaiety of the more frivolous stories with which he had followed them. I looked round me on the room that lay in ominous gloom with an almost disagreeable sensation. I took my pistols now with an undefined apprehension that they might be really needed before my return tonight. This feeling, be it understood, in no wise chilled my ardour. Never had my enthusiasm mounted higher. My adventure absorbed and carried me away; but it added a strange and stern excitement to the expedition.

I loitered for a time in my room. I had ascertained the exact point at which the little churchyard lay. It was about a mile away. I did not wish to reach it earlier than necessary.

I stole quietly out, and sauntered along the road to my left, and thence entered a narrower track, still to my left, which, skirting the park wall, and describing a circuitous route all the way, under grand old trees, passes the ancient cemetery. That cemetery is embowered in trees, and occupies little more than half an acre of ground to the left of the road interposing between it and the park of the Château de la Carque.

Here, at this haunted spot, I paused and listened. The place was utterly silent. A thick cloud had darkened the moon, so that I could distinguish little more than the outlines of near objects, and that vaguely enough; and sometimes, as it were floating in black fog, the white surface of a tombstone emerged.

Among the forms that met my eye against the iron-grey of the horizon were some of those shrubs or trees that grow like our junipers, some six feet high, in form like a miniature poplar, with the darker foliage of the yew. I do not know the name of the plant, but I have often seen it in such funereal places.

Knowing that I was a little too early, I sat down upon the edge of a tombstone to wait, as, for aught I knew, the beautiful countess might have wise reasons for not caring that I should enter the grounds of the château earlier than she had appointed. In the listless state induced by waiting, I sat there, with my eyes on the object straight before me, which chanced to be the faint black outline of a tree such as I have described. It was right before me, about half a dozen steps away.

The moon now began to escape from under the skirt of the cloud that had hid her face for so long;

and, as the light gradually improved, the tree on which I had been lazily staring began to take a new shape. It was no longer a tree, but a man standing motionless. Brighter and brighter grew the moonlight, clearer and clearer the image became, and at last stood out perfectly distinctly. It was Colonel Gaillarde.

Luckily, he was not looking towards me. I could only see him in profile; but there was no mistaking the white moustache, the *farouche* visage, and the gaunt six-foot stature. There he was, his shoulder towards me, listening and watching, plainly, for some signal or person expected, straight in front of him.

If he were by chance to turn his eyes in my direction, I knew that I must reckon upon an instantaneous renewal of the combat only commenced in the hall of the Belle Etoile. In any case, could malignant fortune have posted, at this place and hour, a more dangerous watcher? What ecstasy to him, by a single discovery, to hit me so hard, and blast the Countess de St Alyre, whom he seemed to hate.

He raised his arm; he whistled softly; I heard an answering whistle as low; and, to my relief, the colonel advanced in the direction of this sound, widening the distance between us at every step; and immediately I heard talking, but in a low and cautious key.

I recognised, I thought, even so, the peculiar voice of Gaillarde.

I stole softly forward in the direction in which those sounds were audible. In doing so, I had, of course, to use the extremest caution.

I thought I saw a hat above a jagged piece of ruined wall, and then a second – yes, I saw two hats conversing; the voices came from under them. They moved off, not in the direction of the park, but of the road, and I lay along the grass, peeping over a grave, as a skirmisher might, observing the enemy. One after the other, the figures emerged full into view as they mounted the stile at the roadside. The colonel, who was last, stood on the wall for awhile, looking about him, and then jumped down on the road. I heard their steps and talk as they moved away together, with their backs towards me, in the direction which led them farther and farther from Le Dragon Volant.

I waited until these sounds were quite lost in distance before I entered the park. I followed the instructions I had received from the Countess de St Alyre and made my way among brushwood and thickets to the point nearest the ruinous temple, and then crossed the short intervening space of open ground rapidly.

I was now once more under the gigantic boughs of the old lime and chestnut trees; softly, and with a heart throbbing fast, I approached the little structure.

The moon was now shining steadily, pouring down its radiance on the soft foliage, and here and there mottling the verdure under my feet.

I reached the steps; I was among its worn marble shafts. She was not there, nor in the inner sanctuary, the arched windows of which were screened almost entirely by masses of ivy. The lady had not yet arrived.

19

The Key

I stood now upon the steps, watching and listening. In a minute or two I heard the crackle of withered sticks trod upon, and, looking in the direction, I saw a figure approaching among the trees, wrapped in a mantle.

I advanced eagerly. It was the countess. She did not speak, but gave me her hand, and I led her to the scene of our last interview. She repressed the ardour of my impassioned greeting with a gentle but peremptory firmness. She removed her hood, shook back her beautiful hair, and, gazing on me with sad and glowing eyes, sighed deeply. Some awful thought seemed to weigh upon her.

'Richard, I must speak plainly. The crisis of my life has come. I am sure you would defend me. I think you pity me; perhaps you even love me.'

At these words I became eloquent, as young mad-men in my plight do. She silenced me, however with the same melancholy firmness.

'Listen, dear friend, and then say whether you can aid me. How madly I am trusting you; and yet my heart tells me how wisely! To meet you here as I do – what insanity it seems! How poorly you must think of me! But when you know all, you will judge me fairly. Without your aid I cannot accomplish my purpose. That purpose unaccomplished, I must die. I am chained to a man whom I despise – whom I abhor. I have resolved to fly. I have jewels, principally diamonds, for which I am offered thirty thousand pounds of your English money. They are my separate property by my marriage settlement; I will take them with me. You are a judge, no doubt, of jewels. I was counting mine when the hour came, and brought this in my hand to show you. Look.'

'It is magnificent!' I exclaimed, as a collar of diamonds twinkled and flashed in the moonlight, suspended from her pretty fingers. I thought, even at that tragic moment, that she prolonged the show, with a feminine delight in these brilliant toys.

'Yes,' she said, 'I shall part with them all. I will turn them into money, and break, for ever, the unnatural and wicked bonds that tied me, in the name of a sacrament, to a tyrant. A man young, handsome, generous, brave as you, can hardly be rich. Richard, you say you love me; you shall share all this with me. We will fly together to Switzerland; we will evade pursuit; my powerful friends will intervene and arrange a separation, and I shall, at length, be happy and reward my hero.'

You may suppose the style, florid and vehement, in which I poured forth my gratitude, vowed the devotion of my life, and placed myself absolutely at her disposal.

'Tomorrow night,' she said, 'my husband will attend the remains of his cousin, Monsieur de St Amand, to Père Lachaise. The hearse, he says, will leave this at half-past nine. You must be here, where we stand, at nine o'clock.'

I promised punctual obedience.

'I will not meet you here; but you see a red light in the window of the tower at that angle of the château?'

I assented.

'I placed it there that tomorrow night, when it comes, you may recognise it. So soon as that rose-coloured light appears at that window, it will be a signal to you that the funeral has left the château, and that you may approach safely. Come, then, to that window; I will open it and admit you. Five minutes after, a travelling-carriage, with four horses, shall stand ready in the *porte-cochère*. I will place my diamonds in your hands; and so soon as we enter the carriage, our flight commences. We shall have at least five hours' start; and with energy, stratagem and resource, I fear nothing. Are you ready to undertake all this for my sake?'

Again I vowed myself her slave.

'My only difficulty,' she said, 'is how we shall quickly enough convert my diamonds into money; I dare not remove them while my husband is in the house.'

Here was the opportunity I wished for. I now told her that I had in my banker's hands no less a sum than thirty thousand pounds, with which, in the shape of gold and notes, I should come furnished, and thus the risk and loss of disposing of her diamonds in too much haste would be avoided.

'Good heaven!' she exclaimed, with a kind of disappointment. 'You are rich, then? and I have lost the felicity of making my generous friend more happy. Be it so, since so it must be. Let us contribute, each, in equal shares, to our common fund. Bring you, your money; I, my jewels. There is a happiness to me even in mingling my resources with yours.'

On this there followed a romantic colloquy, all poetry and passion, such as I should in vain endeavour to reproduce.

Then came a very special instruction.

'I have come provided, too, with a key, the use of which I must explain.'

It was a double key – a long, slender stem, with a key at each end – one about the size which opens an ordinary room door; the other, as small, almost, as the key of a dressing-case.

'You cannot employ too much caution tomorrow night. An interruption would murder all my hopes. I have learned that you occupy the haunted room in Le Dragon Volant. It is the very room I would have wished you in. I will tell you why – there is a story of a man who, having shut himself up in that room one night, disappeared before morning. The truth is, he wanted, I believe, to escape from creditors; and the host of Le Dragon Volant, at that time, being a rogue, aided him in absconding. My husband investigated the matter, and discovered how his escape was made. It was by means of this key. Here is a memorandum and a plan describing how it is to be applied. I have taken it from the count's escritoire. And now, once more I must leave to your ingenuity how to mystify the people at Le Dragon Volant. Be sure you try the keys first, to see that the locks turn freely. I will have my jewels ready. You, whatever we divide, had better bring your money, because it may be many months before you can revisit Paris, or disclose our place of residence to anyone; and our passports – arrange all that, in what names and whither you please. And now, dear Richard' (she leaned her arm fondly on my shoulder, and looked with ineffable passion in my eyes, with her other hand clasped in mine), 'my very life is in your hands; I have staked all on your fidelity.'

As she spoke the last word, she, on a sudden, grew deadly pale, and gasped, 'Good God! who is here?'

At the same moment she receded through the door in the marble screen, close to which she stood, and behind which was a small roofless chamber, as small as the shrine, the window of which was darkened by a clustering mass of ivy so dense that hardly a gleam of light came through the leaves.

I stood upon the threshold which she had just crossed, looking in the direction in which she had thrown that one terrified glance. No wonder she was frightened. Quite close upon us, not twenty yards away, and approaching at a quick step, very distinctly lighted by the moon, Colonel Gaillarde and his companion were coming. The shadow of the cornice and a piece of wall were upon me. Unconscious of this, I was expecting the moment when, with one of his frantic yells, he should spring forward to assail me.

I made a step backwards, drew one of my pistols from my pocket and cocked it. It was obvious he had not seen me.

I stood, with my finger on the trigger, determined to shoot him dead if he should attempt to enter the place where the countess was. It would, no doubt, have been a murder; but, in my mind, I had no question or qualm about it. When once we engage in secret and guilty practices we are nearer other and greater crimes than we at all suspect.

There's the statue,' said the colonel, in his brief discordant tones. 'That's the figure.'

'Alluded to in the stanzas?' enquired his companion.

'The very thing. We shall see more next time. Forward, monsieur; let us march.'

And, much to my relief, the gallant colonel turned

on his heel, and marched through the trees, with his back towards the château, striding over the grass, as I quickly saw, to the park wall, which they crossed not far from the gables of Le Dragon Volant.

I found the countess trembling in no affected, but a very real terror. She would not hear of my accompanying her towards the château. But I told her that I would prevent the return of the mad colonel; and upon that point, at least, she need fear nothing. She quickly recovered, again bade me a fond and lingering good-night, and left me, gazing after her, with the key in my hand, and such a phantasmagoria floating in my brain as amounted very nearly to madness.

There was I, ready to brave all dangers, all right and reason, plunge into murder itself, on the first summons, and entangle myself in consequences inextricable and horrible (what cared I?) for a woman of whom I knew nothing but that she was beautiful and reckless!

I have often thanked heaven for its mercy in conducting me through the labyrinths in which I had all but lost myself.

20

A High-Cauld-Cap

I was now upon the road, within two or three hundred yards of Le Dragon Volant. I had undertaken an adventure with a vengeance! And by way of prelude, there not improbably awaited me, at my inn, another encounter, perhaps this time not so lucky, with the grotesque sabreur.

I was glad I had my pistols. I certainly was bound by no law to allow a ruffian to cut me down, unresisting.

Stooping boughs from the old park, gigantic poplars on the other side, and the moonlight over all, made the narrow road to the inn-door picturesque.

I could not think very clearly just now; events were succeeding one another so rapidly, and I, involved in the action of a drama so extravagant and guilty, hardly knew myself or believed my own story as I slowly paced towards the still open door of the inn.

No sign of the colonel, visible or audible, was there. In the hall I enquired. No gentleman had arrived at the inn for the last half-hour. I looked into the public room. It was deserted. The clock struck twelve, and I heard the servant barring the great door. I took my candle. The lights in this rural hostelry were by this time out, and the house had the air of one that had settled to slumber for many hours. The cold moon-light streamed in at the window on the landing as I ascended the broad staircase; and I paused for a moment to look over the wooded grounds to the turreted château, to me so full of interest. I bethought me, however, that prying eyes might read a meaning in this midnight gazing, and possibly the count him-self might, in his jealous mood, surmise a signal in this unwonted light in the stair-window of Le Dragon Volant.

On opening my room door, with a little start I met an extremely old woman with the longest face I ever saw; she had what used to be termed a high-cauld-cap on, the white border of which contrasted with her brown and yellow skin and made her wrinkled face more ugly. She raised her curved shoulders, and looked up in my face, with eyes unnaturally black and bright.

'I have lighted a little wood, monsieur, because the night is chill.'

I thanked her, but she did not go. She stood with her candle in her tremulous fingers.

'Excuse an old woman, monsieur,' she said; 'but what on earth can a young English milord, with all Paris at his feet, find to amuse him in Le Dragon Volant?'

Had I been at the age of fairy tales, and in daily intercourse with the delightful Countess d'Aulnois, I should have seen in this withered apparition the *genius loci*, the malignant fairy, at the stamp of whose foot the ill-fated tenants of this very room had, from time to time, vanished. I was past that, however; but the old woman's dark eyes were fixed on mine with a steady meaning that plainly told me that my secret was known. I was embarrassed and alarmed; I never thought of asking her what business that was of hers.

'These old eyes saw you in the park of the château tonight.'

'*I!*' I began, with all the scornful surprise I could affect.

'It avails nothing, monsieur; I know why you stay here; and I tell you to begone. Leave this house tomorrow morning, and never come again.'

She lifted her disengaged hand, as she looked at me with intense horror in her eyes.

'There is nothing on earth – I don't know what you mean,' I answered; 'and why should you care about me?'

'I don't care about you, monsieur – I care about the honour of an ancient family, whom I served in their happier days, when to be noble was to be honoured. But my words are thrown away, monsieur; you are insolent. I will keep my secret, and you, yours; that is all. You will soon find it hard enough to divulge it.'

The old woman went slowly from the room and shut the door, before I had made up my mind to say anything. I was standing where she had left me, nearly five minutes later. The jealousy of Monsieur the Count, I assumed, appears to this old creature about the most terrible thing in creation. Whatever contempt I might entertain for the dangers which this old lady so darkly intimated, it was by no means pleasant, you may suppose, that a secret so dangerous should be so much as suspected by a stranger, and that stranger a partisan of the Count de St Alyre.

Ought I not, at all risks, to apprise the countess, who had trusted me so generously, or, as she said herself, so madly, of the fact that our secret was, at least, suspected by another? But was there not greater danger in attempting to communicate? What did the beldame mean by saying, 'Keep your secret, and I'll keep mine?'

I had a thousand distracting questions before me. My progress seemed like a journey through the Spessart, where at every step some new goblin or monster starts from the ground or steps from behind a tree.

Peremptorily I dismissed these harassing and frightful doubts. I secured my door, sat myself down at my table, and with a candle at each side, placed before me the piece of vellum which contained the drawings and notes on which I was to rely for full instructions as to how to use the key.

When I had studied this for a while, I made my investigation. The angle of the room at the right side of the window was cut off by an oblique turn in the wainscot. I examined this carefully, and, on pressure, a small bit of the frame of the woodwork slid aside, and disclosed a keyhole. On my removing my finger, it shot back to its place again, with a spring. So far I had interpreted my instructions successfully. A similar search, next the door, and directly under this, was rewarded by a like discovery. The small end of the key fitted this, as it had the upper keyhole; and now, with two or three hard jerks at the key, a door in the panel opened, showing a strip of the bare wall, and a narrow, arched doorway, piercing the thickness of the wall, within which I saw a screw staircase of stone.

Candle in hand, I stepped in. I do not know whether the quality of air, long undisturbed, is peculiar; to me it has always seemed so, and the damp smell of the old masonry hung in this atmosphere. My candle faintly lighted the bare stone wall that enclosed the stair, the foot of which I could not see. Down I went, and a few turns brought me to the stone floor. Here was another door, of the simple old oak kind, deep sunk in the thickness of the wall. The large end of the key fitted this. The lock was stiff; I set the candle down upon the stair, and applied both hands; it turned with difficulty, and as it revolved, uttered a shriek that alarmed me for my secret.

For some minutes I did not move. In a little time, however, I took courage and opened the door. The night-air floating in, puffed out the candle. There was a thicket of holly and underwood, as dense as a jungle, close about the door. I should have been in pitch-darkness were it not that through the topmost leaves there twinkled, here and there, a glimmer of moon-shine.

Softly, lest anyone should have opened his window

at the sound of the rusty bolt, I struggled through this till I gained a view of the open grounds. Here I found that the brushwood spread a good way up the park, uniting with the wood that approached the little temple I have described.

A general could not have chosen a more effectually covered approach from Le Dragon Volant to the trysting-place where hitherto I had conferred with the idol of my lawless adoration.

Looking back upon the old inn, I discovered that the stair I had descended was enclosed in one of those slender turrets that decorate such buildings. It was placed at that angle which corresponded with the part of the panelling of my room indicated in the plan I had been studying.

Thoroughly satisfied with my experiment, I made my way back to the door, with some little difficulty remounted to my room, locked my secret door again, kissed the mysterious key that her hand had pressed that night and placed it under my pillow, upon which, very soon after, my giddy head was laid, not, for some time, to sleep soundly.

21

I See Three Men in a Mirror

I awoke very early next morning, and was too excited to sleep again. As soon as I could, without exciting remark, I saw my host. I told him that I was going into town that night, and thence to Rouen, where I had to see some people on business, and requested him to mention my being there to any friend who might call. That I expected to be back in about a week, and that in the meantime my servant, St Clair, would keep the key of my room, and look after my things.

Having prepared this mystification for my landlord, I drove into Paris, and there transacted the financial part of the affair. The problem was to reduce my balance, nearly thirty thousand pounds, to a shape in which it would be not only easily portable, but available, wherever I might go, without involving correspondence or any other incident which would disclose my place of residence for the time being. All these points were as nearly provided for as they could be. I need not trouble you about my arrangements for passports. It is enough to say that the point I selected for our flight was, in the spirit of romance, one of the most beautiful and sequestered nooks in Switzerland.

Luggage, I should start with none. The first considerable town we reached next morning would supply an extemporised wardrobe. It was now two o'clock; only two! How on earth was I to dispose of the remainder of the day?

I had not yet seen the cathedral of Notre Dame and thither I drove. I spent an hour or more there and then visited the Conciergerie, the Palais de Justice and the beautiful Sainte Chapelle. Still there remained some time to get rid of, and I strolled into the narrow streets adjoining the cathedral. I recollect seeing, in one of them, an old house with a mural inscription stating that it had been the residence of Canon Fulbert, the uncle of Abelard's Eloise. I don't know whether these curious old streets, in which I observed fragments of ancient Gothic churches fitted up as

warehouses, are still extant. I lighted, among other
dingy and eccentric shops, upon one that seemed
that of a broker of all sorts of old decorations, armour,
china, furniture. I entered the shop; it was dark, dusty
and low. The proprietor was busy scouring a piece of
inlaid armour, and allowed me to poke about his
shop, and examine the curious things accumulated
there, just as I pleased. Gradually I made my way to
the farther end of it, where there was but one window
with many panes, each with a bull's-eye in it, and
in the dirtiest possible state. When I reached this
window, I turned about, and in a recess, standing at
right angles with the side wall of the shop, was a large
mirror in an old-fashioned dingy frame. Reflected in
this I saw what in old houses I have heard termed an
'alcove', in which, among lumber, and various dusty
articles hanging on the wall, there stood a table, at
which three persons were seated, as it seemed to
me, in earnest conversation. Two of these persons I
instantly recognised; one was Colonel Gaillarde, the
other was the Marquis d'Harmonville. The third,
who was fiddling with a pen, was a lean, pale man,
pitted with the smallpox, with lank black hair, and
about as mean-looking a person as I had ever seen in
my life. The marquis looked up, and his glance was
instantaneously followed by his two companions. For
a moment I hesitated what to do. But it was plain
that I was not recognised, as indeed I could hardly
have been, the light from the window being behind
me and the portion of the shop immediately before
me being very dark indeed.

Perceiving this, I had the presence of mind to affect
being entirely engrossed by the objects before me,
and strolled slowly down the shop again. I paused for

a moment to hear whether I was followed and was relieved when I heard no step. You may be sure I did not waste more time in that shop, where I had just made a discovery so curious and so unexpected.

It was no business of mine to enquire what brought Colonel Gaillarde and the marquis together in so shabby and even dirty a place, or who the mean person biting the feather end of his pen might be. Such employments as the marquis had accepted sometimes make strange bedfellows.

I was glad to get away, and just as the sun set, I reached the steps of Le Dragon Volant and dismissed the vehicle in which I had arrived, carrying in my hand a strong box, of marvellously small dimensions considering all it contained, strapped in a leather cover, which disguised its real character.

When I got to my room, I summoned St Clair. I told him nearly the same story I had already told my host. I gave him fifty pounds, with orders to expend whatever was necessary on himself and in payment for my rooms till my return. I then ate a slight and hasty dinner. My eyes were often upon the solemn old clock over the chimney-piece, which was my sole accomplice in keeping tryst in this iniquitous venture. The sky favoured my design, and darkened all things with a sea of clouds.

The innkeeper met me in the hall, to ask whether I should want a vehicle to Paris? I was prepared for this question, and instantly answered that I meant to walk to Versailles, and take a carriage there. I called St Clair.

'Go,' said I, 'and drink a bottle of wine with your friends. I shall call you if I should want anything; in the meantime, here is the key of my room; I shall be writing some notes, so don't allow anyone to disturb

146

me for at least half an hour. At the end of that time you will probably find that I have left for Versailles; should you not find me in the room, you may take that for granted; thereupon take charge of everything, and lock the door, you understand?'

St Clair took his leave, wishing me all happiness and no doubt promising himself some little amusement with my money. With my candle in my hand, I hastened upstairs. It wanted now but five minutes to the appointed time. I do not think there is anything of the coward in my nature; but I confess, as the crisis approached, I felt something of the suspense and awe of a soldier going into action. Would I have receded? Not for all this earth could offer.

I bolted my door, put on my greatcoat and placed my pistols one in each pocket. I now applied my key to the secret locks, drew the wainscot door a little open, took my strong box under my arm, extinguished my candle, unbolted my door, listened at it for a few moments to be sure that no one was approaching, and then crossed the floor of my room swiftly, entered the secret door and closed the spring lock after me. I was upon the screw-stair in total darkness, the key in my fingers. Thus far the undertaking was successful.

22

Rapture

Down the screw-stair I went in utter darkness; and having reached the stone floor, I discerned the door and groped out the keyhole. With more caution and less noise than upon the night before, I opened the door, and stepped out into the thick brushwood. It was almost as dark in this jungle.

Having secured the door, I slowly pushed my way through the bushes, which soon became less dense. Then, with more ease, but still under thick cover, I pursued in the track of the wood, keeping near its edge.

At length, in the darkened air, about fifty yards away, the shafts of the marble temple rose like phantoms before me, seen through the trunks of the old trees. Everything favoured my enterprise. I had effectually mystified my servant and the people of Le Dragon Volant, and so dark was the night that even had I alarmed the suspicions of all the tenants of the inn, I might safely defy their united curiosity, though posted at every window of the house.

Through the trunks, over the roots of the old trees, I reached the appointed place of observation. I laid my treasure, in its leathern case, in the embrasure, and leaning my arms upon it, looked steadily in the direction of the château. The outline of the building was scarcely discernible, blending dimly, as it did, with the sky. No light in any window was visible. I was plainly to wait; but for how long?

Leaning on my box of treasure, gazing toward the massive shadow that represented the château, in the midst of my ardent and elated longings, there came upon me an odd thought – which you will think might well have struck me long before. It came on a sudden, and as it came the darkness deepened, and a chill stole into the air around me. Suppose I were to disappear finally, like those other men whose stories I had listened to! Had I not been at all the pains that mortal could to obliterate every trace of my real proceedings, and to mislead everyone to whom I spoke as to the direction in which I had gone?

This icy, snakelike thought stole through my mind, and was gone.

Did I not rejoice in the full-blooded season of youth, conscious strength, rashness, passion, pursuit, the adventure! Here were a pair of double-barrelled pistols, four lives in my hands? What could possibly happen? The count – except for the sake of my Dulcinea, what was it to me whether the old coward whom I had seen in an ague of terror before the brawling colonel interposed or not? I was assuming the worst that could happen. But with an ally so clever and courageous as my beautiful countess, could any such misadventure befall? Bah! I laughed at all such fancies.

As I communed with myself, the signal light sprang up. The rose-coloured light, *couleur de rose*, emblem of sanguine hope and the dawn of a happy day.

Clear, soft and steady glowed the light from the window. The stone shafts showed black against it. Murmuring words of passionate love as I gazed upon the signal, I grasped my strong box under my arm and with rapid strides approached the Château de la Carque. No sign of light or life, no human voice, no tread of foot, no bark of dog indicated a chance of interruption. A blind was down; and as I came close to the tall window, I found that half a dozen steps led up to it, and that a large lattice, answering for a door, lay open.

A shadow from within fell upon the blind; it was drawn aside, and as I ascended the steps, a soft voice murmured – 'Richard, dearest Richard, come, oh, come! how I have longed for this moment!'

Never did she look so beautiful. My love rose to passionate enthusiasm. I only wished there were some real danger in the adventure worthy of such a creature. When the first tumultuous greeting was over, she made me sit beside her on a sofa. There we talked for a minute or two. She told me that the count had gone and was by that time more than a mile on his way, with the funeral, to Père Lachaise. Here were her diamonds. She exhibited, hastily, an open casket containing a profusion of the largest brilliants.

'What is this?' she asked.

'A box containing money to the amount of thirty thousand pounds,' I answered.

'What! all that money?' she exclaimed.

'Every sou.'

'Was it not unnecessary to bring so much, seeing all these,' she said, touching her diamonds. 'It would have been kind of you to allow me to provide for us both, for a time at least. It would have made me happier even than I am.'

'Dearest, generous angel!' Such was my extravagant declamation. 'You forget that it may be necessary, for a long time, to observe silence as to where we are, and impossible to communicate safely with anyone.'

'You have then here this great sum – are you certain; have you counted it?'

'Yes, certainly; I received it today,' I answered, perhaps showing a little surprise in my face. 'I counted it, of course, on drawing it from my bankers.'

'It makes me feel a little nervous, travelling with so much money; but these jewels make as great a danger; *that* can add but little to it. Place them side by side; you shall take off your greatcoat when we are ready to go, and with it manage to conceal these boxes. I should not like the drivers to suspect that we were conveying such a treasure. I must ask you now to close the curtains of that window, and bar the shutters.'

I had hardly done this when a knock was heard at the room door.

'I know who this is,' she said, in a whisper to me. I saw that she was not alarmed. She went softly to the door, and a whispered conversation for a minute followed.

'My trusty maid, who is coming with us. She says we cannot safely go sooner than ten minutes. She is bringing some coffee to the next room.'

She opened the door and looked in.

'I must tell her not to take too much luggage. She is so odd! Don't follow – stay where you are – it is better that she should not see you.'

She left the room with a gesture of caution.

A change had come over the manner of this beautiful woman. For the last few minutes a shadow had been stealing over her, an air of abstraction, a look bordering on suspicion. Why was she pale? Why had there come that dark look in her eyes? Why had her very voice become changed? Had anything gone suddenly wrong? Did some danger threaten?

This doubt, however, speedily quieted itself. If there had been anything of the kind, she would, of course, have told me. It was only natural that, as the crisis approached, she should become more and more nervous. She did not return quite so soon as I had expected. To a man in my situation absolute quietude is next to impossible. I moved restlessly about the room. It was a small one. There was a door at the other end. I opened it, rashly enough. I listened, it

was perfectly silent. I was in an excited, eager state
with every faculty focused on what lay ahead and, in
so far, detached from the immediate present. I can't
account, in any other way, for my having done so
many foolish things that night, for I was, naturally, by
no means deficient in cunning. About the most stupid
of those was that instead of immediately closing that
door, which I never ought to have opened, I actually
took a candle and walked into the room.

There I made, quite unexpectedly, a rather startling
discovery.

23

A Cup of Coffee

The room was carpetless. On the floor were a quantity
of shavings and some score of bricks. Beyond these,
on a narrow table, lay an object, which I could hardly
believe I saw aright.

I approached and drew from it a sheet which had
very slightly disguised its shape. There was no mistake
about it. It was a coffin; and on the lid was a plate,
with the inscription in French:

PIERRE DE LA ROCHE ST AMAND
AGÉ DE XXIII ANS

I drew back with a double shock. So, then, the
funeral after all had not yet left! Here lay the body. I
had been deceived. This, no doubt, accounted for the
embarrassment so manifest in the countess's manner.
She would have done more wisely had she told me
the true state of the case.

I drew back from this melancholy room, and closed the door. Her distrust of me was the worst rashness she could have committed. There is nothing more dangerous than misapplied caution. In entire ignorance of the fact I had entered the room, and there I might have lighted upon some of the very persons it was our special anxiety that I should avoid.

These reflections were interrupted, almost as soon as begun, by the return of the Countess de St Alyre. I saw at a glance that she detected in my face some evidence of what had happened, for she threw a hasty look towards the door.

'Have you seen anything – anything to disturb you, dear Richard? Have you been out of this room?'

I answered promptly, 'Yes,' and told her frankly what had happened.

'Well, I did not like to make you more uneasy than necessary. Besides, it is disgusting and horrible. The body is there; but the count had departed a quarter of an hour before I lighted the coloured lamp and prepared to receive you. The body did not arrive till eight or ten minutes after he had set out. He was afraid lest the people at Père Lachaise should suppose that the funeral was postponed. He knew that the remains of poor Pierre would certainly reach here tonight, although an unexpected delay had occurred; and there are reasons why he wishes the funeral completed before tomorrow. The hearse with the body must leave here in ten minutes. So soon as it is gone, we shall be free to set out upon our wild and happy journey. The horses are to the carriage in the *porte-cochère*. As for this *funeste* horror' (she shuddered very prettily), 'let us think of it no more.'

She bolted the door of communication, and when

she turned, it was with such a pretty penitence in her face and attitude that I was ready to throw myself at her feet.

'It is the last time,' she said, in a sweet sad little pleading, 'I shall ever practise a deception on my brave and beautiful Richard – my hero! Am I forgiven?'

There was another scene of passionate effusion, and lovers' raptures and declamations, but only murmured, lest the ears of listeners should be busy.

At length, on a sudden, she raised her hand as if to prevent my stirring, her eyes fixed on me and her ear towards the door of the room in which the coffin was placed, and remained breathless in that attitude for a few moments. Then, with a little nod towards me, she moved on tiptoe to the door and listened, extending her hand backward as if to warn me against advancing; and, after a little time, she returned, still on tiptoe, and whispered to me, 'They are removing the coffin – come with me.'

I accompanied her into the room from which her maid, as she told me, had spoken to her. Coffee and some old china cups, which appeared to me quite beautiful, stood on a silver tray; and some liqueur glasses, with a flask, which turned out to be noyeau, on a salver beside it.

'I shall attend you. I'm to be your servant here; I am to have my own way; I shall not think myself forgiven by my darling if he refuses to indulge me in anything.'

She filled a cup with coffee and handed it to me with her left hand; her right arm she fondly passed over my shoulder, and with her fingers through my curls caressingly, she whispered, 'Take this, I shall take some just now.'

It was excellent; and when I had done she handed me the liqueur, which I also drank.

'Come back, dearest, to the next room,' she said. 'By this time those terrible people must have gone away, and we shall be safer there, for the present, than here.'

'You shall direct, and I obey; you shall command me, not only now, but always, and in all things, my beautiful queen!' I murmured.

My heroics were unconsciously, I dare say, founded upon my ideal of the French school of lovemaking. I am, even now, ashamed as I recall the bombast to which I treated the Countess de St Alyre.

'There, you shall have another miniature glass – a fairy glass – of noyeau,' she said gaily. In this volatile creature, the funereal gloom of the moment before, and the suspense of an adventure on which all her future was staked, disappeared in a moment. She ran and returned with another tiny glass, which, with an eloquent or tender little speech, I placed to my lips and sipped.

I kissed her hand, I kissed her lips, I gazed in her beautiful eyes and kissed her again unresisting.

'You call me Richard, by what name am I to call my beautiful divinity?' I asked.

'You must call me Eugénie, it is my name. Let us be quite real; that is, if you love as entirely as I do.'

'Eugénie!' I exclaimed, and broke into a new rapture upon the name. It ended by my telling her how impatient I was to set out upon our journey; and, as I spoke, suddenly an odd sensation overcame me. It was not in the slightest degree like faintness. I can find no phrase to describe it except as a sudden constraint of the brain; it was as if the membrane in which it lies, if there be such a thing, contracted, and became inflexible.

'Dear Richard! what is the matter?' she exclaimed, with terror in her looks. 'Good heavens! are you ill? I conjure you, sit down; sit in this chair.' She almost forced me into one; I was in no condition to offer the least resistance. I recognised but too truly the sensations that supervened. I was lying back in the chair without the power, by this time, of uttering a syllable, of closing my eyelids, of moving my eyes, of stirring a muscle. I had in a few seconds glided into precisely the state in which I had passed so many appalling hours when approaching Paris in my night-drive with the Marquis d'Harmonville.

Great and loud was the lady's agony. She seemed to have lost all sense of fear. She called me by my name, shook me by the shoulder, raised my arm and let it fall, all the time imploring of me, in distracting sentences, to make the slightest sign of life, and vowing that if I did not, she would make away with herself.

These ejaculations, after a minute or two, suddenly subsided. The lady was perfectly silent and cool. In a very businesslike way she took a candle and stood before me, pale indeed, very pale, but with an expression only of intense scrutiny with a dash of horror in it. She moved the candle before my eyes slowly, evidently watching the effect. She then set it down, and rang a handbell two or three times sharply. She placed the two cases (I mean hers containing the jewels, and my strong box) side by side on the table; and I saw her carefully lock the door that gave access to the room in which I had just now sipped my coffee.

24

Hope

She had scarcely set down my heavy box, which she seemed to have considerable difficulty in raising on the table, when the door of the room in which I had seen the coffin opened, and a sinister and unexpected apparition entered.

It was the Count de St Alyre, who had been, as I have told you, reported to me to be, for some considerable time, on his way to Père Lachaise. He stood before me for a moment, with the frame of the doorway and a background of darkness enclosing him, like a portrait. His slight, mean figure was draped in the deepest mourning. He had in his hand a pair of black gloves and his hat with crape round it.

When he was not speaking his face showed signs of agitation; his mouth was puckering and working. He looked damnably wicked and frightened.

'Well, my dear Eugénie? Well, child – eh? Well, it all goes admirably?'

'Yes,' she answered, in a low, hard tone. 'But you and Planard should not have left that door open.'

This she said sternly. 'He went in there and looked about wherever he liked; it was fortunate he did not move aside the lid of the coffin.'

'Planard should have seen to that,' said the count, sharply. '*Ma foi!* I can't be everywhere!' He advanced half a dozen short quick steps into the room toward me, and placed his glasses to his eyes.

'Monsieur Beckett,' he cried sharply, two or three times, 'Hi! don't you know me?'

He approached and peered more closely in my face; raised my hand and shook it, calling me again, then let it drop, and said – 'It has set in admirably, my pretty *mignonne*. When did it commence?'

The countess came and stood beside him, and looked at me steadily for some seconds.

You can't conceive the effect of the silent gaze of those two pairs of evil eyes.

The lady glanced to where, I recollected, the mantelpiece stood, and upon it a clock, the regular click of which I sharply heard.

'Four – five – six minutes and a half,' she said slowly, in a cold hard way.

'Brava! Bravissima! my beautiful queen! my little Venus! my Joan of Arc! my heroine! my paragon of women!'

He was gloating on me with an odious curiosity, smiling, as he groped backwards with his thin brown fingers to find the lady's hand; but she, not (I dare say) caring for his caresses, drew back a little.

'Come, *ma chère*, let us count his things. What is it? Pocket-book? Or – or – what?'

'It is that!' said the lady, pointing with a look of disgust to the box, which lay in its leather case on the table.

'Oh! Let us see – let us count – let us see,' he said, as he was unbuckling the straps with his tremulous fingers. 'We must count all – we must see to it. I have pencil and pocket-book – but – where's the key? See this cursed lock! My faith! What is it? Where's the key?' He was standing before the countess, shuffling his feet, with his hands extended and all his fingers quivering.

'I have not got it; how could I? It is in his pocket, of course,' said the lady.

In another instant the fingers of the old miscreant were in my pockets; he plucked out everything they contained, and some keys among the rest.

I lay in precisely the state in which I had been during my drive with the marquis to Paris. This wretch I knew was about to rob me. The whole drama, and the countess's role in it, I could not yet comprehend. I could not be sure – so much more presence of mind and histrionic resource have women than fall to the lot of our clumsy sex – whether the return of the count was not, in truth, a surprise to her; and this scrutiny of the contents of my strong box, an extempore undertaking of the count's. But it was clearing more and more every moment: and I was destined, very soon, to comprehend minutely my appalling situation.

I had not the power of turning my eyes this way or that the smallest fraction of a hair's breadth. But let anyone, placed as I was at the end of a room, ascertain for himself by experiment how wide is the field of sight, without the slightest alteration in the line of vision, he will find that it takes in the entire breadth of a large room, and that up to a very short distance before him; and imperfectly, by a refraction, I believe, in the eye itself, to a point very near indeed. Next to nothing that passed in the room, therefore, was hidden from me.

The old man had, by this time, found the key. The leather case was open. The box cramped round with iron was next unlocked. He turned out its contents upon the table.

'*Rouleaux* of a hundred Napoleons each. One, two, three. Yes, quick. Write down a thousand Napoleons. One, two; yes, right. Another thousand, *write*!' And so on and on still he rapidly counted. Then came the notes.

'Ten thousand francs. *Write*. Ten thousand francs again: is it written? Another ten thousand francs: is it down? Smaller notes would have been better. They should have been smaller. These are horribly embarrassing. Bolt that door again; Planard would become unreasonable if he knew the amount. Why did you not tell him to get it in smaller notes? No matter now – go on – it can't be helped – write – another ten thousand francs – another – another.' And so on, till my treasure was counted out, before my face, while I saw and heard all that passed with the sharpest distinctness, and my mental perceptions were horribly vivid. But in all other respects I was dead.

He had replaced in the box every note and *rouleau* as he counted it, and now having ascertained the sum total, he locked it, replaced it, very methodically, in its cover, opened a buffet in the wainscoting, and, having placed the countess's jewel-case and my strong box in it, he locked it; and immediately on completing these arrangements he began to complain with fresh acrimony and maledictions of Planard's delay.

He unbolted the door, looked in the dark room beyond, and listened. He closed the door again and returned. The old man was in a fever of suspense.

'I have kept ten thousand francs for Planard,' said the count, touching his waistcoat pocket.

'Will that satisfy him?' asked the lady.

'Why – curse him!' screamed the count. 'Has he no conscience? I'll swear to him it's half the entire thing.'

He and the lady again came and looked at me anxiously for a while, in silence; and then the old count began to grumble again about Planard, and to compare his watch with the clock. The lady seemed less impatient; she sat no longer looking at me, but across the room, so that her profile was towards me – and strangely changed, dark and witchlike it looked. My last hope died as I beheld that jaded face from which the mask had dropped. I was certain that they intended to crown their robbery by murder. Why did they not dispatch me at once? What object could there be in postponing the catastrophe which would expedite their own safety. I cannot recall, even to myself, adequately the horrors unutterable that I underwent. You must suppose a real nightmare – I mean a nightmare in which the objects and the danger are real, and the spell of corporal death appears to be protractable at the pleasure of the persons who preside at your unearthly torments. I could have no doubt as to the cause of the state in which I was.

In this agony, to which I could not give the slightest expression, I saw the door of the room where the coffin had been open slowly, and the Marquis d'Harmonville entered the room.

25

Despair

A moment's hope, hope violent and fluctuating, hope that was nearly torture, and then came a dialogue and with it the terrors of despair.

'Thank heaven, Planard, you have come at last,' said the count, taking him with both hands by the arm and clinging to it and drawing him towards me.

'See, look at him. It has all gone sweetly, sweetly, sweetly up to this. Shall I hold the candle for you?'

My friend d'Harmonville, Planard, whoever he was, came to me, pulling off his gloves, which he popped into his pocket.

'The candle, a little this way,' he said, and stooping over me he looked earnestly in my face. He touched my forehead, drew his hand across it, and then looked in my eyes for a time.

'Well, doctor, what do you think?' whispered the count.

'How much did you give him?' said the marquis, thus suddenly stunted down to a doctor.

'Seventy drops,' said the lady.

'In the hot coffee?'

'Yes; sixty in a hot cup of coffee and ten in the liqueur.'

Her voice, low and hard, seemed to me to tremble a little. It takes a long course of guilt to subjugate nature completely, and prevent those exterior signs of agitation that outlive all good.

The doctor, however, was treating me as coolly as he might a subject which he was about to place on the dissecting-table for a lecture.

He looked into my eyes again for a while, took my wrist and applied his fingers to the pulse.

'That action suspended,' he said to himself.

Then again he placed something that, for the moment I saw it, looked like a piece of gold-beater's leaf to my lips, holding his head so far that his own breathing could not affect it.

'Yes,' he said in soliloquy, very low.

Then he plucked my shirt-breast open and applied the stethoscope, shifted it from point to point, listened with his ear to its end, as if for a very far-off sound, raised his head, and said, in like manner, softly to himself, 'All appreciable action of the lungs has subsided.'

Then turning from the sound, as I conjectured, he said: 'Seventy drops, allowing ten for waste, ought to hold him fast for six hours and a half – that is ample. The experiment I tried in the carriage was only thirty drops, and showed a highly sensitive brain. It would not do to kill him, you know. You are certain you did not exceed seventy?'

'Perfectly,' said the lady.

'If he were to die the evaporation would be arrested, and foreign matter, some of it poisonous, would be found in the stomach, don't you see? If you are doubtful, it would be well to use the stomach-pump.'

'Dearest Eugénie, be frank, be frank, do be frank,' urged the count.

'I am *not* doubtful, I am *certain*,' she answered.

'How long ago, exactly? I told you to observe the time.'

'I did; the minute-hand was exactly there, under the point of that cupid's foot.'

'It will last, then, probably for seven hours. He will recover then; the evaporation will be complete, and not one particle of the fluid will remain in the stomach.'

It was reassuring, at all events, to hear that there was no intention to murder me. No one who has not tried it knows the terror of the approach of death, when the mind is clear, the instincts of life unimpaired, and no excitement to disturb the appreciation of that entirely new horror.

The nature and purpose of this tenderness was very, very peculiar, and as yet I had not a suspicion of it.

'You leave France, I suppose?' said the ex-marquis.

'Yes, certainly, tomorrow,' answered the count.

'And where do you mean to go?'

'That I have not yet settled,' he answered quickly.

'You won't tell a friend, eh?'

'I can't till I know. This has turned out an un-profitable affair.'

'We shall settle that by and by.'

'It is time we should get him lying down, eh,' said the count, indicating me with one finger.

'Yes, we must proceed rapidly now. Are his night-shirt and nightcap – you understand – here?'

'All ready,' said the count.

'Now, madame,' said the doctor, turning to the lady, and making her, in spite of the emergency, a bow, 'it is time you should retire.'

The lady passed into the room in which I had taken my cup of treacherous coffee, and I saw her no more.

The count took a candle, and passed through the door at the farther end of the room, returning with a roll of linen in his hand. He bolted first one door then the other.

They now, in silence, proceeded to undress me rapidly. They were not many minutes in accomplishing this.

What the doctor had termed my nightshirt, a long garment which reached below my feet, was now on, and a cap that resembled a female nightcap more than anything I had ever seen upon a male head was fitted upon mine and tied under my chin.

And now, I thought, I shall be laid in a bed to recover how I can, and, in the meantime, the conspirators will have escaped with their booty and pursuit be in vain.

This was my best hope at the time; but it was soon clear that their plans were very different.

The count and Planard now went together into the room that lay straight before me. I heard them talking low, and a sound of shuffling feet; then a long rumble; it suddenly stopped; it recommenced; it continued; side by side they came in at the door, their backs toward me. They were dragging something along the floor that made a continued boom and rumble, but they were interposed between me and it, so that I could not see it until they had dragged it almost beside me; and then, merciful heaven! I saw it plainly enough. It was the coffin I had seen in the next room. It now lay flat on the floor, its edge against the chair in which I sat. Planard removed the lid. The coffin was empty.

26

Catastrophe

'Those seem to be good horses, and we change on the way,' said Planard. 'You give the men a Napoleon or two; we must do it within three hours and a quarter. Now, come; I'll lift him upright so as to place his feet in their proper berth, and you must keep them together, and draw the white shirt well down over them.'

In another moment I was placed, as he described, sustained in Planard's arms, standing at the foot of the coffin, and so lowered backwards, gradually, till I lay my length in it. Then the man, whom the count called Planard, stretched my arms by my sides, and carefully arranged the frills at my breast, and the folds of the shroud, and after that, taking his stand at the foot of the coffin, made a survey which seemed to satisfy him.

The count, who was very methodical, took my clothes which had just been removed, folded them rapidly together and locked them up, as I afterwards heard, in one of the three presses which opened by doors in the panel.

I now understood their frightful plan. This coffin had been prepared for *me*; the funeral of St Amand was a sham to mislead enquiry; I had myself given the order at Père Lachaise, signed it, and paid the fees for the interment of the fictitious Pierre de St Amand, whose place I was to take, to lie in his coffin with his name on the plate above my breast, and with a ton of clay packed down upon me; to waken from this catalepsy, after I had been for hours in the grave, there to perish by a death the most horrible that imagination can conceive.

If, hereafter, by any caprice of curiosity or suspicion, the coffin should be exhumed and the body it enclosed examined, no chemistry could detect a trace of poison, nor the most cautious examination the slightest mark of violence.

I had myself been at the utmost pains to mystify enquiry, should my disappearance excite surmises, and had even written to my few correspondents in England to tell them that they were not to look for a letter from me for three weeks at least.

In the moment of my guilty elation death had caught me, and there was no escape. I tried to pray to God in my unearthly panic, but only thoughts of terror, judgement and eternal anguish crossed the distraction of my immediate doom.

I must not try to recall what is indeed indescribable – the multiform horrors of my own thoughts. I will relate, simply, what befell, every detail of which remains sharp in my memory as if cut in steel.

'The undertaker's men are in the hall,' said the count.

'They must not come till this is fixed,' answered Planard. 'Be good enough to take hold of the lower part while I take this end.' I was not left long to conjecture what was coming, for in a few seconds more something slid across, a few inches above my face, and entirely excluded the light, and muffled sound so that nothing that was not very distinct reached my ears henceforward; but very distinctly came the working of a turnscrew, and the crunching home of screws in succession. Than these vulgar sounds no doom spoken in thunder could have been more tremendous.

The rest I must relate, not as it then reached my ears, which was too imperfectly and interruptedly to supply a connected narrative, but as it was afterwards told me by other people.

The coffin-lid being screwed down, the two gentlemen arranged the room and adjusted the coffin so that it lay perfectly straight along the boards, the count being specially anxious that there should be no appearance of hurry or disorder in the room, which might have excited remark and conjecture.

When this was done, Dr Planard said he would go to the hall to summon the men who were to carry the coffin out and place it in the hearse. The count pulled on his black gloves, and held his white handkerchief in his hand, a very impressive chief-mourner. He stood a little behind the head of the coffin, awaiting the arrival of the persons who accompanied Planard, and whose fast steps he soon heard approaching.

Planard came first. He entered the room through the apartment in which the coffin had been originally placed. His manner was changed; there was something of a swagger in it.

'Monsieur le Comte,' he said, as he strode through the door, followed by half a dozen persons. 'I am sorry to have to announce a most unseasonable interruption. Here is Monsieur Carmaignac, a gentleman holding an office in the police department, who has information to the effect that large quantities of smuggled English and other goods have been distributed in this neighbourhood and that a portion of them is concealed in your house. I have ventured to assure him, of my own knowledge, that nothing can be more false than that information, and that you would be only too happy to throw open for his inspection, at a moment's notice, every room, closet and cupboard in your house.'

'Most assuredly,' exclaimed the count, with a stout voice, but a very white face. 'Thank you, my good friend, for having anticipated me. I will place my house and keys at his disposal, for the purpose of his scrutiny, so soon as he is good enough to inform me of what specific contraband goods he comes in search.'

'The Count de St Alyre will pardon me,' answered Carmaignac, a little drily. 'I am forbidden by my instructions to make that disclosure; and that I am instructed to make a general search, this warrant will satisfy Monsieur le Comte.'

'Monsieur Carmaignac, may I hope,' interposed

Planard, 'that you will permit the Count de St Alyre to attend the funeral of his kinsman, who lies here, as you see' (he pointed to the plate upon the coffin), 'and to convey whom to Père Lachaise, a hearse waits at this moment at the door?'

'That, I regret to say, I cannot permit. My instructions are precise; but the delay, I trust, will be but trifling. Monsieur le Comte will not suppose for a moment that I suspect him; but we have a duty to perform, and I must act as if I did. When I am ordered to search, I search; things are sometimes hid in such bizarre places. I can't say, for instance, what that coffin may contain.'

'The body of my kinsman, Monsieur Pierre de St Amand,' answered the count, loftily.

'Oh! then you've seen him?'

'Seen him? Often, too often!' The count was evidently a good deal moved.

'I mean the body?'

The count stole a quick glance at Planard.

'N–no, monsieur – that is, I mean only for a moment.' Another quick glance at Planard.

'But quite long enough, I fancy, to recognise him?' insinuated that gentleman.

'Of course – of course; instantly – perfectly. What! Pierre de St Amand? Not know him at a glance? No, no, poor fellow, I know him too well for that.'

'The things I am in search of,' said Monsieur Carmaignac, 'would fit in a narrow compass – servants are so ingenious sometimes. Let us raise the lid.'

'Pardon me, monsieur,' said the count, peremptorily, advancing to the side of the coffin, and extending his arm across it, 'I cannot permit that indignity – that desecration.'

'There shall be none, sir – simply the raising of the lid; you shall remain in the room. If it should prove as we all hope, you shall have the pleasure of one final look, really the last, upon your beloved kinsman.'

'But, sir, I can't.'

'But, monsieur, I must.'

'But, besides, the thing, the turnscrew, broke when the last screw was turned; and I give you my sacred honour there is nothing but the body in this coffin.'

'Of course, Monsieur le Comte believes all that; but he does not know so well as I the legerdemain in use among servants who are accustomed to smuggling. Here, Philippe, you must take off the lid of that coffin.'

The count protested; but Philippe – a man with a bald head, and a smirched face, looking like a working blacksmith – placed on the floor a leather bag of tools, from which, having looked at the coffin and picked with his nail at the screw-heads, he selected a turnscrew; after a few deft twirls at each of the screws, they stood up like little rows of mushrooms, and the lid was raised. I saw the light, of which I thought I had seen my last, once more; but the axis of vision remained fixed. As I was reduced to the cataleptic state in a position nearly perpendicular, I continued looking straight before me, and thus my gaze was now fixed upon the ceiling. I saw the face of Carmaignac leaning over me with a curious frown. It seemed to me that there was no recognition in his eyes. Oh, heaven! that I could have uttered were it but one cry! I saw the dark, mean mask of the little count staring down at me from the other side; the face of the pseudo-marquis also peering at me, but not so full in the line of vision; there were other faces also.

'I see, I see,' said Carmaignac, withdrawing. 'Nothing of the kind there.'

'You will be good enough to direct your man to readjust the lid of the coffin, and to fix the screws,' said the count, taking courage; 'and – and – really the funeral must proceed. It is not fair to the people who have but moderate fees for night-work, to keep them hour after hour beyond the time.'

'Count de St Alyre, you shall go in a very few minutes. I will direct, just now, all about the coffin.'

The count looked toward the door, and there saw a gendarme; and two or three more grave and stalwart specimens of the same force were also in the room. The count was very uncomfortably excited; it was growing insupportable.

'As this gentleman makes a difficulty about my attending the obsequies of my kinsman, I will ask you, Planard, to accompany the funeral in my stead.'

'In a few minutes,' answered the incorrigible Carmaignac. 'I must first trouble you for the key that opens that press.'

He pointed directly at the press in which my clothes had just been locked up.

'I – I have no objection,' said the count – 'none, of course; only they have not been used for an age. I'll direct someone to look for the key.'

'If you have not got it about you, it is quite unnecessary. Philippe, try your skeleton-keys with that press. I want it opened. Whose clothes are these?' enquired Carmaignac, when, the press having been opened, he took out the suit that had been placed there scarcely two minutes since.

'I can't say,' answered the count. 'I know nothing of the contents of that press. A roguish servant, named

Lablais, whom I dismissed about a year ago, had the key. I have not seen it open for ten years or more. The clothes are probably his.'

'Here are visiting cards, see, and here a marked pocket-handkerchief – "R. B." upon it. He must have stolen them from a person named Beckett – R. Beckett. "Mr Beckett, Berkeley Square", the card says; and, my faith! here's a watch and a bunch of seals; one of them with the initials "R. B" upon it. That servant, Lablais, must have been a consummate rogue!'

'So he was; you are right, sir.'

'It strikes me that he possibly stole these clothes,' continued Carmaignac, 'from the man in the coffin, who, in that case, would be Monsieur Beckett, and not Monsieur de St Amand. For, wonderful to relate, monsieur, the watch is still going! That man in the coffin, I believe is not dead, but simply drugged. And for having robbed and intended to murder him, I arrest you, Nicolas de la Marque, Count de St Alyre.'

In another moment the old villain was a prisoner. I heard his discordant voice break quaveringly into sudden vehemence and volubility, now croaking, now shrieking, as he oscillated between protests, threats and impious appeals to the God who will 'judge the secrets of men'! And thus lying and raving, he was removed from the room, and placed in the same coach with his beautiful and abandoned accomplice, already arrested; and, with two gendarmes sitting beside them, they were immediately driving at a rapid pace towards the Conciergerie.

There were now added to the general chorus two voices, very different in quality; one was that of the Gasconading Colonel Gaillarde, who had with difficulty been kept in the background up to this; the other was that of my jolly friend Whistlewick, who had come to identify me.

I shall tell you, just now, how this project against my property and life, so ingenious and monstrous, was exploded. I must first say a word about myself. I was placed in a hot bath, under the direction of Planard, as consummate a villain as any of the gang, but now thoroughly in the interests of the prosecution. Thence I was laid in a warm bed, the window of the room being open. These simple measures restored me in about three hours; I should otherwise, probably, have continued under the spell for nearly seven.

The practices of these nefarious conspirators had been carried on with consummate skill and secrecy. Their dupes were led, as I was, to be themselves auxiliary to the mystery which made their own destruction both safe and certain.

A search was, of course, instituted. Graves were opened in Père Lachaise. The bodies exhumed had lain there too long, and were too much decomposed to be recognised. One only was identified. The notice for the burial, in this particular case, had been signed, the order given and the fees paid by Gabriel Gaillarde, who was known to the official clerk who had to transact with him this little funereal business. The very trick that had been arranged for me, had been successfully practised in his case. The person for whom the grave had been ordered was purely fictitious; and Gabriel Gaillarde himself filled the coffin, on the cover of which that false name was inscribed as well as upon a tombstone over the grave. Possibly, the same honour, under my pseudonym, may have been intended for me.

The identification was curious. This Gabriel Gaillarde had had a bad fall from a runaway horse, about five years before his mysterious disappearance. He had lost an eye and some teeth, in this accident, besides sustaining a fracture of the right leg, immediately above the ankle. He had kept the injuries to his face as profound a secret as he could. The result was that the glass eye which had done duty for the one he had lost remained in the socket, slightly displaced, of course, but recognisable by the 'artist' who had supplied it.

More pointedly recognisable were the teeth, peculiar in workmanship, which one of the ablest dentists in Paris had himself adapted to the chasms, the cast of which, owing to peculiarities in the accident, he happened to have preserved. This cast precisely fitted the gold plate found in the mouth of the skull. The mark, also, above the ankle, in the bone, where it had reunited, corresponded exactly with the place where the fracture had knit in the limb of Gabriel Gaillarde.

The colonel, his younger brother, had been furious about the disappearance of Gabriel, and still more so about that of his money, which he had long regarded as his proper keepsake whenever death should remove his brother from the vexations of living. He had suspected for a long time, for certain adroitly discovered reasons, that the Count de St Alyre and the beautiful lady, his companion, countess, or whatever else she was, had pigeoned him. To this suspicion were added some others of a still darker kind – but in their first shape, rather the exaggerated reflections of his fury, ready to believe anything, than well-defined conjectures.

At length an accident had placed the colonel very nearly upon the right scent; a chance, possibly lucky for himself, had apprised the scoundrel Planard that the conspirators – himself among the number – were in danger. The result was that he made terms for himself, became an informer, and concerted with the police this visit made to the Château de la Carque at the critical moment, when every measure had been completed that was necessary to construct a perfect case against his guilty accomplices.

I need not describe the minute industry or fore-thought with which the police agents collected all the details necessary to support the case. They had brought an able physician, who, even had Planard failed, would have supplied the necessary medical evidence.

My trip to Paris, you will believe, had not turned out quite so agreeably as I had anticipated. I was the principal witness for the prosecution in this *cause célèbre*, with all the *agrément* that attends that enviable position. Having had an escape, as my friend Whistle-wick said, 'within a squeak' of my life, I innocently fancied that I should have been an object of con-siderable interest to Parisian society; but, a good deal to my mortification, I discovered that I was the object of a good-natured but contemptuous merriment. I was a *balourd*, a *benêt*, *un âne*, and figured even in caricatures. I became a sort of public character, a figure of fun, 'unto which I was not born' and from which I fled as soon as I conveniently could, without even paying my friend, the Marquis d'Harmonville, a visit at his hospitable château.

The marquis escaped scot-free. His accomplice, the count, was executed. The fair Eugénie, under extenuating circumstances – consisting, so far as I could discover, of her good looks – got off with six years' imprisonment.

Colonel Gaillarde recovered some of his brother's money, out of the not very affluent estate of the count and *soi-disant* countess. This, and the execution of the count, put him in high good humour. So far from insisting on a hostile meeting, he shook me very graciously by the hand and told me that he looked upon the wound to his head, inflicted by the knob of my stick, as having been received in an honourable though irregular duel, in which he had no disadvantage or unfairness to complain of.

I think I have only two additional details to mention. The bricks discovered in the room with the coffin had been packed in it, in straw, to supply the weight of a dead body and to prevent the suspicions and contradictions that might have been excited by the arrival of an empty coffin at the château.

Secondly, the countess's magnificent brilliants were examined by a lapidary and pronounced to be worth about five pounds to a tragedy queen who happened to be in want of a suite of paste.

The countess had figured some years before as one of the cleverest actresses on the minor stage of Paris, where she had been picked up by the count and used as his principal accomplice.

She it was who, admirably disguised, had rifled my papers in the carriage on my memorable night-journey to Paris. She also had figured as the interpreting magician of the palanquin at the ball at Versailles. So far as I was affected by that elaborate mystification it was intended to reanimate my interest, which, they feared, might flag, in the beautiful countess. It had its design and action upon other intended victims also; but of them there is, at present, no need to speak. The introduction of a real corpse – procured from a person who supplied the Parisian anatomists – involved no real danger, while it heightened the mystery and kept the prophet alive in the gossip of the town and in the thoughts of the noodles with whom he had conferred.

I divided the remainder of the summer and autumn between Switzerland and Italy.

As the well-worn phrase goes, I was a sadder if not a wiser man. A great deal of the horrible impression left upon my mind was due, of course, to the mere action of nerves and brain. But serious feelings of another and deeper kind remained. My after life was ultimately formed by the shock I had then received. Those impressions led me – but not till after many years – to happier though not less serious thoughts; and I have deep reason to be thankful to the all-merciful Ruler of Events, for an early and terrible lesson in the ways of sin.

SHERIDAN LE FANU

Madam Crowl's Ghost

I'm an old woman now; and I was but thirteen my
last birthday, the night I came to Applewale House.
My aunt was the housekeeper there, and a sort o'
one-horse carriage was down at Lexhoe to take me
and my box up to Applewale.

I was a bit frightened by the time I got to Lexhoe,
and when I saw the carriage and horse, I wished
myself back again with my mother at Hazelden. I was
crying when I got into the 'shay' – that's what we
used to call it and old John Mulbery that drove it, and
was a good-natured fellow, bought me a handful of
apples at the Golden Lion, to cheer me up a bit; and
he told me that there was a currant-cake, and tea, and
pork-chops, waiting for me, all hot, in my aunt's room
at the great house. It was a fine moonlight night and I
eat the apples, lookin' out o' the shay winda.

It is a shame for gentlemen to frighten a poor foolish
child like I was. I sometimes think it might be tricks.
There was two on 'em on the tap o' the coach beside
me. And they began to question me after nightfall,
when the moon rose, where I was going to. Well, I
told them it was to wait on Dame Arabella Crowl, of
Applewale House, near by Lexhoe.

'Ho, then,' says one of them, 'you'll not be long
there!'

And I looked at him as much as to say, 'Why not?' for I had spoke out when I told them where I was goin', as if 'twas something clever I had to say.

'Because,' says he – 'and don't you for your life tell no one, only watch her and see – she's possessed by the devil, and more an half a ghost. Have you got a Bible?'

'Yes, sir,' says I. For my mother put my little Bible in my box, and I knew it was there and by the same token, though the print's too small for my old eyes, I have it in my press to this hour.

As I looked up at him, saying 'Yes, sir,' I thought I saw him winkin' at his friend; but I could not be sure.

'Well,' says he, 'be sure you put it under your bolster every night, it will keep the old girl's claws aff ye.'

And I got such a fright when he said that, you wouldn't fancy! And I'd a liked to ask him a lot about the old lady, but I was too shy, and he and his friend began talkin' together about their own consarns, and dowly enough I got down, as I told ye, at Lexhoe. My heart sank as I drove into the dark avenue. The trees stands very thick and big, as old as the old house almost, and four people, with their arms out and fingertips touchin', barely girds round some of them.

Well, my neck was stretched out o' the winda, looking for the first view o' the great house; and, all at once we pulled up in front of it.

A great white-and-black house it is, wi' great black beams across and right up it, and gables lookin' out, as white as a sheet, to the moon, and the shadows o' the trees, two or three up and down upon the front, you could count the leaves on them, and all the little diamond-shaped winda-panes, glimmering on the great hall winda, and great shutters, in the old fashion, hinged on the wall outside, boulted across all the rest o' the windas in front, for there was but three or four servants, and the old lady in the house, and most o' t'rooms was locked up.

My heart was in my mouth when I sid the journey was over, and this, the great house afore me, and I sa near my aunt that I never sid till noo, and Dame Crowl, that I was come to wait upon, and was afeard on already.

My aunt kissed me in the hall, and brought me to her room. She was tall and thin, wi' a pale face and black eyes, and long thin hands wi' black mittins on. She was past fifty, and her word was short; but her word was law. I hev no complaints to make of her; but she was a hard woman, and I think she would hev bin kinder to me if I had bin her sister's child in place of her brother's. But all that's o' no consequence noo.

The squire – his name was Mr Chevenix Crowl, he was Dame Crowl's grandson – came down there, by way of seeing that the old lady was well treated, about twice or thrice in the year. I sid him but twice all the time I was at Applewale House.

I can't say but she was well taken care of, notwithstandin', but that was because my aunt and Meg Wyvern, that was her maid, had a conscience, and did their duty by her.

Mrs Wyvern – Meg Wyvern my aunt called her to herself, and Mrs Wyvern to me – was a fat, jolly lass of fifty, a good height and a good breadth, always good-humoured, and walked slow. She had fine wages, but she was a bit stingy, and kept all her fine clothes under lock and key, and wore, mostly, a twilled chocolate cotton, wi' red, and yellow, and green sprigs and balls on it, and it lasted wonderful.

She never gave me nout, not the vally o' a brass thimble, all the time I was there; but she was good-humoured, and always laughin', and she talked no end o' proas over her tea; and, seeing me sa sackless and dowly, she roused me up wi' her laughin' and stories; and I think I liked her better than my aunt – children is so taken wi' a bit o' fun or a story – though my aunt was very good to me, but a hard woman about some things, and silent always.

My aunt took me into her bedchamber, that I might rest myself a bit while she was settin' the tea in her room. But first she patted me on the shouther, and said I was a tall lass o' my years, and had spired up well, and asked me if I could do plain work and stitchin'; and she looked in my face, and said I was like my father, her brother, that was dead and gone, and she hoped I was a better Christian, and wad na du a' that lids.

It was a hard sayin' the first time I set my foot in her room, I thought.

When I went into the next room, the housekeeper's room – very comfortable, yak (oak) all round – there was a fine fire blazin' away, wi' coal, and peat, and wood, all in a low together, and tea on the table, and hot cake, and smokin' meat; and there was Mrs Wyvern, fat, jolly, and talkin' away, more in an hour than my aunt would in a year.

While I was still at my tea my aunt went upstairs to see Madam Crowl.

'She's agone up to see that old Judith Squailes is awake,' says Mrs Wyvern. 'Judith sits with Madam Crowl when me and Mrs Shutters' – that was my aunt's name – 'is away. She's a troublesome old lady.

Ye'll hev to be sharp wi' her, or she'll be into the fire,
or out o' t' winda. She goes on wires, she does, old
though she be.'

'How old, ma'am?' says I.

'Ninety-three her last birthday, and that's eight
months gone,' says she; and she laughed. 'And don't
be askin' questions about her before your aunt –
mind, I tell ye; just take her as you find her, and that's
all.'

'And what's to be my business about her, please
ma'am?' says I.

'About the old lady? Well,' says she, 'your aunt,
Mrs Shutters, will tell you that; but I suppose you'll
hev to sit in the room with your work, and see she's at
no mischief, and let her amuse herself with her things
on the table, and get her her food or drink as she calls
for it, and keep her out o' mischief, and ring the bell
hard if she's troublesome.'

'Is she deaf, ma'am?'

'No, nor blind,' says she; 'as sharp as a needle,
but she's gone quite aupy, and can't remember nout
rightly; and Jack the Giant Killer, or Goody Twoshoes
will please her as well as the King's court, or the
affairs of the nation.'

'And what did the little girl go away for, ma'am,
that went on Friday last? My aunt wrote to my mother
she was to go.'

'Yes; she's gone.'

'What for?' says I again.

'She didn't answer Mrs Shutters, I do suppose,'
says she. 'I don't know. Don't be talkin'; your aunt
can't abide a talkin' child.'

'And please, ma'am, is the old lady well in health?'
says I.

'It ain't no harm to ask that,' says she. 'She's torflin' a bit lately, but better this week past, and I dare say she'll last out her hundred years yet. Hish! Here's your aunt coming down the passage.'

In comes my aunt, and begins talkin' to Mrs Wyvern, and I, beginnin' to feel more comfortable and at home like, was walkin' about the room lookin' at this thing and at that. There was pretty old china things on the cupboard, and pictures again the wall; and there was a door open in the wainscot, and I sees a queer old leathern jacket, wi' straps and buckles to it, and sleeves as long as the bedpost, hangin' up inside.

'What's that you're at, child?' says my aunt, sharp enough, turning about when I thought she least minded. 'What's that in your hand?'

'This, ma'am?' says I, turning about with the leathern jacket. 'I don't know what it is, ma'am.'

Pale as she was, the red came up in her cheeks, and her eyes flashed wi' anger, and I think only she had half a dozen steps to take, between her and me, she'd a gov me a sizzup. But she did give me a shake by the shouther, and she plucked the thing out o' my hand, and says she, 'While ever you stay here, don't ye meddle wi' nout that don't belong to ye,' and she hung it up on the pin that was there, and shut the door wi' a bang and locked it fast.

Mrs Wyvern was liftin' up her hands and laughin' all this time, quietly in her chair, rolling herself a bit in it, as she used when she was kinkin'.

The tears was in my eyes, and she winked at my aunt, and says she, dryin' her own eyes that was wet wi' the laughin', 'Tut, the child meant no harm – come here to me, child. It's only a pair o' crutches for

lame ducks, and ask us no questions mind, and we'll
tell ye no lies; and come here and sit down, and drink
a mug o' beer before ye go to your bed.'

My room, mind ye, was upstairs, next to the old
lady's, and Mrs Wyvern's bed was near hers in her
room and I was to be ready at call, if need should be.

The old lady was in one of her tantrums that night
and part of the day before. She used to take fits o' the
sulks. Sometimes she would not let them dress her,
and other times she would not let them take her
clothes off. She was a great beauty, they said, in her
day. But there was no one about Applewale that
remembered her in her prime. And she was dreadful
fond o' dress, and had thick silks, and stiff satins, and
velvets, and laces, and all sorts, enough to set up
seven shops at the least. All her dresses was old
fashioned and queer, but worth a fortune.

Well, I went to my bed. I lay for a while awake; for
a' things was new to me; and I think the tea was in my
nerves, too, for I wasn't used to it, except now and
then on a holiday, or the like. And I heard Mrs
Wyvern talkin', and I listened with my hand to my
ear; but I could not hear Mrs Crowl, and I don't
think she said a word.

There was great care took of her. The people at
Applewale knew that when she died they would everyone get the sack; and their situations was well paid
and easy.

The doctor come twice a week to see the old lady,
and you may be sure they all did as he bid them. One
thing was the same every time; they were never to
cross or frump her in any way, but to humour and
please her in everything.

So she lay in her clothes all that night, and next

day, not a word she said, and I was at my needlework all that day, in my own room, except when I went down to my dinner.

I would a liked to see the old lady, and even to hear her speak. But she might as well a'bin in Lunnon a' the time for me.

When I had my dinner my aunt sent me out for a walk for an hour. I was glad when I came back, the trees was so big, and the place so dark and lonesome, and 'twas a cloudy day, and I cried a deal, thinkin' of home, while I was walkin' alone there. That evening, the candles bein' alight, I was sittin' in my room, and the door was open into Madam Crowl's chamber, where my aunt was. It was, then, for the first time I heard what I suppose was the old lady talking.

It was a queer noise like, I couldn't well say which, a bird, or a beast, only it had a bleatin' sound in it, and was very small.

I pricked my ears to hear all I could. But I could not make out one word she said. And my aunt answered: 'The evil one can't hurt no one, ma'am, bout the Lord permits.'

Then the same queer voice from the bed says something more that I couldn't make head nor tail on.

And my aunt med answer again: 'Let them pull faces, ma'am, and say what they will; if the Lord be for us, who can be against us?'

I kept listenin' with my ear turned to the door, holdin' my breath, but not another word or sound came in from the room. In about twenty minutes, as I was sittin' by the table, lookin' at the pictures in the old Aesop's Fables, I was aware o' something moving at the door, and lookin' up I sid my aunt's face lookin' in at the door, and her hand raised.

'Hish!' says she, very soft, and comes over to me on tiptoe, and she says in a whisper: 'Thank God, she's asleep at last, and don't ye make no noise till I come back, for I'm going' down to take my cup o' tea, and I'll be back i' noo – me and Mrs Wyvern, and she'll be sleepin' in the room, and you can run down when we come up, and Judith will gie ye yaur supper in my room.'

And with that away she goes.

I kep' looking at the picture-book, as before, listenin' every noo and then, but there was no sound, not a breath, that I could hear; an' I began whisperin' to the pictures and talkin' to myself to keep my heart up, for I was growin' feared in that big room.

And at last up I got, and began walkin' about the room, lookin' at this and peepin' at that, to amuse my mind, ye'll understand. And at last what sud I do but peeps into Madame Crowl's bedchamber.

A grand chamber it was, wi' a great four-poster, wi' flowered silk curtains as tall as the ceilin', and foldin' down on the floor, and drawn close all round. There was a lookin'-glass, the biggest I ever sid before, and the room was a blaze o' light. I counted twenty-two wax-candles, all alight. Such was her fancy, and no one dared say her nay.

I listened at the door, and gaped and wondered all round. When I heard there was not a breath, and did not see so much as a stir in the curtains, I took heart, and I walked into the room on tiptoe and looked round again. Then I takes a keek at myself in the big glass; and at last it came in my head, 'Why couldn't I ha' a keek at the old lady herself in the bed?'

Ye'd think me a fule if ye knew half how I longed to see Dame Crowl, and I thought to myself if I didn't peep now I might wait many a day before I got so gude a chance again.

Well, my dear, I came to the side o' the bed, the curtains bein' close, and my heart a'most failed me. But I took courage, and I slips my finger in between the thick curtains, and then my hand. So I waits a bit, but all was still as death. So, softly, softly I draws the curtain, and there, sure enough, I sid before me, stretched out like the painted lady on the tombstean in Lexhoe Church, the famous Dame Crowl, of Applewale House. There she was, dressed out. You never sid the like in they days. Satin and silk, and scarlet and green, and gold and pint lace; by Jen! 'twas a sight! A big powdered wig, half as high as herself, was a-top o' her head, and, wow! – was ever such wrinkles? – and her old baggy throat all powdered white, and her cheeks rouged, and mouse-skin eyebrows, that Mrs Wyvern used to stick on, and there she lay grand and stark, wi' a pair o' clocked silk hose on, and heels to her shoon as tall as nine-pins. Lawk! But her nose was crooked and thin, and half the whites o' her eyes was open. She used to stand, dressed as she was, gigglin' and dribblin' before the lookin'-glass, wi' a fan in her hand, and a big nosegay in her bodice. Her wrinkled little hands was stretched down by her sides, and such long nails, all cut into points, I never sid in my days. Could it ever a bin the fashion for grit fowk to wear their fingernails so?

Well, I think ye'd a-bin frightened yourself if ye'd a sid such a sight. I couldn't let go the curtain, nor move an inch, not take my eyes off her; my very heart stood still. And in an instant she opens her eyes, and up she sits, and spins herself round, and down wi' her, wi' a clack on her two tall heels on the floor, facin' me, ogglin' in my face wi' her two great glassy eyes, and a wicked simper wi' her old wrinkled lips, and lang fause teeth.

Well, a corpse is a natural thing; but this was the dreadfullest sight I ever sid. She had her fingers straight out pointin' at me, and her back was crooked, round again wi' age. Says she: 'Ye little limb! what for did ye say I killed the boy? I'll tickle ye till ye're stiff!'

If I'd a thought an instant, I'd a turned about and run. But I couldn't take my eyes off her, and I backed from her as soon as I could; and she came clatterin' after, like a thing on wires, with her fingers pointing to my throat, and she makin' all the time a sound with her tongue like zizz-zizz-zizz.

I kept backin' and backin' as quick as I could, and her fingers was only a few inches away from my throat, and I felt I'd lose my wits if she touched me.

I went back this way, right into the corner, and I gev a yellock, ye'd think saul and body was partin', and that minute my aunt, from the door, calls out wi' a blare, and the old lady turns round on her, and I turns about, and ran through my room, and down the back stairs, as hard as my legs could carry me.

I cried hearty, I can tell you, when I got down to the housekeeper's room. Mrs Wyvern laughed a deal when I told her what happened. But she changed her key when she heard the old lady's words.

'Say them again,' says she.

So I told her.

'Ye little limb! What for did ye say I killed the boy? I'll tickle ye till ye're stiff.'

'And did ye say she killed a boy?' says she.

'Not I, ma'am,' says I.

Judith was always up with me, after that, when the two elder women was away from her. I would a jumped out at winda, rather than stay alone in the same room wi' her.

It was about a week after, as well as I can remember, Mrs Wyvern, one day when me and her was alone, told me a thing about Madam Crowl that I did not know before.

She being young, and a great beauty, full seventy years before, had married Squire Crowl of Applewale. But he was a widower, and had a son about nine year old.

There never was tale or tidings of this boy after one mornin'. No one could say where he went to. He was allowed too much liberty, and used to be off in the morning, one day, to the keeper's cottage, and breakfast wi' him, and away to the warren, and not home, mayhap, till evening, and another time down to the lake, and bathe there, and spend the day fishin' there, or paddlin' about in the boat. Well, no one could say what was gone wi' him; only this, that his hat was found by the lake, under a haathorn that grows thar to this day, and 'twas thought he was drowned bathin'. And the squire's son, by his second marriage, by this Madam Crowl that lived sa dreadful lang, came in for the estates. It was his son, the old lady's grandson, Squire Chevenix Crowl, that owned the estates at the time I came to Applewale.

There was a deal o' talk lang before my aunt's time about it; and 'twas said the stepmother knew more than she was like to let out. And she managed her husband, the old squire, wi' her whiteheft and flatteries. And as the boy was never seen more, in course of time the thing died out of fowks' minds.

I'm going' to tell ye noo about what I sid wi' my own een.

I was not there six months, and it was winter time, when the old lady took her last sickness.

The doctor was afeard she might a took a fit o' madness, as she did, fifteen years before, and was buckled up, many a time, in a strait-waistcoat, which was the very leathern jerkin' I sid in the closet, off my aunt's room.

Well, she didn't. She pined, and windered, and went off, torflin', torflin', quiet enough, till a day or two before her flittin', and then she took to rabblin', and sometimes skirlin' in the bed, ye'd think a robber had a knife to her throat, and she used to work out o' the bed, and not being strong enough, then, to walk or stand, she'd fall on the flure, wi' her old wizened hands stretched before her face, and skirlin' still for mercy.

Ye may guess I didn't go into the room, and I used to be shiverin' in my bed wi' fear, at her skirlin' and scrafflin' on the flure, and blarin' out words that id make your skin turn blue.

My aunt, and Mrs Wyvern, and Judith Squailes, and a woman from Lexhoe, was always about her. At last she took fits, and they wore her out.

T' sir (parson) was there, and prayed for her; but she was past praying with. I suppose it was right, but none could think there was much good in it, and sa at lang last she made her flittin', and a' was over, and old Dame Crowl was shrouded and coffined and Squire Chevenix was wrote for. But he was away in France, and the delay was sa lang, that t' sir and doctor both agreed it would not du to keep her langer out o' her place, and no one cared but just them two, and my aunt and the rest o' us, from Applewale, to go to the buryin'. So the old lady of Applewale was laid in the vault under Lexhoe Church; and we lived up at the great house till such time as the squire should come to tell his will about us, and pay off such as he chose to discharge.

I was put into another room, two doors away from what was Dame Crowl's chamber, after her death, and this thing happened the night before Squire Chevenix came to Applewale.

The room I was in now was a large square chamber, covered wi' yak panels, but unfurnished except for my bed, which had no curtains to it, and a chair and a table, so, that looked nothing at all in such a big room. And the big looking-glass, that the old lady used to keek into and admire herself from head to heel, now that there was na mair o' that wark, was put out of the way, and stood against the wall in my room, for there was shiftin' o' many things in her chambers ye may suppose, when she came to be coffined.

The news had come that day that the squire was to be down next morning at Applewale; and not sorry was I, for I thought I was sure to be sent home again to my mother. And right glad was I, and I was thinkin' of a' at hame, and my sister, Janet, and the kitten and the pymag, and Trimmer the tike, and all the rest, and I got sa fidgetty, I couldn't sleep, and the clock struck twelve, and me wide awake, and the room as dark as pick. My back was turned to the door, and my eyes toward the wall opposite.

Well, it could na be a full quarter past twelve, when I sees a lightin' on the wall before me, as if something took fire behind, and the shadas o' the bed, and the chair, and my gown, that was hangin' from the wall, was dancin' up and down, on the ceilin' beams and the yak panels; and I turns my head ower my shouther quick, thinkin' something must a gone a' fire.

And what sud I see, by Jen! but the likeness o' the old beldame, bedisened out in her satins and velvets, on her dead body, simperin', wi' her eyes as wide as saucers, and her face like the fiend himself. 'Twas a red light that rose about her in a fuffin low, as if her dress round her feet was blazin'. She was drivin' on right for me, wi' her old shrivelled hands crooked as if she was goin' to claw me. I could not stir, but she passed me straight by, wi' a blast o' cald air, and I sid her, at the wall, in the alcove as my aunt used to call it, which was a recess where the state bed used to stand in old times, wi' a door open wide, and her hands gropin' in at somethin' was there. I never sid that door before. And she turned round to me, like a thing on a pivot, flyrin' (grinning), and all at once the room was dark, and I standin' at the far side o' the bed; I don't know how I got there, and I found my tongue at last, and if I did na blare a yellock, rennin' down the gallery and almost pulled Mrs Wyvern's door, off t'hooks, and frightened her half out o' her wits.

Ye may guess I did na sleep that night; and wi' the first light, down wi' me to my aunt, as fast as my two legs cud carry me.

Well, my aunt did na frump or flite me, as I thought she would, but she held me by the hand, and looked hard in my face all the time. And she telt me not to be feared; and says she: 'Hed the appearance a key in its hand?'

'Yes,' says I, bringin' it to mind, 'a big key in a queer brass handle.'

'Stop a bit,' says she, lettin' go ma hand, and openin' the cupboard-door. 'Was it like this?' says she, takin' one out in her fingers and showing it to me, with a dark look in my face.

'That was it,' says I, quick enough.

'Are ye sure?' she says, turnin' it round.

'Sart,' says I, and I felt like I was gain' to faint when I sid it.

'Well, that will do, child,' says she, saftly thinkin', and she locked it up again.

'The squire himself will be here today, before twelve o'clock, and ye must tell him all about it,' says she, thinkin', 'and I suppose I'll be leavin' soon, and so the best thing for the present is, that ye should go home this afternoon, and I'll look out another place for you when I can.'

Fain was I, ye may guess, at that word.

My aunt packed up my things for me, and the three pounds that was due to me, to bring home, and Squire Crowl himself came down to Applewale that day, a handsome man, about thirty years old. It was the second time I sid him. But this was the first time he spoke to me.

My aunt talked wi' him in the housekeeper's room, and I don't know what they said. I was a bit feared on the squire, he bein' a great gentleman down in Lexhoe, and I darn't go near till I was called. And says he, smilin': 'What's a' this ye a sen, child? it mun be a dream, for ye know there's na sic a thing as a bo or a freet in a' the world. But whatever it was, ma little maid, sit ye down and tell us all about it from first to last.'

Well, so soon as I med an end, he thought a bit, and says he to my aunt: 'I mind the place well. In old Sir Oliver's time lame Wyndel told me there was a door in that recess, to the left, where the lassie dreamed she saw my grandmother open it. He was past eighty when he telt me that, and I but a boy. It's twenty year sen. The plate and jewels used to be kept there, long ago, before the iron closet was made in the arras chamber, and he told me the key had a brass handle, and this ye say was found in the bottom o' the kist where she kept her old fans. Now, would not it be a queer thing if we found some spoons or diamonds forgot there? Ye mun come up wi' us, lassie, and point to the very spot.'

Loth was I, and my heart in my mouth, and fast I held by my aunt's hand as I stepped into that awsome room, and showed them both how she came and passed me by, and the spot where she stood, and where the door seemed to open.

There was an old empty press against the wall then, and shoving it aside, sure enough there was the tracing of a door in the wainscot, and a keyhole stopped with wood, and planed across as smooth as the rest, and the joining of the door all stopped wi' putty the colour o' yak, and, but for the hinges that showed a bit when the press was shoved aside, ye would not consayt there was a door there at all.

'Ha!' says he, wi' a queer smile, 'this looks like it.'

It took some minutes wi' a small chisel and hammer to pick the bit o' wood out o' the keyhole. The key fitted, sure enough, and, wi' a strang twist and a lang skreeak, the boult went back and he pulled the door open.

There was another door inside, stranger than the

first, but the lacks was gone, and it opened easy. Inside was a narrow floor and walls and vault o' brick; we could not see what was in it, for 'twas dark as pick.

When my aunt had lighted the candle the squire held it up and stepped in.

My aunt stood on tiptoe tryin' to look over his shouther, and I did na see nout.

'Ha! ha!' says the squire, steppin' backward. 'What's that? Gi'ma the poker – quick!' says he to my aunt. And as she went to the hearth I peeps beside his arm, and I sid squat down in the far corner a monkey or a flayin' on the chest, or else the maist shrivelled up, wizzened old wife that ever was sen on yearth.

'By Jen!' says my aunt, as, puttin' the poker in his hand, she keeked by his shouther, and sid the ill-favoured thing, 'hae a care sir, what ye're doin'. Back wi' ye, and shut to the door!'

But in place o' that he steps in saftly, wi' the poker pointed like a swoord, and he gies it a poke, and down it a' tumbles together, head and a', in a heap o' bayans and dust, little meyar an' a hatful.

'Twas the bayans o' a child; a' the rest went to dust at a touch. They said nout for a while, but he turns round the skull as it lay on the floor.

Young as I was I consayted I knew well enough what they was thinkin' on.

'A dead cat!' says he, pushin' back and blowin' out the can'le, and shuttin' to the door. 'We'll come back, you and me, Mrs Shutters, and look on the shelves by and by. I've other matters first to speak to ye about; and this little girl's going' hame, ye say. She has her wages, and I mun mak' her a present,' says he, pattin' my shoulder wi' his hand.

And he did gimma a goud pound, and I went aff to

Lexhoe about an hour after, and sa hame by the stagecoach, and fain was I to be at hame again; and I never sa old Dame Crowl o' Applewale, God be thanked, either in appearance or in dream, at-efter. But when I was grown to be a woman my aunt spent a day and night wi' me at Littleham, and she telt me there was na doubt it was the poor little boy that was missing sa lang sen that was shut up to die thar in the dark by that wicked beldame, whar his skirls, or his prayers, or his thumpin' cud na be heard, and his hat was left by the water's edge, whoever did it, to mak' belief he was drowned. The clothes, at the first touch, a' ran into a snuff o' dust in the cell whar the bayans was found. But there was a handful o' jet buttons, and a knife with a green handle, together wi' a couple o' pennies the poor little fella had in his pocket, I suppose, when he was decoyed in thar, and sid his last o' the light. And there was, amang the squire's papers, a copy o' the notice that was prented after he was lost, when the old squire thought he might 'a run away, or bin took by gypsies, and it said he had a green-hefted knife wi' him, and that his buttons were o' cut jet. Sa that is a' I hev to say consarnin' old Dame Crowl, o' Applewale House.

SHERIDAN LE FANU

Squire Toby's Will

A Ghost Story

Many persons accustomed to travel the old York and London road, in the days of stagecoaches, will remember passing, in the afternoon, say, of an autumn day, in their journey to the capital, about three miles south of the town of Applebury, and a mile and a half before you reach the Old Angel Inn, a large black-and-white house, as those old fashioned cage-work habitations are termed, dilapidated and weather-stained, with broad lattice windows glimmering all over in the evening sun with little diamond panes, and thrown into relief by a dense background of ancient elms. A wide avenue, now overgrown like a churchyard with grass and weeds, and flanked by double rows of the same dark trees, old and gigantic, with here and there a gap in their solemn files, and sometimes a fallen tree lying across on the avenue, leads up to the hall-door.

Looking up its sombre and lifeless avenue from the top of the London coach, as I have often done, you are struck with so many signs of desertion and decay, the tufted grass sprouting in the chinks of the steps and window-stones, the smokeless chimneys over which the jackdaws are wheeling, the absence of human life and all its evidence, that you conclude at once that the place is uninhabited and abandoned to decay. The name of this ancient house is Gylingden Hall. Tall hedges and old timber quickly shroud the old place from view, and about a quarter of a mile further on you pass, embowered in melancholy trees, a small and ruinous Saxon chapel, which, time out of mind, has been the burying-place of the family of Marston, and partakes of the neglect and desolation which brood over their ancient dwelling-place.

The grand melancholy of the secluded valley of Gylingden, lonely as an enchanted forest, in which the crows returning to their roosts among the trees, and the straggling deer who peep from beneath their branches, seem to hold a wild and undisturbed dominion, heightens the forlorn aspect of Gylingden Hall.

Of late years repairs have been neglected, and here and there the roof is stripped, and 'the stitch in time' has been wanting. At the side of the house exposed to the gales that sweep through the valley like a torrent through its channel, there is not a perfect window left, and the shutters but imperfectly exclude the rain. The ceilings and walls are mildewed and green with damp stains. Here and there, where the drip falls from the ceiling, the floors are rotting. On stormy nights, as the guard described, you can hear the doors clapping in the old house, as far away as old Gryston bridge, and the howl and sobbing of the wind through its empty galleries.

About seventy years ago died the old Squire, Toby Marston, famous in that part of the world for his hounds, his hospitality, and his vices. He had done kind things, and he had fought duels: he had given away money and he had horse-whipped people. He carried with him some blessings and a good many curses, and left behind him an amount of debts and charges upon the estates which appalled his two sons, who had no taste for business or accounts, and had never suspected, till that wicked, open-handed, and swearing old gentleman died, how very nearly he had run the estates into insolvency.

They met at Gylingden Hall. They had the will before them, and lawyers to interpret, and information without stint, as to the encumbrances with which the deceased had saddled them. The will was so framed as to set the two brothers instantly at deadly feud.

These brothers differed in some points; but in one material characteristic they resembled one another, and also their departed father. They never went into a quarrel by halves, and once in, they did not stick at trifles.

The elder, Scroope Marston, the more dangerous man of the two, had never been a favourite of the old Squire. He had no taste for the sports of the field and the pleasures of a rustic life. He was no athlete, and he certainly was not handsome. All this the Squire resented. The young man, who had no respect for him, and outgrew his fear of his violence as he came to manhood, retorted. This aversion, therefore, in the ill-conditioned old man grew into positive hatred. He used to wish that d—d pippin-squeezing, hump-backed rascal Scroope, out of the way of better men – meaning his younger son Charles; and in his cups would talk in a way which even the old and young fellows who followed his hounds, and drank his port, and could stand a reasonable amount of brutality, did not like.

Scroope Marston was slightly deformed, and he had the lean sallow face, piercing black eyes, and black lank hair, which sometimes accompany deformity.

'I'm no feyther o' that hog-backed creature. I'm no sire of hisn, d_n him! I'd as soon call that tongs son o' mine,' the old man used to bawl, in allusion to his son's long, lank limbs: 'Charlie's a man, but that's a jack-an-ape. He has no good-nature; there's nothing handy, nor manly, nor no one turn of a Marston in him.'

And when he was pretty drunk, the old Squire used to swear he should never 'sit at the head o' that board; nor frighten away folk from Gylingden Hall wi' his d—d hatchet-face – the black loon!'

Handsome Charlie was the man for his money. He knew what a horse was, and could sit to his bottle; and the lasses were all clean *wad* about him. He was a Marston every inch of his six foot two.

Handsome Charlie and he, however, had also had a row or two. The old Squire was free with his horsewhip as with his tongue, and on occasion when neither weapon was quite practicable, had been known to give a fellow 'a tap o' his knuckles.' Handsome Charlie, however, thought there was a period at which personal chastisement should cease; and one night, when the port was flowing, there was some allusion to Marion Hayward, the miller's daughter, which for some reason the old gentleman did not like. Being 'in liquor,' and having clearer ideas about pugilism than self-government, he struck out, to the surprise of all present, at Handsome Charlie. The youth threw back his head scientifically, and nothing followed but the crash of a decanter on the floor. But the old Squire's blood was up, and he bounced from his chair. Up jumped Handsome Charlie, resolved to stand no nonsense. Drunken Squire Lilbourne, intending to mediate, fell flat on the floor, and cut his ear among the glasses. Handsome Charlie caught the thump which the old Squire discharged at him upon his open hand, and catching him by the cravat, swung him with his back to the wall. They said the old man never looked so purple, nor his eyes so goggle before; and then Handsome Charlie pinioned him tight to the wall by both arms.

'Well, I say – come, don't you talk no more nonsense o' that sort, and I won't lick you,' croaked the old Squire. 'You stopped that un clever, you did. Didn't he? Come, Charlie, man, gie us your hand, I say, and sit down again, lad.'

And so the battle ended; and I believe it was the last time the Squire raised his hand to Handsome Charlie.

But those days were over. Old Toby Marston lay cold and quiet enough now, under the drip of the mighty ash tree within the Saxon ruin where so many of the old Marston race returned to dust, and were forgotten. The weather-stained top-boots and leather-breeches, the three-cornered cocked hat to which old gentlemen of that day still clung, and the well-known red waistcoat that reached below his hips, and the fierce pug face of the old Squire, were now but a picture of memory. And the brothers between whom he had planted an irreconcilable quarrel, were now in their new mourning suits, with the gloss still on, debating furiously across the table in the great oak parlour, which had so often resounded to the banter and coarse songs, the oaths and laughter of the congenial neighbours whom the old Squire of Gylingden Hall loved to assemble there.

These young gentlemen, who had grown up in Gylingden Hall, were not accustomed to bridle their tongues, nor, if need be, to hesitate about a blow. Neither had been at the old man's funeral. His death had been sudden. Having been helped to his bed in that hilarious and quarrelsome state which was induced by port and punch, he was found dead in the morning – his head hanging over the side of the bed, and his face very black and swollen.

Now the Squire's will despoiled his eldest son of Gylingden, which had descended to the heir time out of mind. Scroope Marston was furious. His deep stern voice was heard inveighing against his dead father and living brother, and the heavy thumps on the table with which he enforced his stormy recriminations resounded through the large chamber. Then broke in Charles's rougher voice, and then came a quick alternation of short sentences, and then both voices together in growing loudness and anger, and at last, swelling the tumult, the expostulations of pacific and frightened lawyers, and at last a sudden break up of the conference. Scroope broke out of the room, his pale furious face showing whiter against his long black hair, his dark fierce eyes blazing, his hands clenched, and looking more ungainly and deformed than ever in the convulsions of his fury.

Very violent words must have passed between them; for Charlie, though he was the winning man, was almost as angry as Scroope. The elder brother was for holding possession of the house, and putting his rival to legal process to oust him. But his legal advisers were clearly against it. So, with a heart boiling over with gall, up he went to London, and found the firm who had managed his father's business fair and communicative enough. They looked into the settlements, and found that Gylingden was excepted. It was very odd, but so it was, specially excepted; so that the right of the old Squire to deal with it by his will could not be questioned.

Notwithstanding all this, Scroope, breathing vengeance and aggression, and quite willing to wreck himself provided he could run his brother down, assailed Handsome Charlie, and battered old Squire Toby's will in the Prerogative Court and also at common law, and the feud between the brothers was knit, and every month their exasperation was heightened.

Scroope was beaten, and defeat did not soften him. Charles might have forgiven hard words; but he had been himself worsted during the long campaign in some of those skirmishes, special motions, and so forth, that constitute the episodes of a legal epic like that in which the Marston brothers figured as opposing combatants; and the blight of law-costs had touched him, too, with the usual effect upon the temper of a man of embarrassed means.

Years flew, and brought no healing on their wings. On the contrary, the deep corrosion of this hatred bit deeper by time. Neither brother married. But an accident of a different kind befell the younger, Charles Marston, which abridged his enjoyments very materially.

This was a bad fall from his hunter. There were severe fractures, and there was concussion of the brain. For some time it was thought that he could not recover. He disappointed these evil auguries, however. He did recover, but changed in two essential particulars. He had received an injury in his hip, which doomed him never more to sit in the saddle. And the rollicking animal spirits which hitherto had never failed him, had now taken flight for ever.

He had been for five days in a state of coma – absolute insensibility – and when he recovered consciousness he was haunted by an indescribable anxiety.

Tom Cooper, who had been butler in the palmy days of Gylingden Hall, under old Squire Toby, still maintained his post with old-fashioned fidelity, in these days of faded splendour and frugal housekeeping. Twenty years had passed since the death of his old master. He had grown lean, and stooped, and his face, dark with the peculiar brown of age, furrowed and gnarled, and his temper, except with his master, had waxed surly.

His master had visited Bath and Buxton, and came back, as he went, lame, and halting gloomily about with the aid of a stick. When the hunter was sold, the last tradition of the old life at Gylingden disappeared. The young Squire, as he was still called, excluded by his mischance from the hunting field, dropped into a solitary way of life, and halted slowly and solitarily about the old place, seldom raising his eyes, and with an appearance of indescribable gloom.

Old Cooper could talk freely on occasion with his master; and one day he said, as he handed him his hat and stick in the hall: 'You should rouse yourself up a bit, Master Charles!'

'It's past rousing with me, old Cooper.'

'It's just this, I'm thinking: there's something on your mind, and you won't tell no one. There's no good keeping it on your stomach. You'll be a deal lighter if you tell it. Come, now, what is it, Master Charlie?'

The Squire looked with his round grey eyes straight into Cooper's eyes. He felt that there was a sort of spell broken. It was like the old rule of the ghost who can't speak till it is spoken to. He looked earnestly into old Cooper's face for some seconds, and sighed deeply.

'It ain't the first good guess you've made in your day, old Cooper, and I'm glad you've spoke. It's bin on my mind, sure enough, ever since I had that fall. Come in here after me, and shut the door.'

The Squire pushed open the door of the oak parlour, and looked round on the pictures abstractedly. He had not been there for some time, and, seating himself on the table, he looked again for a while in Cooper's face before he spoke.

'It's not a great deal, Cooper, but it troubles me, and I would not tell it to the parson nor the doctor; for, God knows what they'd say, though there's nothing to signify in it. But you were always true to the family, and I don't mind if I tell you.'

' 'Tis as safe with Cooper, Master Charles, as if 'twas locked in a chest, and sunk in a well.'

'It's only this,' said Charles Marston, looking down on the end of his stick, with which he was tracing lines and circles, 'all the time I was lying like dead, as you thought, after that fall, I was with the old master.' He raised his eyes to Cooper's again as he spoke, and with an awful oath he repeated – 'I was with him, Cooper!'

'He was a good man, sir, in his way,' repeated old Cooper, returning his gaze with awe. 'He was a good master to me, and a good father to you, and I hope he's happy. May God rest him!'

'Well,' said Squire Charles, 'it's only this: the whole

of that time I was with him, or he was with me – I
don't know which. The upshot is, we were together,
and I thought I'd never get out of his hands again,
and all the time he was bullying me about some one
thing; and if it was to save my life, Tom Cooper, by –
from the time I waked I never could call to mind
what it was; and I think I'd give that hand to know;
and if you can think of anything it might be – for
God's sake! don't be afraid, Tom Cooper, but speak
it out, for he threatened me hard, and it was surely
him.'

Here ensued a silence.

'And what did you think it might be yourself,
Master Charles?' said Cooper.

'I han't thought of aught that's likely. I'll never hit
on't – *never*. I thought it might happen he knew something about that d—d humpbacked villain, Scroope,
that swore before Lawyer Gingham I made away with
a paper of settlements – me and father; and, as I hope
to be saved, Tom Cooper, there never was a bigger
lie! I'd a had the law of him for them identical words,
and cast him for more than he's worth; only Lawyer
Gingham never goes into nothing for me since money
grew scarce in Gylingden; and I can't change my
lawyer, I owe him such a hatful of money. But he did,
he swore he'd hang me yet for it. He said it in them
identical words – he'd never rest till he *hanged* me for
it, and I think it was, like enough, something about
that, the old master was troubled; but it's enough to
drive a man mad. I *can't* bring it to mind – I can't
remember a word he said, only he threatened awful,
and looked – Lord a mercy on us! – frightful bad.'

'There's no need he should. May the Lord a-mercy
on him!' said the old butler.

'No, of course; and you're not to tell a soul, Cooper – not a living soul, mind, that I said he looked bad, nor nothing about it.'

'God forbid!' said old Cooper, shaking his head. 'But I was thinking, sir, it might ha' been about the slight that's bin so long put on him by having no stone over him, and never a scratch o' a chisel to say who he is.'

'Ay! Well, I didn't think o' that. Put on your hat, old Cooper, and come down wi' me; for I'll look after that, at any rate.'

There is a bye-path leading by a turnstile to the park, and thence to the picturesque old burying-place, which lies in a nook by the roadside, embowered in ancient trees. It was a fine autumnal sunset, and melancholy lights and long shadows spread their peculiar effects over the landscape as 'Handsome Charlie' and the old butler made their way slowly toward the place where Handsome Charlie was himself to lie at last.

'Which of the dogs made that howling all last night?' asked the Squire, when they had got on a little way.

' 'Twas a strange dog, Master Charlie, in front of the house; ours was all in the yard – a white dog wi' a black head, he looked to be, and he was smelling round them mounting-steps the old master, God be wi' him! set up the time his knee was bad. When the tyke got up a' top of them, howlin' up at the windows, I'd a liked to shy something at him.'

'Hullo! Is that like him?' said the Squire, stopping short, and pointing with his stick at a dirty-white dog with a large black head, which was scampering round them in a wide circle, half crouching with that air of uncertainty and deprecation which dogs so well know how to assume.

He whistled the dog up. He was a large, half-starved bulldog.

'That fellow has made a long journey – thin as a whipping-post, and stained all over, and his claws worn to the stumps,' said the Squire, musingly. 'He isn't a bad dog, Cooper. My poor father liked a good bulldog, and knew a cur from a good 'un.'

The dog was looking up into the Squire's face with the peculiar grim visage of his kind, and the Squire was thinking irreverently how strong a likeness it presented to the character of his father's fierce pug features when he was clutching his horsewhip and swearing at a keeper.

'If I did right I'd shoot him. He'll worry the cattle, and kill our dogs,' said the Squire. 'Hey, Cooper? I'll tell the keeper to look after him. That fellow could pull down a sheep, and he shan't live on my mutton.'

But the dog was not to be shaken off. He looked wistfully after the Squire, and after they had got a little way on, he followed timidly.

It was vain trying to drive him off. The dog ran round them in wide circles, like the infernal dog in 'Faust'; only he left no track of thin flame behind him. These manoeuvres were executed with a sort of beseeching air, which flattered and touched the object of this odd preference. So he called him up again, patted him, and then and there in a manner adopted him.

The dog now followed their steps dutifully, as if he had belonged to Handsome Charlie all his days. Cooper unlocked the little iron door, and the dog walked in close behind their heels, and followed them as they visited the roofless chapel.

The Marstons were lying under the floor of this little building in rows. There is not a vault. Each has his distinct grave enclosed in a lining of masonry. Each is surmounted by a stone kist, on the upper flag of which is enclosed his epitaph, except that of poor old Squire Toby. Over him was nothing but the grass and the line of masonry which indicate the site of the kist, whenever his family should afford him one like the rest.

'Well, it does look shabby. It's the elder brother's business; but if he won't, I'll see to it myself, and I'll take care, old boy, to cut sharp and deep in it, that the elder son having refused to lend a hand the stone was put there by the younger.'

They strolled round this little burial-ground. The sun was now below the horizon, and the red metallic glow from the clouds, still illuminated by the departed sun, mingled luridly with the twilight. When Charlie peeped again into the little chapel, he saw the ugly dog stretched upon Squire Toby's grave, looking at least twice his natural length, and performing such antics as made the young Squire stare. If you have ever seen a cat stretched on the floor, with a bunch of Valerian, straining, writhing, rubbing its jaws in long-drawn caresses, and in the absorption of a sensual ecstasy, you have seen a phenomenon resembling that which Handsome Charlie witnessed on looking in.

The head of the brute looked so large, its body so long and thin, and its joints so ungainly and dis-located, that the Squire, with old Cooper beside him, looked on with a feeling of disgust and astonishment, which, in a moment or two more, brought the

Squire's stick down upon him with a couple of heavy thumps. The beast awakened from his ecstasy, sprang to the head of the grave, and there on a sudden, thick and bandy as before, confronted the Squire, who stood at its foot, with a terrible grin, and eyes that glared with the peculiar green of canine fury.

The next moment the dog was crouching abjectly at the Squire's feet.

'Well, he's a rum 'un!' said old Cooper, looking hard at him.

'I like him,' said the Squire.

'I don't,' said Cooper.

'But he shan't come in here again,' said the Squire.

'I shouldn't wonder if he was a witch,' said old Cooper, who remembered more tales of witchcraft than are now current in that part of the world.

'He's a good dog,' said the Squire, dreamily. 'I remember the time I'd a given a handful for him – but I'll never be good for nothing again. Come along.'

And he stooped down and patted him. So up jumped the dog and looked up in his face, as if watching for some sign, ever so slight, which he might obey.

Cooper did not like a bone in that dog's skin. He could not imagine what his master saw to admire in him. He kept him all night in the gunroom, and the dog accompanied him in his halting rambles about the place. The fonder his master grew of him, the less did Cooper and the other servants like him.

'He hasn't a point of a good dog about him,' Cooper would growl. 'I think Master Charlie be blind. And old Captain (an old red parrot, who sat chained to a perch in the oak parlour, and conversed with himself, and nibbled at his claws and bit his perch all day), – old Captain, the only living thing, except one or two of us, and the Squire himself, that remembers the old master, the minute he saw the dog, screeched as if he was struck, shakin' his feathers out quite wild, and drops down, poor old soul, a-hangin' by his foot, in a fit.'

But there is no accounting for fancies, and the Squire was one of those dogged persons who persist more obstinately in their whims the more they are opposed. But Charles Marston's health suffered by his lameness. The transition from habitual and violent exercise to such a life as his privation now consigned him to, was never made without a risk to health; and a host of dyspeptic annoyances, the existence of which he had never dreamed of before, now beset him in sad earnest. Among these was the now not unfrequent troubling of his sleep with dreams and nightmares. In these his canine favourite invariably had a part and was generally a central, and sometimes a solitary figure. In these visions the dog seemed to stretch himself up the side of the Squire's bed, and in dilated proportions to sit at his feet, with a horrible likeness to the pug features of old Squire Toby, with his tricks of wagging his head and throwing up his chin; and then he would talk to him about Scroope, and tell him 'all wasn't straight', and that he 'must make it up wi' Scroope', that he, the old Squire, had 'served him an ill turn', that 'time was nigh up', and that 'fair was fair', and he was 'troubled where he was, about Scroope'.

Then in his dream this semi-human brute would approach his face to his, crawling and crouching up his body, heavy as lead, till the face of the beast was laid on his, with the same odious caresses and stretchings and writhings which he had seen over the old Squire's grave. Then Charlie would wake up with a gasp and a howl, and start upright in the bed, bathed in a cold moisture, and fancy he saw something white sliding off the foot of the bed. Sometimes he thought it might be the curtain with white lining that slipped down, or the coverlet disturbed by his uneasy turnings; but he always fancied, at such moments, that he saw something white sliding hastily off the bed; and always when he had been visited by such dreams the dog next morning was more than usually caressing and servile, as if to obliterate, by a more than ordinary welcome, the sentiment of disgust which the horror of the night had left behind it.

The doctor half satisfied the Squire that there was nothing in these dreams, which, in one shape or another, invariably attended forms of indigestion such as he was suffering from.

For a while, as if to corroborate this theory, the dog ceased altogether to figure in them. But at last there came a vision in which, more unpleasantly than before, he did resume his old place.

In his nightmare the room seemed all but dark; he heard what he knew to be the dog walking from the door round his bed slowly, to the side from which he always had come upon it. A portion of the room was uncarpeted, and he said he distinctly heard the peculiar tread of a dog, in which the faint clatter of the claws is audible. It was a light stealthy step, but at every tread the whole room shook heavily; he felt something place itself at the foot of his bed, and saw a pair of green eyes staring at him in the dark, from which he could not remove his own. Then he heard, as he thought, the old Squire Toby say – 'The eleventh hour be passed, Charlie, and ye've done nothing – you and I 'a done Scroope a wrong!' and then came a good deal more, and then – 'The time's nigh up, it's going to strike.' And with a long low growl, the thing began to creep up upon his feet; the growl continued, and he saw the reflection of the up-turned green eyes upon the bedclothes, as it began slowly to stretch itself up his body towards his face. With a loud scream, he waked. The light, which of late the Squire was accustomed to have in his bedroom, had accidentally gone out. He was afraid to get up, or even to look about the room for some time; so sure did he feel of seeing the green eyes in the dark fixed on him from some corner. He had hardly recovered from the first agony which nightmare leaves behind it, and was beginning to collect his thoughts, when he heard the clock strike twelve. And he bethought him of the words 'the eleventh hour be passed – time's nigh up – it's going to strike!' and he almost feared that he would hear the voice reopening the subject.

Next morning the Squire came down looking ill.

'Do you know a room, old Cooper,' said he, 'they used to call King Herod's Chamber?'

'Ay, sir; the story of King Herod was on the walls o't when I was a boy.'

'There's a closet off it – is there?'

'I can't be sure o' that; but 'tisn't worth your looking at, now; the hangings was rotten, and took off the walls, before you was born; and there's nou't there but some old broken things and lumber. I seed them put there myself by poor Twinks; he was blind of an eye, and footman afterwards. You'll remember Twinks? He died here, about the time o' the great snow. There was a deal o' work to bury him, poor fellow!'

'Get the key, old Cooper; I'll look at the room,' said the Squire.

'And what the devil can you want to look at it for?' said Cooper, with the old-world privilege of a rustic butler.

'And what the devil's that to you? But I don't mind if I tell you. I don't want that dog in the gunroom, and I'll put him somewhere else; and I don't care if I put him there.'

'A bulldog in a bedroom! Oons, sir! the folks 'ill say you're clean mad!'

'Well, let them; get you the key, and let us look at the room.'

'You'd shoot him if you did right, Master Charlie. You never heard what a noise he kept up all last night in the gunroom, walking to and fro growling like a tiger in a show; and, say what you like, the dog's not worth his feed; he hasn't a point of a dog; he's a bad dog.'

'I know a dog better than you – and he's a good dog!' said the Squire, testily.

'If you was a judge of a dog you'd hang that 'un,' said Cooper.

'I'm not a-going to hang him, so there's an end. Go you, and get the key; and don't be talking, mind, when you go down. I may change my mind.'

Now this freak of visiting King Herod's room had, in truth, a totally different object from that pretended by the Squire. The voice in his nightmare had uttered a particular direction, which haunted him, and would give him no peace until he had tested it. So far from liking that dog today, he was beginning to regard it with a horrible suspicion; and if old Cooper had not stirred his obstinate temper by seeming to dictate,

I dare say he would have got rid of that inmate effectually before evening.

Up to the third storey, long disused, he and old Cooper mounted. At the end of a dusty gallery, the room lay. The old tapestry, from which the spacious chamber had taken its name, had long given place to modern paper, and this was mildewed, and in some places hanging from the walls. A thick mantle of dust lay over the floor. Some broken chairs and boards, thick with dust, lay, along with other lumber, piled together at one end of the room.

They entered the closet, which was quite empty. The Squire looked round, and you could hardly have said whether he was relieved or disappointed.

'No furniture here,' said the Squire, and looked through the dusty window. 'Did you say anything to me lately – I don't mean this morning – about this room, or the closet – or anything – I forget – '

'Lor' bless you! Not I. I han't been thinkin' o' this room this forty year.'

'Is there any sort of old furniture called a *buffet* – do you remember?' asked the Squire.

'A buffet? why, yes – to be sure – there was a buffet, sure enough, in this closet, now you bring it to my mind,' said Cooper. 'But it's papered over.'

'And what is it?'

'A little cupboard in the wall,' answered the old man.

'Ho – I see – and there's such a thing here, is there, under the paper? Show me whereabouts it was.'

'Well – I think it was somewhere about here,' answered he, rapping his knuckles along the wall opposite the window. 'Ay, there it is,' he added, as the hollow sound of a wooden door was returned to his knock.

The Squire pulled the loose paper from the wall, and disclosed the doors of a small press, about two feet square, fixed in the wall.

'The very thing for my buckles and pistols, and the rest of my gimcracks,' said the Squire. 'Come away, we'll leave the dog where he is. Have you the key of that little press?'

No, he had not. The old master had emptied and locked it up, and desired that it should be papered over, and that was the history of it.

Down came the Squire, and took a strong turn-screw from his gun-case; and quietly he reascended to King Herod's room, and, with little trouble, forced the door of the small press in the closet wall. There were in it some letters and cancelled leases, and also a parchment deed which he took to the window and read with much agitation. It was a supplemental deed executed about a fortnight after the others, and previously to his father's marriage, placing Gylingden under strict settlement to the elder son, in what is called 'tail male'. Handsome Charlie, in his fraternal litigation, had acquired a smattering of technical knowledge, and he perfectly well knew that the effect of this would be not only to transfer the house and lands to his brother Scroope, but to leave him at the mercy of that exasperated brother, who might recover from him personally every guinea he had ever received by way of rent, from the date of his father's death.

It was a dismal, clouded day, with something threatening in its aspect, and the darkness, where he stood, was made deeper by the top of one of the huge old trees over-hanging the window.

In a state of awful confusion he attempted to think over his position. He placed the deed in his pocket, and nearly made up his mind to destroy it. A short time ago he would not have hesitated for a moment under such circumstances; but now his health and his nerves were shattered, and he was under a super-natural alarm which the strange discovery of this deed had powerfully confirmed.

In this state of profound agitation he heard a sniffing at the closet-door, and then an impatient scratch and a long low growl. He screwed his courage up, and, not knowing what to expect, threw the door open and saw the dog, not in his dream-shape, but wriggling with joy, and crouching and fawning with eager submission; and then wandering about the closet, the brute growled awfully into the corners of it, and seemed in an unappeasable agitation.

Then the dog returned and fawned and crouched again at his feet.

After the first moment was over, the sensations of abhorrence and fear began to subside, and he almost reproached himself for requiting the affection of this poor friendless brute with the antipathy which he had really done nothing to earn.

The dog pattered after him down the stairs. Oddly enough, the sight of this animal, after the first revul-sion, reassured him; it was, in his eyes, so attached, so good-natured, and palpably so mere a dog.

By the hour of evening the Squire had resolved on a middle course; he would not inform his brother of his discovery, nor yet would he destroy the deed. He would never marry. He was past that time. He would leave a letter, explaining the discovery of the deed, addressed to the only surviving trustee – who had probably forgotten everything about it – and having seen out his own tenure, he would provide that all

should be set right after his death. Was not that fair?
at all events it quite satisfied what he called his conscience, and he thought it a devilish good compromise
for his brother; and he went out, towards sunset, to
take his usual walk.

Returning in the darkening twilight, the dog, as
usual attending him, began to grow frisky and wild, at
first scampering round him in great circles, as before,
nearly at the top of his speed, his great head between
his paws as he raced. Gradually more excited grew
the pace and narrower his circuit, louder and fiercer
his continuous growl, and the Squire stopped and
grasped his stick hard, for the lurid eyes and grin of
the brute threatened an attack. Turning round and
round as the excited brute encircled him, and striking
vainly at him with his stick, he grew at last so tired
that he almost despaired of keeping him longer at
bay; when on a sudden the dog stopped short and
crawled up to his feet wriggling and crouching sub-
missively.

Nothing could be more apologetic and abject; and
when the Squire dealt him two heavy thumps with his
stick, the dog whimpered only, and writhed and licked
his feet. The Squire sat down on a prostrate tree; and
his dumb companion, recovering his wonted spirits
immediately, began to sniff and nuzzle among the
roots. The Squire felt in his breast-pocket for the
deed – it was safe; and again he pondered, in this
loneliest of spots, on the question whether he should
preserve it for restoration after his death to his
brother, or destroy it forthwith. He began rather to
lean toward the latter solution, when the long low
growl of the dog not far off startled him.

He was sitting in a melancholy grove of old trees,

that slants gently westward. Exactly the same odd effect of light I have before described – a faint red glow reflected downward from the upper sky, after the sun had set, now gave to the growing darkness a lurid uncertainty. This grove, which lies in a gentle hollow, owing to its circumscribed horizon on all but one side, has a peculiar character of loneliness.

He got up and peeped over a sort of barrier, accidentally formed of the trunks of felled trees laid one over the other, and saw the dog straining up the other side of it, and hideously stretched out, his ugly head looking in consequence twice the natural size. His dream was coming over him again. And now between the trunks the brute's ungainly head was thrust, and the long neck came straining through, and the body, twining after it like a huge white lizard; and as it came striving and twisting through, it growled and glared as if it would devour him.

As swiftly as his lameness would allow, the Squire hurried from this solitary spot towards the house. What thoughts exactly passed through his mind as he did so, I am sure he could not have told. But when the dog came up with him it seemed appeased, and even in high good-humoured, and no longer resembled the brute that haunted his dreams.

That night, near ten o'clock, the Squire, a good deal agitated, sent for the keeper, and told him that he believed the dog was mad, and that he must shoot him. He might shoot the dog in the gunroom, where he was – a grain of shot or two in the wainscot did not matter, and the dog must not have a chance of getting out.

The Squire gave the gamekeeper his double-barrelled gun, loaded with heavy shot. He did not go with him beyond the hall. He placed his hand on the keeper's arm; the keeper said his hand trembled, and that he looked 'as white as curds'.

'Listen a bit!' said the Squire under his breath.

They heard the dog in a state of high excitement in the room – growling ominously, jumping on the window-stool and down again, and running round the room.

'You'll need to be sharp, mind – don't give him a chance – slip in edgeways, d'ye see? and give him both barrels!'

'Not the first mad dog I've knocked over, sir,' said the man, looking very serious as he cocked the gun.

As the keeper opened the door, the dog had sprung into the empty grate. He said he 'never see sich a stark, staring devil.' The beast made a twist round, as if, he thought, to jump up the chimney – 'but that wasn't to be done at no price,' – and he made a yell – not like a dog – like a man caught in a mill-crank, and before he could spring at the keeper, he fired one barrel into him. The dog leaped towards him, and rolled over, receiving the second barrel in his head, as he lay snorting at the keeper's feet!

'I never seed the like; I never heard a screech like that!' said the keeper, recoiling. 'It makes a fellow feel queer.'

'Quite dead?' asked the Squire.

'Not a stir in him, sir,' said the man, pulling him along the floor by the neck.

'Throw him outside the hall-door now,' said the Squire; 'and mind you pitch him outside the gate tonight – old Cooper says he's a witch,' and the pale Squire smiled, 'so he shan't lie in Gylingden.'

Never was man more relieved than the Squire, and

he slept better for a week after this than he had done for many weeks before.

It behoves us all to act promptly on our good resolutions. There is a determined gravitation towards evil, which, if left to itself, will bear down first intentions. If at one moment of superstitious fear, the Squire had made up his mind to a great sacrifice, and resolved in the matter of that deed so strangely recovered, to act honestly by his brother, that resolution very soon gave place to the compromise with fraud, which so conveniently postponed the restitution to the period when further enjoyment on his part was impossible. Then came more tidings of Scroope's violent and minatory language, with always the same burthen – that he would leave no stone unturned to show that there had existed a deed which Charles had either secreted or destroyed, and that he would never rest till he had hanged him.

This of course was wild talk. At first it had only enraged him; but, with his recent guilty knowledge and suppression, had come fear. His danger was the existence of the deed, and little by little he brought himself to a resolution to destroy it. There were many falterings and recoils before he could bring himself to commit this crime. At length, however, he did it, and got rid of the custody of that which at any time might become the instrument of disgrace and ruin. There was relief in this, but also the new and terrible sense of actual guilt.

He had got pretty well rid of his supernatural qualms. It was a different kind of trouble that agitated him now.

But this night, he imagined, he was awakened by a violent shaking of his bed. He could see, in the very imperfect light, two figures at the foot of it, holding each a bedpost. One of these he half fancied was his brother Scroope, but the other was the old Squire – of that he was sure – and he fancied that they had shaken him up from his sleep. Squire Toby was talking as Charlie wakened, and he heard him say: 'Put out of our own house by you! It won't hold for long. We'll come in together, friendly, and stay. Forewarned, wi' yer eyes open, ye did it; and now Scroope'll hang you! We'll hang you together! Look at me, you devil's limb.'

And the old Squire tremblingly stretched his face, torn with shot and bloody, and growing every moment more and more into the likeness of the dog, and began to stretch himself out and climb the bed over the foot-board; and he saw the figure at the other side, little more than a black shadow, begin also to scale the bed; and there was instantly a dreadful confusion and uproar in the room, and such a gabbling and laughing; he could not catch the words; but, with a scream, he woke, and found himself standing on the floor. The phantoms and the clamour were gone, but a crash and ringing of fragments was in his ears. The great china bowl, from which for generations the Marstons of Gylingden had been baptised, had fallen from the mantelpiece, and was smashed on the hearthstone.

'I've bin dreamin' all night about Mr Scroope, and I wouldn't wonder, old Cooper, if he was dead,' said the Squire, when he came down in the morning.

'God forbid! I was adreamed about him, too, sir: I dreamed he was dammin' and sinkin' about a hole was burnt in his coat, and the old master, God be wi' him! said – quite plain – I'd 'a swore 'twas himself –

"Cooper, get up, ye d—d land-loupin' thief, and lend a hand to hang him – for he's a daft cur, and no dog o' mine." 'Twas the dog shot over night, I do suppose, as was runnin' in my old head. I thought old master gied me a punch wi' his knuckles, and says I, wakenin' up, "At yer service, sir"; and for a while I couldn't get it out o' my head, master was in the room still.'

Letters from town soon convinced the Squire that his brother Scroope, so far from being dead, was particularly active; and Charlie's attorney wrote to say, in serious alarm, that he had heard, accidentally, that he intended setting up a case, of a supplementary deed of settlement, of which he had secondary evidence, which would give him Gylingden. And at this menace Handsome Charlie snapped his fingers, and wrote courageously to his attorney; abiding what might follow with, however, a secret foreboding.

Scroope threatened loudly now, and swore after his bitter fashion, and reiterated his old promise of hanging that cheat at last. In the midst of these menaces and preparations, however, a sudden peace proclaimed itself: Scroope died, without time even to make provisions for a posthumous attack upon his brother. It was one of those cases of disease of the heart in which death is as sudden as by a bullet.

Charlie's exultation was undisguised. It was shocking. Not, of course, altogether malignant. For there was the expansion consequent on the removal of a secret fear. There was also the comic piece of luck, that only the day before Scroope had destroyed his old will, which left to a stranger every farthing he possessed, intending in a day or two to execute another to the same person, charged with the express condition of prosecuting the suit against Charlie.

The result was, that all his possessions went uncon-
ditionally to his brother Charles as his heir. Here were
grounds for abundance of savage elation. But there
was also the deep-seated hatred of half a life of mutual
and persistent aggression and revilings; and Handsome
Charlie was capable of nursing a grudge, and enjoying
a revenge with his whole heart.

He would gladly have prevented his brother's being
buried in the old Gylingden chapel, where he wished
to lie; but his lawyers doubted his power, and he was
not quite proof against the scandal which would
attend his turning back the funeral, which would, he
knew, be attended by some of the country gentry and
others, with an hereditary regard for the Marstons.

But he warned his servants that not one of them
were to attend it; promising, with oaths and curses
not to be disregarded, that any one of them who did
so, should find the door shut in his face on his return.

I don't think, with the exception of old Cooper,
that the servants cared for this prohibition, except as
it baulked a curiosity always strong in the solitude of
the country. Cooper was very much vexed that the
eldest son of the old Squire should be buried in the
old family chapel, and no sign of decent respect from
Gylingden Hall. He asked his master, whether he
would not, at least, have some wine and refreshments
in the oak parlour, in case any of the country gentlemen who paid this respect to the old family should
come up to the house? But the Squire only swore at
him, told him to mind his own business, and ordered
him to say, if such a thing happened, that he was out,
and no preparations made, and, in fact, to send them
away as they came. Cooper expostulated stoutly, and
the Squire grew angrier; and after a tempestuous

scene, took his hat and stick and walked out, just as the funeral descending the valley from the direction of the Old Angel Inn came in sight.

Old Cooper prowled about disconsolately, and counted the carriages as well as he could from the gate. When the funeral was over, and they began to drive away, he returned to the hall, the door of which lay open, and as usual deserted. Before he reached it quite, a mourning coach drove up, and two gentlemen in black cloaks, and with crapes to their hats, got out, and without looking to the right or the left, went up the steps into the house. Cooper followed them slowly. The carriage had, he supposed, gone round to the yard, for, when he reached the door, it was no longer there.

So he followed the two mourners into the house. In the hall he found a fellow-servant, who said he had seen two gentlemen, in black cloaks, pass through the hall, and go up the stairs without removing their hats, or asking leave of anyone. This was very odd, old Cooper thought, and a great liberty; so upstairs he went to make them out.

But he could not find them then, nor ever. And from that hour the house was troubled.

In a little time there was not one of the servants who had not something to tell. Steps and voices followed them sometimes in the passages, and tittering whispers, always minatory, scared them at corners of the galleries, or from dark recesses; so that they would return panic-stricken to be rebuked by thin Mrs Beckett, who looked on such stories as worse than idle. But Mrs Beckett herself, a short time after, took a very different view of the matter.

She had herself begun to hear these voices, and

with this formidable aggravation, that they came always when she was at her prayers, which she had been punctual in saying all her life, and utterly interrupted them. She was scared at such moments by dropping words and sentences, which grew, as she persisted, into threats and blasphemies.

These voices were not always in the room. They called, as she fancied, through the walls, very thick in that old house, from the neighbouring apartments, sometimes on one side, sometimes on the other; sometimes they seemed to holloa from distant lobbies, and came muffled, but threateningly, through the long panelled passages. As they approached they grew furious, as if several voices were speaking together. Whenever, as I said, this worthy woman applied herself to her devotions, these horrible sentences came hurrying towards the door, and, in panic, she would start from her knees, and all then would subside except the thumping of her heart against her stays, and the dreadful tremors of her nerves.

What these voices said, Mrs Beckett never could quite remember one minute after they had ceased speaking; one sentence chased another away; gibe and menace and impious denunciation, each hideously articulate, were lost as soon as heard. And this added to the effect of these terrifying mockeries and invectives, that she could not, by any effort, retain their exact import, although their horrible character remained vividly present to her mind.

For a long time the Squire seemed to be the only person in the house absolutely unconscious of these annoyances. Mrs Beckett had twice made up her mind within the week to leave. A prudent woman, however, who has been comfortable for more than twenty years in a place, thinks oftener than twice before she leaves it. She and old Cooper were the only servants in the house who remembered the good old housekeeping in Squire Toby's day. The others were few, and such as could hardly be accounted regular servants. Meg Dobbs, who acted as housemaid, would not sleep in the house, but walked home, in trepidation, to her father's, at the gatehouse, under the escort of her little brother, every night. Old Mrs Beckett, who was high and mighty with the makeshift servants of fallen Gylingden, let herself down all at once, and made Mrs Kymes and the kitchen-maid move their beds into her large and faded room, and there, very frankly, shared her nightly terrors with them.

Old Cooper was testy and captious about these stories. He was already uncomfortable enough by reason of the entrance of the two muffled figures into the house, about which there could be no mistake. His own eyes had seen them. He refused to credit the stories of the women, and affected to think that the two mourners might have left the house and driven away, on finding no one to receive them.

Old Cooper was summoned at night to the oak parlour, where the Squire was smoking.

'I say, Cooper,' said the Squire, looking pale and angry, 'what for ha' you been frightenin' they crazy women wi' your plaguy stories? d—n me, if you see ghosts here it's no place for you, and it's time you should pack. I won't be left without servants. Here has been old Beckett, wi' the cook and the kitchenmaid, as white as pipeclay, all in a row, to tell me I must have a parson to sleep among them, and preach down the devil! Upon my soul, you're a wise old body, filling their heads wi' maggots! and Meg goes down to the lodge every night, afeared to lie in the house – all your doing, wi' your old wives' stories, – ye withered old Tom o' Bedlam!'

'I'm not to blame, Master Charles. 'Tisn't along o' no stories o' mine, for I'm never done tellin' 'em it's all vanity and vapours. Mrs Beckett 'ill tell you that, and there's been many a wry word betwixt us on the head o't. Whate'er I may *think*,' said old Cooper, significantly, and looking askance, with the sternness of fear in the Squire's face.

The Squire averted his eyes, and muttered angrily to himself, and turned away to knock the ashes out of his pipe on the hob, and then turning suddenly round upon Cooper again, he spoke, with a pale face, but not quite so angrily as before.

'I know you're no fool, old Cooper, when you like. Suppose there was such a thing as a ghost here, don't you see, it ain't to them snipe-headed women it 'id go to tell its story. What ails you, man, that you should think aught about it, but just what *I* think? You had a good headpiece o' yer own once, Cooper, don't be you clappin' a goosecap over it, as my poor father used to say; d— it, old boy, you mustn't let 'em be fools, settin' one another wild wi' their blether, and makin' the folk talk what they shouldn't, about Gylingden and the family. I don't think ye'd like that, old Cooper, I'm sure ye wouldn't. The women has gone out o' the kitchen, make up a bit o' fire, and get your pipe. I'll go to you, when I finish this one, and we'll smoke a bit together, and a glass o' brandy and water.'

Down went the old butler, not altogether unused to such condescensions in that disorderly and lonely household; and let not those who can choose their company, be too hard on the Squire who couldn't.

When he had got things tidy, as he said, he sat down in that big old kitchen, with his feet on the fender, the kitchen candle burning in a great brass candlestick, which stood on the deal table at his elbow, with the brandy bottle and tumblers beside it, and Cooper's pipe also in readiness. And these preparations completed, the old butler, who had remembered other generations and better times, fell into rumination, and so, gradually, into a deep sleep.

Old Cooper was half awakened by someone laughing low, near his head. He was dreaming of old times in the Hall, and fancied one of 'the young gentlemen' going to play him a trick, and he mumbled something in his sleep, from which he was awakened by a stern deep voice, saying, 'You wern't at the funeral; I might take your life, I'll take your ear.' At the same moment, the side of his head received a violent push, and he started to his feet.

The fire had gone down, and he was chilled. The candle was expiring in the socket, and threw on the white wall long shadows, that danced up and down from the ceiling to the ground, and their black outlines he fancied resembled the two men in cloaks, whom he remembered with a profound horror.

He took the candle, with all the haste he could, getting along the passage, on whose walls the same dance of black shadows was continued, very anxious to reach his room before the light should go out. He was startled half out of his wits by the sudden clang of his master's bell, close over his head, ringing furiously.

'Ha, ha! There it goes – yes, sure enough,' said Cooper, reassuring himself with the sound of his own voice, as he hastened on, hearing more and more distinct every moment the same furious ringing. 'He's fell asleep, like me; that's it, and his lights is out, I lay you fifty – '

When he turned the handle of the door of the oak parlour, the Squire wildly called, 'Who's *there*?' in the tone of a man who expects a robber.

'It's me, old Cooper, all right, Master Charlie, you didn't come to the kitchen after all, sir.'

'I'm very bad, Cooper; I don't know how I've been. Did you meet anything?' asked the Squire.

'No,' said Cooper.

They stared on one another.

'Come here – stay here! Don't you leave me! Look round the room, and say is all right; and gie us your hand, old Cooper, for I must hold it.' The Squire's was damp and cold, and trembled very much. It was not very far from daybreak now.

After a time he spoke again: 'I 'a done many a thing I shouldn't; I'm not fit to go, and wi' God's blessin' I'll look to it – why shouldn't I? I'm as lame as old Billy – I'll never be able to do any good no more, and I'll give over drinking, and marry, as I ought to 'a done long ago – none o' yer fine ladies, but a good homely wench; there's Farmer Crump's youngest daughter, a good lass, and discreet. What for shouldn't I take her? She'd take care o' me, and wouldn't bring a head full o' romances here, and mantua-makers' trumpery, and I'll talk with the parson, and I'll do what's fair wi' everyone; and mind, I said I'm sorry for many a thing I 'a done.'

A wild cold dawn had by this time broken. The Squire, Cooper said, looked 'awful bad,' as he got his hat and stick, and sallied out for a walk, instead of going to his bed, as Cooper besought him, looking so wild and distracted, that it was plain his object was simply to escape from the house. It was twelve o'clock when the Squire walked into the kitchen, where he was sure of finding some of the servants, looking as if ten years had passed over him since yesterday. He pulled a stool by the fire, without speaking a word, and sat down. Cooper had sent to Applebury for the doctor, who had just arrived, but the Squire would not go to him. 'If he wants to see me, he may come here,' he muttered as often as Cooper urged him. So the doctor did come, charily enough, and found the Squire very much worse than he had expected.

The Squire resisted the order to get to his bed. But the doctor insisted under a threat of death, at which his patient quailed.

'Well, I'll do what you say – only this – you must let old Cooper and Dick Keeper stay wi' me. I mustn't be left alone, and they must keep awake o' nights; and stay a while, do *you*. When I get round a bit, I'll go and live in a town. It's dull livin' here, now that I can't do nou't, as I used, and I'll live a better life, mind ye; ye heard me say that, and I don't care who laughs, and I'll talk wi' the parson. I like 'em to laugh, hang 'em, it's a sign I'm doin' right, at last.'

The doctor sent a couple of nurses from the County Hospital, not choosing to trust his patient to the management he had selected, and he went down himself to Gylingden to meet them in the evening. Old Cooper was ordered to occupy the dressing-room, and sit up at night, which satisfied the Squire, who was in a strangely excited state, very low, and threatened, the doctor said, with fever.

The clergyman came, an old, gentle, 'book-learned'

man, and talked and prayed with him late that evening. After he had gone the Squire called the nurses to his bedside, and said: 'There's a fellow sometimes comes; you'll never mind him. He looks in at the door and beckons, – a thin, humpbacked chap in mourning, wi' black gloves on; ye'll know him by his lean face, as brown as the wainscot: don't ye mind his smilin'. You don't go out to him, nor ask him in; he won't say nout; and if he grows anger'd and looks awry at ye, don't ye be afeared, for he can't hurt ye, and he'll grow tired waitin', and go away; and for God's sake mind ye don't ask him in, nor go out after him!'

The nurses put their heads together when this was over, and held afterwards a whispering conference with old Cooper. 'Law bless ye! – no, there's no madman in the house,' he protested; 'not a soul but what ye saw, – it's just a trifle o' the fever in his head – no more.'

The Squire grew worse as the night wore on. He was heavy and delirious, talking of all sorts of things – of wine, and dogs, and lawyers; and then he began to talk, as it were, to his brother Scroope. As he did so, Mrs Oliver, the nurse, who was sitting up alone with him, heard, as she thought, a hand softly laid on the door handle outside, and a stealthy attempt to turn it. 'Lord bless us! who's there?' she cried, and her heart jumped into her mouth, as she thought of the humpbacked man in black, who was to put in his head smiling and beckoning – 'Mr Cooper! sir! are you there?' she cried. 'Come here, Mr Cooper, please – do, sir, quick!'

Old Cooper, called up from his doze by the fire, stumbled in from the dressing-room, and Mrs Oliver seized him tightly as he emerged.

'The man with the hump has been atryin' the door, Mr Cooper, as sure as I am here.' The Squire was moaning and mumbling in his fever, understanding nothing, as she spoke. 'No, no! Mrs Oliver, ma'am, it's impossible, for there's no sich man in the house: what is Master Charlie sayin'?'

'He's saying *Scroope* every minute, whatever he means by that, and – and – hisht! – listen – there's the handle again,' and, with a loud scream, she added – 'Look at his head and neck in at the door!' and in her tremor she strained old Cooper in an agonising embrace.

The candle was flaring, and there was a wavering shadow at the door that looked like the head of a man with a long neck, and a longish sharp nose, peeping in and drawing back.

'Don't be a d—n fool, ma'am!' cried Cooper, very white, and shaking her with all his might. 'It's only the candle, I tell you – nothing in life but that. Don't you see?' and he raised the light; 'and I'm sure there was no one at the door, and I'll try, if you let me go.'

The other nurse was asleep on a sofa, and Mrs Oliver called her up in a panic, for company, as old Cooper opened the door. There was no one near it, but at the angle of the gallery was a shadow resembling that which he had seen in the room. He raised the candle a little, and it seemed to beckon with a long hand as the head drew back. 'Shadow from the candle!' exclaimed Cooper aloud, resolved not to yield to Mrs Oliver's panic; and, candle in hand, he walked to the corner. There was nothing. He could not forbear peeping down the long gallery from this point, and as he moved the light, he saw precisely the same sort of shadow, a little further down, and as he advanced the

233

same withdrawal, and beckon. 'Gammon!' said he; 'it is nout but the candle.' And on he went, growing half angry and half frightened at the persistency with which this ugly shadow – a literal shadow he was sure it was – presented itself. As he drew near the point where it now appeared, it seemed to collect itself, and nearly dissolve in the central panel of an old carved cabinet which he was now approaching.

In the centre panel of this is a sort of boss carved into a wolf's head. The light fell oddly upon this, and the fugitive shadow seemed to be breaking up, and rearranging itself as oddly. The eyeball gleamed with a point of reflected light, which glittered also upon the grinning mouth, and he saw the long, sharp nose of Scroope Marston, and his fierce eye looking at him, he thought, with a steadfast meaning.

Old Cooper stood gazing upon this sight, unable to move, till he saw the face, and the figure that belonged to it, begin gradually to emerge from the wood. At the same time he heard voices approaching rapidly up a side gallery, and Cooper, with a loud 'Lord a-mercy on us!' turned and ran back again, pursued by a sound that seemed to shake the old house like a mighty gust of wind.

Into his master's room burst old Cooper, half wild with fear, and clapped the door and turned the key in a twinkling, looking as if he had been pursued by murderers.

'Did you hear it?' whispered Cooper, now standing near the dressing-room door. They all listened, but not a sound from without disturbed the utter stillness of night. 'God bless us! I doubt it's my old head that's gone crazy!' exclaimed Cooper.

He would tell them nothing but that he was himself

'an old fool,' to be frightened by their talk, and that 'the rattle of a window, or the dropping o' a pin' was enough to scare him now; and so he helped himself through that night with brandy, and sat up talking by his master's fire.

The Squire recovered slowly from his brain fever, but not perfectly. A very little thing, the doctor said, would suffice to upset him. He was not yet sufficiently strong to remove for change of scene and air, which were necessary for his complete restoration.

Cooper slept in the dressing-room, and was now his only nightly attendant. The ways of the invalid were odd: he liked, half sitting up in his bed, to smoke his churchwarden o' nights, and made old Cooper smoke, for company, at the fireside. As the Squire and his humble friend indulged in it, smoking is a taciturn pleasure, and it was not until the Master of Gylingden had finished his third pipe that he essayed conversation, and when he did, the subject was not such as Cooper would have chosen.

'I say, old Cooper, look in my face, and don't be afeared to speak out,' said the Squire, looking at him with a steady, cunning smile; 'you know all this time, as well as I do, who's in the house. You needn't deny – hey? – Scroope and my father?'

'Don't you be talking like that, Charlie,' said old Cooper, rather sternly and frightened, after a long silence; still looking in his face, which did not change.

'What's the good o' shammin', Cooper? Scroope's took the hearin' o' yer right ear – you know he did. He's looking angry. He's nigh took my life wi' this fever. But he's not done wi' me yet, and he looks awful wicked. Ye saw him – ye know ye did.'

Cooper was awfully frightened, and the odd smile

on the Squire's lips frightened him still more. He dropped his pipe, and stood gazing in silence at his master, and feeling as if he were in a dream.

'If ye think so, ye should not be smiling like that,' said Cooper, grimly.

'I'm tired, Cooper, and it's as well to smile as t'other thing; so I'll even smile while I can. You know what they mean to do wi' me. That's all I wanted to say. Now, lad, go on wi' yer pipe – I'm going' asleep.'

So the Squire turned over in his bed, and lay down serenely, with his head on the pillow. Old Cooper looked at him, and glanced at the door, and then half filled his tumbler with brandy, and drank it off, and felt better, and got to his bed in the dressing-room.

In the dead of night he was suddenly awakened by the Squire, who was standing, in his dressing-gown and slippers, by his bed.

'I've brought you a bit o' a present. I got the rents o' Hazelden yesterday, and ye'll keep that for yourself – it's a fifty – and give t' other to Nelly Carwell, tomorrow; I'll sleep the sounder; and I saw Scroope since; he's not such a bad 'un after all, old fellow! He's got a crape over his face – for I told him I couldn't bear it; and I'd do many a thing for him now. I never could stand shillyshally. Good-night, old Cooper!'

And the Squire laid his trembling hand kindly on the old man's shoulder, and returned to his own room. 'I don't half like how he is. Doctor don't come half often enough. I don't like that queer smile o' his, and his hand was as cold as death. I hope in God his brain's not a-turnin'!'

With these reflections, he turned to the pleasanter subject of his present, and at last fell asleep.

In the morning, when he went into the Squire's room, the Squire had left his bed. 'Never mind; he'll come back, like a bad shillin',' thought old Cooper, preparing the room as usual. But he did not return. Then began an uneasiness, succeeded by a panic, when it began to be plain that the Squire was not in the house. What had become of him? None of his clothes, but his dressing-down and slippers, were missing. Had he left the house, in his present sickly state, in that garb? and, if so, could he be in his right senses; and was there a chance of his surviving a cold, damp night, so passed, in the open air?

Tom Edwards was up to the house, and told them, that, walking a mile or so that morning, at four o'clock – there being no moon – along with Farmer Nokes, who was driving his cart to market, in the dark, three men walked, in front of the horse, not twenty yards before them, all the way from near Gylingden Lodge to the burial-ground, the gate of which was opened for them from within, and the three men entered, and the gate was shut. Tom Edwards thought they were gone in to make preparation for a funeral of some member of the Marston family. But the occurrence seemed to Cooper, who knew there was no such thing, horribly ominous.

He now commenced a careful search, and at last bethought him of the lonely upper storey, and King Herod's chamber. He saw nothing changed there, but the closet door was shut, and, dark as was the morning, something, like a large white knot sticking out over the door, caught his eye.

The door resisted his efforts to open it for a time; some great weight forced it down against the floor; at length, however, it did yield a little, and a heavy crash, shaking the whole floor, and sending an echo flying through all the silent corridors, with a sound like receding laughter, half stunned him.

When he pushed open the door, his master was lying dead upon the floor. His cravat was drawn halter-wise tight round his throat, and had done its work well. The body was cold, and had been long dead.

In due course the coroner held his inquest, and the jury pronounced, 'that the deceased, Charles Marston, had died by his own hand, in a state of temporary insanity.' But old Cooper had his own opinion about the Squire's death, though his lips were sealed, and he never spoke about it. He went and lived for the residue of his days in York, where there are still people who remember him, a taciturn and surly old man, who attended church regularly, and also drank a little, and was known to have saved some money.

SHERIDAN LE FANU

The Child that went with the Fairies

Eastward of the old city of Limerick, about ten Irish miles under the range of mountains known as the Slieveelim hills, famous as having afforded Sarsfield a shelter among their rocks and hollows, when he crossed them in his gallant descent upon the cannon and ammunition of King William, on its way to the beleaguering army, there runs a very old and narrow road. It connects the Limerick road to Tipperary with the old road from Limerick to Dublin, and runs by bog and pasture, hill and hollow, straw-thatched village, and roofless castle, not far from twenty miles.

Skirting the heathy mountains of which I have spoken, at one part it becomes singularly lonely. For more than three Irish miles it traverses a deserted country. A wide, black bog, level as a lake, skirted with copse, spreads at the left, as you journey northward, and the long and irregular line of mountain rises at the right, clothed in heath, broken with lines of grey rock that resemble the bold and irregular outlines of fortifications, and riven with many a gully, expanding here and there into rocky and wooded glens, which open as they approach the road.

A scanty pasturage, on which browsed a few scattered sheep or kine, skirts this solitary road for some miles, and under shelter of a hillock, and of two or three great ash trees, stood, not many years ago, the little thatched cabin of a widow named Mary Ryan.

Poor was this widow in a land of poverty. The thatch had acquired the grey tint and sunken outlines, that show how the alternations of rain and sun have told upon that perishable shelter.

But whatever other dangers threatened, there was one well provided against by the care of other times. Round the cabin stood half a dozen mountain ashes, as the rowans, inimical to witches, are there called. On the worn planks of the door were nailed two horseshoes, and over the lintel and spreading along the thatch, grew, luxuriant, patches of that ancient cure for many maladies, and prophylactic against the machinations of the evil one, the house-leek. Descending into the doorway, in the *chiaroscuro* of the interior, when your eye grew sufficiently accustomed to that dim light, you might discover, hanging at the head of the widow's wooden-roofed bed, her beads and a phial of holy water.

Here certainly were defences and bulwarks against the intrusion of that unearthly and evil power, of whose vicinity this solitary family were constantly reminded by the outline of Lisnavoura, that lonely hill-haunt of the 'good people', as the fairies are called euphemistically, whose strangely domelike summit rose not half a mile away, looking like an outwork of the long line of mountain that sweeps by it.

It was at the fall of the leaf, and an autumnal sunset threw the lengthening shadow of haunted Lisnavoura, close in front of the solitary little cabin, over the undulating slopes and sides of Slieveelim. The birds were singing among the branches in the thinning leaves of the melancholy ash trees that grew at the roadside in front of the door. The widow's three younger children were playing on the road, and their voices mingled with the evening song of the birds. Their elder sister, Nell, was 'within in the house', as their phrase is, seeing after the boiling of the potatoes for supper.

Their mother had gone down to the bog, to carry up a hamper of turf on her back. It is, or was at least, a charitable custom – and if not disused, long may it continue – for the wealthier people when cutting their turf and stacking it in the bog, to make a smaller stack for the behoof of the poor, who were welcome to take from it so long as it lasted, and thus the potato pot was kept boiling, and the hearth warm that would have been cold enough but for that good-natured bounty, through wintry months.

Moll Ryan trudged up the steep 'bohereen' whose banks were overgrown with thorn and brambles, and stooping under her burden, re-entered her door, where her dark-haired daughter Nell met her with a welcome, and relieved her of her hamper.

Moll Ryan looked round with a sigh of relief, and drying her forehead, uttered the Munster ejaculation: 'Eiah, wisha! It's tired I am with it, God bless it. And where's the craythurs, Nell?'

'Playin' out on the road, mother; didn't ye see them and you comin' up?'

'No; there was no one before me on the road,' she said, uneasily; 'not a soul, Nell; and why didn't ye keep an eye on them?'

'Well, they're in the haggard, playin' there, or round by the back o' the house. Will I call them in?'

'Do so, good girl, in the name o' God. The hens is

comin' home, see, and the sun was just down over Knockdoulah, an' I comin' up.'

So out ran tall, dark-haired Nell, and standing on the road, looked up and down it; but not a sign of her two little brothers, Con and Bill, or her little sister, Peg, could she see. She called them; but no answer came from the little haggard, fenced with straggling bushes. She listened, but the sound of their voices was missing. Over the stile, and behind the house she ran – but there all was silent and deserted.

She looked down toward the bog, as far as she could see; but they did not appear. Again she listened – but in vain. At first she had felt angry, but now a different feeling overcame her, and she grew pale. With an undefined boding she looked toward the heathy boss of Lisnavoura, now darkening into the deepest purple against the flaming sky of sunset.

Again she listened with a sinking heart, and heard nothing but the farewell twitter and whistle of the birds in the bushes around. How many stories had she listened to by the winter hearth, of children stolen by the fairies, at nightfall, in lonely places! With this fear she knew her mother was haunted.

No one in the country round gathered her little flock about her so early as this frightened widow, and no door 'in the seven parishes' was barred so early.

Sufficiently fearful, as all young people in that part of the world are of such dreaded and subtle agents, Nell was even more than usually afraid of them, for her terrors were infected and redoubled by her mother's. She was looking towards Lisnavoura in a trance of fear, and crossed herself again and again, and whispered prayer after prayer. She was interrupted by her mother's voice on the road calling her loudly. She answered, and ran round to the front of the cabin, where she found her standing.

'And where in the world's the craythurs – did ye see sight o' them anywhere?' cried Mrs Ryan, as the girl came over the stile.

'Arrah! mother, 'tis only what they're run down the road a bit. We'll see them this minute coming back. It's like goats they are, climbin' here and runnin' there; an' if I had them here, in my hand, maybe I wouldn't give them a hiding all round.'

'May the Lord forgive you, Nell! the childers gone. They're took, and not a soul near us, and Father Tom three miles away! And what'll I do, or who's to help us this night? Oh, wirristhru, wirristhru! The craythurs is gone!'

'Whisht, mother, be aisy: don't ye see them comin' up.'

And then she shouted in menacing accents, waving her arm, and beckoning the children, who were seen approaching on the road, which some little way off made a slight dip, which had concealed them. They were approaching from the westward, and from the direction of the dreaded hill of Lisnavoura.

But there were only two of the children, and one of them, the little girl, was crying. Their mother and sister hurried forward to meet them, more alarmed than ever.

'Where is Billy – where is he?' cried the mother, nearly breathless, so soon as she was within hearing.

'He's gone – they took him away; but they said he'll come back again,' answered little Con, with the dark brown hair.

'He's gone away with the grand ladies,' blubbered the little girl.

'What ladies – where? Oh, Leum, asthora! My darlin', are you gone away at last? Where is he? Who took him? What ladies are you talkin' about? What way did he go?' she cried in distraction.

'I couldn't see where he went, mother; 'twas like as if he was going to Lisnavoura.'

With a wild exclamation the distracted woman ran on towards the hill alone, clapping her hands, and crying aloud the name of her lost child.

Scared and horrified, Nell, not daring to follow, gazed after her, and burst into tears; and the other children raised high their lamentations in shrill rivalry.

Twilight was deepening. It was long past the time when they were usually barred securely within their habitation. Nell led the younger children into the cabin, and made them sit down by the turf fire, while she stood in the open door, watching in great fear for the return of her mother.

After a long while they did see their mother return. She came in and sat down by the fire, and cried as if her heart would break.

'Will I bar the doore, mother?' asked Nell.

'Ay, do – didn't I lose enough, this night, without lavin' the doore open, for more o' yez to go; but first take an' sprinkle a dust o' the holy waters over ye, acuishla, and bring it here till I throw a taste iv it over myself and the craythurs; an' I wondher, Nell, you'd forget to do the like yourself, lettin' the craythurs out so near nightfall. Come here and sit on my knees, asthora, come to me, mavourneen, and hould me fast, in the name o' God, and I'll hould you fast that none can take yez from me, and tell me all about it, and what it was – the Lord between us and harm – an' how it happened, and who was in it.'

244

And the door being barred, the two children, sometimes speaking together, often interrupting one
another, often interrupted by their mother, managed
to tell this strange story, which I had better relate
connectedly and in my own language.

The Widow Ryan's three children were playing,
as I have said, upon the narrow old road in front of
her door. Little Bill or Leum, about five years old,
with golden hair and large blue eyes, was a very
pretty boy, with all the clear tints of healthy child-
hood, and that gaze of earnest simplicity which
belongs not to town children of the same age. His
little sister Peg, about a year elder, and his brother
Con, a little more than a year elder than she, made
up the little group.

Under the great old ash trees, whose last leaves were
falling at their feet, in the light of an October sunset,
they were playing with the hilarity and eagerness of
rustic children, clamouring together, and their faces
were turned toward the west and storeyed hill of
Lisnavoura.

Suddenly a startling voice with a screech called to
them from behind, ordering them to get out of the
way, and turning, they saw a sight, such as they never
beheld before. It was a carriage drawn by four horses
that were pawing and snorting, in impatience, as if
just pulled up. The children were almost under their
feet, and scrambled to the side of the road next their
own door.

This carriage and all its appointments were old
fashioned and gorgeous, and presented to the children,
who had never seen anything finer than a turf car, and
once, an old chaise that passed that way from Killaloe,
a spectacle perfectly dazzling.

Here was antique splendour. The harness and trappings were scarlet, and blazing with gold. The horses were huge, and snow white, with great manes, that as they tossed and shook them in the air, seemed to stream and float sometimes longer and sometimes shorter, like so much smoke – their tails were long, and tied up in bows of broad scarlet and gold ribbon. The coach itself was glowing with colours, gilded and emblazoned. There were footmen in gay liveries, and three-cocked hats, like the coachman's; but he had a great wig, like a judge's, and their hair was frizzed out and powdered, and a long thick 'pigtail,' with a bow to it, hung down the back of each.

All these servants were diminutive, and ludicrously out of proportion with the enormous horses of the equipage, and had sharp, sallow features, and small, restless fiery eyes, and faces of cunning and malice that chilled the children. The little coachman was scowling and showing his white fangs under his cocked hat, and his little blazing beads of eyes were quivering with fury in their sockets as he whirled his whip round and round over their heads, till the lash of it looked like a streak of fire in the evening sun, and sounded like the cry of a legion of 'fillapoueeks' in the air.

'Stop the princess on the highway!' cried the coachman, in a piercing treble.

'Stop the princess on the highway!' piped each footman in turn, scowling over his shoulder down on the children, and grinding his keen teeth.

The children were so frightened they could only gape and turn white in their panic. But a very sweet voice from the open window of the carriage reassured them, and arrested the attack of the lackeys.

A beautiful and 'very grand-looking' lady was smiling from it on them, and they all felt pleased in the strange light of that smile.

'The boy with the golden hair, I think,' said the lady, bending her large and wonderfully clear eyes on little Leum.

The upper sides of the carriage were chiefly of glass, so that the children could see another woman inside, whom they did not like so well.

This was a black woman, with a wonderfully long neck, hung round with many strings of large variously-coloured beads, and on her head was a sort of turban of silk striped with all the colours of the rainbow, and fixed in it was a golden star.

This black woman had a face as thin almost as a death's-head, with high cheekbones, and great goggle eyes, the whites of which, as well as her wide range of teeth, showed in brilliant contrast with her skin, as she looked over the beautiful lady's shoulder, and whispered something in her ear.

'Yes; the boy with the golden hair, I think,' repeated the lady.

And her voice sounded sweet as a silver bell in the children's ears, and her smile beguiled them like the light of an enchanted lamp, as she leaned from the window with a look of ineffable fondness on the golden-haired boy, with the large blue eyes; insomuch that little Billy, looking up, smiled in return with a wondering fondness, and when she stooped down, and stretched her jewelled arms towards him, he stretched his little hands up, and how they touched the other children did not know; but, saying, 'Come and give me a kiss, my darling,' she raised him, and he seemed to ascend in her small fingers as lightly as a

247

feather, and she held him in her lap and covered him with kisses.

Nothing daunted, the other children would have been only too happy to change places with their favoured little brother. There was only one thing that was unpleasant, and a little frightened them, and that was the black woman, who stood and stretched forward, in the carriage as before. She gathered a rich silk and gold handkerchief that was in her fingers up to her lips, and seemed to thrust ever so much of it, fold after fold, into her capacious mouth, as they thought to smother her laughter, with which she seemed convulsed, for she was shaking and quivering, as it seemed, with suppressed merriment; but her eyes, which remained uncovered, looked angrier than they had ever seen eyes look before.

But the lady was so beautiful they looked on her instead, and she continued to caress and kiss the little boy on her knee; and smiling at the other children she held up a large russet apple in her fingers, and the carriage began to move slowly on, and with a nod inviting them to take the fruit, she dropped it on the road from the window; it rolled some way beside the wheels, they following, and then she dropped another, and then another, and so on. And the same thing happened to all; for just as either of the children who ran beside had caught the rolling apple, somehow it slipped into a hole or ran into a ditch, and looking up they saw the lady drop another from the window, and so the chase was taken up and continued till they got, hardly knowing how far they had gone, to the old cross-road that leads to Owney. It seemed that there the horses' hoofs and carriage-wheels rolled up a wonderful dust, which being caught in one of those eddies that whirl the dust up into a column, on the calmest day, enveloped the children for a moment, and passed whirling on towards Lisnavoura, the carriage, as they fancied, driving in the centre of it; but suddenly it subsided, the straws and leaves floated to the ground, the dust dissipated itself, but the white horses and the lackeys, the gilded carriage, the lady and their little golden-haired brother were gone.

At the same moment suddenly the upper rim of the clear setting sun disappeared behind the hill of Knock-doula, and it was twilight. Each child felt the transition like a shock – and the sight of the rounded summit of Lisnavoura, now closely overhanging them, struck them with a new fear.

They screamed their brother's name after him, but their cries were lost in the vacant air. At the same time they thought they heard a hollow voice say, close to them, 'Go home.'

Looking round and seeing no one, they were scared, and hand in hand – the little girl crying wildly, and the boy white as ashes, from fear, they trotted homeward, at their best speed, to tell, as we have seen, their strange story.

Molly Ryan never more saw her darling. But something of the lost little boy was seen by his former playmates.

Sometimes when their mother was away earning a trifle at haymaking, and Nelly washing the potatoes for their dinner, or 'beatling' clothes in the little stream that flows in the hollow close by, they saw the pretty face of little Billy peeping in archly at the door, and smiling silently at them, and as they ran to embrace him, with cries of delight, he drew back,

249

still smiling archly, and when they got out into the open day, he was gone, and they could see no trace of him anywhere.

This happened often, with slight variations in the circumstances of the visit. Sometimes he would peep for a longer time, sometimes for a shorter time, sometimes his little hand would come in, and, with bended finger, beckon them to follow; but always he was smiling with the same arch look and wary silence – and always he was gone when they reached the door. Gradually these visits grew less and less frequent, and in about eight months they ceased altogether, and little Billy, irretrievably lost, took rank in their memories with the dead.

One wintry morning, nearly a year and a half after his disappearance, their mother having set out for Limerick soon after cockcrow, to sell some fowls at the market, the little girl, lying by the side of her elder sister, who was fast asleep, just at the grey of the morning heard the latch lifted softly, and saw little Billy enter and close the door gently after him. There was light enough to see that he was barefoot and ragged, and looked pale and famished. He went straight to the fire, and cowered over the turf embers, and rubbed his hands slowly, and seemed to shiver as he gathered the smouldering turf together.

The little girl clutched her sister in terror and whispered, 'Waken, Nelly, waken; here's Billy come back!'

Nelly slept soundly on, but the little boy, whose hands were extended close over the coals, turned and looked toward the bed, it seemed to her, in fear, and she saw the glare of the embers reflected on his thin cheek as he turned toward her. He rose and went, on tiptoe, quickly to the door, in silence, and let himself out as softly as he had come in.

After that, the little boy was never seen any more by any one of his kindred.

'Fairy doctors', as the dealers in the preternatural, who in such cases were called in, are termed, did all that in them lay – but in vain. Father Tom came down, and tried what holier rites could do, but equally without result. So little Billy was dead to mother, brother, and sisters; but no grave received him. Others whom affection cherished, lay in holy ground, in the old churchyard of Abington, with headstone to mark the spot over which the survivor might kneel and say a kind prayer for the peace of the departed soul. But there was no landmark to show where little Billy was hidden from their loving eyes, unless it was in the old hill of Lisnavoura, that cast its long shadow at sunset before the cabin-door; or that, white and filmy in the moonlight, in later years, would occupy his brother's gaze as he returned from fair or market, and draw from him a sigh and a prayer for the little brother he had lost so long ago, and was never to see again.

SHERIDAN LE FANU

An Account of Some Strange Disturbances in Aungier Street

It is not worth telling, this story of mine – at least, not worth writing. Told, indeed, as I have sometimes been called upon to tell it, to a circle of intelligent and eager faces, lighted up by a good after-dinner fire on a winter's evening, with a cold wind rising and wailing outside, and all snug and cosy within, it has gone off – though I say it, who should not – indifferent well. But it is a venture to do as you would have me. Pen, ink, and paper are cold vehicles for the marvellous, and a 'reader' decidedly a more critical animal than a 'listener.' If, however, you can induce your friends to read it after nightfall, and when the fireside talk has run for a while on thrilling tales of shapeless terror; in short, if you will secure me the *mollia tempora fandi*, I will go to my work, and say my say, with better heart. Well, then, these conditions presupposed, I shall waste no more words, but tell you simply how it all happened.

My cousin (Tom Ludlow) and I studied medicine together. I think he would have succeeded, had he stuck to the profession; but he preferred the Church, poor fellow, and died early, a sacrifice to contagion, contracted in the noble discharge of his duties. For my present purpose, I say enough of his character when I mention that he was of a sedate but frank and cheerful nature; very exact in his observance of truth, and not by any means like myself – of an excitable or nervous temperament.

My Uncle Ludlow – Tom's father – while we were attending lectures, purchased three or four old houses in Aungier Street, one of which was unoccupied. *He* resided in the country, and Tom proposed that we should take up our abode in the untenanted house, so long as it should continue unlet; a move which would accomplish the double end of settling us nearer alike to our lecture-rooms and to our amusements, and of relieving us from the weekly charge of rent for our lodgings.

Our furniture was very scant – our whole equipage remarkably modest and primitive; and, in short, our arrangements pretty nearly as simple as those of a bivouac. Our new plan was, therefore, executed almost as soon as conceived. The front drawing-room was our sitting-room. I had the bedroom over it, and Tom the back bedroom on the same floor, which nothing could have induced me to occupy.

The house, to begin with, was a very old one. It had been, I believe, newly fronted about fifty years before; but with this exception, it had nothing modern about it. The agent who bought it and looked into the titles for my uncle, told me that it was sold, along with much other forfeited property, at Chichester House, I think, in 1702; and had belonged to Sir Thomas Hacket, who was Lord Mayor of Dublin in James II's time. How old it was *then*, I can't say; but, at all events, it had seen years and changes enough to have contracted all that mysterious and saddened air, at once exciting and depressing, which belongs to most old mansions.

There had been very little done in the way of modernising details; and, perhaps, it was better so; for there was something queer and bygone in the very walls and ceilings – in the shape of doors and windows – in the odd diagonal site of the chimney-pieces – in the beams and ponderous cornices – not to mention the singular solidity of all the woodwork, from the bannisters to the window-frames, which hopelessly defied disguise, and would have emphatically proclaimed their antiquity through any conceivable amount of modern finery and varnish.

An effort had, indeed, been made, to the extent of papering the drawing-rooms; but somehow, the paper looked raw and out of keeping; and the old woman, who kept a little dirt-pie of a shop in the lane, and whose daughter – a girl of two and fifty – was our solitary handmaid, coming in at sunrise, and chastely receding again as soon as she had made all ready for tea in our state apartment; – this woman, I say, remembered it, when old Judge Horrocks (who, having earned the reputation of a particularly 'hanging judge,' ended by hanging himself, as the coroner's jury found, under an impulse of 'temporary insanity,' with a child's skipping-rope, over the massive old bannisters) resided there, entertaining good company, with fine venison and rare old port. In those halcyon days, the drawing-rooms were hung with gilded leather, and, I dare say, cut a good figure, for they were really spacious rooms.

The bedrooms were wainscoted, but the front one was not gloomy; and in it the cosiness of antiquity quite overcame its sombre associations. But the back bedroom, with its two queerly-placed melancholy windows, staring vacantly at the foot of the bed, and with the shadowy recess to be found in most old houses in Dublin, like a large ghostly closet, which, from congeniality of temperament, had amalgamated with the bedchamber, and dissolved the partition. At night-time, this 'alcove' – as our 'maid' was wont to call it – had, in my eyes, a specially sinister and suggestive character. Tom's distant and solitary candle glimmered vainly into its darkness. *There* it was always overlooking him – always itself impenetrable. But this was only part of the effect. The whole room was, I can't tell how, repulsive to me. There was, I suppose, in its proportions and features, a latent discord – a certain mysterious and indescribable relation, which jarred indistinctly upon some secret sense of the fitting and the safe, and raised indefinable suspicions and apprehensions of the imagination. On the whole, as I began by saying, nothing could have induced me to pass a night alone in it.

I had never pretended to conceal from poor Tom my superstitious weakness; and he, on the other hand, most unaffectedly ridiculed my tremors. The sceptic was, however, destined to receive a lesson, as you shall hear.

We had not been very long in occupation of our respective dormitories, when I began to complain of uneasy nights and disturbed sleep. I was, I suppose, the more impatient under this annoyance, as I was usually a sound sleeper, and by no means prone to nightmares. It was now, however, my destiny, instead of enjoying my customary repose, every night to 'sup full of horrors'. After a preliminary course of disagreeable and frightful dreams, my troubles took a definite form, and the same vision, without an appreciable variation in a single detail, visited me at least (on an average) every second night in the week.

Now, this dream, nightmare, or infernal illusion –
which you please – of which I was the miserable sport,
was on this wise – I saw, or thought I saw, with the
most abominable distinctness, although at the time
in profound darkness, every article of furniture and
accidental arrangement of the chamber in which I
lay. This, as you know, is incidental to ordinary nightmare. Well, while in this clairvoyant condition, which
seemed but the lighting up of the theatre in which
was to be exhibited the monotonous tableau of horror,
which made my nights insupportable, my attention
invariably became, I know not why, fixed upon the
windows opposite the foot of my bed; and, uniformly
with the same effect, a sense of dreadful anticipation
always took slow but sure possession of me. I became
somehow conscious of a sort of horrid but undefined
preparation going forward in some unknown quarter,
and by some unknown agency, for my torment; and,
after an interval, which always seemed to me of the
same length, a picture suddenly flew up to the window,
where it remained fixed, as if by an electrical attraction,
and my discipline of horror then commenced, to last
perhaps for hours. The picture thus mysteriously glued
to the window-panes, was the portrait of an old man,
in a crimson flowered silk dressing-gown, the folds
of which I could now describe, with a countenance
embodying a strange mixture of intellect, sensuality,
and power, but withal sinister and full of malignant
omen. His nose was hooked, like the beak of a vulture;
his eyes large, grey, and prominent, and lighted up
with a more than mortal cruelty and coldness. These
features were surmounted by a crimson velvet cap,
the hair that peeped from under which was white
with age, while the eyebrows retained their original

STRANGE DISTURBANCES IN AUNGIER STREET

blackness. Well I remember every line, hue, and shadow of that stony countenance, and well I may! The gaze of this hellish visage was fixed upon me, and mine returned it with the inexplicable fascination of nightmare, for what appeared to me to be hours of agony. At last – 'The cock he crew, away then flew', the fiend who had enslaved me through the awful watches of the night; and, harassed and nervous, I rose to the duties of the day.

I had – I can't say exactly why, but it may have been from the exquisite anguish and profound impressions of unearthly horror, with which this strange phantasmagoria was associated – an insurmountable antipathy to describing the exact nature of my nightly troubles to my friend and comrade. Generally, however, I told him that I was haunted by abominable dreams; and, true to the imputed materialism of medicine, we put our heads together to dispel my horrors, not by exorcism, but by a tonic.

I will do this tonic justice, and frankly admit that the accursed portrait began to intermit its visits under its influence. What of that? Was this singular apparition – as full of character as of terror – therefore the creature of my fancy, or the invention of my poor stomach? Was it, in short, *subjective* (to borrow the technical slang of the day) and not the palpable aggression and intrusion of an external agent? That, good friend, as we will both admit, by no means follows. The evil spirit, who enthralled my senses in the shape of that portrait, may have been just as near me, just as energetic, just as malignant, though I saw him not. What means the whole moral code of revealed religion regarding the due keeping of our own bodies, soberness, temperance, etc.? here is an obvious connection between the material and the invisible; the healthy tone of the system, and its unimpaired energy, may, for aught we can tell, guard us against influences which would otherwise render life itself terrific. The mesmerist and the electrobiologist will fail upon an average with nine patients out of ten – so may the evil spirit. Special conditions of the corporeal system are indispensable to the production of certain spiritual phenomena. The operation succeeds sometimes – sometimes fails – that is all.

I found afterwards that my would-be sceptical companion had his troubles too. But of these I knew nothing yet. One night, for a wonder, I was sleeping soundly, when I was roused by a step on the lobby outside my room, followed by the loud clang of what turned out to be a large brass candlestick, flung with all his force by poor Tom Ludlow over the banisters, and rattling with a rebound down the second flight of stairs; and almost concurrently with this, Tom burst open my door, and bounced into my room backwards, in a state of extraordinary agitation.

I had jumped out of bed and clutched him by the arm before I had any distinct idea of my own whereabouts. There we were – in our shirts – standing before the open door – staring through the great old banister opposite, at the lobby window, through which the sickly light of a clouded moon was gleaming.

'What's the matter, Tom? What's the matter with you? What the devil's the matter with you, Tom?' I demanded shaking him with nervous impatience.

He took a long breath before he answered me, and then it was not very coherently.

'It's nothing, nothing at all – did I speak? – what

did I say? – where's the candle, Richard? It's dark; I – I had a candle!'

'Yes, dark enough,' I said; 'but what's the matter? – what is it? – why don't you speak, Tom? – have you lost your wits? – what is the matter?'

'The matter? – oh, it is all over. It must have been a dream – nothing at all but a dream – don't you think so? It could not be anything more than a dream.'

'Of *course*,' said I, feeling uncommonly nervous, 'it *was* a dream.'

'I thought,' he said, 'there was a man in my room, and – and I jumped out of bed; and – and – where's the candle?'

'In your room, most likely,' I said, 'shall I go and bring it?'

'No; stay here – don't go; it's no matter – don't, I tell you; it was all a dream. Bolt the door, Dick; I'll stay here with you – I feel nervous. So, Dick, like a good fellow, light your candle and open the window – I am in a *shocking state*.'

I did as he asked me, and robing himself like Granuaile in one of my blankets, he seated himself close beside my bed.

Everybody knows how contagious is fear of all sorts, but more especially that particular kind of fear under which poor Tom was at that moment labouring. I would not have heard, nor I believe would he have recapitulated, just at that moment, for half the world, the details of the hideous vision which had so unmanned him.

'Don't mind telling me anything about your non-sensical dream, Tom,' said I, affecting contempt, really in a panic; 'let us talk about something else; but it is quite plain that this dirty old house disagrees with us both, and hang me if I stay here any longer, to be pestered with indigestion and – and – bad nights, so we may as well look out for lodgings – don't you think so? – at once.'

Tom agreed, and, after an interval, said – 'I have been thinking, Richard, that it is a long time since I saw my father, and I have made up my mind to go down tomorrow and return in a day or two, and you can take rooms for us in the meantime.'

I fancied that this resolution, obviously the result of the vision which had so profoundly scared him, would probably vanish next morning with the damps and shadows of night. But I was mistaken. Off went Tom at peep of day to the country, having agreed that so soon as I had secured suitable lodgings, I was to recall him by letter from his visit to my Uncle Ludlow.

Now, anxious as I was to change my quarters, it so happened, owing to a series of petty procrastinations and accidents, that nearly a week elapsed before my bargain was made and my letter of recall on the wing to Tom; and, in the meantime, a trifling adventure or two had occurred to your humble servant, which, absurd as they now appear, diminished by distance, did certainly at the time serve to whet my appetite for change considerably.

A night or two after the departure of my comrade, I was sitting by my bedroom fire, the door locked, and the ingredients of a tumbler of hot whisky-punch upon the crazy spider-table; for, as the best mode of keeping the

> Black spirits and white,
> Blue spirits and grey,

with which I was environed, at bay, I had adopted

the practice recommended by the wisdom of my ancestors, and 'kept my spirits up by pouring spirits down.' I had thrown aside my volume of Anatomy, and was treating myself by way of a tonic, preparatory to my punch and bed, to half a dozen pages of the *Spectator*, when I heard a step on the flight of stairs descending from the attics. It was two o'clock, and the streets were as silent as a churchyard – the sounds were, therefore, perfectly distinct. There was a slow, heavy tread, characterised by the emphasis and deliberation of age, descending by the narrow staircase from above; and, what made the sound more singular, it was plain that the feet which produced it were perfectly bare, measuring the descent with something between a pound and a flop, very ugly to hear.

I knew quite well that my attendant had gone away many hours before, and that nobody but myself had any business in the house. It was quite plain also that the person who was coming downstairs had no intention whatever of concealing his movements; but, on the contrary, appeared disposed to make even more noise, and proceed more deliberately, than was at all necessary. When the step reached the foot of the stairs outside my room, it seemed to stop; and I expected every moment to see my door open spontaneously, and give admission to the original of my detested portrait. I was, however, relieved in a few seconds by hearing the descent renewed, just in the same manner, upon the staircase leading down to the drawing-rooms, and thence, after another pause, down the next flight, and so on to the hall, whence I heard no more.

Now, by the time the sound had ceased, I was wound up, as they say, to a very unpleasant pitch of excitement. I listened, but there was not a stir. I screwed up my courage to a decisive experiment – opened my door, and in a stentorian voice bawled over the banisters, 'Who's there?' There was no answer but the ringing of my own voice through the empty old house, – no renewal of the movement; nothing, in short, to give my unpleasant sensations a definite direction. There is, I think, something most disagreeably disenchanting in the sound of one's own voice under such circumstances, exerted in solitude, and in vain. It redoubled my sense of isolation and my misgivings increased on perceiving that the door, which I certainly thought I had left open, was closed behind me; in a vague alarm, lest my retreat should be cut off, I got again into my room as quickly as I could, where I remained in a state of imaginary blockade, and very uncomfortable indeed, till morning.

Next night brought no return of my barefooted fellow-lodger; but the night following, being in my bed, and in the dark – somewhere, I suppose, about the same hour as before, I distinctly heard the old fellow again descending from the garrets.

This time I had had my punch, and the *morale* of the garrison was consequently excellent. I jumped out of bed, clutched the poker as I passed the expiring fire, and in a moment was upon the lobby. The sound had ceased by this time – the dark and chill were discouraging; and, guess my horror, when I saw, or thought I saw, a black monster, whether in the shape of a man or a bear I could not say, standing, with its back to the wall, on the lobby, facing me, with a pair of great greenish eyes shining dimly out. Now, I must be frank, and confess that the cupboard which displayed our plates and cups stood just there, though at the moment I did not recollect it. At the same time I must honestly say, that making every allowance for an excited imagination, I never could satisfy myself that I was made the dupe of my own fancy in this matter; for this apparition, after one or two shiftings of shape, as if in the act of incipient transformation, began, as it seemed on second thoughts, to advance upon me in its original form. From an instinct of terror rather than of courage, I hurled the poker, with all my force, at its head; and to the music of a horrid crash made my way into my room, and double-locked the door. Then, in a minute more, I heard the horrid bare feet walk down the stairs, till the sound ceased in the hall, as on the former occasion.

If the apparition of the night before was an ocular delusion of my fancy sporting with the dark outlines of our cupboard, and if its horrid eyes were nothing but a pair of inverted teacups, I had, at all events, the satisfaction of having launched the poker with admirable effect, and in true 'fancy' phrase, 'knocked its two daylights into one', as the commingled fragments of my tea-service testified. I did my best to gather comfort and courage from these evidences; but it would not do. And then what could I say of those horrid bare feet, and the regular tramp, tramp, tramp, which measured the distance of the entire staircase through the solitude of my haunted dwelling, and at an hour when no good influence was stirring? Confound it! – the whole affair was abominable. I was out of spirits, and dreaded the approach of night.

It came, ushered ominously in with a thunderstorm and dull torrents of depressing rain. Earlier than usual the streets grew silent; and by twelve o'clock nothing but the comfortless pattering of the rain was to be heard.

I made myself as snug as I could. I lighted *two* candles instead of one. I forswore bed, and held myself in readiness for a sally, candle in hand; for, *coute qui coute*, I was resolved to *see* the being, if visible at all, who troubled the nightly stillness of my mansion. I was fidgetty and nervous and, tried in vain to interest myself with my books. I walked up and down my room, whistling in turn martial and hilarious music, and listening ever and anon for the dreaded noise. I sate down and stared at the square label on the solemn and reserved-looking black bottle, until 'Flanagan & Co.'s Best Old Malt Whisky' grew into a sort of subdued accompaniment to all the fantastic and horrible speculations which chased one another through my brain.

Silence, meanwhile, grew more silent, and darkness darker. I listened in vain for the rumble of a vehicle, or the dull clamour of a distant row. There was nothing but the sound of a rising wind, which had succeeded the thunderstorm that had travelled over the Dublin mountains quite out of hearing. In the middle of this great city I began to feel myself alone with nature, and Heaven knows what beside. My courage was ebbing. Punch, however, which makes beasts of so many, made a man of me again – just in time to hear with tolerable nerve and firmness the lumpy, flabby, naked feet deliberately descending the stairs again.

I took a candle, not without a tremor. As I crossed the floor I tried to extemporise a prayer, but stopped short to listen, and never finished it. The steps continued. I confess I hesitated for some seconds at the door before I took heart of grace and opened it. When

I peeped out the lobby was perfectly empty – there was no monster standing on the staircase; and as the detested sound ceased, I was reassured enough to venture forward nearly to the banisters. Horror of horrors! within a stair or two beneath the spot where I stood the unearthly tread smote the floor. My eye caught something in motion; it was about the size of Goliah's foot – it was grey, heavy, and flapped with a dead weight from one step to another. As I am alive, it was the most monstrous grey rat I ever beheld or imagined.

Shakespeare says – 'Some men there are cannot abide a gaping pig, and some that are mad if they behold a cat.' I went well-nigh out of my wits when I beheld this *rat*; for, laugh at me as you may, it fixed upon me, I thought, a perfectly human expression of malice; and, as it shuffled about and looked up into my face almost from between my feet, I saw, I could swear it – I felt it then, and know it now, the infernal gaze and the accursed countenance of my old friend in the portrait, transfused into the visage of the bloated vermin before me.

I bounced into my room again with a feeling of loathing and horror I cannot describe, and locked and bolted my door as if a lion had been at the other side. D—n him or *it*; curse the portrait and its original! I felt in my soul that the rat – yes, the *rat*, the rat I had just seen, was that evil being in masquerade, and rambling through the house upon some infernal night lark.

Next morning I was early trudging through the miry streets; and, among other transactions, posted a peremptory note recalling Tom. On my return, however, I found a note from my absent 'chum,' announcing his intended return next day. I was doubly rejoiced at this, because I had succeeded in getting rooms; and because the change of scene and return of my comrade were rendered specially pleasant by the last night's half ridiculous half horrible adventure.

I slept extemporaneously in my new quarters in Digges' Street that night, and next morning returned for breakfast to the haunted mansion, where I was certain Tom would call immediately on his arrival.

I was quite right – he came; and almost his first question referred to the primary object of our change of residence.

'Thank God,' he said with genuine fervour, on hearing that all was arranged. 'On *your* account I am delighted. As to myself, I assure you that no earthly consideration could have induced me ever again to pass a night in this disastrous old house.'

'Confound the house!' I ejaculated, with a genuine mixture of fear and detestation, 'we have not had a pleasant hour since we came to live here'; and so I went on, and related incidentally my adventure with the plethoric old rat.

'Well, if that were *all*,' said my cousin, affecting to make light of the matter, 'I don't think I should have minded it very much.'

'Ay, but its eye – its countenance, my dear Tom,' – urged I; 'if you had seen that, *you* would have felt it might be *anything* but what it seemed.'

'I inclined to think the best conjurer in such a case would be an able-bodied cat,' he said, with a provoking chuckle.

'But let us hear your own adventure,' I said tartly.

At this challenge he looked uneasily round him. I had poked up a very unpleasant recollection.

'You shall hear it, Dick; I'll tell it to you,' he said.

'Begad, sir, I should feel quite queer, though, telling it *here*, though we are too strong a body for ghosts to meddle with just now.'

Though he spoke this like a joke, I think it was serious calculation. Our Hebe was in a corner of the room, packing our cracked delft tea and dinner-services in a basket. She soon suspended operations, and with mouth and eyes wide open became an absorbed listener. Tom's experiences were told nearly in these words: 'I saw it three times, Dick – three distinct times; and I am perfectly certain it meant me some infernal harm. I was, I say, in danger – in *extreme* danger; for, if nothing else had happened, my reason would most certainly have failed me, unless I had escaped so soon. Thank God. I *did* escape.

'The first night of this hateful disturbance, I was lying in the attitude of sleep, in that lumbering old bed. I hate to think of it. I was really wide awake, though I had put out my candle, and was lying as quietly as if I had been asleep; and although accidentally restless, my thoughts were running in a cheerful and agreeable channel.

'I think it must have been two o'clock at least when I thought I heard a sound in that – that odious dark recess at the far end of the bedroom. It was as if someone was drawing a piece of cord slowly along the floor, lifting it up, and dropping it softly down again in coils. I sate up once or twice in my bed, but could see nothing, so I concluded it must be mice in the wainscot. I felt no emotion graver than curiosity, and after a few minutes ceased to observe it.

'While lying in this state, strange to say; without at first a suspicion of anything supernatural, on a sudden I saw an old man, rather stout and square, in a sort of roan-red dressing-gown, and with a black cap on his head, moving stiffly and slowly in a diagonal direction, from the recess, across the floor of the bedroom, passing my bed at the foot, and entering the lumber-closet at the left. He had something under his arm; his head hung a little at one side; and, merciful God! when I saw his face.'

Tom stopped for a while, and then said: 'That awful countenance, which living or dying I never can forget, disclosed what he was. Without turning to the right or left, he passed beside me, and entered the closet by the bed's head.

'While this fearful and indescribable type of death and guilt was passing, I felt that I had no more power to speak or stir than if I had been myself a corpse. For hours after it had disappeared, I was too terrified and weak to move. As soon as daylight came, I took courage, and examined the room, and especially the course which the frightful intruder had seemed to take, but there was not a vestige to indicate anybody's having passed there; no sign of any disturbing agency visible among the lumber that strewed the floor of the closet.

'I now began to recover a little. I was fagged and exhausted, and at last, overpowered by a feverish sleep. I came down late; and finding you out of spirits, on account of your dreams about the portrait, whose *original* I am now certain disclosed himself to me, I did not care to talk about the infernal vision. In fact, I was trying to persuade myself that the whole thing was an illusion, and I did not like to revive in their intensity the hated impressions of the past night – or, to risk the constancy of my scepticism, by recounting the tale of my sufferings.

'It required some nerve, I can tell you, to go to my haunted chamber next night, and lie down quietly in the same bed,' continued Tom. 'I did so with a degree of trepidation, which, I am not ashamed to say, a very little matter would have sufficed to stimulate to downright panic. This night, however, passed off quietly enough, as also the next; and so too did two or three more. I grew more confident, and began to fancy that I believed in the theories of spectral illusions, with which I had at first vainly tried to impose upon my convictions.

'The apparition had been, indeed, altogether anomalous. It had crossed the room without any recognition of my presence: I had not disturbed *it*, and *it* had no mission to *me*. What, then, was the imaginable use of its crossing the room in a visible shape at all? Of course it might have *been* in the closet instead of *going* there, as easily as it introduced itself into the recess without entering the chamber in a shape discernible by the senses. Besides, how the deuce *had* I seen it? It was a dark night; I had no candle; there was no fire; and yet I saw it as distinctly, in colouring and outline, as ever I beheld human form! A cataleptic dream would explain it all; and I was determined that a dream it should be.

'One of the most remarkable phenomena connected with the practice of mendacity is the vast number of deliberate lies we tell ourselves, whom, of all persons, we can least expect to deceive. In all this, I need hardly tell you, Dick, I was simply lying to myself, and did not believe one word of the wretched humbug. Yet I went on, as men will do, like persevering charlatans and impostors, who tire people into credulity by the mere force of reiteration; so I hoped to win myself over at last to a comfortable scepticism about the ghost.

'He had not appeared a second time – that certainly was a comfort; and what, after all, did I care for him, and his queer old toggery and strange looks? Not a fig! I was nothing the worse for having seen him, and a good story the better. So I tumbled into bed, put out my candle, and, cheered by a loud drunken quarrel in the back lane, went fast asleep.

'From this deep slumber I awoke with a start. I knew I had had a horrible dream; but what it was I could not remember. My heart was thumping furiously; I felt bewildered and feverish; I sate up in the bed and looked about the room. A broad flood of moonlight came in through the curtainless window; everything was as I had last seen it; and though the domestic squabble in the back lane was, unhappily for me, allayed, I yet could hear a pleasant fellow singing, on his way home, the then popular comic ditty called, "Murphy Delany". Taking advantage of this diversion I lay down again, with my face towards the fireplace, and closing my eyes, did my best to think of nothing else but the song, which was every moment growing fainter in the distance:

'Twas Murphy Delany, so funny and frisky,
     Stepped into a shebeen shop to get his skin full;
He reeled out again pretty well lined with whiskey,
     As fresh as a shamrock, as blind as a bull.

'The singer, whose condition I dare say resembled that of his hero, was soon too far off to regale my ears any more; and as his music died away, I myself sank into a doze, neither sound nor refreshing. Somehow the song had got into my head, and I went meandering on through the adventures of my respectable fellow-countryman, who, on emerging from the "shebeen shop," fell into a river, from which he was fished up to be "sat upon" by a coroner's jury, who having learned from a "horse-doctor" that he was "dead as a doornail, so there was an end," returned their verdict accordingly, just as he returned to his senses, when an angry altercation and a pitched battle between the body and the coroner winds up the lay with due spirit and pleasantry.

'Through this ballad I continued with a weary monotony to plod, down to the very last line, and then *da capo*, and so on, in my uncomfortable half sleep, for how long, I can't conjecture. I found myself at last, however, muttering, "*dead* as a doornail, so there was an end"; and something like another voice within me, seemed to say, very faintly, but sharply, "dead! dead! *dead!* and may the Lord have mercy on your soul!" and instantaneously I was wide awake, and staring right before me from the pillow.

'Now – will you believe it, Dick? – I saw the same accursed figure standing full front, and gazing at me with its stony and fiendish countenance, not two yards from the bedside.'

Tom stopped here, and wiped the perspiration from his face. I felt very queer. The girl was as pale as Tom; and, assembled as we were in the very scene of these adventures, we were all, I dare say, equally grateful for the clear daylight and the resuming bustle out of doors.

'For about three seconds only I saw it plainly; then it grew indistinct; but, for a long time, there was something like a column of dark vapour where it had been standing, between me and the wall; and I felt sure that he was still there. After a good while, this appearance went too. I took my clothes downstairs to the hall, and dressed there, with the door half open; then went out into the street, and walked about the town till morning when I came back, in a miserable state of nervousness and exhaustion. I was such a fool, Dick, as to be ashamed to tell you how I came to be so upset. I thought you would laugh at me; especially as I had always talked philosophy, and treated your ghosts with contempt. I concluded you would give me no quarter; and so kept my tale of horror to myself.

'Now, Dick, you will hardly believe me, when I assure you, that for many nights after this last experience, I did not go to my room at all. I used to sit up for a while in the drawing-room after you had gone up to your bed; and then steal down softly to the hall-door, let myself out, and sit in the "Robin Hood" tavern until the last guest went off; and then I got through the night like a sentry, pacing the streets till morning.

'For more than a week I never slept in bed. I sometimes had a snooze on a form in the "Robin Hood", and sometimes a nap in a chair during the day; but regular sleep I had absolutely none.

'I was quite resolved that we should get into another house; but I could not bring myself to tell you the reason, and I somehow put it off from day to day, although my life was, during every hour of this pro-crastination, rendered as miserable as that of a felon with the constables on his track. I was growing absolutely ill from this wretched mode of life.

'One afternoon I determined to enjoy an hour's sleep upon your bed. I hated mine; so that I had never, except in a stealthy visit every day to unmake it, lest Martha should discover the secret of my nightly absence, entered the ill-omened chamber.

'As ill-luck would have it, you had locked your bedroom, and taken away the key. I went into my own to unsettle the bedclothes, as usual, and give the bed the appearance of having been slept in. Now, a variety of circumstances concurred to bring about the dreadful scene through which I was that night to pass. In the first place, I was literally overpowered with fatigue, and longing for sleep; in the next place, the effect of this extreme exhaustion upon my nerves resembled that of a narcotic, and rendered me less susceptible than, perhaps I should in any other condition have been, of the exciting fears which had become habitual to me. Then again, a little bit of the window was open, a pleasant freshness pervaded the room, and, to crown all, the cheerful sun of day was making the room quite pleasant. What was to prevent my enjoying an hour's nap *here*? The whole air was resonant with the cheerful hum of life, and the broad matter-of-fact light of day filled every corner of the room.

'I yielded – stifling my qualms – to the almost overpowering temptation; and merely throwing off my coat, and loosening my cravat, I lay down, limiting myself to *half* an hour's doze in the unwonted enjoyment of a feather bed, a coverlet, and a bolster.

'It was horribly insidious; and the demon, no doubt, marked my infatuated preparations. Dolt that I was, I fancied, with mind and body worn out for want of sleep, and an arrear of a full week's rest to my credit, that such measure as *half* an hour's sleep, in such a situation, was possible. My sleep was deathlike, long, and dreamless.

'Without a start or fearful sensation of any kind, I waked gently, but completely. It was, as you have good reason to remember, long past midnight – I believe, about two o'clock. When sleep has been deep and long enough to satisfy nature thoroughly, one often wakens in this way, suddenly, tranquilly, and completely.

'There was a figure seated in that lumbering, old sofa-chair, near the fireplace. Its back was rather towards me, but I could not be mistaken; it turned slowly round, and, merciful heavens! there was the stony face, with its infernal lineaments of malignity and despair, gloating on me. There was now no doubt as to its consciousness of my presence, and the hellish malice with which it was animated, for it arose, and drew close to the bedside. There was a rope about its neck, and the other end, coiled up, it held stiffly in its hand.

'My good angel nerved me for this horrible crisis. I remained for some seconds transfixed by the gaze of this tremendous phantom. He came close to the bed, and appeared on the point of mounting upon it. The next instant I was upon the floor at the far side, and in a moment more was, I don't know how, upon the lobby.

'But the spell was not yet broken; the valley of the shadow of death was not yet traversed. The abhorred phantom was before me there; it was standing near the banisters, stooping a little, and with one end of the rope round its own neck, was poising a noose at the other, as if to throw over mine; and while engaged in this baleful pantomime, it wore a smile so sensual, so unspeakably dreadful, that my senses were nearly overpowered. I saw and remember nothing more, until I found myself in your room.

'I had a wonderful escape, Dick – there is no disputing *that* – an escape for which, while I live, I shall bless the mercy of heaven. No one can conceive or imagine what it is for flesh and blood to stand in the presence of such a thing, but one who has had the terrific experience. Dick, Dick, a shadow has passed over me – a chill has crossed my blood and marrow, and I will never be the same again – never, Dick – never!'

Our handmaid, a mature girl of two-and-fifty, as I have said, stayed her hand, as Tom's story proceeded, and by little and little drew near to us, with open mouth, and her brows contracted over her little, beady black eyes, till stealing a glance over her shoulder now and then, she established herself close behind us. During the relation, she had made various earnest comments, in an undertone; but these and her ejaculations, for the sake of brevity and simplicity, I have omitted in my narration.

'It's often I heard tell of it,' she now said, 'but I never believed it rightly till now – though, indeed, why should not I? Does not my mother, down there in the lane, know quare stories, God bless us, beyant telling about it? But you ought not to have slept in the back bedroom. She was loath to let me be going in and out of that room even in the day time, let alone for any Christian to spend the night in it; for sure she says it was his own bedroom.'

'*Whose* own bedroom?' we asked, in a breath.

'Why, *his* – the ould Judge's – Judge Horrock's, to be sure, God rest his sowl'; and she looked fearfully round.

'Amen!' I muttered. 'But did he die there?'

'Die there! No, not quite *there*,' she said. 'Shure,

was not it over the bannisters he hung himself, the ould sinner, God be merciful to us all? and was not it in the alcove they found the handles of the skipping-rope cut off, and the knife where he was settling the cord, God bless us, to hang himself with? It was his housekeeper's daughter owned the rope, my mother often told me, and the child never throve after, and used to be starting up out of her sleep, and screeching in the night time, wid dhrames and frights that cum an her; and they said how it was the speerit of the ould Judge that was tormentin' her; and she used to be roaring and yelling out to hould back the big ould fellow with the crooked neck; and then she'd screech "Oh, the master! the master! he's stampin' at me, and beckoning to me! Mother, darling, don't let me go!" And so the poor crathure died at last, and the docthers said it was wather on the brain, for it was all they could say.'

'How long ago was all this?' I asked.

'Oh, then, how would I know?' she answered. 'But it must be a wondherful long time ago, for the house-keeper was an ould woman, with a pipe in her mouth, and not a tooth left, and better nor eighty years ould when my mother was first married; and they said she was a rale buxom, fine-dressed woman when the ould Judge come to his end; an', indeed, my mother's not far from eighty years ould herself this day; and what made it worse for the unnatural ould villain, God rest his soul, to frighten the little girl out of the world the way he did, was what was mostly thought and believed by everyone. My mother says how the poor little crathure was his own child; for he was by all accounts an ould villain every way, an' the hangin'est judge that ever was known in Ireland's ground.'

'From what you said about the danger of sleeping in that bedroom,' said I, 'I suppose there were stories about the ghost having appeared there to others.'

'Well, there *was* things said – quare things, surely,' she answered, as it seemed, with some reluctance. 'And why would not there? Sure was it not up in that same room he slept for more than twenty years? and was it not in the *alcove* he got the rope ready that done his own business at last, the way he done many a betther man's in his lifetime? – and was not the body lying in the same bed after death, and put in the coffin there, too, and carried out to his grave from it in Pether's churchyard, after the coroner was done? But there was quare stories – my mother has them all – about how one Nicholas Spaight got into trouble on the head of it.'

'And what did they say of this Nicholas Spaight?' I asked.

'Oh, for that matther, it's soon told,' she answered.

And she certainly did relate a very strange story, which so piqued my curiosity, that I took occasion to visit the ancient lady, her mother, from whom I learned many very curious particulars. Indeed, I am tempted to tell the tale, but my fingers are weary, and I must defer it. But if you wish to hear it another time, I shall do my best.

When we had heard the strange tale I have *not* told you, we put one or two further questions to her about the alleged spectral visitations, to which the house had, ever since the death of the wicked old Judge, been subjected.

'No one ever had luck in it,' she told us. 'There was always cross accidents, sudden deaths, and short times in it. The first that tuck it was a family – I forget their name – but at any rate there was two young ladies and their papa. He was about sixty, and a stout healthy gentleman as you'd wish to see at that age. Well, he slept in that unlucky back bedroom; and, God between us an' harm! sure enough he was found dead one morning, half out of the bed, with his head as black as a sloe, and swelled like a puddin', hanging down near the floor. It was a fit, they said. He was as dead as a mackerel, and so *he* could not say what it was; but the ould people was all sure that it was nothing at all but the ould Judge, God bless us! that frightened him out of his senses and his life together.

'Some time after there was a rich old maiden lady took the house. I don't know which room *she* slept in, but she lived alone; and at any rate, one morning, the servants going down early to their work, found her sitting on the passage-stairs, shivering and talkin' to herself, quite mad; and never a word more could any of *them* or her friends get from her ever afterwards but, "Don't ask me to go, for I promised to wait for him." They never made out from her who it was she meant by *him*, but of course those that knew all about the ould house were at no loss for the meaning of all that happened to her.

'Then afterwards, when the house was let out in lodgings, there was Micky Byrne that took the same room, with his wife and three little children; and sure I heard Mrs Byrne myself telling how the children used to be lifted up in the bed at night, she could not see by what mains; and how they were starting and screeching every hour, just all as one as the housekeeper's little girl that died, till at last one night poor Micky had a dhrop in him, the way he used now and again; and what do you think in the middle of the night he thought he heard a noise on the stairs, and being in liquor, nothing less id do him but out he must go himself to see what was wrong. Well, after that, all she ever heard of him was himself sayin', "Oh, God!" and a tumble that shook the very house; and there, sure enough, he was lying on the lower stairs, under the lobby, with his neck smashed double undher him, where he was flung over the banisters.'

Then the handmaiden added: 'I'll go down to the lane, and send up Joe Gavvey to pack up the rest of the taythings, and bring all the things across to your new lodgings.'

And so we all sallied out together, each of us breathing more freely, I have no doubt, as we crossed that ill-omened threshold for the last time.

Now, I may add thus much, in compliance with the immemorial usage of the realm of fiction, which sees the hero not only through his adventures, but fairly out of the world. You must have perceived that what the flesh, blood, and bone hero of romance proper is to the regular compounder of fiction, this old house of brick, wood, and mortar is to the humble recorder of this true tale. I, therefore, relate, as in duty bound, the catastrophe which ultimately befell it, which was simply this – that about two years subsequently to my story it was taken by a quack doctor, who called himself Baron Duhlstoerf, and filled the parlour windows with bottles of indescribable horrors preserved in brandy, and the newspapers with the usual grandiloquent and mendacious advertisements. This gentleman among his virtues did not reckon sobriety, and one night, being overcome with much wine, he set fire to his bed curtains, partially burned himself, and totally consumed the house. It was afterwards rebuilt, and for a time an undertaker established himself in the premises.

I have now told you my own and Tom's adventures, together with some valuable collateral particulars; and having acquitted myself of my engagement, I wish you a very good-night, and pleasant dreams.

SHERIDAN LE FANU

Ghost Stories of Chapelizod

Take my word for it, there is no such thing as an
ancient village, especially if it has seen better days,
unillustrated by its legends of terror. You might as
well expect to find a decayed cheese without mites,
or an old house without rats, as an antique and
dilapidated town without an authentic population of
goblins. Now, although this class of inhabitants are
in nowise amenable to the police authorities, yet, as
their demeanour directly affects the comforts of her
Majesty's subjects, I cannot but regard it as a grave
omission that the public have hitherto been left without any statistical returns of their numbers, activity,
etc., etc. And I am persuaded that a Commission to
enquire into and report upon the numerical strength,
habits, haunts, etc., etc., of supernatural agents
resident in Ireland, would be a great deal more
innocent and entertaining than half the Commissions
for which the country pays, and at least as instructive.
This I say, more from a sense of duty, and to deliver
my mind of a grave truth, than with any hope of
seeing the suggestion adopted. But, I am sure, my
readers will deplore with me that the comprehensive
powers of belief, and apparently illimitable leisure,
possessed by parliamentary commissions of enquiry,
should never have been applied to the subject I have

named, and that the collection of that species of information should be confided to the gratuitous and desultory labours of individuals, who, like myself, have other occupations to attend to. This, however, by the way.

Among the village outposts of Dublin, Chapelizod once held a considerable, if not a foremost rank. Without mentioning its connection with the history of the great Kilmainham Preceptory of the Knights of St John, it will be enough to remind the reader of its ancient and celebrated Castle, not one vestige of which now remains, and of the fact that it was for, we believe, some centuries, the summer residence of the Viceroys of Ireland. The circumstance of its being up, we believe, to the period at which that corps was disbanded, the headquarters of the Royal Irish Artillery, gave it also a consequence of an humbler, but not less substantial kind. With these advantages in its favour, it is not wonderful that the town exhibited at one time an air of substantial and semi-aristocratic prosperity unknown to Irish villages in modern times.

A broad street, with a well-paved footpath, and houses as lofty as were at that time to be found in the fashionable streets of Dublin; a goodly stone-fronted barrack; an ancient church, vaulted beneath, and with a tower clothed from its summit to its base with the richest ivy; an humble Roman Catholic chapel; a steep bridge spanning the Liffey, and a great old mill at the near end of it, were the principal features of the town. These, or at least most of them, remain still, but the greater part in a very changed and forlorn condition. Some of them indeed are superseded, though not obliterated by modern erections, such as the bridge, the chapel, and the church in part; the rest forsaken by the order who originally raised them, and delivered up to poverty, and in some cases to absolute decay.

The village lies in the lap of the rich and wooded valley of the Liffey, and is overlooked by the high grounds of the beautiful Phoenix Park on the one side, and by the ridge of the Palmerstown hills on the other. Its situation, therefore, is eminently pictur-esque; and factory-fronts and chimneys notwith-standing, it has, I think, even in its decay, a sort of melancholy picturesqueness of its own. Be that as it may, I mean to relate two or three stories of that sort which may be read with very good effect by a blazing fire on a shrewd winter's night, and are all directly connected with the altered and somewhat melan-choly little town I have named. The first I shall relate concerns

THE VILLAGE BULLY

About thirty years ago there lived in the town of Chapelizod an ill-conditioned fellow of herculean strength, well known throughout the neighbourhood by the title of Bully Larkin. In addition to this remark-able physical superiority, this fellow had acquired a degree of skill as a pugilist which alone would have made him formidable. As it was, he was the autocrat of the village, and carried not the sceptre in vain. Conscious of his superiority, and perfectly secure of impunity, he lorded it over his fellows in a spirit of cowardly and brutal insolence, which made him hated even more profoundly than he was feared.

Upon more than one occasion he had deliberately forced quarrels upon men whom he had singled out for the exhibition of his savage prowess; and in every encounter his over-matched antagonist had received an amount of 'punishment' which edified and appalled the spectators, and in some instances left ineffaceable scars and lasting injuries after it.

Bully Larkin's pluck had never been fairly tried. For, owing to his prodigious superiority in weight, strength, and skill, his victories had always been certain and easy; and in proportion to the facility with which he uniformly smashed an antagonist, his pugnacity and insolence were inflamed. He thus became an odious nuisance in the neighbourhood, and the terror of every mother who had a son, and of every wife who had a husband who possessed a spirit to resent insult, or the smallest confidence in his own pugilistic capabilities.

Now it happened that there was a young fellow named Ned Moran better known by the soubriquet of 'Long Ned', from his slender, lathy proportions at that time living in the town. He was, in truth, a mere lad, nineteen years of age, and fully twelve years younger than the stalwart bully. This, however, as the reader will see secured for him no exemption from the dastardly provocations of the ill-conditioned pugilist. Long Ned, in an evil hour, had thrown eyes of affection upon a certain buxom damsel, who, notwithstanding Bully Larkin's amorous rivalry, inclined to reciprocate them.

I need not say how easily the spark of jealousy, once kindled, is blown into a flame, and how naturally, in a coarse and ungoverned nature, it explodes in acts of violence and outrage.

'The bully' watched his opportunity, and contrived to provoke Ned Moran, while drinking in a public-house with a party of friends, into an altercation, in the course of which he failed not to put such insults upon his rival as manhood could not tolerate. Long Ned, though a simple, good-natured sort of fellow, was by no means deficient in spirit, and retorted in a tone of defiance which edified the more timid, and gave his opponent the opportunity he secretly coveted.

Bully Larkin challenged the heroic youth, whose pretty face he had privately consigned to the mangling and bloody discipline he was himself so capable of administering. The quarrel, which he had himself contrived to get up, to a certain degree covered the ill blood and malignant premeditation which inspired his proceedings, and Long Ned, being full of generous ire and whiskey punch, accepted the gauge of battle on the instant. The whole party, accompanied by a mob of idle men and boys, and in short by all who could snatch a moment from the calls of business, proceeded in slow procession through the old gate into the Phoenix Park, and mounting the hill overlooking the town, selected near its summit a level spot on which to decide the quarrel.

The combatants stripped, and a child might have seen in the contrast presented by the slight, lank form and limbs of the lad, and the muscular and massive build of his veteran antagonist, how desperate was the chance of poor Ned Moran.

'Seconds' and 'bottle-holders' – selected of course for their love of the game – were appointed, and 'the fight' commenced.

I will not shock my readers with a description of the cool-blooded butchery that followed. The result of the combat was what anybody might have predicted. At the eleventh round, poor Ned refused to 'give in';

the brawny pugilist, unhurt, in good wind, and pale with concentrated and as yet unslaked revenge, had the gratification of seeing his opponent seated upon his second's knee, unable to hold up his head, his left arm disabled; his face a bloody, swollen, and shapeless mass; his breast scarred and bloody, and his whole body panting and quivering with rage and exhaustion.

'Give in Ned, my boy,' cried more than one of the bystanders.

'Never, never,' shrieked he, with a voice hoarse and choking.

Time being 'up,' his second placed him on his feet again. Blinded with his own blood, panting and staggering, he presented but a helpless mark for the blows of his stalwart opponent. It was plain that a touch would have been sufficient to throw him to the earth. But Larkin had no notion of letting him off so easily. He closed with him without striking a blow (the effect of which, prematurely dealt, would have been to bring him at once to the ground, and so put an end to the combat), and getting his battered and almost senseless head under his arm, fast in that peculiar 'fix' known to the fancy pleasantly by the name of 'chancery,' he held him firmly, while with monotonous and brutal strokes he beat his fist, as it seemed, almost into his face. A cry of 'shame' broke from the crowd, for it was plain that the beaten man was now insensible, and supported only by the herculean arm of the bully. The round and the fight ended by his hurling him upon the ground, falling upon him at the same time with his knee upon his chest.

The bully rose, wiping the perspiration from his white face with his blood-stained hands, but Ned lay stretched and motionless upon the grass. It was impossible to get him upon his legs for another round. So he was carried down, just as he was, to the pond which then lay close to the old Park gate, and his head and body were washed beside it. Contrary to the belief of all he was not dead. He was carried home, and after some months to a certain extent recovered. But he never held up his head again, and before the year was over he had died of consumption. Nobody could doubt how the disease had been induced, but there was no actual proof to connect the cause and effect, and the ruffian Larkin escaped the vengeance of the law. A strange retribution, however, awaited him.

After the death of Long Ned, he became less quarrelsome than before, but more sullen and reserved. Some said 'he took it to heart', and others, that his conscience was not at ease about it. Be this as it may, however, his health did not suffer by reason of his presumed agitations, nor was his worldly prosperity marred by the blasting curses with which poor Moran's enraged mother pursued him; on the contrary, he had rather risen in the world, and obtained regular and well-remunerated employment from the Chief Secretary's gardener, at the other side of the Park. He still lived in Chapelizod, whither, on the close of his day's work, he used to return across the Fifteen Acres.

It was about three years after the catastrophe we have mentioned, and late in the autumn, when, one night, contrary to his habit, he did not appear at the house where he lodged, neither had he been seen anywhere, during the evening, in the village. His hours of return had been so very regular, that his absence excited considerable surprise, though, of course, no actual alarm; and, at the usual hour, the house was closed for the night, and the absent lodger consigned to the mercy of the elements, and the care of his presiding star. Early in the morning, however, he was found lying in a state of utter helplessness upon the slope immediately overlooking the Chapelizod gate. He had been smitten with a paralytic stroke: his right side was dead; and it was many weeks before he had recovered his speech sufficiently to make himself at all understood.

He then made the following relation: He had been detained, it appeared, later than usual, and darkness had closed before he commenced his homeward walk across the Park. It was a moonlit night, but masses of ragged clouds were slowly drifting across the heavens. He had not encountered a human figure, and no sounds but the softened rush of the wind sweeping through bushes and hollows met his ear. These wild and monotonous sounds, and the utter solitude which surrounded him, did not however, excite any of those uneasy sensations which are ascribed to superstition, although he said he did feel depressed, or, in his own phraseology, 'lonesome.' Just as he crossed the brow of the hill which shelters the town of Chapelizod, the moon shone out for some moments with unclouded lustre, and his eye, which happened to wander by the shadowy enclosures which lay at the foot of the slope, was arrested by the sight of a human figure climbing, with all the haste of one pursued, over the churchyard wall, and running up the steep ascent directly towards him. Stories of 'resurrectionists' crossed his recollection, as he observed this suspicious-looking figure. But he began, momentarily, to be aware with a sort of fearful instinct which he could not explain, that the running figure was directing his steps, with a sinister purpose, towards himself.

The form was that of a man with a loose coat about him, which, as he ran, he disengaged, and as well as Larkin could see, for the moon was again wading in clouds, threw from him. The figure thus advanced until within some two score yards of him, it arrested its speed, and approached with a loose, swaggering gait. The moon again shone out bright and clear, and, gracious God! what was the spectacle before him? He saw as distinctly as if he had been presented there in the flesh, Ned Moran, himself, stripped naked from the waist upward, as if for pugilistic combat, and drawing towards him in silence. Larkin would have shouted, prayed, cursed, fled across the Park, but he was absolutely powerless; the apparition stopped within a few steps, and leered on him with a ghastly mimicry of the defiant stare with which pugilists strive to cow one another before combat. For a time, which he could not so much as conjecture, he was held in the fascination of that unearthly gaze, and at last the thing, whatever it was, on a sudden swaggered close up to him with extended palms. With an impulse of horror, Larkin put out his hand to keep the figure off, and their palms touched – at least, so he believed – for a thrill of unspeakable agony, running through his arm, pervaded his entire frame, and he fell senseless to the earth.

Though Larkin lived for many years after, his punishment was terrible. He was incurably maimed; and being unable to work, he was forced, for existence, to beg alms of those who had once feared and flattered him. He suffered, too, increasingly, under his own horrible interpretation of the preternatural encounter which was the beginning of all his miseries. It was vain to endeavour to shake his faith in the reality of the apparition, and equally vain, as some compassionately did, to try to persuade him that the greeting with which his vision closed was intended, while inflicting a temporary trial, to signify a compensating reconciliation.

'No, no,' he used to say, 'all won't do. I know the meaning of it well enough; it is a challenge to meet him in the other world – in Hell, where I am going – that's what it means, and nothing else.'

And so, miserable and refusing comfort, he lived on for some years, and then died, and was buried in the same narrow churchyard which contains the remains of his victim.

I need hardly say, how absolute was the faith of the honest inhabitants, at the time when I heard the story, in the reality of the preternatural summons which, through the portals of terror, sickness, and misery, had summoned Bully Larkin to his long, last home, and that, too, upon the very ground on which he had signalised the guiltiest triumph of his violent and vindictive career.

I recollect another story of the preternatural sort, which made no small sensation, some five-and-thirty years ago, among the good gossips of the town; and, with your leave, courteous reader, I shall relate it.

Those who remember Chapelizod a quarter of a century ago, or more, may possibly recollect the parish sexton. Bob Martin was held much in awe by truant boys who sauntered into the churchyard on Sundays, to read the tombstones, or play leap frog over them, or climb the ivy in search of bats or sparrows' nests, or peep into the mysterious aperture under the eastern window, which opened a dim perspective of descending steps losing themselves among profounder darkness, where lidless coffins gaped horribly among tattered velvet, bones, and dust, which time and mortality had strewn there. Of such horribly curious, and otherwise enterprising juveniles, Bob was, of course, the special scourge and terror. But terrible as was the official aspect of the sexton, and repugnant as his lank form, clothed in rusty, sable vesture, his small, frosty visage, suspicious grey eyes, and rusty, brown scratch-wig, might appear to all notions of genial frailty; it was yet true, that Bob Martin's severe morality sometimes nodded, and that Bacchus did not always solicit him in vain.

Bob had a curious mind, a memory well stored with 'merry tales', and tales of terror. His profession familiarised him with graves and goblins, and his tastes with weddings, wassail, and sly frolics of all sorts. And as his personal recollections ran back nearly three score years into the perspective of the village history, his fund of local anecdote was copious, accurate, and edifying.

As his ecclesiastical revenues were by no means considerable, he was not unfrequently obliged, for the indulgence of his tastes, to arts which were, at the best, undignified.

He frequently invited himself when his entertainers had forgotten to do so; he dropped in accidentally upon small drinking parties of his acquaintance in public-houses, and entertained them with stories, queer or terrible, from his inexhaustible reservoir, never scrupling to accept an acknowledgment in the shape of hot whiskey-punch, or whatever else was going.

There was at that time a certain atrabilious publican, called Philip Slaney, established in a shop nearly opposite the old turnpike. This man was not, when left to himself, immoderately given to drinking; but being naturally of a saturnine complexion, and his spirits constantly requiring a fillip, he acquired a prodigious liking for Bob Martin's company. The sexton's society, in fact, gradually became the solace of his existence, and he seemed to lose his constitutional melancholy in the fascination of his sly jokes and marvellous stories.

This intimacy did not redound to the prosperity or reputation of the convivial allies. Bob Martin drank a good deal more punch than was good for his health, or consistent with the character of an ecclesiastical functionary. Philip Slaney, too, was drawn into similar indulgences, for it was hard to resist the genial seductions of his gifted companion; and as he was obliged to pay for both, his purse was believed to have suffered even more than his head and liver.

Be this as it may, Bob Martin had the credit of having made a drunkard of 'black Phil Slaney' – for by this cognomen was he distinguished; and Phil Slaney had also the reputation of having made the sexton, if possible, a 'bigger bliggard' than ever. Under these circumstances, the accounts of the concern opposite the turnpike became somewhat entangled; and it came to pass one drowsy summer morning, the weather being at once sultry and cloudy, that Phil Slaney went into a small back parlour, where he kept his books, and which commanded, through its dirty window-panes, a full view of a dead wall, and having bolted the door, he took a loaded pistol, and clapping the muzzle in his mouth, blew the upper part of his skull through the ceiling.

This horrid catastrophe shocked Bob Martin extremely; and partly on this account, and partly because having been, on several late occasions, found at night in a state of abstraction, bordering on insensibility, upon the high road, he had been threatened with dismissal; and, as some said, partly also because of the difficulty of finding anybody to 'treat' him as poor Phil Slaney used to do, he for a time forswore alcohol in all its combinations, and became an eminent example of temperance and sobriety.

Bob observed his good resolutions, greatly to the comfort of his wife, and the edification of the neighbourhood, with tolerable punctuality. He was seldom tipsy, and never drunk, and was greeted by the better part of society with all the honours of the prodigal son.

Now it happened, about a year after the grisly event we have mentioned, that the curate having received, by the post, due notice of a funeral to be consummated in the churchyard of Chapelizod, with certain instructions respecting the site of the grave, despatched a summons for Bob Martin, with a view to communicate to that functionary these official details.

It was a lowering autumn night: piles of lurid thunderclouds, slowly rising from the earth, had loaded the sky with a solemn and boding canopy of storm. The growl of the distant thunder was heard afar off upon the dull, still air, and all nature seemed, as it were, hushed and cowering under the oppressive influence of the approaching tempest.

It was past nine o'clock when Bob, putting on his official coat of seedy black, prepared to attend his professional superior.

'Bobby, darlin',' said his wife, before she delivered the hat she held in her hand to his keeping, 'sure you won't, Bobby, darlin' – you won't – you know what.'

'I *don't* know what,' he retorted, smartly, grasping at his hat.

'You won't be throwing up the little finger, Bobby, acushla?' she said, evading his grasp.

'Arrah, why would I, woman? there, give me my hat, will you?'

'But won't you promise me, Bobby darlin' – won't you, alanna?'

'Ay, ay, to be sure I will – why not? – there, give me my hat, and let me go.'

'Ay, but you're not promisin', Bobby, mavourneen; you're not promisin' all the time.'

'Well, divil carry me if I drink a drop till I come back again,' said the sexton, angrily; 'will that do you? And *now* will you give me my hat?'

'Here it is, darlin',' she said, 'and God send you safe back.'

And with this parting blessing she closed the door upon his retreating figure, for it was now quite dark, and resumed her knitting till his return, very much relieved; for she thought he had of late been oftener tipsy than was consistent with his thorough reformation, and feared the allurements of the half-dozen 'publics' which he had at that time to pass on his way to the other end of the town.

They were still open, and exhaled a delicious reek of whiskey, as Bob glided wistfully by them; but he stuck his hands in his pockets and looked the other way, whistling resolutely, and filling his mind with the image of the curate and anticipations of his coming fee. Thus he steered his morality safely through these rocks of offence, and reached the curate's lodging in safety.

He had, however, an unexpected sick call to attend, and was not at home, so that Bob Martin had to sit in the hall and amuse himself with the devil's tattoo until his return. This, unfortunately, was very long delayed, and it must have been fully twelve o'clock when Bob Martin set out upon his homeward way. By this time the storm had gathered to a pitchy darkness, the bellowing thunder was heard among the rocks and hollows of the Dublin mountains, and the pale, blue lightning shone upon the staring fronts of the houses.

By this time, too, every door was closed; but as Bob trudged homeward, his eye mechanically sought the public-house which had once belonged to Phil Slaney. A faint light was making its way through the shutters and the glass panes over the doorway, which made a sort of dull, foggy halo about the front of the house.

As Bob's eyes had become accustomed to the obscurity by this time, the light in question was quite sufficient to enable him to see a man in a sort of loose riding-coat seated upon a bench which, at that time, was fixed under the window of the house. He wore his hat very much over his eyes, and was smoking a long pipe. The outline of a glass and a quart bottle were also dimly traceable beside him; and a large horse saddled, but faintly discernible, was patiently awaiting his master's leisure.

There was something odd, no doubt, in the appearance of a traveller refreshing himself at such an hour in the open street; but the sexton accounted for it easily by supposing that, on the closing of the house for the night, he had taken what remained of his refection to the place where he was now discussing it alfresco.

At another time Bob might have saluted the stranger as he passed with a friendly 'good-night'; but, somehow, he was out of humour and in no genial mood, and was about passing without any courtesy of the sort, when the stranger, without taking the pipe from his mouth, raised the bottle, and with it beckoned him familiarly, while, with a sort of lurch of the head and shoulders, and at the same time shifting his seat to the end of the bench, he pantomimically invited him to share his seat and his cheer. There was a divine fragrance of whiskey about the spot, and Bob half relented; but he remembered his promise just as he began to waver, and said: 'No, I thank you, sir, I can't stop tonight.'

The stranger beckoned with vehement welcome, and pointed to the vacant space on the seat beside him.

'I thank you for your polite offer,' said Bob, 'but it's what I'm too late as it is, and haven't time to spare, so I wish you a good-night.'

The traveller jingled the glass against the neck of the bottle, as if to intimate that he might at least swallow a dram without losing time. Bob was mentally quite of the same opinion; but, though his mouth watered, he remembered his promise, and shaking his head with incorruptible resolution, walked on.

The stranger, pipe in mouth, rose from his bench, the bottle in one hand, and the glass in the other, and followed at the Sexton's heels, his dusky horse keeping close in his wake.

There was something suspicious and unaccountable in this importunity.

Bob quickened his pace, but the stranger followed close. The sexton began to feel queer, and turned about. His pursuer was behind, and still inviting him with impatient gestures to taste his liquor.

'I told you before,' said Bob, who was both angry and frightened, 'that I would not taste it, and that's enough. I don't want to have anything to say to you or your bottle; and in God's name,' he added, more vehemently, observing that he was approaching still closer, 'fall back and don't be tormenting me this way.'

These words, as it seemed, incensed the stranger, for he shook the bottle with violent menace at Bob Martin; but, notwithstanding this gesture of defiance, he suffered the distance between them to increase. Bob, however, beheld him dogging him still in the distance, for his pipe shed a wonderful red glow, which duskily illuminated his entire figure like the lurid atmosphere of a meteor.

'I wish the devil had his own, my boy,' muttered the excited sexton, 'and I know well enough where you'd be.'

The next time he looked over his shoulder, to his dismay he observed the importunate stranger as close as ever upon his track.

'Confound you,' cried the man of skulls and shovels, almost beside himself with rage and horror, 'what is it you want of me?'

The stranger appeared more confident, and kept wagging his head and extending both glass and bottle toward him as he drew near, and Bob Martin heard the horse snorting as it followed in the dark.

'Keep it to yourself, whatever it is, for there is neither grace nor luck about you,' cried Bob Martin, freezing with terror; 'leave me alone, will you.'

And he fumbled in vain among the seething confusion of his ideas for a prayer or an exorcism. He quickened his pace almost to a run; he was now close to his own door, under the impending bank by the river side.

'Let me in, let me in, for God's sake; Molly, open the door,' he cried, as he ran to the threshold, and leant his back against the plank. His pursuer confronted him upon the road; the pipe was no longer in his mouth, but the dusky red glow still lingered round him. He uttered some inarticulate cavernous sounds, which were wolfish and indescribable, while he seemed employed in pouring out a glass from the bottle.

The sexton kicked with all his force against the door, and cried at the same time with a despairing voice.

'In the name of God Almighty, once for all, leave me alone.'

His pursuer furiously flung the contents of the bottle at Bob Martin; but instead of fluid it issued out in a stream of flame, which expanded and whirled round them, and for a moment they were both enveloped in a faint blaze; at the same instant a sudden gust whisked off the stranger's hat, and the sexton beheld that his skull was roofless. For an instant he beheld the gaping aperture, black and shattered, and then he fell senseless into his own doorway, which his affrighted wife had just unbarred.

I need hardly give my reader the key to this most intelligible and authentic narrative. The traveller was acknowledged by all to have been the spectre of the suicide, called up by the Evil One to tempt the convivial sexton into a violation of his promise, sealed, as it was, by an imprecation. Had he succeeded, no doubt the dusky steed, which Bob had seen saddled in attendance, was destined to have carried back a double burden to the place from whence he came.

As an attestation of the reality of this visitation, the old thorn tree which overhung the doorway was found in the morning to have been blasted with the infernal fires which had issued from the bottle, just as if a thunderbolt had scorched it.

The moral of the above tale is upon the surface, apparent, and, so to speak, *self-acting* – a circumstance which happily obviates the necessity of our discussing it together. Taking our leave, therefore, of honest Bob Martin, who now sleeps soundly in the same solemn dormitory where, in his day, he made so many beds for others, I come to a legend of the Royal Irish Artillery, whose headquarters were for so long a time in the town of Chapelizod. I don't mean to say that I cannot tell a great many more stories, equally authentic and marvellous, touching this old town;

but as I may possibly have to perform a like office for other localities, and as Anthony Poplar is known, like Atropos, to carry a shears, wherewith to snip across all 'yarns' which exceed reasonable bounds, I consider it, on the whole, safer to despatch the traditions of Chapelizod with one tale more.

Let me, however, first give it a name; for an author can no more despatch a tale without a title, than an apothecary can deliver his physic without a label. We shall, therefore, call it –

THE SPECTRE LOVERS

There lived some fifteen years since in a small and ruinous house, little better than a hovel, an old woman who was reported to have considerably exceeded her eightieth year, and who rejoiced in the name of Alice, or popularly, Ally Moran. Her society was not much courted, for she was neither rich, nor, as the reader may suppose, beautiful. In addition to a lean cur and a cat she had one human companion, her grandson, Peter Brien, whom, with laudable good nature, she had supported from the period of his orphanage down to that of my story, which finds him in his twentieth year. Peter was a good-natured slob of a fellow, much more addicted to wrestling, dancing, and lovemaking, than to hard work, and fonder of whiskey punch than good advice. His grandmother had a high opinion of his accomplishments, which indeed was but natural, and also of his genius, for Peter had of late years begun to apply his mind to politics; and as it was plain that he had a mortal hatred of honest labour, his grandmother predicted, like a true fortune-teller, that he was born to marry an heiress, and Peter himself (who had no mind to forego his freedom even on such terms) that he was destined to find a pot of gold. Upon one point both agreed, that being unfitted by the peculiar bias of his genius for work, he was to acquire the immense fortune to which his merits entitled him by means of a pure run of good luck. This solution of Peter's future had the double effect of reconciling both himself and his grandmother to his idle courses, and also of maintaining that even flow of hilarious spirits which made him everywhere welcome, and which was in truth the natural result of his consciousness of approaching affluence.

It happened one night that Peter had enjoyed himself to a very late hour with two or three choice spirits near Palmerstown. They had talked politics and love, sung songs, and told stories, and, above all, had swallowed, in the chastened disguise of punch, at least a pint of good whiskey, every man.

It was considerably past one o'clock when Peter bid his companions goodbye, with a sigh and a hiccough, and lighting his pipe set forth on his solitary homeward way.

The bridge of Chapelizod was pretty nearly the midway point of his night march, and from one cause or another his progress was rather slow, and it was past two o'clock by the time he found himself leaning over its old battlements, and looking up the river, over whose winding current and wooded banks the soft moonlight was falling.

The cold breeze that blew lightly down the stream was grateful to him. It cooled his throbbing head, and he drank it in at his hot lips. The scene, too, had, without his being well sensible of it, a secret fascination. The village was sunk in the profoundest slumber, not a mortal stirring, not a sound afloat, a soft haze covered it all, and the fairy moonlight hovered over the entire landscape.

In a state between rumination and rapture, Peter continued to lean over the battlements of the old bridge, and as he did so he saw, or fancied he saw, emerging one after another along the river bank in the little gardens and enclosures in the rear of the street of Chapelizod, the queerest little white-washed huts and cabins he had ever seen there before. They had not been there that evening when he passed the bridge on the way to his merry tryst. But the most remarkable thing about it was the odd way in which these quaint little cabins showed themselves. First he saw one or two of them just with the corner of his eye, and when he looked full at them, strange to say, they faded away and disappeared. Then another and another came in view, but all in the same coy way, just appearing and gone again before he could well fix his gaze upon them; in a little while, however, they began to bear a fuller gaze, and he found, as it seemed to himself, that he was able by an effort of attention to fix the vision for a longer and a longer time, and when they waxed faint and nearly vanished, he had the power of recalling them into light and substance, until at last their vacillating indistinctness became less and less, and they assumed a permanent place in the moonlit landscape.

'Be the hokey,' said Peter, lost in amazement, and dropping his pipe into the river unconsciously, 'them is the quarist bits iv mud cabins I ever seen, growing up like musharoons in the dew of an evening, and poppin' up here and down again there, and up again in another place, like so many white rabbits in a warren; and there they stand at last as firm and fast as if they were there from the Deluge; bedad it's enough to make a man a'most believe in the fairies.'

This latter was a large concession from Peter, who was a bit of a free-thinker, and spoke contemptuously in his ordinary conversation of that class of agencies.

Having treated himself to a long last stare at these mysterious fabrics, Peter prepared to pursue his homeward way; having crossed the bridge and passed the mill, he arrived at the corner of the main street of the little town, and casting a careless look up the Dublin road, his eye was arrested by a most unexpected spectacle.

This was no other than a column of foot-soldiers, marching with perfect regularity towards the village, and headed by an officer on horseback. They were at the far side of the turnpike, which was closed; but much to his perplexity he perceived that they marched on through it without appearing to sustain the least check from that barrier.

On they came at a slow march; and what was most singular in the matter was, that they were drawing several cannons along with them; some held ropes, others spoked the wheels, and others again marched in front of the guns and behind them, with muskets shouldered, giving a stately character of parade and regularity to this, as it seemed to Peter, most unmilitary procedure.

It was owing either to some temporary defect in Peter's vision, or to some illusion attendant upon mist and moonlight, or perhaps to some other cause, that the whole procession had a certain waving and vapoury character which perplexed and tasked his eyes not a little. It was like the pictured pageant of a phantasmagoria reflected upon smoke. It was as if every breath disturbed it; sometimes it was blurred, sometimes obliterated; now here, now there. Sometimes, while the upper part was quite distinct, the legs of the column would nearly fade away or vanish outright, and then again they would come out into clear relief, marching on with measured tread, while the cocked hats and shoulders grew, as it were, transparent, and all but disappeared.

Notwithstanding these strange optical fluctuations, however, the column continued steadily to advance. Peter crossed the street from the corner near the old bridge, running on tiptoe, and with his body stooped to avoid observation, and took up a position upon the raised footpath in the shadow of the houses, where, as the soldiers kept the middle of the road, he calculated that he might, himself undetected, see them distinctly enough as they passed.

'What the div—, what on airth,' he muttered, checking the irreligious ejaculation with which he was about to start, for certain queer misgivings were hovering about his heart, notwithstanding the factitious courage of the whiskey bottle. 'What on airth is the manin' of all this? is it the French that's landed at last to give us a hand and help us in airnest to this blessed repale? If it is not them, I simply ask who the div—, I mane who on airth are they, for such sogers as them I never seen before in my born days?'

By this time the foremost of them were quite near, and truth to say they were the queerest soldiers he had ever seen in the course of his life. They wore long gaiters and leather breeches, three-cornered hats, bound with silver lace, long blue coats, with scarlet facings and linings, which latter were shown by a fastening which held together the two opposite corners of the skirt behind; and in front the breasts were in like manner connected at a single point, where and below which they sloped back, disclosing a long-flapped waistcoat of snowy whiteness; they had very large, long cross-belts, and wore enormous pouches of white leather hung extraordinarily low, and on each of which a little silver star was glittering. But what struck him as most grotesque and outlandish in their costume was their extraordinary display of shirt-frill in front, and of ruffle about their wrists, and the strange manner in which their hair was frizzled out and powdered under their hats, and clubbed up into great rolls behind. But one of the party was mounted. He rode a tall white horse, with high action and arching neck; he had a snow-white feather in his three-cornered hat, and his coat was shimmering all over with a profusion of silver lace. From these circumstances Peter concluded that he must be the commander of the detachment, and examined him as he passed attentively. He was a slight, tall man, whose legs did not half fill his leather breeches, and he appeared to be at the wrong side of sixty. He had a shrunken, weather-beaten, mulberry-coloured face, carried a large black patch over one eye, and turned neither to the right nor to the left, but rode on at the head of his men, with a grim, military inflexibility.

The countenances of these soldiers, officers as well as men, seemed all full of trouble, and, so to speak, scared and wild. He watched in vain for a single contented or comely face. They had, one and all, a melancholy and hang-dog look; and as they passed by, Peter fancied that the air grew cold and thrilling.

He had seated himself upon a stone bench, from which, staring with all his might, he gazed upon the grotesque and noiseless procession as it filed by him. Noiseless it was; he could neither hear the jingle of accoutrements, the tread of feet, nor the rumble of the wheels; and when the old colonel turned his horse a little, and made as though he were giving the word of command, and a trumpeter, with a swollen blue nose and white feather fringe round his hat, who was walking beside him, turned about and put his bugle to his lips, still Peter heard nothing, although it was plain the sound had reached the soldiers, for they instantly changed their front to three abreast.

'Botheration!' muttered Peter, 'is it deaf I'm growing?'

But that could not be, for he heard the sighing of the breeze and the rush of the neighbouring Liffey plain enough.

'Well,' said he, in the same cautious key, 'by the piper, this bangs Banagher fairly! It's either the Frinch army that's in it, come to take the town iv Chapelizod by surprise, an' makin' no noise for feard iv wakenin' the inhabitants; or else it's – it's – what it's – somethin' else. But, tundher-an-ouns, what's gone wid Fitzpatrick's shop across the way?'

The brown, dingy stone building at the opposite side of the street looked newer and cleaner than he had been used to see it; the front door of it stood open, and a sentry, in the same grotesque uniform, with shouldered musket, was pacing noiselessly to and fro before it. At the angle of this building, in like manner, a wide gate (of which Peter had no recollection whatever) stood open, before which, also,

a similar sentry was gliding, and into this gateway the
whole column gradually passed, and Peter finally lost
sight of it.

'I'm not asleep; I'm not dhramin',' said he, rubbing
his eyes, and stamping slightly on the pavement, to
assure himself that he was wide awake. 'It is a quare
business, whatever it is; an' it's not alone that, but
everything about the town looks strange to me.
There's Tresham's house new painted, bedad, an'
them flowers in the windies! An' Delany's house, too,
that had not a whole pane of glass in it this morning,
and scarce a slate on the roof of it! It is not possible it's
what it's dhrunk I am. Sure there's the big tree, and
not a leaf of it changed since I passed, and the stars
overhead, all right. I don't think it is in my eyes it is.'

And so looking about him, and every moment
finding or fancying new food for wonder, he walked
along the pavement, intending, without further delay,
to make his way home.

But his adventures for the night were not concluded. He had nearly reached the angle of the short
lane that leads up to the church, when for the first
time he perceived that an officer, in the uniform he
had just seen, was walking before, only a few yards in
advance of him.

The officer was walking along at an easy, swinging
gait, and carried his sword under his arm, and was
looking down on the pavement with an air of reverie.

In the very fact that he seemed unconscious of
Peter's presence, and disposed to keep his reflections
to himself, there was something reassuring. Besides,
the reader must please to remember that our hero
had a *quantum sufficit* of good punch before his
adventure commenced, and was thus fortified against

those qualms and terrors under which, in a more reasonable state of mind, he might not impossibly have sunk.

The idea of the French invasion revived in full power in Peter's fuddled imagination, as he pursued the nonchalant swagger of the officer.

'Be the powers iv Moll Kelly, I'll ax him what it is,' said Peter, with a sudden accession of rashness. 'He may tell me or not, as he plases, but he can't be offinded, anyhow.'

With this reflection having inspired himself, Peter cleared his voice and began: 'Captain!' said he, 'I ax your pardon, captain, an' maybe you'd be so condescindin' to my ignorance as to tell me, if it's plasin' to yer honour, whether your honour is not a Frinchman, if it's plasin' to you.'

This he asked, not thinking that, had it been as he suspected, not one word of his question in all probability would have been intelligible to the person he addressed. He was, however, understood, for the officer answered him in English, at the same time slackening his pace and moving a little to the side of the pathway, as if to invite his interrogator to take his place beside him.

'No; I am an Irishman,' he answered.

'I humbly thank your honour,' said Peter, drawing nearer – for the affability and the nativity of the officer encouraged him – 'but maybe your honour is in the *sarvice* of the King of France?'

'I serve the same King as you do,' he answered, with a sorrowful significance which Peter did not comprehend at the time; and, interrogating in turn, he asked, 'But what calls you forth at this hour of the day?'

'The *day*, your honour! – the night, you mane.'

'It was always our way to turn night into day, and we keep to it still,' remarked the soldier. 'But, no matter, come up here to my house; I have a job for you, if you wish to earn some money easily. I live here.'

As he said this, he beckoned authoritatively to Peter, who followed almost mechanically at his heels, and they turned up a little lane near the old Roman Catholic chapel, at the end of which stood, in Peter's time, the ruins of a tall, stone-built house.

Like everything else in the town, it had suffered a metamorphosis. The stained and ragged walls were now erect, perfect, and covered with pebble-dash; windowpanes glittered coldly in every window; the green hall-door had a bright brass knocker on it. Peter did not know whether to believe his previous or his present impressions; seeing is believing, and Peter could not dispute the reality of the scene. All the records of his memory seemed but the images of a tipsy dream. In a trance of astonishment and per-plexity, therefore, he submitted himself to the chances of his adventure.

The door opened, the officer beckoned with a melancholy air of authority to Peter, and entered. Our hero followed him into a sort of hall, which was very dark, but he was guided by the steps of the soldier, and, in silence, they ascended the stairs. The moonlight, which shone in at the lobbies, showed an old, dark wainscoting, and a heavy, oak banister. They passed by closed doors at different landing-places, but all was dark and silent as, indeed, became that late hour of the night.

Now they ascended to the topmost floor. The

captain paused for a minute at the nearest door, and, with a heavy groan, pushing it open, entered the room. Peter remained at the threshold. A slight female form in a sort of loose, white robe, and with a great deal of dark hair hanging loosely about her, was standing in the middle of the floor, with her back towards them.

The soldier stopped short before he reached her, and said, in a voice of great anguish, 'Still the same, sweet bird – sweet bird! still the same.' Whereupon, she turned suddenly, and threw her arms about the neck of the officer, with a gesture of fondness and despair, and her frame was agitated as if by a burst of sobs. He held her close to his breast in silence; and honest Peter felt a strange terror creep over him, as he witnessed these mysterious sorrows and endearments.

'Tonight, tonight – and then ten years more – ten long years another ten years.'

The officer and the lady seemed to speak these words together; her voice mingled with his in a musical and fearful wail, like a distant summer wind, in the dead hour of night, wandering through ruins. Then he heard the officer say, alone, in a voice of anguish: 'Upon me be it all, for ever, sweet birdie, upon me.'

And again they seemed to mourn together in the same soft and desolate wail, like sounds of grief heard from a great distance.

Peter was thrilled with horror, but he was also under a strange fascination; and an intense and dreadful curiosity held him fast.

The moon was shining obliquely into the room, and through the window Peter saw the familiar slopes of the Park, sleeping mistily under its shimmer. He could also see the furniture of the room with tolerable distinctness – the old balloon-backed chairs, a four-post bed in a sort of recess, and a rack against the wall, from which hung some military clothes and accoutrements; and the sight of all these homely objects reassured him somewhat, and he could not help feeling unspeakably curious to see the face of the girl whose long hair was streaming over the officer's epaulet.

Peter, accordingly, coughed, at first slightly, and afterward more loudly, to recall her from her reverie of grief; and, apparently, he succeeded; for she turned round, as did her companion, and both, standing hand in hand, gazed upon him fixedly. He thought he had never seen such large, strange eyes in all his life; and their gaze seemed to chill the very air around him, and arrest the pulses of his heart. An eternity of misery and remorse was in the shadowy faces that looked upon him.

If Peter had taken less whisky by a single thimbleful, it is probable that he would have lost heart altogether before these figures, which seemed every moment to assume a more marked and fearful, though hardly definable, contrast to ordinary human shapes.

'What is it you want with me?' he stammered.

'To bring my lost treasure to the churchyard,' replied the lady, in a silvery voice of more than mortal desolation.

The word 'treasure' revived the resolution of Peter, although a cold sweat was covering him, and his hair was bristling with horror; he believed, however, that he was on the brink of fortune, if he could but command nerve to brave the interview to its close.

'And where,' he gasped, 'is it hid – where will I find it?'

They both pointed to the sill of the window, through which the moon was shining at the far end of the room, and the soldier said: 'Under that stone.'

Peter drew a long breath, and wiped the cold dew from his face, preparatory to passing to the window, where he expected to secure the reward of his protracted terrors. But looking steadfastly at the window, he saw the faint image of a new-born child sitting upon the sill in the moonlight, with its little arms stretched toward him, and a smile so heavenly as he never beheld before.

At sight of this, strange to say, his heart entirely failed him, he looked on the figures that stood near, and beheld them gazing on the infantine form with a smile so guilty and distorted, that he felt as if he were entering alive among the scenery of hell, and shuddering, he cried in an irrepressible agony of horror: 'I'll have nothing to say with you, and nothing to do with you; I don't know what yez are or what yez want iv me, but let me go this minute, everyone of yez, in the name of God.'

With these words there came a strange rumbling and sighing about Peter's ears; he lost sight of everything, and felt that peculiar and not unpleasant sensation of falling softly, that sometimes supervenes in sleep, ending in a dull shock. After that he had neither dream nor consciousness till he wakened, chill and stiff, stretched between two piles of old rubbish, among the black and roofless walls of the ruined house.

We need hardly mention that the village had put on its wonted air of neglect and decay, or that Peter looked around him in vain for traces of those novelties which had so puzzled and distracted him upon the previous night.

'Ay, ay,' said his grandmother, removing her pipe, as he ended his description of the view from the bridge, 'sure enough I remember myself, when I was a slip of a girl, these little white cabins among the gardens by the river side. The artillery sogers that was married, or had not room in the barracks, used to be in them, but they're all gone long ago.'

'The Lord be merciful to us!' she resumed, when he had described the military procession, 'it's often I seen the regiment marchin' into the town, jist as you saw it last night, acushla. Oh, voch, but it makes my heart sore to think iv them days; they were pleasant times, sure enough; but is not it terrible, avick, to think its what it was the ghost of the rigiment you seen? The Lord betune us an' harm, for it was nothing else, as sure as I'm sittin' here.'

When he mentioned the peculiar physiognomy and figure of the old officer who rode at the head of the regiment: '*That*,' said the old crone, dogmatically, 'was ould Colonel Grimshaw, the Lord presarve us! he's buried in the churchyard iv Chapelizod, and well I remember him, when I was a young thing, an' a cross ould floggin' fellow he was wid the men, an' a devil's boy among the girls – rest his soul!'

'Amen!' said Peter; 'it's often I read his tombstone myself; but he's a long time dead.'

'Sure, I tell you he died when I was no more nor a slip iv a girl – the Lord betune us and harm!'

'I'm afeard it is what I'm not long for this world myself, afther seeing such a sight as that,' said Peter, fearfully.

'Nonsinse, avourneen,' retorted his grandmother, indignantly, though she had herself misgivings on the subject; 'sure there was Phil Doolan, the ferryman, that seen black Ann Scanlan in his own boat, and what harm ever kem of it?'

Peter proceeded with his narrative, but when he came to the description of the house, in which his adventure had had so sinister a conclusion, the old woman was at fault.

'I know the house and the ould walls well, an' I can remember the time there was a roof on it, and the doors an' windows in it, but it had a bad name about being haunted, but by who, or for what, I forget intirely.'

'Did you ever hear was there goold or silver there?' he enquired.

'No, no, avick, don't be thinking about the likes; take a fool's advice, and never go next or near them ugly black walls again the longest day you have to live; an' I'd take my davy, it's what it's the same word the priest himself I'd be afther sayin' to you if you wor to ax his raverence consarnin' it, for it's plain to be seen it was nothing good you seen there, and there's neither luck nor grace about it.'

Peter's adventure made no little noise in the neighbourhood, as the reader may well suppose; and a few evenings after it, being on an errand to old Major Vandeleur, who lived in a snug old fashioned house, close by the river, under a perfect bower of ancient trees, he was called on to relate the story in the parlour.

The Major was, as I have said, an old man; he was small, lean, and upright, with a mahogany complexion, and a wooden inflexibility of face; he was a man, besides, of few words, and if *he* was old, it follows plainly that his mother was older still. Nobody could guess or tell *how* old, but it was admitted that her own generation had long passed away, and that she had not a competitor left. She had French blood in her veins, and although she did not retain her charms quite so well as Ninon de l'Enclos, she was in full possession of all her mental activity, and talked quite enough for herself and the Major.

'So, Peter,' she said, 'you have seen the dear, old Royal Irish again in the streets of Chapelizod. Make him a tumbler of punch, Frank; and Peter, sit down, and while you take it let us have the story.'

Peter accordingly, seated near the door, with a tumbler of the nectarian stimulant steaming beside him, proceeded with marvellous courage, considering they had no light but the uncertain glare of the fire, to relate with minute particularity his awful adventure. The old lady listened at first with a smile of good-natured incredulity; her cross examination touching the drinking-bout at Palmerstown had been teasing, but as the narrative proceeded she became attentive, and at length absorbed, and once or twice she uttered ejaculations of pity or awe. When it was over, the old lady looked with a somewhat sad and stern abstraction on the table, patting her cat assiduously meanwhile, and then suddenly looking upon her son, the Major, she said; 'Frank, as sure as I live he has seen the wicked Captain Devereux.'

The Major uttered an inarticulate expression of wonder.

'The house was precisely that he has described. I have told you the story often, as I heard it from your dear grandmother, about the poor young lady he ruined, and the dreadful suspicion about the little baby. *She*, poor thing, died in that house heart-broken, and you know he was shot shortly after in a duel.'

This was the only light that Peter ever received respecting his adventure. It was supposed, however, that he still clung to the hope that treasure of some sort was hidden about the old house, for he was often seen lurking about its walls, and at last his fate overtook him, poor fellow, in the pursuit; for climbing near the summit one day, his holding gave way, and he fell upon the hard uneven ground, fracturing a leg and a rib, and after a short interval died, and he, like the other heroes of these true tales, lies buried in the little churchyard of Chapelizod.

SHERIDAN LE FANU

The Vision of Tom Chuff

At the edge of melancholy Catstean Moor, in the north of England, with half a dozen ancient poplar trees with rugged and hoary stems around, one smashed across the middle by a flash of lightning thirty summers before, and all by their great height dwarfing the abode near which they stand, there squats a rude stone house, with a thick chimney, a kitchen and bedroom on the ground floor, and a loft, accessible by a ladder, under the shingle roof, divided into two rooms.

Its owner was a man of ill repute. Tom Chuff was his name. A shock-headed, broad-shouldered, powerful man, though somewhat short, with lowering brows and a sullen eye. He was a poacher, and hardly made an ostensible pretence of earning his bread by any honest industry. He was a drunkard. He beat his wife, and led his children a life of terror and lamentation, when he was at home. It was a blessing to his frightened little family when he absented himself, as he sometimes did, for a week or more together.

On the night I speak of he knocked at the door with his cudgel at about eight o'clock. It was winter, and the night was very dark. Had the summons been that of a bogie from the moor, the inmates of this small house could hardly have heard it with greater terror.

His wife unbarred the door in fear and haste. Her hunchbacked sister stood by the hearth, staring toward the threshold. The children cowered behind.

Tom Chuff entered with his cudgel in his hand, without speaking, and threw himself into a chair opposite the fire. He had been away two or three days. He looked haggard, and his eyes were bloodshot. They knew he had been drinking.

Tom raked and knocked the peat fire with his stick, and thrust his feet close to it. He signed towards the little dresser, and nodded to his wife, and she knew he wanted a cup, which in silence she gave him. He pulled a bottle of gin from his coat-pocket, and nearly filling the teacup, drank off the dram at a few gulps.

He usually refreshed himself with two or three drams of this kind before beating the inmates of his house. His three little children, cowering in a corner, eyed him from under a table, as Jack did the ogre in the nursery tale. His wife, Nell, standing behind a chair, which she was ready to snatch up to meet the blow of the cudgel, which might be levelled at her at any moment, never took her eyes off him; and hunchbacked Mary showed the whites of a large pair of eyes, similarly employed, as she stood against the oaken press, her dark face hardly distinguishable in the distance from the brown panel behind it.

Tom Chuff was at his third dram, and had not yet spoken a word since his entrance, and the suspense was growing dreadful, when, on a sudden, he leaned back in his rude seat, the cudgel slipped from his hand, a change and a deathlike pallor came over his face.

For a while they all stared on; such was their fear of

him, they dared not speak or move, lest it should prove to have been but a doze, and Tom should wake up and proceed forthwith to gratify his temper and exercise his cudgel.

In a very little time, however, things began to look so odd, that they ventured, his wife and Mary, to exchange glances full of doubt and wonder. He hung so much over the side of the chair, that if it had not been one of cyclopean clumsiness and weight, he would have borne it to the floor. A leaden tint was darkening the pallor of his face. They were becoming alarmed, and finally braving everything his wife timidly said, 'Tom!' and then more sharply repeated it, and finally cried the appellative loudly, and again and again, with the terrified accompaniment, 'He's dying – he's dying!' her voice rising to a scream, as she found that neither it nor her plucks and shakings of him by the shoulder had the slightest effect in recalling him from his torpor.

And now from sheer terror of a new kind the children added their shrilly piping to the talk and cries of their seniors; and if anything could have called Tom up from his lethargy, it might have been the piercing chorus that made the rude chamber of the poacher's habitation ring again. But Tom continued unmoved, deaf, and stirless.

His wife sent Mary down to the village, hardly a quarter of a mile away, to implore of the doctor, for whose family she did duty as laundress, to come down and look at her husband, who seemed to be dying.

The doctor, who was a good-natured fellow, arrived. With his hat still on, he looked at Tom, examined him, and when he found that the emetic he had brought with him, on conjecture from Mary's

description, did not act, and that his lancet brought
no blood, and that he felt a pulseless wrist, he shook
his head, and inwardly thought: 'What the plague is
the woman crying for? Could she have desired a
greater blessing for her children and herself than the
very thing that has happened?'

Tom, in fact, seemed quite gone. At his lips no
breath was perceptible. The doctor could discover no
pulse. His hands and feet were cold, and the chill was
stealing up into his body.

The doctor, after a stay of twenty minutes, had
buttoned up his greatcoat again and pulled down his
hat, and told Mrs Chuff that there was no use in his
remaining any longer, when, all of a sudden, a little
rill of blood began to trickle from the lancet-cut in
Tom Chuff's temple.

'That's very odd,' said the doctor. 'Let us wait a
little.'

I must describe now the sensations which Tom
Chuff had experienced.

With his elbows on his knees, and his chin upon his
hands, he was staring into the embers, with his gin
beside him, when suddenly a swimming came in his
head, he lost sight of the fire, and a sound like one
stroke of a loud church bell smote his brain.

Then he heard a confused humming, and the
leaden weight of his head held him backward as he
sank in his chair, and consciousness quite forsook
him.

When he came to himself he felt chilled, and was
leaning against a huge leafless tree. The night was
moonless, and when he looked up he thought he had
never seen stars so large and bright, or sky so black.
The stars, too, seemed to blink down with longer

intervals of darkness, and fiercer and more dazzling emergence, and something, he vaguely thought, of the character of silent menace and fury.

He had a confused recollection of having come there, or rather of having been carried along, as if on men's shoulders, with a sort of rushing motion. But it was utterly indistinct; the imperfect recollection simply of a sensation. He had seen or heard nothing on his way.

He looked round. There was not a sign of a living creature near. And he began with a sense of awe to recognise the place.

The tree against which he had been leaning was one of the noble old beeches that surround at irregular intervals the churchyard of Shackleton, which spreads its green and wavy lap on the edge of the Moor of Catstean, at the opposite side of which stands the rude cottage in which he had just lost consciousness. It was six miles or more across the moor to his habitation, and the black expanse lay before him, disappearing dismally in the darkness. So that, looking straight before him, sky and land blended together in an undistinguishable and awful blank.

There was a silence quite unnatural over the place. The distant murmur of the brook, which he knew so well, was dead; not a whisper in the leaves above him; the air, earth, everything about and above was indescribably still; and he experienced that quaking of the heart that seems to portend the approach of something awful. He would have set out upon his return across the moor, had he not an undefined presentiment that he was waylaid by something he dared not pass.

The old grey church and tower of Shackleton stood

like a shadow in the rear. His eye had grown accustomed to the obscurity, and he could just trace its outline. There were no comforting associations in his mind connected with it; nothing but menace and misgiving. His early training in his lawless calling was connected with this very spot. Here his father used to meet two other poachers, and bring his son, then but a boy, with him.

Under the church porch, towards morning, they used to divide the game they had taken, and take account of the sales they had made on the previous day, and make partition of the money, and drink their gin. It was here he had taken his early lessons in drinking, cursing and lawlessness. His father's grave was hardly eight steps from the spot where he stood. In his present state of awful dejection, no scene on earth could have so helped to heighten his fear.

There was one object close by which added to his gloom. About a yard away, in rear of the tree, behind himself, and extending to his left, was an open grave, the mould and rubbish piled on the other side. At the head of this grave stood the beech tree; its columnar stem rose like a huge monumental pillar. He knew every line and crease on its smooth surface. The initial letters of his own name, cut in its bark long ago, had spread out and wrinkled like the grotesque capitals of a fanciful engraver, and now with a sinister significance overlooked the open grave, as if answering his mental question, 'Who for is t' grave cut?'

He felt still a little stunned, and there was a faint tremor in his joints that disinclined him to exert himself; and, further, he had a vague apprehension that take what direction he might, there was danger around him worse than that of staying where he was.

On a sudden the stars began to blink more fiercely, a faint wild light overspread for a minute the bleak landscape, and he saw approaching from the moor a figure at a kind of swinging trot, with now and then a zig-zag hop or two, such as men accustomed to cross such places make, to avoid the patches of slob or quag that meet them here and there. This figure resembled his father's, and like him, whistled through his finger by way of signal as he approached; but the whistle sounded not now shrilly and sharp, as in old times, but immensely far away, and seemed to sing strangely through Tom's head. From habit or from fear, in answer to the signal, Tom whistled as he used to do five-and-twenty years ago and more, although he was already chilled with an unearthly fear.

Like his father, too, the figure held up the bag that was in his left hand as he drew near, when it was his custom to call out to him what was in it. It did not reassure the watcher, you may be certain, when a shout unnaturally faint reached him, as the phantom dangled the bag in the air, and he heard with a faint distinctness the words, 'Tom Chuff's soul!'

Scarcely fifty yards away from the low churchyard fence at which Tom was standing, there was a wider chasm in the peat, which there threw up a growth of reeds and bulrushes, among which, as the old poacher used to do on a sudden alarm, the approaching figure suddenly cast itself down.

From the same patch of tall reeds and rushes emerged instantaneously what he at first mistook for the same figure creeping on all-fours, but what he soon perceived to be an enormous black dog with a rough coat like a bear's, which at first sniffed about, and then started towards him in what seemed to be a sportive amble, bouncing this way and that, but as it drew near it displayed a pair of fearful eyes that glowed like live coals, and emitted from the monstrous expanse of its jaws a terrifying growl.

This beast seemed on the point of seizing him, and Tom recoiled in panic and fell into the open grave behind him. The edge which he caught as he tumbled gave way, and down he went, expecting almost at the same instant to reach the bottom. But never was such a fall! Bottomless seemed the abyss! Down, down, down, with immeasurable and still increasing speed, through utter darkness, with hair streaming straight upward, breathless, he shot with a rush of air against him, the force of which whirled up his very arms, second after second, minute after minute, through the chasm downward he flew, the icy perspiration of horror covering his body, and suddenly, as he expected to be dashed into annihilation, his descent was in an instant arrested with a tremendous shock, which, however, did not deprive him of consciousness even for a moment.

He looked about him. The place resembled a smoke-stained cavern or catacomb, the roof of which, except for a ribbed arch here and there faintly visible, was lost in darkness. From several rude passages, like the galleries of a gigantic mine, which opened from this centre chamber, was very dimly emitted a dull glow as of charcoal, which was the only light by which he could imperfectly discern the objects immediately about him.

What seemed like a projecting piece of the rock, at the corner of one of these murky entrances, moved on a sudden, and proved to be a human figure, that beckoned to him. He approached, and saw his father.

He could barely recognise him, he was so monstrously altered.

'I've been looking for you, Tom. Welcome home, lad; come along to your place.'

Tom's heart sank as he heard these words, which were spoken in a hollow and, he thought, derisive voice that made him tremble. But he could not help accompanying the wicked spirit, who led him into a place, in passing which he heard, as it were from within the rock, dreadful cries and appeals for mercy.

'What is this?' said he.

'Never mind.'

'Who are they?'

'New-comers, like yourself, lad,' answered his father apathetically. 'They give over that work in time, finding it is no use.'

'What shall I do?' said Tom, in an agony.

'It's all one.'

'But what shall I do?' reiterated Tom, quivering in every joint and nerve.

'Grin and bear it, I suppose.'

'For God's sake, if ever you cared for me, as I am your own child, let me out of this!'

'There's no way out.'

'If there's a way in there's a way out, and for Heaven's sake let me out of this.'

But the dreadful figure made no further answer, and glided backwards by his shoulder to the rear; and others appeared in view, each with a faint red halo round it, staring on him with frightful eyes, images, all in hideous variety, of eternal fury or derision. He was growing mad, it seemed, under the stare of so many eyes, increasing in number and drawing closer every moment, and at the same time myriads and myriads of voices were calling him by his name, some far away, some near, some from one point, some from another, some from behind, close to his ears. These cries were increased in rapidity and multitude, and mingled with laughter, with flitting blasphemies, with broken insults and mockeries, succeeded and obliterated by others, before he could half catch their meaning.

All this time, in proportion to the rapidity and urgency of these dreadful sights and sounds, the epilepsy of terror was creeping up to his brain, and with a long and dreadful scream he lost consciousness.

When he recovered his senses, he found himself in a small stone chamber, vaulted above, and with a ponderous door. A single point of light in the wall, with a strange brilliancy illuminated this cell.

Seated opposite to him was a venerable man with a snowy beard of immense length; an image of awful purity and severity. He was dressed in a coarse robe, with three large keys suspended from his girdle. He might have filled one's idea of an ancient porter of a city gate; such spiritual cities, I should say, as John Bunyan loved to describe.

This old man's eyes were brilliant and awful, and fixed on him as they were, Tom Chuff felt himself helplessly in his power. At length he spoke: 'The command is given to let you forth for one trial more. But if you are found again drinking with the drunken, and beating your fellow-servants, you shall return through the door by which you came, and go out no more.'

With these words the old man took him by the wrist and led him through the first door, and then unlocking one that stood in the cavern outside, he struck Tom Chuff sharply on the shoulder, and the door shut behind him with a sound that boomed peal after peal of thunder near and far away, and all round and above, till it rolled off gradually into silence. It was totally dark, but there was a fanning of fresh cool air that overpowered him. He felt that he was in the upper world again.

In a few minutes he began to hear voices which he knew, and first a faint point of light appeared before his eyes, and gradually he saw the flame of the candle, and, after that, the familiar faces of his wife and children, and he heard them faintly when they spoke to him, although he was as yet unable to answer.

He also saw the doctor, like an isolated figure in the dark, and heard him say: 'There, now, you have him back. He'll do, I think.'

His first words, when he could speak and saw clearly all about him, and felt the blood on his neck and shirt, were: 'Wife, forgie me. I'm a changed man. Send for 't sir.'

Which last phrase means, 'Send for the clergyman.'

When the vicar came and entered the little bedroom where the scared poacher, whose soul had died within him, was lying, still sick and weak, in his bed, and with a spirit that was prostrate with terror, Tom Chuff feebly beckoned the rest from the room, and, the door being closed, the good parson heard the strange confession, and with equal amazement the man's earnest and agitated vows of amendment, and his helpless appeals to him for support and counsel.

These, of course, were kindly met; and the visits of the rector, for some time, were frequent.

One day, when he took Tom Chuff's hand on bidding him goodbye, the sick man held it still, and said: 'Ye'r vicar o' Shackleton, sir, and if I sud dee, ye'll promise me a'e thing, as I a promised ye a many. I a said I'll never gie wife, nor barn, nor folk o' no sort, skelp nor sizzup more, and ye'll know o' me no more among the sipers. Nor never will Tom draw trigger, nor set a snare again, but in an honest way, and after that ye'll no make it a bootless bene for me, but bein', as I say, vicar o' Shackleton, and able to do as ye list, ye'll no let them bury me within twenty good yerd-wands measure o' the a'd beech trees that's round the churchyard of Shackleton.'

'I see; you would have your grave, when your time really comes, a good way from the place where lay the grave you dreamed of.'

'That's jest it. I'd lie at the bottom o' a marl-pit liefer! And I'd be laid in anither churchyard just to be shut o' my fear o' that, but that a' my kinsfolk is buried beyond in Shackleton, and ye'll gie me yer promise, and no break yer word.'

'I do promise, certainly. I'm not likely to outlive you; but, if I should, and still be vicar of Shackleton, you shall be buried somewhere as near the middle of the churchyard as we can find space.'

'That'll do.'

And so content they parted.

The effect of the vision upon Tom Chuff was powerful, and promised to be lasting. With a sore effort he exchanged his life of desultory adventure and comparative idleness for one of regular industry. He gave up drinking; he was as kind as an originally surly nature would allow to his wife and family; he went to church; in fine weather they crossed the moor to Shackleton Church; the vicar said he came there to look at the scenery of his vision, and to fortify his good resolutions by the reminder.

Impressions upon the imagination, however, are but transitory, and a bad man acting under fear is not a free agent; his real character does not appear. But as the images of the imagination fade, and the action of fear abates, the essential qualities of the man reassert themselves.

So, after a time, Tom Chuff began to grow weary of his new life; he grew lazy, and people began to say that he was catching hares, and pursuing his old contraband way of life, under the rose.

He came home one hard night, with signs of the bottle in his thick speech and violent temper. Next day he was sorry, or frightened, at all events repentant, and for a week or more something of the old horror returned, and he was once more on his good behaviour. But in a little time came a relapse, and another repentance, and then a relapse again, and gradually the return of old habits and the flooding in of all his old way of life, with more violence and gloom, in proportion as the man was alarmed and exasperated by the remembrance of his despised, but terrible, warning.

With the old life returned the misery of the cottage. The smiles, which had begun to appear with the unwonted sunshine, were seen no more. Instead, returned to his poor wife's face the old pale and heartbroken look. The cottage lost its neat and cheerful air, and the melancholy of neglect was visible. Sometimes at night were overheard, by a chance passer-by, cries and sobs from that ill-omened dwelling. Tom Chuff was now often drunk, and not very often at home, except when he came in to sweep away his poor wife's earnings.

Tom had long lost sight of the honest old parson. There was shame mixed with his degradation. He had grace enough left when he saw the thin figure of 't' sir' walking along the road to turn out of his way and avoid meeting him. The clergyman shook his head, and sometimes groaned, when his name was mentioned. His horror and regret were more for the poor wife than for the relapsed sinner, for her case was pitiable indeed.

Her brother, Jack Everton, coming over from Hexley, having heard stories of all this, determined to beat Tom, for his ill-treatment of his sister, within an inch of his life. Luckily, perhaps, for all concerned, Tom happened to be away upon one of his long excursions, and poor Nell besought her brother, in extremity of terror, not to interpose between them. So he took his leave and went home muttering and sulky.

Now it happened a few months later that Nelly Chuff fell sick. She had been ailing, as heartbroken people do, for a good while. But now the end had come.

There was a coroner's inquest when she died, for the doctor had doubts as to whether a blow had not, at least, hastened her death. Nothing certain, however, came of the enquiry. Tom Chuff had left his home more than two days before his wife's death. He was absent upon his lawless business still when the coroner had held his quest.

Jack Everton came over from Hexley to attend the dismal obsequies of his sister. He was more incensed than ever with the wicked husband, who, one way or other, had hastened Nelly's death. The inquest had closed early in the day. The husband had not appeared.

An occasional companion – perhaps I ought to say accomplice – of Chuff's happened to turn up. He had left him on the borders of Westmoreland, and said he would probably be home next day. But Everton affected not to believe it. Perhaps it was to Tom Chuff, he suggested, a secret satisfaction to crown the history of his bad married life with the scandal of his absence from the funeral of his neglected and abused wife.

Everton had taken on himself the direction of the melancholy preparations. He had ordered a grave to be opened for his sister beside her mother's, in Shackleton churchyard, at the other side of the moor. For the purpose, as I have said, of marking the callous neglect of her husband, he determined that the funeral should take place that night. His brother Dick had accompanied him, and they and his sister, with Mary and the children, and a couple of the neighbours, formed the humble cortège.

Jack Everton said he would wait behind, on the chance of Tom Chuff coming in time, that he might tell him what had happened, and make him cross the moor with him to meet the funeral. His real object, I think, was to inflict upon the villain the drubbing he had so long wished to give him. Anyhow, he was resolved, by crossing the moor, to reach the churchyard in time to anticipate the arrival of the funeral, and to have a few words with the vicar, clerk, and sexton, all old friends of his, for the parish of Shackleton was the place of his birth and early recollections.

But Tom Chuff did not appear at his house that night. In surly mood, and without a shilling in his pocket, he was making his way homeward. His bottle of gin, his last investment, half emptied, with its neck protruding, as usual on such returns, was in his coat-pocket.

His way home lay across the moor of Catstean, and the point at which he best knew the passage was from the churchyard of Shackleton. He vaulted the low wall that forms its boundary, and strode across the graves, and over many a flat, half-buried tombstone, toward the side of the churchyard next Catstean Moor.

The old church of Shackleton and its tower rose, close at his right, like a black shadow against the sky. It was a moonless night, but clear. By this time he had reached the low boundary wall, at the other side, that overlooks the wide expanse of Catstean Moor. He stood by one of the huge old beech trees, and leaned his back to its smooth trunk. Had he ever seen the sky look so black, and the stars shine out and blink so vividly? There was a deathlike silence over the scene, like the hush that precedes thunder in sultry weather. The expanse before him was lost in utter blackness. A strange quaking unnerved his heart. It was the sky and scenery of his vision! The same horror and misgiving. The same invincible fear of venturing from the spot where he stood. He would have prayed if he dared. His sinking heart demanded a restorative of some sort, and he grasped the bottle in his coat-pocket. Turning to his left, as he did so, he saw the piled-up mould of an open grave that gaped with its head close to the base of the great tree against which he was leaning.

He stood aghast. His dream was returning and slowly enveloping him. Everything he saw was weaving itself into the texture of his vision. The chill of horror stole over him.

A faint whistle came shrill and clear over the moor, and he saw a figure approaching at a swinging trot, with a zig-zag course, hopping now here and now there, as men do over a surface where one has need to choose their steps. Through the jungle of reeds and bulrushes in the foreground this figure advanced; and with the same unaccountable impulse that had coerced him in his dream, he answered the whistle of the advancing figure.

On that signal it directed its course straight toward him. It mounted the low wall, and, standing there, looked into the graveyard.

'Who med answer?' challenged the new-comer from his post of observation.

'Me,' answered Tom.

'Who are you?' repeated the man upon the wall.

'Tom Chuff; and who's this grave cut for?' He answered in a savage tone, to cover the secret shudder of his panic.

'I'll tell you that, ye villain!' answered the stranger, descending from the wall, 'I a' looked for you far and near, and waited long, and now you're found at last.'

Not knowing what to make of the figure that advanced upon him, Tom Chuff recoiled, stumbled, and fell backward into the open grave. He caught at the sides as he fell, but without retarding his fall.

An hour after, when lights came with the coffin, the corpse of Tom Chuff was found at the bottom of the grave. He had fallen direct upon his head, and his neck was broken. His death must have been simultaneous with his fall. Thus far his dream was accomplished.

It was his brother-in-law who had crossed the moor and approached the churchyard of Shackleton, exactly in the line which the image of his father had seemed to take in his strange vision. Fortunately for Jack Everton, the sexton and clerk of Shackleton church were, unseen by him, crossing the churchyard toward the grave of Nelly Chuff, just as Tom the poacher stumbled and fell. Suspicion of direct violence would otherwise have inevitably attached to the exasperated brother. As it was, the catastrophe was followed by no legal consequences.

The good vicar kept his word, and the grave of Tom Chuff is still pointed out by the old inhabitants of Shackleton pretty nearly in the centre of the churchyard. This conscientious compliance with the entreaty of the panic-stricken man as to the place of his sepulture gave a horrible and mocking emphasis to the strange combination by which fate had defeated his precaution, and fixed the place of his death.

The story was for many a year, and we believe still is, told round many a cottage hearth, and though it appeals to what many would term superstition, it yet sounded, in the ears of a rude and simple audience, a thrilling, and, let us hope, not altogether fruitless homily.

W. B. YEATS

The Curse

One summer night, when there was peace, a score
of Puritan troopers, under the pious Sir Frederick
Hamilton, broke through the door of the Abbey of
the White Friars which stood over the Gara Lough at
Sligo. As the door fell with a crash they saw a little
knot of friars, gathered about the altar, their white
habits glimmering in the steady light of the holy
candles. All the monks were kneeling except the
abbot, who stood upon the altar steps with a great
brazen crucifix in his hand. 'Shoot them!' cried Sir
Frederick Hamilton, but none stirred, for all were
new converts and feared the crucifix and the holy
candles. The white lights from the altar threw the
shadows of the troopers up on to roof and wall. As
the troopers moved about, the shadows began a
fantastic dance among the corbels and the memorial
tablets. For a little while all was silent, and then five
troopers who were the bodyguard of Sir Frederick
Hamilton lifted their muskets and shot down five of
the friars. The noise and the smoke drove away the
mystery of the pale altar lights and the other troopers
took courage and began to strike. In a moment the
friars lay about the altar steps, their white habits
stained with blood. 'Set fire to the house!' cried Sir
Frederick Hamilton, and at his word one went out

and came in again carrying a heap of dry straw and piled it against the western wall, and, having done this, fell back, for the fear of the crucifix and of the holy candles was still in his heart. Seeing this, the five troopers who were Sir Frederick Hamilton's body-guard darted forward, and taking each a holy candle set the straw in a blaze. The red tongues of fire rushed up and flickered from corbel to corbel and from tablet to tablet, and crept along the floor, setting in a blaze the seats and benches. The dance of the shadows passed away, and the dance of the fires began. The troopers fell back towards the door in the southern wall, and watched those yellow dancers springing hither and thither.

For a time the altar stood safe and apart in the midst of its white light; the eyes of the troopers turned upon it. The abbot whom they had thought dead had risen to his feet and now stood before it with the crucifix lifted in both hands high above his head. Suddenly he cried with a loud voice, 'Woe unto all who smite those who dwell within the Light of the Lord, for they shall wander among the ungovernable shadows, and follow the ungovernable fires!' And having so cried he fell on his face dead, and the brazen crucifix rolled down the steps of the altar. The smoke had now grown very thick, so that it drove the troopers out into the open air. Before them were burning houses. Behind them shone the painted windows of the abbey filled with saints and martyrs, awakened, as from a sacred trance, into an angry and animated life. The eyes of the troopers were dazzled, and for a while could see nothing but the flaming faces of saints and martyrs. Presently, however, they saw a man covered with dust who came running towards them. 'Two messengers,' he cried, 'have been sent by the defeated Irish to raise against you the whole country about Manor Hamilton, and if you do not stop them you will be overpowered in the woods before you reach home again! They ride north-east between Ben Bulben and Cashel-na-Gael.'

Sir Frederick Hamilton called to him the five troopers who had first fired upon the monks and said, 'Mount quickly, and ride through the woods towards the mountain, and get before these men, and kill them.'

In a moment the troopers were gone, and before many moments they had splashed across the river at what is now called Buckley's Ford, and plunged into the woods. They followed a beaten track that wound along the northern bank of the river. The boughs of the birch and quicken trees mingled above, and hid the cloudy moonlight, leaving the pathway in almost complete darkness. They rode at a rapid trot, now chatting together, now watching some stray weasel or rabbit scuttling away in the darkness. Gradually, as the gloom and silence of the woods oppressed them, they drew closer together, and began to talk rapidly; they were old comrades and knew each other's lives. One was married, and told how glad his wife would be to see him return safe from this hare-brained expedition against the White Friars, and to hear how fortune had made amends for rashness. The oldest of the five, whose wife was dead, spoke of a flagon of wine which awaited him upon an upper shelf; while the third, who was the youngest, had a sweetheart watching for his return, and he rode a little way before the others, not talking at all. Suddenly the young man stopped, and they saw that his horse was trembling. 'I saw something,' he said, 'and yet I do not know but it may have been one of the shadows. It looked like a great worm with a silver crown upon his head.' One of the five put his hand up to his forehead as if about to cross himself, but remembering that he had changed his religion he put it down, and said: 'I am certain it was but a shadow, for there are a great many about us, and of very strange kinds.' Then they rode on in silence. It had been raining in the earlier part of the day, and the drops fell from the branches, wetting their hair and their shoulders. In a little they began to talk again. They had been in many battles against many a rebel together, and now told each other over again the story of their wounds, and so awakened in their hearts the strongest of all fellowships, the fellowship of the sword, and half forgot the terrible solitude of the woods.

Suddenly the first two horses neighed, and then stood still, and would go no farther. Before them was a glint of water, and they knew by the rushing sound that it was a river. They dismounted, and after much tugging and coaxing brought the horses to the riverside. In the midst of the water stood a tall old woman with grey hair flowing over a grey dress. She stood up to her knees in the water, and stooped from time to time as though washing. Presently they could see that she was washing something that half floated. The moon cast a flickering light upon it, and they saw that it was the dead body of a man, and, while they were looking at it, an eddy of the river turned the face towards them, and each of the five troopers recognised at the same moment his own face. While they stood dumb and motionless with horror, the woman began to speak, saying slowly and loudly: 'Did you see my son? He has a crown of silver on his head, and there are rubies in the crown.' Then the oldest of the troopers, he who had been most often wounded, drew his sword and cried: 'I have fought for the truth of my God, and need not fear the shadows of Satan,' and with that rushed into the water. In a moment he returned. The woman had vanished, and though he had thrust his sword into air and water he had found nothing.

The five troopers remounted, and set their horses at the ford, but all to no purpose. They tried again and again, and went plunging hither and thither, the horses foaming and rearing. 'Let us,' said the old trooper, 'ride back a little into the wood, and strike the river higher up.' They rode in under the boughs, the ground-ivy crackling under the hoofs, and the branches striking against their steel caps. After about twenty minutes' riding they came out again upon the river, and after another ten minutes found a place where it was possible to cross without sinking below the stirrups. The wood upon the other side was very thin, and broke the moonlight into long streams. The wind had arisen and had begun to drive the clouds rapidly across the face of the moon, so that thin streams of light seemed to be dancing a grotesque dance among the scattered bushes and small fir trees. The tops of the trees began also to moan, and the sound of it was like the voice of the dead in the wind; and the troopers remembered the belief that tells how the dead in purgatory are spitted upon the points of the trees and upon the points of the rocks. They turned a little to the south, in the hope that they might strike the beaten path again, but they could find no trace of it.

Meanwhile, the moaning grew louder and louder, and the dance of the white moon-fires more and more rapid. Gradually they began to be aware of a sound of distant music. It was the sound of a bagpipe, and they rode towards it with great joy. It came from the bottom of a deep, cuplike hollow. In the midst of the hollow was an old man with a red cap and withered face. He sat beside a fire of sticks, and had a burning torch thrust into the earth at his feet, and played an old bagpipe furiously. His red hair dripped over his face like the iron rust upon a rock. 'Did you see my wife?' he cried, looking up a moment; 'she was washing! she was washing!' 'I am afraid of him,' said the young trooper, 'I fear he is one of the Sidhe.' 'No,' said the old trooper, 'he is a man, for I can see the sun-freckles upon his face. We will compel him to be our guide'; and at that he drew his sword, and the others did the same. They stood in a ring round the piper, and pointed their swords at him, and the old trooper then told him that they must kill two rebels, who had taken the road between Ben Bulben and the great mountain spur that is called Cashel-na-Gael, and that he must get up before one of them and be their guide, for they had lost their way. The piper turned, and pointed to a neighbouring tree, and they saw an old white horse ready bitted, bridled and saddled. He slung the pipe across his back, and, taking the torch in his hand, got upon the horse, and started off before them, as hard as he could go.

The wood grew thinner and thinner, and the ground began to slope up toward the mountain. The moon had already set, and the little white flames of the stars had come out everywhere. The ground sloped more and more until at last they rode far above the woods upon the wide top of the mountain. The woods lay spread out mile after mile below, and away to the south shot up the red glare of the burning town. But before and above them were the little white flames. The guide drew rein suddenly, and pointing upwards with the hand that did not hold the torch, shrieked out, 'Look; look at the holy candles!' and then plunged forward at a gallop, waving the torch hither and thither. 'Do you hear the hoofs of the messengers?' cried the guide. 'Quick, quick! or they will be gone out of your hands!' and he laughed as with delight of the chase. The troopers thought they could hear far off, and as if below them, the rattle of hoofs; but now the ground began to slope more and more, and the speed grew more headlong moment by moment. They tried to pull up, but in vain, for the horses seemed to have gone mad. The guide had thrown the reins on to the neck of the old white horse, and was waving his arms and singing a wild Gaelic song. Suddenly they saw the thin gleam of a river, at an immense distance below, and knew that they were upon the brink of the abyss that is now called Lug-na-Gael or, in English, the Stranger's Leap. The six horses sprang forward, and five screams went up into the air; a moment later five men and horses fell with a dull crash upon the green slopes at the foot of the rocks.

W. B. YEATS

Hanraham's Vision

It was in the month of June Hanrahan was on the
road near Sligo, but he did not go into the town but
turned towards Beinn Bulben; for there were thoughts
of the old times coming upon him, and he had no
mind to meet with common men. And as he walked
he was singing to himself a song that had come to
him one time in his dreams:

'O Death's old bony finger
Will never find us there
In the high hollow townland
Where love's to give and to spare;
Where boughs have fruit and blossom
At all times of the year;
Where rivers are running over
With red beer and brown beer.
An old man plays the bagpipes
In a gold and silver wood;
Queens, their eyes blue like the ice,
Are dancing in a crowd.

'The little fox he murmured,
"O what of the world's bane?"
The sun was laughing sweetly,
The moon plucked at my rein;
But the little red fox murmured,

"O do not pluck at his rein,
He is riding to the townland
That is the world's bane."

'When their hearts are so high
That they would come to blows,
They unhook their heavy swords
From golden and silver boughs:
But all that are killed in battle
Awaken to life again:
It is lucky that their story
Is not known among men.
For O, the strong farmers
That would let the spade lie,
Their hearts would be like a cup
That somebody had drunk dry.

'Michael will unhook his trumpet
From a bough overhead,
And blow a little noise
When the supper has been spread.
Gabriel will come from the water
With a fish tail, and talk
Of wonders that have happened
On wet roads where men walk,
And lift up an old horn
Of hammered silver, and drink
Till he has fallen asleep
Upon the starry brink.'

Hanrahan had begun to climb the mountain then,
and he gave over singing, for it was a long climb for
him, and every now and again he had to sit down and
to rest for a while. And one time he was resting he
took notice of a wild briar bush, with blossoms on it,

that was growing beside a rath, and it brought to
mind the wild roses he used to bring to Mary Lavelle,
and to no woman after her. And he tore off a little
branch of the bush, that had buds on it and open
blossoms, and he went on with his song:

> 'The little fox he murmured,
> "O what of the world's bane?"
> The sun was laughing sweetly,
> The moon plucked at my rein;
> But the little red fox murmured,
> "O do not pluck at his rein,
> He is riding to the townland
> That is the world's bane." '

And he went on climbing the hill, and left the rath,
and there came to his mind some of the old poems
that told of lovers, good and bad, and of some that
were awakened from the sleep of the grave itself by
the strength of one another's love, and brought away
to a life in some shadowy place, where they are
waiting for the judgement and banished from the
face of God.

And at last, at the fall of day, he came to the Steep
Gap of the Strangers, and there he laid himself down
along a ridge of rock, and looked into the valley, that
was full of grey mist spreading from mountain to
mountain.

And it seemed to him as he looked that the mist
changed to shapes of shadowy men and women, and
his heart began to beat with the fear and the joy of the
sight. And his hands, that were always restless, began
to pluck off the leaves of the roses on the little branch,
and he watched them as they went floating down into
the valley in a little fluttering troop.

Suddenly he heard a faint music, a music that had more laughter in it and more crying than all the music of this world. And his heart rose when he heard that, and he began to laugh out loud, for he knew that music was made by some who had a beauty and a greatness beyond the people of this world. And it seemed to him that the little soft rose leaves as they went fluttering down into the valley began to change their shape till they looked like a troop of men and women far off in the mist, with the colour of the roses on them. And then that colour changed to many colours, and what he saw was a long line of tall beautiful young men, and of queen-women, that were not going from him but coming towards him and past him, and their faces were full of tenderness for all their proud looks, and were very pale and worn, as if they were seeking and ever seeking for high sorrowful things. And shadowy arms were stretched out of the mist as if to take hold of them, but could not touch them, for the quiet that was about them could not be broken. And before them and beyond them, but at a distance as if in reverence, there were other shapes, sinking and rising and coming and going, and Hanrahan knew them by their whirling flight to be the Sidhe, the ancient defeated gods; and the shadowy arms did not rise to take hold of them, for they were of those that can neither sin nor obey. And they all lessened then in the distance, and they seemed to be going towards the white door that is in the side of the mountain.

The mist spread out before him now like a deserted sea washing the mountains with long grey waves, but while he was looking at it, it began to fill again with a flowing broken witless life that was a part of itself, and arms and pale heads covered with tossing hair appeared in the greyness. It rose higher and higher till it was level with the edge of the steep rock, and then the shapes grew to be solid, and a new procession half lost in mist passed very slowly with uneven steps, and in the midst of each shadow there was something shining in the starlight. They came nearer and nearer, and Hanrahan saw that they also were lovers, and that they had heart-shaped mirrors instead of hearts, and they were looking and ever looking on their own faces in one another's mirrors. They passed on, sinking downward as they passed, and other shapes rose in their place, and these did not keep side by side, but followed after one another, holding out wild beckoning arms, and he saw that those who were followed were women, and as to their heads they were beyond all beauty, but as to their bodies they were but shadows without life, and their long hair was moving and trembling about them, as if it lived with some terrible life of its own. And then the mist rose of a sudden and hid them, and then a light gust of wind blew them away towards the north-east, and covered Hanrahan at the same time with a white wing of cloud.

He stood up trembling and was going to turn away from the valley, when he saw two dark and half-hidden forms standing as if in the air just beyond the rock, and one of them that had the sorrowful eyes of a beggar said to him in a woman's voice, 'Speak to me, for no one in this world or any other world has spoken to me for seven hundred years.'

'Tell me who are those that have passed by,' said Hanrahan.

'Those that passed first,' the woman said, 'are the

lovers that had the greatest name in the old times, Blanad and Deirdre and Grania and their dear comrades, and a great many that are not so well known but are as well loved. And because it was not only the blossom of youth they were looking for in one another, but the beauty that is as lasting as the night and the stars, the night and the stars hold them for ever from the warring and the perishing, in spite of the wars and the bitterness their love brought into the world. And those that came next,' she said, 'and that still breathe the sweet air and have the mirrors in their hearts, are not put in songs by the poets, because they sought only to triumph one over the other, and so to prove their strength and beauty, and out of this they made a kind of love. And as to the women with shadow-bodies, they desired neither to triumph nor to love but only to be loved, and there is no blood in their hearts or in their bodies until it flows through them from a kiss, and their life is but for a moment. All these are unhappy, but I am the unhappiest of all, for I am Dervadilla, and this is Dermot, and it was our sin brought the Norman into Ireland. And the curses of all the generations are upon us, and none are punished as we are punished. It was but the blossom of the man and of the woman we loved in one another, the dying beauty of the dust and not the everlasting beauty. When we died there was no lasting unbreakable quiet about us, and the bitterness of the battles we brought into Ireland turned to our own punishment. We go wandering together for ever, but Dermot that was my lover sees me always as a body that has been a long time in the ground, and I know that is the way he sees me. Ask me more, ask me more, for all the years have left their wisdom in my

347

heart, and no one has listened to me for seven hundred years.'

A great terror had fallen upon Hanrahan, and lifting his arms above his head he screamed out loud three times, and the cattle in the valley lifted their heads and lowed, and the birds in the wood at the edge of the mountain awaked out of their sleep and fluttered through the trembling leaves. But a little below the edge of the rock, the troop of rose leaves still fluttered in the air, for the gateway of Eternity had opened and shut again in one beat of the heart.

BRAM STOKER

The Judge's House

When the time for his examination drew near Malcolm Malcolmson made up his mind to go somewhere to read by himself. He feared the attractions of the sea-side, and also he feared completely rural isolation, for of old he knew its charms, and so he determined to find some unpretentious little town where there would be nothing to distract him. He refrained from asking suggestions from any of his friends, for he argued that each would recommend some place of which he had knowledge, and where he had already acquaintances. As Malcolmson wished to avoid friends he had no wish to encumber himself with the attention of friends' friends, and so he determined to look out for a place for himself. He packed a portmanteau with some clothes and all the books he required, and then took ticket for the first name on the local timetable which he did not know.

When at the end of three hours' journey he alighted at Benchurch, he felt satisfied that he had so far obliterated his tracks as to be sure of having a peaceful opportunity of pursuing his studies. He went straight to the one inn which the sleepy little place contained, and put up for the night. Benchurch was a market town, and once in three weeks was crowded to excess, but for the remainder of the twenty-one days it was as

349

attractive as a desert. Malcolmson looked around the day after his arrival to try to find quarters more isolated than even so quiet an inn as the Good Traveller afforded. There was only one place which took his fancy, and it certainly satisfied his wildest ideas regarding quiet; in fact, quiet was not the proper word to apply to it – desolation was the only term conveying any suitable idea of its isolation. It was an old rambling, heavy-built house of the Jacobean style, with heavy gables and windows, unusually small, and set higher than was customary in such houses, and was surrounded with a high brick wall massively built. Indeed, on examination, it looked more like a fortified house than an ordinary dwelling. But all these things pleased Malcolmson. 'Here,' he thought, 'is the very spot I have been looking for, and if I can only get opportunity of using it I shall be happy.' His joy was increased when he realised beyond doubt that it was not at present inhabited.

From the post-office he got the name of the agent, who was rarely surprised at the application to rent a part of the old house. Mr Carnford, the local lawyer and agent, was a genial old gentleman, and frankly confessed his delight at anyone being willing to live in the house.

'To tell you the truth,' said he, 'I should be only too happy, on behalf of the owners, to let anyone have the house rent free for a term of years if only to accustom the people here to see it inhabited. It has been so long empty that some kind of absurd prejudice has grown up about it, and this can be best put down by its occupation – if only,' he added with a sly glance at Malcolmson, 'by a scholar like yourself, who wants its quiet for a time.'

Malcolmson thought it needless to ask the agent about the 'absurd prejudice'; he knew he would get more information, if he should require it, on that subject from other quarters. He paid his three months' rent, got a receipt, and the name of an old woman who would probably undertake to 'do' for him, and came away with the keys in his pocket. He then went to the landlady of the inn, who was a cheerful and most kindly person, and asked her advice as to such stores and provisions as he would be likely to require. She threw up her hands in amazement when he told her where he was going to settle himself.

'Not in the Judge's House!' she said and grew pale as she spoke. He explained the locality of the house, saying that he did not know its name. When he had finished, she answered: 'Aye, sure enough – sure enough the very place. It is the Judge's House sure enough.' He asked her to tell him about the place, why so called, and what there was against it. She told him that it was so called locally because it had been many years before – how long she could not say, as she was herself from another part of the country, but she thought it must have been a hundred years or more – the abode of a judge who was held in great terror on account of his harsh sentences and his hostility to prisoners at Assizes. As to what there was against the house itself she could not tell. She had often asked, but no one could inform her; but there was a general feeling that there was *something*, and for her own part she would not take all the money in Drinkwater's Bank and stay in the house an hour by herself. Then she apologised to Malcolmson for her disturbing talk.

'It is too bad of me, sir, and you – and a young

351

gentleman, too – if you will pardon me saying it, going to live there all alone. If you were my boy – and you'll excuse me for saying it – you wouldn't sleep there a night, not if I had to go there myself and pull the big alarm bell that's on the roof!' The good creature was so manifestly in earnest, and was so kindly in her intentions, that Malcolmson, although amused, was touched. He told her kindly how much he appreciated her interest in him, and added: 'But, my dear Mrs Witham, indeed you need not be concerned about me! A man who is reading for the Mathematical Tripos has too much to think of to be disturbed by any of these mysterious "somethings", and his work is of too exact and prosaic a kind to allow of his having any corner in his mind for mysteries of any kind. Harmonical Progression, Permutations and Combinations, and Elliptic Functions have sufficient mysteries for me!' Mrs Witham kindly undertook to see after his commissions, and he went himself to look for the old woman who had been recommended to him. When he returned to the Judge's House with her, after an interval of a couple of hours, he found Mrs Witham herself waiting with several men and boys carrying parcels, and an upholsterer's man with a bed in a cart, for she said, though tables and chairs might be all very well, a bed that hadn't been aired for maybe fifty years was not proper for young ones to lie on. She was evidently curious to see the inside of the house; and though manifestly so afraid of the 'somethings' that at the slightest sound she clutched on to Malcolmson, whom she never left for a moment, went over the whole place.

After his examination of the house, Malcolmson decided to take up his abode in the great dining-room, which was big enough to serve for all his requirements; and Mrs Witham, with the aid of the charwoman, Mrs Dempster, proceeded to arrange matters. When the hampers were brought in and unpacked, Malcolmson saw that with much kind forethought she had sent from her own kitchen sufficient provisions to last for a few days. Before going she expressed all sorts of kind wishes; and at the door turned and said: 'And perhaps, sir, as the room is big and drafty it might be well to have one of those big screens put round your bed at night – though, truth to tell, I would die myself if I were to be so shut in with all kinds of – of "things" that put their heads round the sides, or over the top, and look on me!' The image which she had called up was too much for her nerves, and she fled incontinently.

Mrs Dempster sniffed in a superior manner as the landlady disappeared, and remarked that for her own part she wasn't afraid of all the bogies in the kingdom.

'I'll tell you what it is, sir,' she said, 'bogies is all kinds and sorts of things – except bogies! Rats and mice, and beetles; and creaky doors, and loose slates, and broken panes, and stiff drawer handles, that stay out when you pull them and then fall down in the middle of the night. Look at the wainscot of the room! It is old – hundreds of years old! Do you think there's no rats and beetles there! And do you imagine, sir, that you won't see none of them! Rats is bogies, I tell you, and bogies is rats; and don't you get to think anything else!'

'Mrs Dempster,' said Malcolmson gravely, making her a polite bow, 'you know more than a Senior Wrangler! And let me say, that, as a mark of esteem for your indubitable soundness of head and heart, I shall, when I go, give you possession of this house, and let you stay here by yourself for the last two months of my tenancy, for four weeks will serve my purpose.'

'Thank you kindly, sir!' she answered, 'but I couldn't sleep away from home a night. I am in Greenhow's Charity, and if I slept a night away from my rooms I should lose all I have got to live on. The rules is very strict; and there's too many watching for a vacancy for me to run any risks in the matter. Only for that, sir, I'd gladly come here and attend on you altogether during your stay.'

'My good woman,' said Malcolmson hastily, 'I have come here on a purpose to obtain solitude; and believe me that I am grateful to the late Greenhow for having organised his admirable charity – whatever it is – that I am perforce denied the opportunity of suffering from such a form of temptation! St Anthony himself could not be more rigid on the point!'

The old woman laughed harshly. 'Ah, you young gentlemen,' she said, 'you don't fear for naught; and belike you'll get all the solitude you want here.' She set to work with her cleaning; and by nightfall, when Malcolmson returned from his walk – he always had one of his books to study as he walked – he found the room swept and tidied, a fire burning on the old hearth, the lamp lit, and the table spread for supper with Mrs Witham's excellent fare. 'This is comfort, indeed,' he said, as he rubbed his hands.

When he had finished his supper, and lifted the tray to the other end of the great oak dining-table, he got out his books again, put fresh wood on the fire, trimmed his lamp, and set himself down to a spell of real hard work. He went on without a pause till about eleven o'clock, when he knocked off for a bit to fix his fire and lamp and to make himself a cup of tea. He had always been a tea-drinker, and during his college life had sat late at work and had taken tea late. The rest was a great luxury to him, and he enjoyed it with a sense of delicious, voluptuous ease. The renewed fire leaped and sparkled, and threw quaint shadows through the great old room; and as he sipped his hot tea he revelled in the sense of isolation from his kind. Then it was that he began to notice for the first time what a noise the rats were making.

'Surely,' he thought, 'they cannot have been at it all the time I was reading. Had they been, I must have noticed it!' Presently, when the noise increased, he satisfied himself that it was really new. It was evident that at first the rats had been frightened at the presence of a stranger, and the light of fire and lamp; but that as the time went on they had grown bolder and were now disporting themselves as was their wont.

How busy they were! and hark to the strange noises! Up and down behind the old wainscot, over the ceiling and under the floor they raced, and gnawed, and scratched! Malcolmson smiled to himself as he recalled to mind the saying of Mrs Dempster, 'Bogies is rats, and rats is bogies!' The tea began to have its effect of intellectual and nervous stimulus, he saw with joy another long spell of work to be done before the night was past, and in the sense of security which it gave him, he allowed himself the luxury of a good look round the room. He took his lamp in one hand, and went all round, wondering that so quaint and beautiful an old house had been so long neglected. The carving of the oak on the panels of the wainscot

355

was fine, and on and round the doors and windows it was beautiful and of rare merit. There were some old pictures on the walls, but they were coated so thick with dust and dirt that he could not distinguish any detail of them, though he held his lamp as high as he could over his head. Here and there as he went round he saw some crack or hole blocked for a moment by the face of a rat with its bright eyes glittering in the light, but in an instant it was gone, and a squeak and a scamper followed. The thing that most struck him, however, was the rope of the great alarm bell on the roof, which hung down in a corner of the room on the right-hand side of the fireplace. He pulled up close to the hearth a great high-backed carved oak chair, and sat down to his last cup of tea. When this was done he made up the fire, and went back to his work, sitting at the corner of the table, having the fire to his left. For a little while the rats disturbed him somewhat with their perpetual scampering, but he got accustomed to the noise as one does to the ticking of the clock or to the roar of moving water; and he became so immersed in his work that everything in the world, except the problem which he was trying to solve, passed away from him.

He suddenly looked up, his problem was still unsolved, and there was in the air that sense of the hour before the dawn, which is so dread to doubtful life. The noise of the rats had ceased. Indeed it seemed to him that it must have ceased but lately and that it was the sudden cessation which had disturbed him. The fire had fallen low, but still it threw out a deep red glow. As he looked he started in spite of his *sang froid*.

There on the great high-backed carved oak chair by the right side of the fireplace sat an enormous rat, steadily glaring at him with baleful eyes. He made a motion to it as though to hunt it away, but it did not stir. Then he made the motion of throwing something. Still it did not stir, but showed its great white teeth angrily, and its cruel eyes shone in the lamplight with an added vindictiveness.

Malcolmson felt amazed, and seizing the poker from the hearth ran at it to kill it. Before, however, he could strike it, the rat, with a squeak that sounded like the concentration of hate, jumped upon the floor, and, running up the rope of the alarm bell, disappeared in the darkness beyond the range of the green-shaded lamp. Instantly, strange to say, the noisy scampering of the rats in the wainscot began again.

By this time Malcolmson's mind was quite off the problem; and as a shrill cockcrow outside told him of the approach of morning, he went to bed and to sleep.

He slept so sound that he was not even waked by Mrs Dempster coming in to make up his room. It was only when she had tidied up the place and got his breakfast ready and tapped on the screen which closed in his bed that he woke. He was a little tired still after his night's hard work, but a strong cup of tea soon freshened him up and, taking his book, he went out for his morning walk, bringing with him a few sandwiches lest he should not care to return till dinner time. He found a quiet walk between high elms some way outside the town, and here he spent the greater part of the day studying his Laplace. On his return he looked in to see Mrs Witham and to thank her for her kindness. When she saw him coming through the diamond-paned bay window of her sanctum, she came out to meet him and asked him in. She looked at him searchingly and shook her head as she said:

'You must not overdo it, sir. You are paler this morning than you should be. Too late hours and too hard work on the brain isn't good for any man! But tell me, sir, how did you pass the night? Well, I hope? But, my heart! sir, I was glad when Mrs Dempster told me this morning that you were all right and sleeping sound when she went in.'

'Oh, I was all right,' he answered smiling; 'the "somethings" didn't worry me, as yet. Only the rats; and they had a circus, I tell you, all over the place. There was one wicked looking old devil that sat up on my own chair by the fire and wouldn't go till I took the poker to him, and then he ran up the rope of the alarm bell and got to somewhere up the wall or the ceiling – I couldn't see where, it was so dark.'

'Mercy on us,' said Mrs Witham, 'an old devil, and sitting on a chair by the fireside! Take care, sir! take care! There's many a true word spoken in jest.'

'How do you mean? 'Pon my word I don't understand.'

'An old devil! The old devil, perhaps. There! sir, you needn't laugh,' for Malcolmson had broken into a hearty peal. 'You young folks think it easy to laugh at things that makes older ones shudder. Never mind, sir! never mind. Please God, you'll laugh all the time. It's what I wish you myself!' and the good lady beamed all over in sympathy with his enjoyment, her fears gone for a moment.

'Oh, forgive me!' said Malcolmson presently. 'Don't think me rude, but the idea was too much for me – that the old devil himself was on the chair last night!' And at the thought he laughed again. Then he went home to dinner.

This evening the scampering of the rats began

earlier; indeed it had been going on before his arrival, and only ceased whilst his presence by its freshness disturbed them. After dinner he sat by the fire for a while and had a smoke; and then, having cleared his table, began to work as before. Tonight the rats disturbed him more than they had done on the previous night. How they scampered up and down and under and over! How they squeaked, and scratched, and gnawed! How they, getting bolder by degrees, came to the mouths of their holes and to the chinks and cracks and crannies in the wainscoting till their eyes shone like tiny lamps as the firelight rose and fell. But to him, now doubtless accustomed to them, their eyes were not wicked; only their playfulness touched him. Sometimes the boldest of them made sallies out on the floor or along the mouldings of the wainscot. Now and again as they disturbed him Malcolmson made a sound to frighten them, smiting the table with his hand or giving a fierce 'Hsh, hsh,' so that they fled straightway to their holes.

And so the early part of the night wore on; and despite the noise Malcolmson got more and more immersed in his work.

All at once he stopped, as on the previous night, being overcome by a sudden sense of silence. There was not the faintest sound of gnaw, or scratch, or squeak. The silence was as of the grave. He remembered the odd occurrence of the previous night, and instinctively he looked at the chair standing close by the fireside. And then a very odd sensation thrilled through him.

There, on the great old high-backed carved oak chair beside the fireplace sat the same enormous rat, steadily glaring at him with baleful eyes.

Instinctively he took the nearest thing to his hand, a book of logarithms, and flung it at it. The book was badly aimed and the rat did not stir, so again the poker performance of the previous night was repeated; and again the rat, being closely pursued, fled up the rope of the alarm bell. Strangely, too, the departure of this rat was instantly followed by the renewal of the noise made by the general rat community. On this occasion, as on the previous one, Malcolmson could not see at what part of the room the rat disappeared, for the green shade of his lamp left the upper part of the room in darkness, and the fire had burned low.

On looking at his watch he found it was close on midnight and, not sorry for the *divertissement*, he made up his fire and made himself his nightly pot of tea. He had got through a good spell of work, and thought himself entitled to a cigarette; and so he sat on the great carved oak chair before the fire and enjoyed it. Whilst smoking he began to think that he would like to know where the rat disappeared to, for he had certain ideas for the morrow not entirely disconnected with a rat trap. Accordingly he lit another lamp and placed it so that it would shine well into the right-hand corner of the wall by the fireplace. Then he got all the books he had with him, and placed them handy to throw at the vermin. Finally he lifted the rope of the alarm bell and placed the end of it on the table, fixing the extreme end under the lamp. As he handled it he could not help noticing how pliable it was, especially for so strong a rope, and one not in use. 'You could hang a man with it,' he thought to himself. When his preparations were made he looked around, and said complacently: 'There now, my friend, I think we shall learn something of you this time!' He began his work again, and though as before somewhat disturbed at first by the noise of the rats, soon lost himself in his proposition and problems.

Again he was called to his immediate surroundings suddenly. This time it might not have been the sudden silence only which took his attention; there was a slight movement of the rope, and the lamp moved. Without stirring, he looked to see if his pile of books was within range, and then cast his eye along the rope. As he looked he saw the great rat drop from the rope on the oak armchair and sit there glaring at him. He raised a book in his right hand, and taking careful aim, flung it at the rat. The latter, with a quick movement, sprang aside and dodged the missile. He then took another book, and a third, and flung them one after another at the rat, but each time unsuccessfully. At last, as he stood with a book poised in his hand to throw, the rat squeaked and seemed afraid. This made Malcolmson more than ever eager to strike, and the book flew and struck the rat a resounding blow. It gave a terrified squeak, and turning on his pursuer a look of terrible malevolence, ran up the chair-back and made a great jump to the rope of the alarm bell and ran up it like lightning. The lamp rocked under the sudden strain, but it was a heavy one and did not topple over. Malcolmson kept his eyes on the rat, and saw it by the light of the second lamp leap to a moulding of the wainscot and disappear through a hole in one of the great pictures which hung on the wall, obscured and invisible through its coating of dirt and dust.

'I shall look up my friend's habitation in the morning,' said the student, as he went over to collect his books. 'The third picture from the fireplace; I shall not forget.' He picked up the books one by one, commenting on them as he lifted them. *Conic Sections* he does not mind, nor *Cycloidal Oscillations*, nor the *Principia*, nor *Quaternions*, nor *Thermodynamics*. Now for a book that fetched him!' Malcolmson took it up and looked at it. As he did so he started, and a sudden pallor overspread his face. He looked round uneasily and shivered slightly, as he murmured to himself: 'The Bible my mother gave me! What an odd coincidence.' He sat down to work again, and the rats in the wainscot renewed their gambols. They did not disturb him, however; somehow their presence gave him a sense of companionship. But he could not attend to his work, and after striving to master the subject on which he was engaged, gave it up in despair, and went to bed as the first streak of dawn stole in through the eastern window.

He slept heavily but uneasily, and dreamed much; and when Mrs Dempster woke him late in the morning he seemed ill at ease, and for a few minutes did not seem to realise exactly where he was. His first request rather surprised the servant.

'Mrs Dempster, when I am out today I wish you would get the steps and dust or wash those pictures – specially that one the third from the fireplace – I want to see what they are.'

Late in the afternoon Malcolmson worked at his books in the shaded walk, and the cheerfulness of the previous day came back to him as the day wore on, and he found that his reading was progressing well. He had worked out to a satisfactory conclusion all the problems which had as yet baffled him, and it was in a state of jubilation that he paid a visit to Mrs Witham at the Good Traveller. He found a stranger in the cozy sitting-room with the landlady, who was introduced to him as Dr Thornhill. She was not quite at ease, and this, combined with the doctor's plunging at once into a series of questions, made Malcolmson come to the conclusion that his presence was not an accident, so without preliminary he said: 'Dr Thornhill, I shall with pleasure answer you any question you may choose to ask me if you will answer me one question first.'

The doctor seemed surprised, but he smiled and answered at once, 'Done! What is it?'

'Did Mrs Witham ask you to come here and see me and advise me?'

Dr Thornhill for a moment was taken aback, and Mrs Witham got fiery red and turned away; but the doctor was a frank and ready man, and he answered at once and openly: 'She did, but she didn't intend you to know it. I suppose it was my clumsy haste that made you suspect. She told me that she did not like the idea of your being in that house all by yourself, and that she thought you took too much strong tea. In fact, she wants me to advise you if possible to give up the tea and the very late hours. I was a keen student in my time, so I suppose I may take the liberty of a college man, and without offence, advise you not quite as a stranger.'

Malcolmson with a bright smile held out his hand. 'Shake! as they say in America,' he said. 'I must thank you for your kindness and Mrs Witham too, and your kindness deserves a return on my part. I promise to take no more strong tea – no tea at all till you let me – and I shall go to bed tonight at one o'clock at latest. Will that do?'

'Capital,' said the doctor. 'Now tell us all that you

noticed in the old house,' and so Malcolmson then and there told in minute detail all that had happened in the last two nights. He was interrupted every now and then by some exclamation from Mrs Witham, till finally when he told of the episode of the Bible the landlady's pent-up emotions found vent in a shriek; and it was not till a stiff glass of brandy and water had been administered that she grew composed again. Dr Thornhill listened with a face of growing gravity, and when the narrative was complete and Mrs Witham had been restored, he asked: 'The rat always went up the rope of the alarm bell?'

'I suppose you know,' said the doctor after a pause, 'what the rope is?'

'It is,' said the doctor slowly, 'the very rope which the hangman used for all the victims of the judge's judicial rancour!' Here he was interrupted by another scream from Mrs Witham, and steps had to be taken for her recovery. Malcolmson having looked at his watch, and found that it was close to his dinner hour, had gone home before her complete recovery.

When Mrs Witham was herself again she almost assailed the doctor with angry questions as to what he meant by putting such horrible ideas into the poor young man's mind. 'He has quite enough there already to upset him,' she added. Dr Thornhill replied: 'My dear madam, I had a distinct purpose in it! I wanted to draw his attention to the bell rope, and to fix it there. It may be that he is in a highly overwrought state, and has been studying too much, although I am bound to say that he seems as sound and healthy a young man, mentally and bodily, as ever I saw – but then the rats – and that suggestion of the devil.' The doctor shook his head and went on. 'I would have offered to go and stay the first night with him but that I felt sure it would have been a cause of offence. He may get in the night some strange fright or hallucination and if he does I want him to pull that rope. All alone as he is, it will give us warning, and we may reach him in time to be of service. I shall be sitting up pretty late tonight and shall keep my ears open. Do not be alarmed if Benchurch gets a surprise before morning.'

'Oh, doctor, what do you mean? What do you mean?'

'I mean this; that possibly – nay, more probably – we shall hear the great alarm bell from the Judge's House tonight,' and the doctor made about as effective an exit as could be thought of.

When Malcolmson arrived home he found that it was a little after his usual time, and Mrs Dempster had gone away – the rules of Greenhow's Charity were not to be neglected. He was glad to see that the place was bright and tidy with a cheerful fire and a well-trimmed lamp. The evening was colder than might have been expected in April, and a heavy wind was blowing with such rapidly-increasing strength that there was every promise of a storm during the night. For a few minutes after his entrance the noise of the rats ceased; but so soon as they became accustomed to his presence they began again. He was glad to hear them, for he felt once more the feeling of companionship in their noise, and his mind ran back to the strange fact that they only ceased to manifest themselves when that other – the great rat with the baleful eyes – came upon the scene. The reading-lamp only was lit and its green shade kept the ceiling and the upper part of the room in darkness, so that the cheerful light from the hearth spreading over the floor and shining on the white cloth laid over the end of the table was warm and cheery. Malcolmson sat down to his dinner with a good appetite and a buoyant spirit. After his dinner and a cigarette he sat steadily down to work, determined not to let anything disturb him, for he remembered his promise to the doctor, and made up his mind to make the best of the time at his disposal.

For an hour or so he worked all right, and then his thoughts began to wander from his books. The actual circumstances around him, the calls on his physical attention, and his nervous susceptibility were not to be denied. By this time the wind had become a gale, and the gale a storm. The old house, solid though it was, seemed to shake to its foundations, and the storm roared and raged through its many chimneys and its queer old gables, producing strange, unearthly sounds in the empty rooms and corridors. Even the great alarm bell on the roof must have felt the force of the wind, for the rope rose and fell slightly, as though the bell were moved a little from time to time, and the limber rope fell on the oak floor with a hard and hollow sound.

As Malcolmson listened to it he bethought himself of the doctor's words, 'It is the rope which the hangman used for the victims of the judge's judicial rancour,' and he went over to the corner of the fireplace and took it in his hand to look at it. There seemed a sort of deadly interest in it, and as he stood there he lost himself for a moment in speculation as to who these victims were, and the grim wish of the judge to have such a ghastly relic ever under his eyes. As he stood there the swaying of the bell on the roof still lifted the rope now and again; but presently there came a new sensation – a sort of tremor in the rope, as though something was moving along it.

Looking up instinctively Malcolmson saw the great rat coming slowly down towards him, glaring at him steadily. He dropped the rope and started back with a muttered curse, and the rat turning ran up the rope again and disappeared, and at the same instant Malcolmson became conscious that the noise of the other rats, which had ceased for a while, began again.

All this set him thinking, and it occurred to him that he had not investigated the lair of the rat or looked at the pictures, as he had intended. He lit the other lamp without the shade, and, holding it up, went and stood opposite the third picture from the fireplace on the right-hand side where he had seen the rat disappear on the previous night.

At the first glance he started back so suddenly that he almost dropped the lamp, and a deadly pallor overspread his face. His knees shook, and heavy drops of sweat came on his forehead, and he trembled like an aspen. But he was young and plucky, and pulled himself together, and after the pause of a few seconds stepped forward again, raised the lamp, and examined the picture which had been dusted and washed, and now stood out clearly.

It was of a judge dressed in his robes of scarlet and ermine. His face was strong and merciless, evil, crafty, and vindictive, with a sensual mouth, hooked nose of ruddy colour, and shaped like the beak of a bird of prey. The rest of the face was of a cadaverous colour. The eyes were of peculiar brilliance and with a terribly malignant expression. As he looked at them, Malcolmson grew cold, for he saw there the very counterpart of the eyes of the great rat. The lamp almost fell from his hand, he saw the rat with its baleful eyes peering out through the hole in the corner of the picture, and noted the sudden cessation of the noise of the other rats. However, he pulled himself together, and went on with his examination of the picture.

The judge was seated in a great high-backed carved oak chair, on the right-hand side of a great stone fireplace where, in the corner, a rope hung down from the ceiling, its end lying coiled on the floor. With a feeling of something like horror, Malcolmson recognised the scene of the room as it stood, and gazed around him in an awestruck manner as though he expected to find some strange presence behind him. Then he looked over to the corner of the fireplace – and with a loud cry he let the lamp fall from his hand.

There, in the judge's armchair, with the rope hanging behind, sat the rat with the judge's baleful eyes, now intensified and with a fiendish leer. Save for the howling of the storm without there was silence.

The fallen lamp recalled Malcolmson to himself. Fortunately it was of metal, and so the oil was not spilt. However, the practical need of attending to it settled at once his nervous apprehensions. When he had turned it out, he wiped his brow and thought for a moment.

'This will not do,' he said to himself. 'If I go on like this I shall become a crazy fool. This must stop! I promised the doctor I would not take tea. Faith, he was pretty right! My nerves must have been getting into a queer state. Funny I did not notice it. I never felt better in my life. However, it is all right now, and I shall not be such a fool again.'

Then he mixed himself a good stiff glass of brandy and water and resolutely sat down to his work.

It was nearly an hour later when he looked up from his book, disturbed by the sudden stillness. Without, the wind howled and roared louder then ever, and the rain drove in sheets against the windows, beating like hail on the glass; but within there was no sound whatever save the echo of the wind as it roared in the great chimney, and now and then a hiss as a few raindrops found their way down the chimney in a lull of the storm. The fire had fallen low and had ceased to flame, though it threw out a red glow. Malcolmson listened attentively, and presently heard a thin, squeaking noise, very faint. It came from the corner of the room where the rope hung down, and he thought it was the creaking of the rope on the floor as the swaying of the bell raised and lowered it. Looking up, however, he saw in the dim light the great rat clinging to the rope and gnawing it. The rope was already nearly gnawed through – he could see the lighter colour where the strands were laid bare. As he looked the job was completed, and the severed end of the rope fell clattering on the oaken floor, whilst for an instant the great rat remained like a knob or tassel at the end of the rope, which now began to sway to and fro. Malcolmson felt for a moment another pang of terror as he thought that now the possibility of calling the outer world to his assistance was cut off, but an intense anger took its place, and seizing the book he was reading he hurled it at the rat. The blow was well aimed, but before the missile could reach him the rat dropped off and struck the floor with a soft thud. Malcolmson instantly rushed over towards him, but it darted away and disappeared in the darkness of the shadows of the room. Malcolmson felt that his work was over for the night, and determined then and there to vary the monotony of the proceedings by a hunt for the rat, and took off the green shade of the lamp so as to insure a wider spreading light. As he did so the gloom of the upper part of the room was relieved, and in the new flood of light, great by comparison with the previous darkness, the pictures on the wall stood out boldly. From where he stood, Malcolmson saw right opposite to him the third picture on the wall from the right of the fireplace. He rubbed his eyes in surprise, and then a great fear began to come upon him.

In the centre of the picture was a great irregular patch of brown canvas, as fresh as when it was stretched on the frame. The background was as before, with chair and chimney-corner and rope, but the figure of the judge had disappeared.

Malcolmson, almost in a chill of horror, turned slowly round, and then he began to shake and tremble like a man in a palsy. His strength seemed to have left him, and he was incapable of action or movement, hardly even of thought. He could only see and hear.

There, on the great high-backed carved oak chair sat the judge in his robes of scarlet and ermine, with his baleful eyes glaring vindictively, and a smile of triumph on the resolute, cruel mouth, as he lifted with his hands a *black cap*. Malcolmson felt as if the blood was running from his heart, as one does in moments of prolonged suspense. There was a ringing in his ears. Without, he could hear the roar and howl of the tempest, and through it, swept on the storm, came the striking of midnight by the great chimes in the marketplace. He stood for a space of time that seemed to him endless still as a statue, and with wide-open, horror-struck eyes, breathless. As the clock struck, so the smile of triumph on the judge's face intensified, and at the last stroke of midnight he placed the black cap on his head.

Slowly and deliberately the judge rose from his chair and picked up the piece of the rope of the alarm bell which lay on the floor, drew it through his hands as if he enjoyed its touch, and then deliberately began to knot one end of it, fashioning it into a noose. This he tightened and tested with his foot, pulling hard at it till he was satisfied and then making a running noose of it, which he held in his hand. Then he began to move along the table on the opposite side to Malcolmson keeping his eyes on him until he had passed him, when with a quick movement he stood in front of the door. Malcolmson then began to feel that he was trapped, and tried to think of what he should do. There was some fascination in the judge's eyes, which he never took off him, and he had, perforce, to look. He saw the judge approach – still keeping between him and the door – and raise the noose and throw it towards him as if to entangle him. With a great effort he made a quick movement to one side, and saw the rope fall beside him, and heard it strike the oaken floor. Again the judge raised the noose and tried to ensnare him, ever keeping his baleful eyes fixed on him, and each time by a mighty effort the student just managed to evade it. So this went on for many times, the judge seeming never discouraged nor discomposed at failure, but playing as a cat does with a mouse. At last in despair, which had reached its climax, Malcolmson cast a quick glance round him. The lamp seemed to have blazed up, and there was a fairly good light in the room. At the many rat-

holes and in the chinks and crannies of the wainscot
he saw the rats' eyes; and this aspect, that was purely
physical, gave him a gleam of comfort. He looked
round and saw that the rope of the great alarm bell
was laden with rats. Every inch of it was covered with
them, and more and more were pouring through the
small circular hole in the ceiling whence it emerged,
so that with their weight the bell was beginning to
sway.

Hark! it had swayed till the clapper had touched
the bell. The sound was but a tiny one, but the bell
was only beginning to sway, and it would increase.

At the sound the judge, who had been keeping his
eyes fixed on Malcolmson, looked up, and a scowl of
diabolical anger overspread his face. His eyes fairly
glowed like hot coals, and he stamped his foot with
a sound that seemed to make the house shake. A
dreadful peal of thunder broke overhead as he raised
the rope again, whilst the rats kept running up and
down the rope as though working against time. This
time, instead of throwing it, he drew close to his
victim, and held open the noose as he approached.
As he came closer there seemed something paralysing
in his very presence, and Malcolmson stood rigid as
a corpse. He felt the judge's icy fingers touch his
throat as he adjusted the rope. The noose tightened –
tightened. Then the judge, taking the rigid form of
the student in his arms, carried him over and placed
him standing in the oak chair, and stepping up beside
him, put his hand up and caught the end of the
swaying rope of the alarm bell. As he raised his hand
the rats fled squeaking, and disappeared through the
hole in the ceiling. Taking the end of the noose
which was round Malcolmson's neck he tied it to

the hanging-bell rope, and then descending pulled away the chair.

* * *

When the alarm bell of the Judge's House began to sound, a crowd soon assembled. Lights and torches of various kinds appeared, and soon a silent crowd was hurrying to the spot. They knocked loudly at the door, but there was no reply. Then they burst in the door, and poured into the great dining room, the doctor at the head.

There at the end of the rope of the great alarm bell hung the body of the student, and on the face of the judge in the picture was a malignant smile.

BRAM STOKER

The Secret of the Growing Gold

When Margaret Delandre went to live at Brent's Rock
the whole neighbourhood awoke to the pleasure of an
entirely new scandal. Scandals in connection with
either the Delandre family or the Brents of Brent's
Rock, were not few; and if the secret history of the
county had been written in full both names would
have been found well represented. It is true that
the status of each was so different that they might
have belonged to different continents – or to different
worlds for the matter of that – for hitherto their orbits
had never crossed. The Brents were accorded by
the whole section of the country a unique social
dominance, and had ever held themselves as high
above the yeoman class to which Margaret Delandre
belonged as a blue-blooded Spanish hidalgo out-
tops his peasant tenantry.

The Delandres had an ancient record and were as
proud of it in their way as the Brents were of theirs.
But the family had never risen above yeomanry;
and although they had been once well-to-do in the
good old times of foreign wars and protection, their
fortunes had withered under the scorching of the free-
trade sun and the 'piping times of peace'. They had,
as the elder members used to assert, 'stuck to the
land', with the result that they had taken root in it,

body and soul. In fact, they, having chosen the life of vegetables, had flourished as vegetation does – blossomed and thrived in the good season and suffered in the bad. Their holding, Dander's Croft, seemed to have been worked out, and to be typical of the family which had inhabited it. The latter had declined generation after generation, sending out now and again some abortive shoot of unsatisfied energy in the shape of a soldier or sailor, who had worked his way to the minor grades of the services and had there stopped, cut short either from unheeding gallantry in action or from that destroying cause to men without breeding or youthful care – the recognition of a position above them which they feel unfitted to fill. So, little by little, the family dropped lower and lower, the men brooding and dissatisfied, and drinking themselves into the grave, the women drudging at home, or marrying beneath them – or worse. In process of time all disappeared, leaving only two in the Croft, Wykham Delandre and his sister Margaret. The man and woman seemed to have inherited in masculine and feminine form respectively the evil tendency of their race, sharing in common the principles, though manifesting them in different ways, of sullen passion, voluptuousness and recklessness.

The history of the Brents had been something similar, but showing the causes of decadence in their aristocratic and not their plebeian forms. They, too, had sent their shoots to the wars; but their positions had been different and they had often attained honour – for without flaw they were gallant, and brave deeds were done by them before the selfish dissipation which marked them had sapped their vigour.

The present head of the family – if family it could now be called when one remained of the direct line – was Geoffrey Brent. He was almost a type of worn out race, manifesting in some ways its most brilliant qualities, and in others its utter degradation. He might be fairly compared with some of those antique Italian nobles whom the painters have preserved to us with their courage, their unscrupulousness, their refinement of lust and cruelty – the voluptuary actual with the fiend potential. He was certainly handsome, with that dark, aquiline, commanding beauty which women so generally recognise as dominant. With men he was distant and cold; but such a bearing never deters womankind. The inscrutable laws of sex have so arranged it that even a timid woman is not afraid of a fierce and haughty man. And so it was that there was hardly a woman of any kind or degree, who lived within view of Brent's Rock, who did not cherish some form of secret admiration for the handsome wastrel. The category was a wide one, for Brent's Rock rose up steeply from the midst of a level region and for a circuit of a hundred miles it lay on the horizon, with its high old towers and steep roofs cutting the level edge of wood and hamlet and far-scattered mansions.

So long as Geoffrey Brent confined his dissipations to London and Paris and Vienna – anywhere out of sight and sound of his home – opinion was silent. It is easy to listen to far off echoes unmoved, and we can treat them with disbelief, or scorn, or disdain, or whatever attitude of coldness may suit our purpose. But when the scandal came close home it was another matter; and the feelings of independence and integrity which are in people of every community which is not utterly spoiled, asserted itself and demanded that condemnation should be expressed. Still there was a certain reticence in all, and no more notice was taken of the existing facts than was absolutely necessary. Margaret Delandre bore herself so fearlessly and so openly – she accepted her position as the justified companion of Geoffrey Brent so naturally – that people came to believe that she was secretly married to him, and therefore thought it wiser to hold their tongues lest time should justify her and also make her an active enemy.

The one person who, by his interference, could have settled all doubts was debarred by circumstances from interfering in the matter. Wykham Delandre had quarrelled with his sister – or perhaps it was that she had quarrelled with him – and they were on terms not merely of armed neutrality but of bitter hatred. The quarrel had been antecedent to Margaret going to Brent's Rock. She and Wykham had almost come to blows. There had certainly been threats on one side and on the other; and in the end Wykham, overcome with passion, had ordered his sister to leave his house. She had risen straightway, and, without waiting to pack up even her own personal belongings, had walked out of the house. On the threshold she had paused for a moment to hurl a bitter threat at Wykham that he would rue in shame and despair to the last hour of his life his act of that day. Some weeks had since passed, and it was understood in the neighbourhood that Margaret had gone to London, when she suddenly appeared driving out with Geoffrey Brent, and the entire neighbourhood knew before nightfall that she had taken up her abode at the Rock. It was no subject of surprise that Brent had come back unexpectedly, for such was his usual custom. Even his own servants never knew when to expect him, for there was a private door, of which he alone had the key, by which he sometimes entered without anyone in the house being aware of his coming. This was his usual method of appearing after a long absence.

Wykham Delandre was furious at the news. He vowed vengeance – and to keep his mind level with his passion drank deeper than ever. He tried several times to see his sister, but she contemptuously refused to meet him. He tried to have an interview with Brent and was refused by him also. Then he tried to stop him in the road, but without avail, for Geoffrey was not a man to be stopped against his will. Several actual encounters took place between the two men, and many more were threatened and avoided. At last Wykham Delandre settled down to a morose, vengeful acceptance of the situation.

Neither Margaret nor Geoffrey was of a pacific temperament, and it was not long before there began to be quarrels between them. One thing would lead to another, and wine flowed freely at Brent's Rock. Now and again the quarrels would assume a bitter aspect, and threats would be exchanged in uncompromising language that fairly awed the listening servants. But such quarrels generally ended where domestic altercations do, in reconciliation, and in a mutual respect for the fighting qualities proportionate to their manifestation. Fighting for its own sake is found by a certain class of persons, all the world over, to be a matter of absorbing interest, and there is no reason to believe that domestic conditions minimise its potency. Geoffrey and Margaret made occasional absences from Brent's Rock, and on each of these occasions Wykham Delandre also absented himself; but as he generally heard of the absence too late to be of any service, he returned home each time in a more bitter and discontented frame of mind than before.

At last there came a time when the absence from Brent's Rock became longer than before. Only a few days earlier there had been a quarrel, exceeding in bitterness anything which had gone before; but this, too, had been made up, and a trip on the Continent had been mentioned before the servants. After a few days Wykham Delandre also went away, and it was some weeks before he returned. It was noticed that he was full of some new importance – satisfaction, exaltation – they hardly knew how to call it. He went straightway to Brent's Rock, and demanded to see Geoffrey Brent, and on being told that he had not yet returned, said, with a grim decision which the servants noted: 'I shall come again. My news is solid – it can wait!' and turned away.

Week after week went by, and month after month; and then there came a rumour, certified later on, that an accident had occurred in the Zermatt valley. Whilst crossing a dangerous pass the carriage containing an English lady and the driver had fallen over a precipice, the gentleman of the party, Mr Geoffrey Brent, having been fortunately saved as he had been walking up the hill to ease the horses. He gave information, and search was made. The broken rail, the excoriated roadway, the marks where the horses had struggled on the decline before finally pitching over into the torrent – all told the sad tale. It was a wet season, and there had been much snow in the winter, so that the river was swollen beyond its usual volume, and the eddies of the stream were packed with ice. All search was made, and finally the wreck of the carriage and the body of one horse were found in an eddy of the river. Later on the body of the driver was found on the sandy, torrent-swept waste near Täsch; but the body of the lady, like that of the other horse, had quite disappeared, and was – what was left of it by that time – whirling amongst the eddies of the Rhone on its way down to the Lake of Geneva.

Wykham Delandre made all the enquiries possible, but could not find any trace of the missing woman. He found, however, in the books of the various hotels the name of 'Mr and Mrs Geoffrey Brent'. And he had a stone erected at Zermatt to his sister's memory, under her married name, and a tablet put up in the church at Bretten, the parish in which both Brent's Rock and Dander's Croft were situated.

There was a lapse of nearly a year, after the excitement of the matter had worn away, and the whole neighbourhood had gone on in its accustomed way. Brent was still absent, and Delandre more drunken, more morose, and more revengeful than before.

Then there was a new excitement. Brent's Rock was being made ready for a new mistress. It was officially announced by Geoffrey himself in a letter to the vicar, that he had been married some months before to an Italian lady, and that they were then on their way home. Then a small army of workmen invaded the house; and hammer and plane sounded, and a general air of size and paint pervaded the atmosphere. One wing of the old house, the south, was entirely re-done; and then the great body of the workmen departed, leaving only materials for the doing of the old hall when Geoffrey Brent should have returned, for he had directed that the decoration was only to be done under his own eyes. He had brought with him accurate drawings of a hall in the house of his bride's father, for he wished to reproduce for her the place to which she had been accustomed. As the moulding had all to be re-done, some scaffolding poles and boards were brought in and laid on one side of the great hall, and also a great wooden tank or box for mixing the lime, which was laid in bags beside it.

When the new mistress of Brent's Rock arrived the bells of the church rang out, and there was a general jubilation. She was a beautiful creature, full of the poetry and fire and passion of the South; and the few English words which she had learned were spoken in such a sweet and pretty broken way that she won the hearts of the people almost as much by the music of her voice as by the melting beauty of her dark eyes.

Geoffrey Brent seemed more happy than he had ever before appeared; but there was a dark, anxious look on his face that was new to those who knew him of old, and he started at times as though at some noise that was unheard by others.

And so months passed and the whisper grew that at last Brent's Rock was to have an heir. Geoffrey was very tender to his wife, and the new bond between them seemed to soften him. He took more interest in his tenants and their needs than he had ever done; and works of charity on his part as well as on his sweet young wife's were not lacking. He seemed to have set all his hopes on the child that was coming, and as he looked deeper into the future the dark shadow that had come over his face seemed to die gradually away.

381

All the time Wykham Delandre nursed his revenge. Deep in his heart had grown up a purpose of vengeance which only waited an opportunity to crystallise and take a definite shape. His vague idea was somehow centred in the wife of Brent, for he knew that he could strike him best through those he loved, and the coming time seemed to hold in its womb the opportunity for which he longed. One night he sat alone in the living-room of his house. It had once been a handsome room in its way, but time and neglect had done their work and it was now little better than a ruin, without dignity or picturesqueness of any kind. He had been drinking heavily for some time and was more than half stupefied. He thought he heard a noise as of someone at the door and looked up. Then he called half-savagely to come in; but there was no response. With a muttered blasphemy he renewed his potations. Presently he forgot all around him, sank into a daze, but suddenly awoke to see standing before him someone or something like a battered, ghostly edition of his sister. For a few moments there came upon him a sort of fear. The woman before him, with distorted features and burning eyes, seemed hardly human, and the only thing that seemed a reality of his sister, as she had been, was her wealth of golden hair, and this was now streaked with grey. She eyed her brother with a long, cold stare; and he, too, as he looked and began to realise the actuality of her presence, found the hatred of her which he had had once again surging up in his heart. All the brooding passion of the past year seemed to find a voice at once as he asked her: 'Why are you here? You're dead and buried.'

'I am here, Wykham Delandre, for no love of you,

but because I hate another even more than I do you!'
A great passion blazed in her eyes.

'Him?' he asked, in so fierce a whisper that even
the woman was for an instant startled till she regained
her calm.

'Yes, him!' she answered. 'But make no mistake,
my revenge is my own; and I merely use you to help
me to it.'

Wykham asked suddenly: 'Did he marry you?'

The woman's distorted face broadened out in a
ghastly attempt at a smile. It was a hideous mockery,
for the broken features and seamed scars took strange
shapes and strange colours, and queer lines of white
showed out as the straining muscles pressed on the
old cicatrices.

'So you would like to know! It would please your
pride to feel that your sister was truly married! Well,
you shall not know. That was my revenge on you,
and I do not mean to change it by a hair's breadth. I
have come here tonight simply to let you know that I
am alive, so that if any violence be done me where I
am going there may be a witness.'

'Where are you going?' demanded her brother.

'That is my affair! and I have not the least intention
of letting you know!' Wykham stood up, but the
drink was on him and he reeled and fell. As he lay on
the floor he announced his intention of following his
sister; and with an outburst of splenetic humour told
her that he would follow her through the darkness by
the light of her hair and of her beauty. At this she
turned on him, and said that there were others beside
him that would rue her hair and her beauty too. 'As
he will,' she hissed; 'for the hair remains though the
beauty be gone. When he withdrew the lynchpin and

383

sent us over the precipice into the torrent, he had little thought of my beauty. Perhaps his beauty would be scarred like mine were he whirled, as I was, among the rocks of the Visp, and frozen on the ice pack in the drift of the river. But let him beware! His time is coming!' and with a fierce gesture she flung open the door and passed out into the night.

* * *

Later on that night, Mrs Brent, who was but half-asleep, became suddenly awake and spoke to her husband: 'Geoffrey, was not that the click of a lock somewhere below our window?'

But Geoffrey – though she thought that he, too, had started at the noise – seemed sound asleep, and breathed heavily. Again Mrs Brent dozed; but this time awoke to the fact that her husband had arisen and was partially dressed. He was deadly pale, and when the light of the lamp which he had in his hand fell on his face, she was frightened at the look in his eyes.

'What is it, Geoffrey? What dost thou?' she asked.

'Hush! little one,' he answered, in a strange, hoarse voice. 'Go to sleep. I am restless, and wish to finish some work I left undone.'

'Bring it here, my husband,' she said; 'I am lonely and I fear when thou art away.'

For reply he merely kissed her and went out, closing the door behind him. She lay awake for a while, and then nature asserted itself, and she slept.

Suddenly she started broad awake with the memory in her ears of a smothered cry from somewhere not far off. She jumped up and ran to the door and listened, but there was no sound. She grew alarmed for her husband, and called out: 'Geoffrey! Geoffrey!'

After a few moments the door of the great hall opened, and Geoffrey appeared at it, but without his lamp.

'Hush!' he said, in a sort of whisper, and his voice was harsh and stern. 'Hush! Get to bed! I am working, and must not be disturbed. Go to sleep, and do not wake the house!'

With a chill in her heart – for the harshness of her husband's voice was new to her – she crept back to bed and lay there trembling, too frightened to cry, and listened to every sound. There was a long pause of silence, and then the sound of some iron implement striking muffled blows! Then there came a clang of a heavy stone falling, followed by a muffled curse. Then a dragging sound, and then more noise of stone on stone. She lay all the while in an agony of fear, and her heart beat dreadfully. She heard a curious sort of scraping sound; and then there was silence. Presently the door opened gently, and Geoffrey appeared. His wife pretended to be asleep; but through her eyelashes she saw him wash from his hands something white that looked like lime.

In the morning he made no allusion to the previous night, and she was afraid to ask any question.

From that day there seemed some shadow over Geoffrey Brent. He neither ate nor slept as he had been accustomed, and his former habit of turning suddenly as though someone were speaking from behind him revived. The old hall seemed to have some kind of fascination for him. He used to go there many times in the day, but grew impatient if anyone, even his wife, entered it. When the builder's foreman came to enquire about continuing his work, Geoffrey was out driving; the man went into the hall, and when

Geoffrey returned the servant told him of his arrival and where he was. With a frightful oath he pushed the servant aside and hurried up to the old hall. The workman met him almost at the door and as Geoffrey burst into the room he ran against him. The man apologised: 'Beg pardon, sir, but I was just going out to make some enquiries. I directed twelve sacks of lime to be sent here, but I see there are only ten.'

'Damn the ten sacks and the twelve too!' was the ungracious and incomprehensible rejoinder.

The workman looked surprised, and tried to turn the conversation.

'I see, sir, there is a little matter which our people must have done; but the governor will of course see it set right at his own cost.'

'What do you mean?'

'That 'ere 'arthstone, sir. Some idiot must have put a scaffold pole on it and cracked it right down the middle, and it's thick enough you'd think to stand hanythink.' Geoffrey was silent for quite a minute, and then said in a constrained voice and with much gentler manner: 'Tell your people that I am not going on with the work in the hall at present. I want to leave it as it is for a while longer.'

'All right, sir. I'll send up a few of our chaps to take away these poles and lime bags and tidy the place up a bit.'

'No! No!' said Geoffrey, 'leave them where they are. I shall send and tell you when you are to get on with the work.' So the foreman went away, and his comment to his master was: 'I'd send in the bill, sir, for the work already done. 'Pears to me that money's a little shaky in that quarter.'

Once or twice Delandre tried to stop Brent on the

road, and at last, finding that he could not attain his object, rode after the carriage, calling out: 'What has become of my sister, your wife?' Geoffrey lashed his horses into a gallop, and the other, seeing from his white face and from his wife's collapse almost into a faint that his object was attained, rode away with a scowl and a laugh.

That night when Geoffrey went into the hall he passed over to the great fireplace, and all at once started back with a smothered cry. Then with an effort he pulled himself together and went away, returning with a light. He bent down over the broken hearthstone to see if the moonlight falling through the storeyed window had in any way deceived him. Then with a groan of anguish he sank to his knees.

There, sure enough, through the crack in the broken stone were protruding a multitude of threads of golden hair just tinged with grey!

He was disturbed by a noise at the door, and looking round, saw his wife standing in the doorway. In the desperation of the moment he took action to prevent discovery, and lighting a match at the lamp, stooped down and burned away the hair that rose through the broken stone. Then rising nonchalantly as he could, he pretended surprise at seeing his wife beside him.

For the next week he lived in an agony; for, whether by accident or design, he could not find himself alone in the hall for any length of time. At each visit the hair had grown afresh through the crack, and he had to watch it carefully lest his terrible secret should be discovered. He tried to find a receptacle for the body of the murdered woman outside the house, but someone always interrupted him; and once, when he was coming out of the private doorway, he was met by his wife, who began to question him about it, and manifested surprise that she should not have before noticed the key which he now reluctantly showed her. Geoffrey dearly and passionately loved his wife, so that any possibility of her discovering his dread secrets, or even of doubting him, filled him with anguish; and after a couple of days had passed, he could not help coming to the conclusion that, at least, she suspected something.

That very evening she came into the hall after her drive and found him there sitting moodily by the deserted fireplace. She spoke to him directly.

'Geoffrey, I have been spoken to by that fellow Delandre, and he says horrible things. He tells me that a week ago his sister returned to his house, the wreck and ruin of her former self, with only her golden hair as of old, and announced some fell intention. He asked me where she is – and oh, Geoffrey, she is dead, she is dead! So how can she have returned? Oh! I am in dread, and I know not where to turn!'

For answer, Geoffrey burst into a torrent of blasphemy which made her shudder. He cursed Wykham Delandre and his sister and all their kind, and in especial he hurled curse after curse on her golden hair.

'Oh, hush! hush!' she said, and was then silent, for she feared her husband when she saw the evil effect of his humour. Geoffrey in the torrent of his anger stood up and moved away from the hearth; but suddenly stopped as he saw a new look of terror in his wife's eyes. He followed their glance, and then he, too, shuddered – for there on the broken hearthstone lay a golden streak as the point of the hair rose though the crack.

'Look, look!' she shrieked. 'Is it some ghost of the dead! Come away – come away!' and seizing her husband by the wrist with the frenzy of madness, she pulled him from the room.

That night she was in a raging fever. The doctor of the district attended her at once, and special aid was telegraphed for to London. Geoffrey was in despair, and in his anguish at the danger to his young wife almost forgot his own crime and its consequences. In the evening the doctor had to leave to attend to others; but he left Geoffrey in charge of his wife. His last words were: 'Remember, you must humour her till I come in the morning, or till some other doctor has her case in hand. What you have to dread is another attack of emotion. See that she is kept warm. Nothing more can be done.'

Late in the evening, when the rest of the household had retired, Geoffrey's wife got up from her bed and called to her husband.

'Come!' she said. 'Come to the old hall! I know where the gold comes from! I want to see it grow!'

Geoffrey would fain have stopped her, but he feared for her life or reason on the one hand, and on the other lest in a paroxysm she should shriek out her terrible suspicion, and seeing that it was useless to try to prevent her, wrapped a warm rug around her and went with her to the old hall. When they entered, she turned and shut the door and locked it.

'We want no strangers among us three tonight!' she whispered with a wan smile.

'We three! nay we are but two,' said Geoffrey with a shudder; he feared to say more.

'Sit here,' said his wife as she put out the light. 'Sit here by the hearth and watch the gold growing. The

389

silver moonlight is jealous! See, it steals along the floor towards the gold – our gold!' Geoffrey looked with growing horror, and saw that during the hours that had passed the golden hair had protruded farther through the broken hearthstone. He tried to hide it by placing his feet over the broken place; and his wife, drawing her chair beside him, leant over and laid her head on his shoulder.

'Now do not stir, dear,' she said; 'let us sit still and watch. We shall find the secret of the growing gold!'

He passed his arm round her and sat silent; and as the moonlight stole along the floor she sank to sleep. He feared to wake her and so sat silent and miserable as the hours stole away and before his horror-struck eyes the golden hair from the broken stone grew and grew; and as it increased, so his heart got colder and colder, till at last he had not power to stir, and sat with eyes full of terror watching his doom.

* * *

In the morning, when the London doctor came, neither Geoffrey nor his wife could be found. Search was made in all the rooms, but without avail. As a last resource the great door of the old hall was broken open, and those who entered saw a grim and sorry sight.

There by the deserted hearth Geoffrey Brent and his young wife sat cold and white and dead. Her face was peaceful, and her eyes were closed in sleep; but his face was a sight that made all who saw it shudder, for there was on it a look of unutterable horror. The eyes were open and stared glassily at his feet, which were twined with tresses of golden hair, streaked with grey, which came through the broken hearthstone.

OSCAR WILDE

The Canterville Ghost

A Hylo-Idealistic Romance

I

When Mr Hiram B. Otis, the American Minister, bought Canterville Chase, everyone told him he was doing a very foolish thing, as there was no doubt at all that the place was haunted. Indeed, Lord Canterville himself, who was a man of the most punctilious honour, had felt it his duty to mention the fact to Mr Otis when they came to discuss terms.

'We have not cared to live in the place ourselves,' said Lord Canterville, 'since my grandaunt, the Dowager Duchess of Bolton, was frightened into a fit, from which she never really recovered, by two skeleton hands being placed on her shoulders as she was dressing for dinner, and I feel bound to tell you, Mr Otis, that the ghost has been seen by several living members of my family, as well as by the rector of the parish, the Reverend Augustus Dampier, who is a Fellow of King's College, Cambridge. After the unfortunate accident to the Duchess, none of our younger servants would stay with us, and Lady Canterville often got very little sleep at night, in consequence of the mysterious noises that came from the corridor and the library.'

'My Lord,' answered the minister, 'I will take the furniture and the ghost at a valuation. I come from a modern country, where we have everything that money can buy; and with all our spry young fellows painting the Old World red, and carrying off your best actresses and prima-donnas, I reckon that if there were such a thing as a ghost in Europe, we'd have it at home in a very short time in one of our public museums, or on the road as a show.'

'I fear that the ghost exists,' said Lord Canterville, smiling, 'though it may have resisted the overtures of your enterprising impresarios. It has been well known for three centuries, since 1584 in fact, and always makes its appearance before the death of any member of our family.'

'Well, so does the family doctor for that matter, Lord Canterville. But there is no such thing, sir, as a ghost, and I guess the laws of nature are not going to be suspended for the British aristocracy.'

'You are certainly very natural in America,' answered Lord Canterville, who did not quite understand Mr Otis's last observation, 'and if you don't mind a ghost in the house, it is all right. Only you must remember I warned you.'

A few weeks after this, the purchase was completed, and at the close of the season the minister and his family went down to Canterville Chase. Mrs Otis, who, as Miss Lucretia R. Tappan, of West 53rd Street, had been a celebrated New York belle, was now a very handsome, middle-aged woman, with fine eyes and a superb profile. Many American ladies on leaving their native land adopt an appearance of chronic ill-health, under the impression that it is a form of European refinement, but Mrs Otis had never fallen into this error. She had a magnificent constitution, and a really wonderful amount of animal spirits. Indeed, in many respects, she was quite English, and was an excellent example of the fact that we have really everything in common with America nowadays, except, of course, language. Her eldest son, christened Washington by his parents in a moment of patriotism, which he never ceased to regret, was a fair-haired, rather good-looking young man, who had qualified himself for American diplomacy by leading the German at the Newport Casino for three successive seasons, and even in London was well known as an excellent dancer. Gardenias and the peerage were his only weaknesses. Otherwise he was extremely sensible. Miss Virginia E. Otis was a little girl of fifteen, lithe and lovely as a fawn, and with a fine freedom in her large blue eyes. She was a wonderful amazon, and had once raced old Lord Bilton on her pony twice round the park, winning by a length and a half, just in front of the Achilles statue, to the huge delight of the young Duke of Cheshire, who proposed for her on the spot, and was sent back to Eton that very night by his guardians, in floods of tears. After Virginia came the twins, who were usually called 'the Stars and Stripes', as they were always getting swished. They were delightful boys, and with the exception of the worthy minister, the only true republicans of the family.

As Canterville Chase is seven miles from Ascot, the nearest railway station, Mr Otis had telegraphed for a waggonette to meet them, and they started on their drive in high spirits. It was a lovely July evening, and the air was delicate with the scent of the pine woods. Now and then they heard a woodpigeon brooding over its own sweet voice, or saw, deep in the rustling fern, the burnished breast of the pheasant. Little squirrels peered at them from the beech trees as they went by, and the rabbits scudded away through the brushwood and over the mossy knolls, with their white tails in the air. As they entered the avenue of Canterville Chase, however, the sky became suddenly overcast with clouds, a curious stillness seemed to hold the atmosphere, a great flight of rooks passed silently over their heads, and, before they reached the house, some big drops of rain had fallen.

Standing on the steps to receive them was an old woman, neatly dressed in black silk, with a white cap and apron. This was Mrs Umney, the housekeeper, whom Mrs Otis, at Lady Canterville's earnest request, had consented to keep on in her former position. She made them each a low curtsey as they alighted and said, in a quaint, old-fashioned manner, 'I bid you welcome to Canterville Chase.' Following her, they passed through the fine Tudor hall into the library, a long, low room, panelled in black oak, at the end of which was a large stained-glass window. Here they found tea laid out for them, and, after taking off their wraps, they sat down and began to look round, while Mrs Umney waited on them.

Suddenly Mrs Otis caught sight of a dull red stain on the floor just by the fireplace and, quite unconscious of what it really signified, said to Mrs Umney, 'I am afraid something has been spilt there.'

'Yes, madam,' replied the old housekeeper in a low voice, 'blood has been spilt on that spot.'

'How horrid,' cried Mrs Otis; 'I don't at all care for bloodstains in a sitting-room. It must be removed at once.'

The old woman smiled, and answered in the same low, mysterious voice, 'It is the blood of Lady Eleanore de Canterville, who was murdered on that very spot by her own husband, Sir Simon de Canterville, in 1575. Sir Simon survived her nine years, and disappeared suddenly under very mysterious circumstances. His body has never been discovered, but his guilty spirit still haunts the Chase. The bloodstain has been much admired by tourists and others, and cannot be removed.'

'That is all nonsense,' cried Washington Otis; 'Pinkerton's Champion Stain Remover and Paragon Detergent will clean it up in no time,' and before the terrified housekeeper could interfere he had fallen upon his knees, and was rapidly scouring the floor with a small stick of what looked like a black cosmetic. In a few moments no trace of the bloodstain could be seen.

'I knew Pinkerton would do it,' he exclaimed triumphantly, as he looked round at his admiring family; but no sooner had he said these words than a terrible flash of lightning lit up the sombre room, a fearful peal of thunder made them all start to their feet, and Mrs Umney fainted.

'What a monstrous climate!' said the American Minister calmly, as he lit a long cheroot. 'I guess the old country is so over-populated that they have not enough decent weather for everybody. I have always been of opinion that emigration is the only thing for England.'

'My dear Hiram,' cried Mrs Otis, 'what can we do with a woman who faints?'

'Charge it to her like breakages,' answered the minister; 'she won't faint after that;' and in a few moments Mrs Umney certainly came to. There was no doubt, however, that she was extremely upset, and she sternly warned Mr Otis to beware of some trouble coming to the house.

'I have seen things with my own eyes, sir,' she said, 'that would make any Christian's hair stand on end, and many and many a night I have not closed my eyes in sleep for the awful things that are done here.' Mr Otis, however, and his wife warmly assured the honest soul that they were not afraid of ghosts, and, after invoking the blessings of Providence on her new master and mistress, and making arrangements for an increase of salary, the old housekeeper tottered off to her own room.

2

The storm raged fiercely all that night, but nothing of particular note occurred. The next morning, however, when they came down to breakfast, they found the terrible stain of blood once again on the floor. 'I don't think it can be the fault of the Paragon Detergent,' said Washington, 'for I have tried it with everything. It must be the ghost.' He accordingly rubbed out the stain a second time, but the second morning it appeared again. The third morning also it was there, though the library had been locked up at night by Mr Otis himself, and the key carried upstairs. The whole family were now quite interested; Mr Otis began to suspect that he had been too dogmatic in his denial of the existence of ghosts, Mrs Otis expressed her intention of joining the Psychical Society, and Washington prepared a long letter to Messrs Myers and Podmore on the subject of the Permanence of Sanguineous Stains when connected with Crime. That night all doubts about the objective existence of phantasmata were removed for ever.

The day had been warm and sunny; and, in the cool of the evening, the whole family went out for a drive. They did not return home till nine o'clock, when they had a light supper. The conversation in no way turned upon ghosts, so there were not even those primary conditions of receptive expectation which so often precede the presentation of psychical phenomena. The subjects discussed, as I have since learned from Mr Otis, were merely such as form the ordinary conversation of cultured Americans of the better class, such as the immense superiority of Miss Fanny Davenport over Sarah Bernhardt as an actress; the difficulty of obtaining green corn, buckwheat cakes and hominy, even in the best English houses; the importance of Boston in the development of the world-soul; the advantages of the baggage-check system in railway travelling; and the sweetness of the New York accent as compared to the London drawl. No mention at all was made of the supernatural, nor was Sir Simon de Canterville alluded to in anyway. At eleven o'clock the family retired, and by half-past all the lights were out. Some time after, Mr Otis was awakened by a curious noise in the corridor, outside his room. It sounded like the clank of metal, and seemed to be coming nearer every moment. He got up at once, struck a match, and looked at the time. It was exactly one o'clock. He was quite calm, and felt his pulse, which was not at all feverish. The strange noise still continued, and with it he heard distinctly the sound of footsteps. He put on his slippers, took a small oblong phial out of his dressing-case, and opened the door. Right in front of him he saw, in the wan moonlight, an old man of terrible aspect. His eyes were as red burning coals; long grey hair fell over his shoulders in matted coils; his garments, which were of antique cut, were soiled and ragged, and from his wrists and ankles hung heavy manacles and rusty gyves.

'My dear sir,' said Mr Otis, 'I really must insist on your oiling those chains, and have brought you for that purpose a small bottle of the Tammany Rising Sun Lubricator. It is said to be completely efficacious upon one application, and there are several testimonials to that effect on the wrapper from some of our most eminent native divines. I shall leave it here for you by the bedroom candles, and will be happy to supply you with more should you require it.' With these words the United States Minister laid the bottle down on a marble table, and, closing his door, retired to rest.

For a moment the Canterville ghost stood quite motionless in natural indignation; then, dashing the bottle violently upon the polished floor, he fled down the corridor, uttering hollow groans, and emitting a ghastly green light. Just, however, as he reached the top of the great oak staircase, a door was flung open, two little white-robed figures appeared, and a large pillow whizzed past his head! There was evidently no time to be lost, so, hastily adopting the Fourth Dimension of Space as a means of escape, he vanished through the wainscoting, and the house became quite quiet.

On reaching a small secret chamber in the left wing, he leaned up against a moonbeam to recover his breath, and began to try and realise his position.

Never, in a brilliant and uninterrupted career of three hundred years, had he been so grossly insulted. He thought of the Dowager Duchess, whom he had frightened into a fit as she stood before the glass in her lace and diamonds; of the four housemaids, who had gone off into hysterics when he merely grinned at them through the curtains of one of the spare bedrooms; of the rector of the parish, whose candle he had blown out as he was coming late one night from the library, and who had been under the care of Sir William Gull ever since, a perfect martyr to nervous disorders; and of old Madame de Tremouillac, who, having wakened up one morning early and seen a skeleton seated in an armchair by the fire reading her diary, had been confined to her bed for six weeks with an attack of brain fever, and, on her recovery, had become reconciled to the church, and broken off her connection with that notorious sceptic Monsieur de Voltaire. He remembered the terrible night when the wicked Lord Canterville was found choking in his dressing-room, with the knave of diamonds halfway down his throat, and confessed, just before he died, that he had cheated Charles James Fox out of £50,000 at Crockford's by means of that very card, and swore that the ghost had made him swallow it. All his great achievements came back to him again, from the butler who had shot himself in the pantry because he had seen a green hand tapping at the window pane, to the beautiful Lady Stutfield, who was always obliged to wear a black velvet band round her throat to hide the mark of five fingers burnt upon her white skin, and who drowned herself at last in the carp-pond at the end of the King's Walk. With the enthusiastic egotism of the true artist he went over his most celebrated performances, and smiled bitterly to himself as he recalled to mind his last appearance as 'Red Ruben, or the Strangled Babe', his début as 'Gaunt Gibeon, the Bloodsucker of Bexley Moor', and the furore he had excited one lovely June evening by merely playing ninepins with his own bones upon the lawn-tennis ground. And after all this, some wretched modern Americans were to come and offer him the Rising Sun Lubricator, and throw pillows at his head! It was quite unbearable. Besides, no ghosts in history had ever been treated in this manner. Accordingly, he determined to have vengeance, and remained till daylight in an attitude of deep thought.

3

The next morning when the Otis family met at breakfast, they discussed the ghost at some length. The United States Minister was naturally a little annoyed to find that his present had not been accepted. 'I have no wish,' he said, 'to do the ghost any personal injury, and I must say that, considering the length of time he has been in the house, I don't think it is at all polite to throw pillows at him' – a very just remark, at which, I am sorry to say, the twins burst into shouts of laughter. 'Upon the other hand,' he continued, 'if he really declines to use the Rising Sun Lubricator, we shall have to take his chains from him. It would be quite impossible to sleep, with such a noise going on outside the bedrooms.'

For the rest of the week, however, they were undisturbed, the only thing that excited any attention being the continual renewal of the bloodstain on the library floor. This certainly was very strange, as the door was always locked at night by Mr Otis, and the windows kept closely barred. The chameleon-like colour, also, of the stain excited a good deal of comment. Some mornings it was a dull (almost Indian) red, then it would be vermilion, then a rich purple, and once when they came down for family prayers, according to the simple rites of the Free American Reformed Episcopalian Church, they found it a bright emerald-green. These kaleidoscopic changes naturally amused the party very much, and bets on the subject were freely made every evening. The only person who did not enter into the joke was little Virginia, who, for some unexplained reason, was always a good deal distressed at the sight of the bloodstain, and very nearly cried the morning it was emerald-green.

The second appearance of the ghost was on Sunday night. Shortly after they had gone to bed they were suddenly alarmed by a fearful crash in the hall. Rushing downstairs, they found that a large suit of old armour had become detached from its stand, and had fallen on the stone floor, while, seated in a high-backed chair, was the Canterville ghost, rubbing his knees with an expression of acute agony on his face. The twins, having brought their peashooters with them, at once discharged two pellets on him, with that accuracy of aim which can only be attained by long and careful practice on a writing-master, while the United States Minister covered him with his revolver, and called upon him, in accordance with Californian etiquette, to hold up his hands! The ghost started up with a wild shriek of rage, and swept through them like a mist, extinguishing Washington Otis's candle as he passed, and so leaving them all in total darkness. On reaching the top of the staircase he recovered himself, and determined to give his celebrated peal of demoniac laughter. This he had on more than one occasion found extremely useful. It was said to have turned Lord Raker's wig grey in a single night, and had certainly made three of Lady Canterville's French governesses give warning before their month was up. He accordingly laughed his most horrible laugh, till the old vaulted roof rang and rang again, but hardly had the fearful echo died away when a door opened, and Mrs Otis came out in a light blue dressing-gown. 'I am afraid you are far from well,' she said, 'and have brought you a bottle of Dr Dobell's tincture. If it is indigestion, you will find it a most excellent remedy.' The ghost glared at her in fury, and began at once to make preparations for turning himself into a large black dog, an accomplishment for which he was justly renowned, and to which the family doctor always attributed the permanent idiocy of Lord Canterville's uncle, the Hon. Thomas Horton. The sound of approaching footsteps, however, made him hesitate in his fell purpose, so he contented himself with becoming faintly phosphorescent, and vanished with a deep churchyard groan, just as the twins had come up to him.

On reaching his room he entirely broke down, and became a prey to the most violent agitation. The vulgarity of the twins, and the gross materialism of Mrs Otis, were naturally extremely annoying, but what really distressed him most was that he had been unable to wear the suit of mail. He had hoped that even modern Americans would be thrilled by the sight of a Spectre In Armour, if for no more sensible reason, at least out of respect for their national poet

Longfellow, over whose graceful and attractive poetry he himself had whiled away many a weary hour when the Cantervilles were up in town. Besides, it was his own suit. He had worn it with great success at the Kenilworth tournament, and had been highly complimented on it by no less a person than the Virgin Queen herself. Yet when he had put it on, he had been completely overpowered by the weight of the huge breastplate and steel casque, and had fallen heavily on the stone pavement, barking both his knees severely, and bruising the knuckles of his right hand.

For some days after this he was extremely ill, and hardly stirred out of his room at all, except to keep the bloodstain in proper repair. However, by taking great care of himself, he recovered, and resolved to make a third attempt to frighten the United States Minister and his family. He selected Friday, the 17th of August, for his appearance, and spent most of that day in looking over his wardrobe, ultimately deciding in favour of a large slouched hat with a red feather, a winding-sheet frilled at the wrists and neck, and a rusty dagger. Towards evening a violent storm of rain came on, and the wind was so high that all the windows and doors in the old house shook and rattled. In fact, it was just such weather as he loved. His plan of action was this. He was to make his way quietly to Washington Otis's room, gibber at him from the foot of the bed, and stab himself three times in the throat to the sound of slow music. He bore Washington a special grudge, being quite aware that it was he who was in the habit of removing the famous Canterville bloodstain, by means of Pinkerton's Paragon Detergent. Having reduced the reckless and foolhardy youth to a condition of abject terror, he was then to proceed to the room occupied by the United States Minister and his wife, and there to place a clammy hand on Mrs Otis's forehead, while he hissed into her trembling husband's ear the awful secrets of the charnel-house. With regard to little Virginia, he had not quite made up his mind. She had never insulted him in any way, and was pretty and gentle. A few hollow groans from the wardrobe, he thought, would be more than sufficient, or, if that failed to wake her, he might grabble at the counterpane with palsy-twitching fingers. As for the twins, he was quite determined to teach them a lesson. The first thing to be done was, of course, to sit upon their chests, so as to produce the stifling sensation of nightmare. Then, as their beds were quite close to each other, to stand between them in the form of a green, icy-cold corpse, till they became paralysed with fear, and, finally, to throw off the winding-sheet, and crawl round the room, with white bleached bones and one rolling eyeball, in the character of 'Dumb Daniel, or the Suicide's Skeleton', a role in which he had on more than one occasion produced a great effect, and which he considered quite equal to his famous part of 'Martin the Maniac, or the Masked Mystery'.

At half-past ten he heard the family going to bed. For some time he was disturbed by wild shrieks of laughter from the twins, who, with the light-hearted gaiety of schoolboys, were evidently amusing themselves before they retired to rest, but at a quarter past eleven all was still, and, as midnight sounded, he sallied forth. The owl beat against the window panes, the raven croaked from the old yew tree, and the wind wandered moaning round the house like a lost soul; but the Otis family slept unconscious of their doom, and high above the rain and storm he could hear the steady snoring of the Minister for the United States. He stepped stealthily out of the wainscoting, with an evil smile on his cruel, wrinkled mouth, and the moon hid her face in a cloud as he stole past the great oriel window, where his own arms and those of his murdered wife were blazoned in azure and gold. On and on he glided, like an evil shadow, the very darkness seeming to loathe him as he passed. Once he thought he heard something call, and stopped; but it was only the baying of a dog from the Red Farm, and he went on, muttering strange sixteenth-century curses, and ever and anon brandishing the rusty dagger in the midnight air. Finally he reached the corner of the passage that led to luckless Washington's room. For a moment he paused there, the wind blowing his long grey locks about his head, and twisting into grotesque and fantastic folds the nameless horror of the dead man's shroud. Then the clock struck the quarter, and he felt the time was come. He chuckled to himself, and turned the corner; but no sooner had he done so, than, with a piteous wail of terror, he fell back, and hid his blanched face in his long, bony hands. Right in front of him was standing a horrible spectre, motionless as a carven image, and monstrous as a madman's dream! Its head was bald and burnished; its face round, and fat, and white; and hideous laughter seemed to have writhed its features into an eternal grin. From the eyes streamed rays of scarlet light, the mouth was a wide well of fire, and a hideous garment, like to his own, swathed with its silent snows the Titan form. On its breast was a placard with strange writing in antique characters, some scroll of shame it seemed, some record of wild sins, some awful calendar of crime, and, with its right hand, it bore aloft a falchion of gleaming steel.

Never having seen a ghost before, he naturally was terribly frightened, and, after a second hasty glance at the awful phantom, he fled back to his room, tripping up in his long winding-sheet as he sped down the corridor, and finally dropping the rusty dagger into the minister's jackboots, where it was found in the morning by the butler. Once in the privacy of his own apartment, he flung himself down on a small pallet-bed, and hid his face under the clothes. After a time, however, the brave old Canterville spirit asserted itself, and he determined to go and speak to the other ghost as soon as it was daylight. Accordingly, just as the dawn was touching the hills with silver, he returned towards the spot where he had first laid eyes on the grisly phantom, feeling that, after all, two ghosts were better than one, and that, by the aid of his new friend, he might safely grapple with the twins. On reaching the spot, however, a terrible sight met his gaze. Something had evidently happened to the spectre, for the light had entirely faded from its hollow eyes, the gleaming falchion had fallen from its hand, and it was leaning up against the wall in a strained and uncomfortable attitude. He rushed forward and seized it in his arms, when, to his horror, the head slipped off and rolled on the floor, the body assumed a recumbent posture, and he found himself clasping a white dimity bed-curtain, with a sweeping-brush, a kitchen cleaver, and a hollow turnip lying at his feet! Unable to understand this curious transformation, he clutched the placard with feverish haste, and there, in the grey morning light, he read these fearful words:

𝕿𝖍𝖊 𝕺𝖙𝖎𝖘 𝕲𝖍𝖔𝖘𝖙𝖊
𝖄𝖊 𝕺𝖓𝖑𝖎𝖊 𝕿𝖗𝖚𝖊 𝖆𝖓𝖉 𝕺𝖗𝖎𝖌𝖎𝖓𝖆𝖑𝖊 𝕾𝖕𝖔𝖔𝖐
𝕭𝖊𝖜𝖆𝖗𝖊 𝖔𝖋 𝖄𝖊 𝕴𝖒𝖎𝖙𝖆𝖙𝖎𝖔𝖓𝖘
𝕬𝖑𝖑 𝖔𝖙𝖍𝖊𝖗𝖘 𝖆𝖗𝖊 𝕮𝖔𝖚𝖓𝖙𝖊𝖗𝖋𝖊𝖎𝖙𝖊

The whole thing flashed across him. He had been tricked, foiled and outwitted! The old Canterville look came into his eyes; he ground his toothless gums together; and, raising his withered hands high above his head, swore, according to the picturesque phraseology of the antique school, that when Chanticleer had sounded twice his merry horn, deeds of blood would be wrought, and Murder walk abroad with silent feet.

Hardly had he finished this awful oath when, from the red-tiled roof of a distant homestead, a cock crew. He laughed a long, low, bitter laugh, and waited. Hour after hour he waited, but the cock, for some strange reason, did not crow again. Finally, at half-past seven, the arrival of the housemaids made him give up his fearful vigil, and he stalked back to his room, thinking of his vain hope and baffled purpose. There he consulted several books of ancient chivalry, of which he was exceedingly fond, and found that, on every occasion on which his oath had been used, Chanticleer had always crowed a second time. 'Perdition seize the naughty fowl,' he muttered. 'I have seen the day when, with my stout spear, I would have run him through the gorge, and made him crow for me as 'twere in death!' He then retired to a comfortable lead coffin, and stayed there till evening.

4

The next day the ghost was very weak and tired. The terrible excitement of the last four weeks was beginning to have its effect. His nerves were completely shattered, and he started at the slightest noise. For five days he kept his room, and at last made up his mind to give up the point of the bloodstain on the library floor. If the Otis family did not want it, they clearly did not deserve it. They were evidently people on a low, material plane of existence, and quite incapable of appreciating the symbolic value of sensuous phenomena. The question of phantasmic apparitions, and the development of astral bodies, was of course quite a different matter, and really not under his control. It was his solemn duty to appear in the corridor once a week, and to gibber from the large oriel window on the first and third Wednesday in every month, and he did not see how he could honourably escape from his obligations. It is quite true that his life had been very evil, but, upon the other hand, he was most conscientious in all things connected with the supernatural. For the next three Saturdays, accordingly, he traversed the corridor as usual between midnight and three o'clock, taking every possible precaution against being either heard or seen. He removed his boots, trod as lightly as possible on the old worm-eaten boards, wore a large black velvet cloak, and was careful to use the Rising Sun Lubricator for oiling his chains. I am bound to acknowledge that it was with a good deal of difficulty that he brought himself to adopt this last mode of protection. However, one night, while the family were at dinner, he slipped into Mr Otis's bedroom and carried off the bottle. He felt a little humiliated at first, but afterwards was sensible enough to see that there was a great deal to be said for the invention, and, to a certain degree, it served his purpose. Still, in spite of everything, he was not left unmolested. Strings were continually being stretched across the corridor, over which he tripped in the dark, and on one occasion, while dressed for the part of 'Black Isaac, or the Hunts-man of Hogley Woods', he met with a severe fall, through treading on a butter-slide, which the twins had constructed from the entrance of the Tapestry Chamber to the top of the oak staircase. This last insult so enraged him, that he resolved to make one final effort to assert his dignity and social position, and determined to visit the insolent young Etonians the next night in his celebrated character of 'Reckless Rupert, or the Headless Earl'.

He had not appeared in this disguise for more than seventy years; in fact, not since he had so frightened pretty Lady Barbara Modish by means of it, that she suddenly broke off her engagement with the present Lord Canterville's grandfather, and ran away to Gretna Green with handsome Jack Castleton, declaring that nothing in the world would induce her to marry into a family that allowed such a horrible phantom to walk up and down the terrace at twilight. Poor Jack was afterwards shot in a duel by Lord Canterville on Wandsworth Common, and Lady Barbara died of a broken heart at Tunbridge Wells before the year was out, so, in every way, it had been a great success. It was, however, an extremely difficult 'make-up', if I may use such a theatrical expression in connection with one of the greatest mysteries of the supernatural, or, to employ a more scientific term, the higher-natural world, and it took him fully three hours to make his preparations. At last everything was ready, and he was very pleased with his appearance. The big leather riding-boots that went with the dress were just a little too large for him, and he could only find one of the two horse-pistols, but, on the whole, he was quite satisfied, and at a quarter past one he glided out of the wainscoting and crept down the corridor. On reaching the room occupied by the twins, which I should mention was called the Blue Bedchamber, on account of the colour of its hangings, he found the door just ajar. Wishing to make an effective entrance, he flung it wide open, when a heavy jug of water fell right down on him, wetting him to the skin, and just missing his left shoulder by a couple of inches. At the same moment he heard stifled shrieks of laughter proceeding from the four-post bed. The shock to his nervous system was so great that he fled back to his room as hard as he could go, and the next day he was laid up with a severe cold. The only thing that at all consoled him in the whole affair was the fact that he had not brought his head with him, for, had he done so, the consequences might have been very serious.

He now gave up all hope of ever frightening this rude American family, and contented himself, as a rule, with creeping about the passages in list slippers, with a thick red muffler round his throat for fear of draughts, and a small arquebuse, in case he should be attacked by the twins. The final blow he received occurred on the 19th of September. He had gone downstairs to the great entrance-hall, feeling sure that there, at any rate, he would be quite unmolested, and was amusing himself by making satirical remarks on the large Saroni photographs of the United States Minister and his wife, which had now taken the place of the Canterville family pictures. He was simply but neatly clad in a long shroud, spotted with churchyard mould, had tied up his jaw with a strip of yellow linen, and carried a small lantern and a sexton's spade. In fact, he was dressed for the character of 'Jonas the Graveless, or the Corpse-Snatcher of Chertsey Barn', one of his most remarkable impersonations, and one which the Cantervilles had every reason to remember, as it was the real origin of their quarrel with their neighbour, Lord Rufford. It was about a quarter past two o'clock in the morning, and, as far as he could ascertain, no one was stirring. As he was strolling towards the library, however, to see if there were any traces left of the bloodstain, suddenly there leaped out on him from a dark corner two figures, who waved their arms wildly above their heads, and shrieked out 'boo!' in his ear.

Seized with a panic, which, under the circumstances, was only natural, he rushed for the staircase, but found Washington Otis waiting for him there with the big garden-syringe; and being thus hemmed in by his enemies on every side, and driven almost to bay, he vanished into the great iron stove which, fortunately for him, was not lit, and had to make his way home through the flues and chimneys, arriving at his own room in a terrible state of dirt, disorder and despair.

After this he was not seen again on any nocturnal expedition. The twins lay in wait for him on several occasions, and strewed the passages with nutshells every night to the great annoyance of their parents and the servants, but it was of no avail. It was quite evident that his feelings were so wounded that he would not appear. Mr Otis consequently resumed his great work on the history of the Democratic Party, on which he had been engaged for some years; Mrs Otis organised a wonderful clam bake, which amazed the whole county; the boys took to lacrosse, euchre, poker, and other American national games; and Virginia rode about the lanes on her pony, accompanied by the young Duke of Cheshire, who had come to spend the last week of his holidays at Canterville Chase. It was generally assumed that the ghost had gone away, and, in fact, Mr Otis wrote a letter to that effect to Lord Canterville, who, in reply, expressed his great pleasure at the news, and sent his best congratulations to the minister's worthy wife.

The Otises, however, were deceived, for the ghost was still in the house, and though now almost an invalid, was by no means ready to let matters rest, particularly as he heard that among the guests was the young Duke of Cheshire, whose granduncle, Lord Francis Stilton, had once bet a hundred guineas with Colonel Carbury that he would play dice with the Canterville ghost, and was found the next morning lying on the floor of the cardroom in such a helpless paralytic state, that though he lived on to a great age, he was never able to say anything again but 'Double Sixes'. The story was well known at the time, though, of course, out of respect for the feelings of the two noble families, every attempt was made to hush it up; and a full account of all the circumstances connected with it will be found in the third volume of Lord Tattle's *Recollections of the Prince Regent and his Friends*. The ghost, then, was naturally very anxious to show that he had not lost his influence over the Stiltons, with whom, indeed, he was distantly connected, his own first cousin having been married *en secondes noces* to the Sieur de Bulkeley, from whom, as everyone knows, the Dukes of Cheshire are lineally descended. Accordingly, he made arrangements for appearing to Virginia's little lover in his celebrated impersonation of 'The Vampire Monk, or the Bloodless Benedictine', a performance so horrible that when old Lady Startup saw it, which she did on one fatal New Year's Eve, in the year 1764, she went off into the most piercing shrieks, which culminated in violent apoplexy, and died in three days, after disinheriting the Cantervilles, who were her nearest relations, and leaving all her money to her London apothecary. At the last moment, however, his terror of the twins prevented his leaving his room, and the little Duke slept in peace under the great feathered canopy in the Royal Bedchamber, and dreamed of Virginia.

5

A few days after this, Virginia and her curly-haired cavalier went out riding on Brockley meadows, where she tore her habit so badly in getting through a hedge, that, on her return home, she made up her mind to go up by the back staircase so as not to be seen. As she was running past the Tapestry Chamber, the door of which happened to be open, she fancied she saw someone inside, and thinking it was her mother's maid, who sometimes used to bring her work there, looked in to ask her to mend her habit. To her immense surprise, however, it was the Canterville

Ghost himself! He was sitting by the window, watching the ruined gold of the yellowing trees fly through the air, and the red leaves dancing madly down the long avenue. His head was leaning on his hand, and his whole attitude was one of extreme depression. Indeed, so forlorn, and so much out of repair did he look, that little Virginia, whose first idea had been to run away and lock herself in her room, was filled with pity, and determined to try and comfort him. So light was her footfall, and so deep his melancholy, that he was not aware of her presence till she spoke to him.

'I am so sorry for you,' she said, 'but my brothers are going back to Eton tomorrow, and then, if you behave yourself, no one will annoy you.'

'It is absurd asking me to behave myself,' he answered, looking round in astonishment at the pretty little girl who had ventured to address him, 'quite absurd. I must rattle my chains, and groan through keyholes, and walk about at night, if that is what you mean. It is my only reason for existing.'

'It is no reason at all for existing, and you know you have been very wicked. Mrs Umney told us, the first day we arrived here, that you had killed your wife.'

'Well, I quite admit it,' said the Ghost petulantly, 'but it was a purely family matter, and concerned no one else.'

'It is very wrong to kill anyone,' said Virginia, who at times had a sweet Puritan gravity, caught from some old New England ancestor.

'Oh, I hate the cheap severity of abstract ethics! My wife was very plain, never had my ruffs properly starched, and knew nothing about cookery. Why, there was a buck I had shot in Hogley Woods, a magnificent pricket, and do you know how she had it sent up to table? However, it is no matter now, for it is all over, and I don't think it was very nice of her brothers to starve me to death, though I did kill her.'

'Starve you to death? Oh, Mr Ghost, I mean Sir Simon, are you hungry? I have a sandwich in my case. Would you like it?'

'No, thank you, I never eat anything now; but it is very kind of you, all the same, and you are much nicer than the rest of your horrid, rude, vulgar, dishonest family.'

'Stop!' cried Virginia, stamping her foot, 'it is you who are rude, and horrid, and vulgar, and as for dishonesty, you know you stole the paints out of my box to try and furbish up that ridiculous bloodstain in the library. First you took all my reds, including the vermilion, and I couldn't do any more sunsets, then you took the emerald-green and the chrome-yellow, and finally I had nothing left but indigo and Chinese white, and could only do moonlight scenes, which are always depressing to look at, and not at all easy to paint. I never told on you, though I was very much annoyed, and it was most ridiculous, the whole thing; for who ever heard of emerald-green blood?'

'Well, really,' said the Ghost, rather meekly, 'what was I to do? It is a very difficult thing to get real blood nowadays, and as your brother began it all with his Paragon Detergent, I certainly saw no reason why I should not have your paints. As for colour, that is always a matter of taste: the Cantervilles have blue blood, for instance, the very bluest in England; but I know you Americans don't care for things of this kind.'

'You know nothing about it, and the best thing you

can do is to emigrate and improve your mind. My
father will be only too happy to give you a free passage,
and though there is a heavy duty on spirits of every
kind, there will be no difficulty about the Custom
House, as the officers are all Democrats. Once in New
York, you are sure to be a great success. I know lots of
people there who would give a hundred thousand
dollars to have a grandfather, and much more than
that to have a family Ghost.'

'I don't think I should like America.'

'I suppose because we have no ruins and no
curiosities,' said Virginia satirically.

'No ruins! No curiosities!' answered the Ghost;
'you have your navy and your manners.'

'Good-evening; I will go and ask papa to get the
twins an extra week's holiday.'

'Please don't go, Miss Virginia,' he cried; 'I am so
lonely and so unhappy, and I really don't know what
to do. I want to go to sleep and I cannot.'

'That's quite absurd! You have merely to go to bed
and blow out the candle. It is very difficult sometimes
to keep awake, especially at church, but there is no
difficulty at all about sleeping. Why, even babies know
how to do that, and they are not very clever.'

'I have not slept for three hundred years,' he said
sadly, and Virginia's beautiful blue eyes opened in
wonder; 'for three hundred years I have not slept,
and I am so tired.'

Virginia grew quite grave, and her little lips trembled
like rose-leaves. She came towards him, and kneeling
down at his side, looked up into his old withered face.

'Poor, poor Ghost,' she murmured; 'have you no
place where you can sleep?'

'Far away beyond the pine woods,' he answered, in

a low dreamy voice, 'there is a little garden. There the grass grows long and deep, there are the great white stars of the hemlock flower, there the nightingale sings all night long. All night long he sings, and the cold, crystal moon looks down, and the yew tree spreads out its giant arms over the sleepers.'

Virginia's eyes grew dim with tears, and she hid her face in her hands.

'You mean the Garden of Death,' she whispered.

'Yes, Death. Death must be so beautiful. To lie in the soft brown earth, with the grasses waving above one's head, and listen to silence. To have no yesterday, and no tomorrow. To forget time, to forgive life, to be at peace. You can help me. You can open for me the portals of Death's house, for Love is always with you, and Love is stronger than Death is.'

Virginia trembled, a cold shudder ran through her, and for a few moments there was silence. She felt as if she was in a terrible dream.

Then the Ghost spoke again, and his voice sounded like the sighing of the wind.

'Have you ever read the old prophecy on the library window?'

'Oh, often,' cried the little girl, looking up; 'I know it quite well. It is painted in curious black letters, and it is difficult to read. There are only six lines:

> 'When a golden girl can win
> Prayer from out the lips of sin,
> When the barren almond bears,
> And a little child gives away its tears,
> Then shall all the house be still
> And peace come to Canterville.

But I don't know what they mean.'

'They mean,' he said sadly, 'that you must weep for me for my sins, because I have no tears, and pray with me for my soul, because I have no faith, and then, if you have always been sweet, and good, and gentle, the Angel of Death will have mercy on me. You will see fearful shapes in darkness, and wicked voices will whisper in your ear, but they will not harm you, for against the purity of a little child the powers of hell cannot prevail.'

Virginia made no answer, and the Ghost wrung his hands in wild despair as he looked down at her bowed golden head. Suddenly she stood up, very pale, and with a strange light in her eyes. 'I am not afraid,' she said firmly, 'and I will ask the Angel to have mercy on you.'

He rose from his seat with a faint cry of joy, and taking her hand bent over it with old-fashioned grace and kissed it. His fingers were as cold as ice, and his lips burned like fire, but Virginia did not falter, as he led her across the dusky room. On the faded green tapestry were broidered little huntsmen. They blew their tasselled horns and with their tiny hands waved to her to go back. 'Go back! little Virginia,' they cried, 'go back!' but the Ghost clutched her hand more tightly, and she shut her eyes against them. Horrible animals with lizard tails, and goggle eyes, blinked at her from the carven chimney-piece, and murmured 'Beware! little Virginia, beware! we may never see you again,' but the Ghost glided on more swiftly, and Virginia did not listen. When they reached the end of the room he stopped, and muttered some words she could not understand. She opened her eyes, and saw the wall slowly fading away like a mist, and a great black cavern in front of her. A bitter cold wind swept round them, and she felt something pulling at her dress. 'Quick, quick,' cried the Ghost, 'or it will be too late,' and, in a moment, the wainscoting had closed behind them, and the Tapestry Chamber was empty.

6

About ten minutes later, the bell rang for tea, and, as Virginia did not come down, Mrs Otis sent up one of the footmen to tell her. After a little time he returned and said that he could not find Miss Virginia anywhere. As she was in the habit of going out to the garden every evening to get flowers for the dinner-table, Mrs Otis was not at all alarmed at first, but when six o'clock struck, and Virginia did not appear, she became really agitated, and sent the boys out to look for her, while she herself and Mr Otis searched every room in the house. At half-past six the boys came back and said that they could find no trace of their sister anywhere. They were all now in the greatest state of excitement, and did not know what to do, when Mr Otis suddenly remembered that, some few days before, he had given a band of gypsies permission to camp in the park. He accordingly at once set off for Blackfell Hollow, where he knew they were, accompanied by his eldest son and two of the farm-servants. The little Duke of Cheshire, who was perfectly frantic with anxiety, begged hard to be allowed to go too, but Mr Otis would not allow him, as he was afraid there might be a scuffle. On arriving at the spot, however, he found that the gypsies had gone, and it was evident that their departure had been rather sudden, as the fire was still burning, and some plates were lying on the grass. Having sent off Washington and the two men to scour the district, he ran home, and despatched telegrams to all the police inspectors in the county, telling them to look out for a little girl who had been kidnapped by tramps or gypsies. He then ordered his horse to be brought round, and, after insisting on his wife and the three boys sitting down to dinner, rode off down the Ascot Road with a groom. He had hardly, however, gone a couple of miles when he heard somebody galloping after him, and, looking round, saw the little Duke coming up on his pony, with his face very flushed and no hat. 'I'm awfully sorry, Mr Otis,' gasped out the boy, 'but I can't eat any dinner as long as Virginia is lost. Please, don't be angry with me; if you had let us be engaged last year, there would never have been all this trouble. You won't send me back, will you? I can't go! I won't go!'

The minister could not help smiling at the handsome young scapegrace, and was a good deal touched at his devotion to Virginia, so leaning down from his horse, he patted him kindly on the shoulders, and said, 'Well, Cecil, if you won't go back I suppose you must come with me, but I must get you a hat at Ascot.'

'Oh, bother my hat! I want Virginia!' cried the little Duke, laughing, and they galloped on to the railway station. There Mr Otis enquired of the station-master if anyone answering the description of Virginia had been seen on the platform, but could get no news of her. The station-master, however, wired up and down the line, and assured him that a strict watch would be kept for her, and, after having bought a hat for the little Duke from a linen-draper, who was just putting up his shutters, Mr Otis rode off to Bexley, a village about four miles away, which he was told was a well-known haunt of the gypsies, as there was a large common next to it. Here they roused up the rural policeman, but could get no information from him, and, after riding all over the common, they turned their horses' heads homewards and reached the Chase about eleven o'clock, dead-tired and almost heart-broken. They found Washington and the twins waiting for them at the gatehouse with lanterns, as the avenue was very dark. Not the slightest trace of Virginia had been discovered. The gypsies had been caught on Brockley meadows, but she was not with them, and they had explained their sudden departure by saying that they had mistaken the date of Chorton Fair, and had gone off in a hurry for fear they might be late. Indeed, they had been quite distressed at hearing of Virginia's disappearance, as they were very grateful to Mr Otis for having allowed them to camp in his park, and four of their number had stayed behind to help in the search. The carp-pond had been dragged, and the whole Chase thoroughly gone over, but without any result. It was evident that, for that night at any rate, Virginia was lost to them; and it was in a state of the deepest depression that Mr Otis and the boys walked up to the house, the groom following behind with the two horses and the pony. In the hall they found a group of frightened servants, and lying on a sofa in the library was poor Mrs Otis, almost out of her mind with terror and anxiety, and having her forehead bathed with eau-de-Cologne by the old housekeeper. Mr Otis at once insisted on her having something to eat, and ordered up supper for the whole party. It was a melancholy meal, as hardly anyone

spoke, and even the twins were awestruck and subdued, as they were very fond of their sister. When
they had finished, Mr Otis, in spite of the entreaties
of the little Duke, ordered them all to bed, saying that
nothing more could be done that night, and that he
would telegraph in the morning to Scotland Yard for
some detectives to be sent down immediately. Just as
they were passing out of the dining-room, midnight
began to boom from the clock tower, and when the
last stroke sounded they heard a crash and a sudden
shrill cry; a dreadful peal of thunder shook the house,
a strain of unearthly music floated through the air, a
panel at the top of the staircase flew back with a loud
noise, and out on the landing, looking very pale
and white, with a little casket in her hand, stepped
Virginia. In a moment they had all rushed up to her.
Mrs Otis clasped her passionately in her arms, the
Duke smothered her with violent kisses, and the twins
executed a wild war-dance round the group.

'Good heavens! child, where have you been?' said
Mr Otis, rather angrily, thinking that she had been
playing some foolish trick on them. 'Cecil and I have
been riding all over the country looking for you, and
your mother has been frightened to death. You must
never play these practical jokes any more.'

'Except on the Ghost! Except on the Ghost!'
shrieked the twins, as they capered about.

'My own darling, thank God you are found; you
must never leave my side again,' murmured Mrs Otis,
as she kissed the trembling child, and smoothed the
tangled gold of her hair.

'Papa,' said Virginia quietly, 'I have been with the
Ghost. He is dead, and you must come and see him.
He had been very wicked, but he was really sorry for

all that he had done, and he gave me this box of beautiful jewels before he died.'

The whole family gazed at her in mute amazement, but she was quite grave and serious; and, turning round, she led them through the opening in the wainscoting down a narrow secret corridor, Washington following with a lighted candle, which he had caught up from the table. Finally, they came to a great oak door, studded with rusty nails. When Virginia touched it, it swung back on its heavy hinges, and they found themselves in a little low room, with a vaulted ceiling, and one tiny grated window. Imbedded in the wall was a huge iron ring, and chained to it was a gaunt skeleton, that was stretched out at full length on the stone floor, and seemed to be trying to grasp with its long fleshless fingers an old-fashioned trencher and ewer, that were placed just out of its reach. The jug had evidently been once filled with water, as it was covered inside with green mould. There was nothing on the trencher but a pile of dust. Virginia knelt down beside the skeleton, and, folding her little hands together, began to pray silently, while the rest of the party looked on in wonder at the terrible tragedy whose secret was now disclosed to them.

'Hallo!' suddenly exclaimed one of the twins, who had been looking out of the window to try and discover in what wing of the house the room was situated. 'Hallo! the old withered almond tree has blossomed. I can see the flowers quite plainly in the moonlight.'

'God has forgiven him,' said Virginia gravely, as she rose to her feet, and a beautiful light seemed to illumine her face.

'What an angel you are!' cried the young Duke, and he put his arm round her neck and kissed her.

7

Four days after these curious incidents a funeral started from Canterville Chase at about eleven o'clock at night. The hearse was drawn by eight black horses, each of which carried on its head a great tuft of nodding ostrich-plumes, and the leaden coffin was covered by a rich purple pall, on which was embroidered in gold the Canterville coat-of-arms. By the side of the hearse and the coaches walked the servants with lighted torches, and the whole procession was wonderfully impressive. Lord Canterville was the chief mourner, having come up specially from Wales to attend the funeral, and sat in the first carriage along with little Virginia. Then came the United States Minister and his wife, then Washington and the three boys, and in the last carriage was Mrs Umney. It was generally felt that, as she had been frightened by the ghost for more than fifty years of her life, she had the right to see the last of him. A deep grave had been dug in the corner of the church-yard, just under the old yew tree, and the service was read in the most impressive manner by the Reverend Augustus Dampier. When the ceremony was over, the servants, according to an old custom observed in the Canterville family, extinguished their torches, and, as the coffin was being lowered into the grave, Virginia stepped forward and laid on it a large cross made of white and pink almond-blossoms. As she did so, the moon came out from behind a cloud, and flooded with its silent silver the little churchyard, and from a distant copse a nightingale began to sing. She thought of the ghost's description of the Garden of Death, her eyes became dim with tears, and she hardly spoke a word during the drive home.

The next morning, before Lord Canterville went up to town, Mr Otis had an interview with him on the subject of the jewels the ghost had given to Virginia. They were perfectly magnificent, especially a certain ruby necklace with old Venetian setting, which was really a superb specimen of sixteenth-century work, and their value was so great that Mr Otis felt considerable scruples about allowing his daughter to accept them.

'My lord,' he said, 'I know that in this country mortmain is held to apply to trinkets as well as to land, and it is quite clear to me that these jewels are, or should be, heirlooms in your family. I must beg you, accordingly, to take them to London with you, and to regard them simply as a portion of your property which has been restored to you under certain strange conditions. As for my daughter, she is merely a child, and has as yet, I am glad to say, but little interest in such appurtenances of idle luxury. I am also informed by Mrs Otis, who, I may say, is no mean authority upon art – having had the privilege of spending several winters in Boston when she was a girl – that these gems are of great monetary worth, and if offered for sale would fetch a tall price. Under these circumstances, Lord Canterville, I feel sure that you will recognise how impossible it would be for me to allow them to remain in the possession of any member of my family; and, indeed, all such vain gauds and toys, however suitable or necessary to the dignity of the British aristocracy, would be completely out of place among those who have been brought up on the severe, and I believe immortal, principles of republican simplicity. Perhaps I should mention that Virginia is very anxious that you should allow her to retain the box as a memento of your unfortunate but misguided ancestor. As it is extremely old, and consequently a good deal out of repair, you may perhaps think fit to comply with her request. For my own part, I confess I am a good deal surprised to find a child of mine expressing sympathy with mediaevalism in any form, and can only account for it by the fact that Virginia was born in one of your London suburbs shortly after Mrs Otis had returned from a trip to Athens.'

Lord Canterville listened very gravely to the worthy minister's speech, pulling his grey moustache now and then to hide an involuntary smile, and when Mr Otis had ended, he shook him cordially by the hand, and said, 'My dear sir, your charming little daughter rendered my unlucky ancestor, Sir Simon, a very important service, and I and my family are much indebted to her for her marvellous courage and pluck. The jewels are clearly hers, and, egad, I believe that if I were heartless enough to take them from her, the wicked old fellow would be out of his grave in a fortnight, leading me the devil of a life. As for their being heirlooms, nothing is an heirloom that is not so mentioned in a will or legal document, and the existence of these jewels has been quite unknown. I assure you I have no more claim on them than your butler, and when Miss Virginia grows up I dare say she will be pleased to have pretty things to wear. Besides, you forget, Mr Otis, that you took the furniture and the ghost at a valuation, and anything that belonged to the ghost passed at once into your possession, as, whatever activity Sir Simon may have shown in the corridor at night, in point of law he was really dead, and you acquired his property by purchase.'

Mr Otis was a good deal distressed at Lord Canterville's refusal, and begged him to reconsider his decision, but the good-natured peer was quite firm, and finally induced the minister to allow his daughter to retain the present the ghost had given her, and when, in the spring of 1890, the young Duchess of Cheshire was presented at the Queen's first drawing-room on the occasion of her marriage, her jewels were the universal theme of admiration. For Virginia received the coronet, which is the reward of all good little American girls, and was married to her boy-lover as soon as he came of age. They were both so charming, and they loved each other so much, that everyone was delighted at the match, except the old Marchioness of Dumbleton, who had tried to catch the Duke for one of her seven unmarried daughters, and had given no less than three expensive dinner-parties for that purpose, and, strange to say, Mr Otis himself. Mr Otis was extremely fond of the young Duke personally, but, theoretically, he objected to titles, and, to use his own words, 'was not without apprehension lest, amid the enervating influences of a pleasure-loving aristocracy, the true principles of republican simplicity should be forgotten'. His objections, however, were completely overruled, and I believe that when he walked up the aisle of St George's, Hanover Square, with his daughter leaning on his arm, there was not a prouder man in the whole length and breadth of England.

The Duke and Duchess, after the honeymoon was over, went down to Canterville Chase, and on the

day after their arrival they walked over in the afternoon to the lonely churchyard by the pine woods.
There had been a great deal of difficulty at first about
the inscription on Sir Simon's tombstone, but finally
it had been decided to engrave on it simply the initials
of the old gentleman's name, and the verse from the
library window. The Duchess had brought with her
some lovely roses, which she strewed upon the grave,
and after they had stood by it for some time they
strolled into the ruined chancel of the old abbey.
There the Duchess sat down on a fallen pillar, while
her husband lay at her feet smoking a cigarette and
looking up at her beautiful eyes. Suddenly he threw
his cigarette away, took hold of her hand, and said to
her, 'Virginia, a wife should have no secrets from her
husband.'

'Dear Cecil! I have no secrets from you.'

'Yes, you have,' he answered, smiling, 'you have
never told me what happened to you when you were
locked up with the ghost.'

'I have never told anyone, Cecil,' said Virginia
gravely.

'I know that, but you might tell me.'

'Please don't ask me, Cecil, I cannot tell you. Poor
Sir Simon! I owe him a great deal. Yes, don't laugh,
Cecil, I really do. He made me see what Life is, and
what Death signifies, and why Love is stronger than
both.'

The Duke rose and kissed his wife lovingly.

'You can have your secret as long as I have your
heart,' he murmured.

'You have always had that, Cecil.'

'And you will tell our children someday, won't you?'

Virginia blushed.

MRS J. H. RIDDELL

The Old House in Vauxhall Walk

'Houseless – homeless – hopeless!'

Many a one who had before him trodden that same street must have uttered the same words – the weary, the desolate, the hungry, the forsaken, the waifs and strays of struggling humanity that are always coming and going, cold, starving and miserable, over the pavements of Lambeth Parish; but it is open to question whether they were ever previously spoken with a more thorough conviction of their truth, or with a feeling of keener self-pity, than by the young man who hurried along Vauxhall Walk one rainy winter's night, with no overcoat on his shoulders and no hat on his head.

A strange sentence for one-and-twenty to give expression to – and it was stranger still to come from the lips of a person who looked like and who was a gentleman. He did not appear either to have sunk very far down in the good graces of Fortune. There was no sign or token which would have induced a passer-by to imagine he had been worsted after a long fight with calamity. His boots were not worn down at the heels or broken at the toes, as many, many boots were which dragged and shuffled and scraped along the pavement. His clothes were good and fashionably cut, and innocent of the rents and patches and tatters that slunk wretchedly by, crouched in doorways, and held out a hand mutely appealing for charity. His face was not pinched with famine or lined with wicked wrinkles, or brutalised by drink and debauchery, and yet he said and thought he was hopeless, and almost in his young despair spoke the words aloud.

It was a bad night to be about with such a feeling in one's heart. The rain was cold, pitiless and increasing. A damp, keen wind blew down the cross streets leading from the river. The fumes of the gasworks seemed to fall with the rain. The roadway was muddy; the pavement greasy; the lamps burned dimly; and that dreary district of London looked its very gloomiest and worst.

Certainly not an evening to be abroad without a home to go to or a sixpence in one's pocket, yet this was the position of the young gentleman who, without a hat, strode along Vauxhall Walk, the rain beating on his unprotected head.

Upon the houses, so large and good – once inhabited by well-to-do citizens, now let out for the most part in floors to weekly tenants – he looked enviously. He would have given much to have had a room, or even part of one. He had been walking for a long time, ever since dark in fact, and dark falls soon in December. He was tired and cold and hungry, and he saw no prospect save of pacing the streets all night.

As he passed one of the lamps, the light falling on his face revealed handsome young features, a mobile, sensitive mouth, and that particular formation of the eyebrows – not a frown exactly, but a certain draw of the brows – often considered to bespeak genius, but which more surely accompanies an impulsive organisation easily pleased, easily depressed, capable of suffering very keenly or of enjoying fully. In his short life he had not enjoyed much, and he had suffered a good deal. That night, when he walked bareheaded through the rain, affairs had come to a crisis. So far as he in his despair felt able to see or reason, the best thing he could do was to die. The world did not want him; he would be better out of it.

The door of one of the houses stood open, and he could see in the dimly lighted hall some few articles of furniture waiting to be removed. A van stood beside the kerb, and two men were lifting a table into it as he, for a second, paused.

'Ah,' he thought, 'even those poor people have some place to go to, some shelter provided, while I have not a roof to cover my head, or a shilling to get a night's lodging.' And he went on fast, as if memory were spurring him, so fast that a man running after had some trouble to overtake him.

'Master Graham! Master Graham!' this man exclaimed, breathlessly; and, thus addressed, the young fellow stopped as if he had been shot.

'Who are you that know me?' he asked, facing round.

'I'm William; don't you remember William, Master Graham? And, Lord's sake, sir, what are you doing out a night like this without your hat?'

'I forgot it,' was the answer; 'and I did not care to go back and fetch it.'

'Then why don't you buy another, sir? You'll catch your death of cold; and besides, you'll excuse me, sir, but it does look odd.'

'I know that,' said Master Graham grimly; 'but I haven't a halfpenny in the world.'

'Have you and the master, then – ' began the man, but there he hesitated and stopped.

'Had a quarrel? Yes, and one that will last us our lives,' finished the other, with a bitter laugh.

'And where are you going now?'

'Going! Nowhere, except to seek out the softest paving stone, or the shelter of an arch.'

'You are joking, sir.'

'I don't feel much in a mood for jesting either.'

'Will you come back with me, Master Graham? We are just at the last of our moving, but there is a spark of fire still in the grate, and it would be better talking out of this rain. Will you come, sir?'

'Come! Of course I will come,' said the young fellow, and, turning, they retraced their steps to the house he had looked into as he passed along.

An old, old house, with long, wide hall, stairs low, easy of ascent, with deep cornices to the ceilings, and oak floorings, and mahogany doors, which still spoke mutely of the wealth and stability of the original owner, who lived before the Tradescants and Ashmoles were thought of, and had been sleeping far longer than they, in St Mary's churchyard, hard by the archbishop's palace.

'Step upstairs, sir,' entreated the departing tenant; 'it's cold down here, with the door standing wide.'

'Had you the whole house, then, William?' asked Graham Coulton, in some surprise.

'The whole of it, and right sorry I, for one, am to leave it; but nothing else would serve my wife. This room, sir,' and with a little conscious pride, William, doing the honours of his late residence, asked his guest into a spacious apartment occupying the full width of the house on the first floor.

Tired though he was, the young man could not repress an exclamation of astonishment.

'Why, we have nothing so large as this at home, William,' he said.

'It's a fine house,' answered William, raking the embers together as he spoke and throwing some wood upon them; 'but, like many a good family, it has come down in the world.'

There were four windows in the room, shuttered close; they had deep, low seats, suggestive of pleasant days gone by, when, well-curtained and well-cushioned, they formed snug retreats for the children, and sometimes for adults also; there was no furniture left, unless an oaken settle beside the hearth, and a large mirror let into the panelling at the opposite end of the apartment, with a black marble console table beneath it, could be so considered; but the very absence of chairs and tables enabled the magnificent proportions of the chamber to be seen to full advantage, and there was nothing to distract the attention from the ornamented ceiling, the panelled walls, the old-world chimney-piece so quaintly carved, and the fireplace lined with tiles, each one of which contained a picture of some scriptural or allegorical subject.

'Had you been staying on here, William,' said Coulton, flinging himself wearily on the settle, 'I'd have asked you to let me stop where I am for the night.'

'If you can make shift, sir, there is nothing as I am aware of to prevent you stopping,' answered the man, fanning the wood into a flame. 'I shan't take the key back to the landlord till tomorrow, and this would be better for you than the cold streets at any rate.'

'Do you really mean what you say?' asked the other eagerly. 'I should be thankful to lie here; I feel dead beat.'

'Then stay, Master Graham, and welcome. I'll fetch a basket of coals I was going to put in the van, and make up a good fire, so that you can warm yourself; then I must run round to the other house for a minute or two, but it's not far, and I'll be back as soon as ever I can.'

'Thank you, William; you were always good to me,' said the young man gratefully. 'This is delightful,' and he stretched his numbed hands over the blazing wood, and looked round the room with a satisfied smile.

'I did not expect to get into such quarters,' he remarked, as his friend in need reappeared, carrying a half-bushel basket full of coals, with which he proceeded to make up a roaring fire. 'I am sure the last thing I could have imagined was meeting with anyone I knew in Vauxhall Walk.'

'Where were you coming from, Master Graham?' asked William curiously.

'From old Melfield's. I was at his school once, you know, and he has now retired, and is living upon the proceeds of years of robbery in Kennington Oval. I thought perhaps he would lend me a pound, or offer me a night's lodging, or even a glass of wine; but, oh dear, no. He took the moral tone, and observed he could have nothing to say to a son who defied his father's authority. He gave me plenty of advice, but nothing else, and showed me out into the rain with a bland courtesy, for which I could have struck him.'

William muttered something under his breath which was not a blessing, and added aloud: 'You are better

434

here, sir, I think, at any rate. I'll be back in less than half an hour.'

Left to himself, young Coulton took off his coat, and shifting the settle a little, hung it over the end to dry. With his handkerchief he rubbed some of the wet out of his hair; then, perfectly exhausted, he lay down before the fire and, pillowing his head on his arm, fell fast asleep.

He was awakened nearly an hour afterwards by the sound of someone gently stirring the fire and moving quietly about the room. Starting into a sitting posture, he looked around him, bewildered for a moment, and then, recognising his humble friend, said laughingly: 'I had lost myself; I could not imagine where I was.'

'I am sorry to see you here, sir,' was the reply; 'but still this is better than being out of doors. It has come on a nasty night. I brought a rug round with me that, perhaps, you would wrap yourself in.'

'I wish, at the same time, you had brought me something to eat,' said the young man, laughing.

'Are you hungry, then, sir?' asked William, in a tone of concern.

'Yes; I have had nothing to eat since breakfast. The governor and I commenced rowing the minute we sat down to luncheon, and I rose and left the table. But hunger does not signify; I am dry and warm, and can forget the other matter in sleep.'

'And it's too late now to buy anything,' soliloquised the man; 'the shops are all shut long ago. Do you think, sir,' he added, brightening, 'you could manage some bread and cheese?'

'Do I think? – I should call it a perfect feast,' answered Graham Coulton. 'But never mind about

435

food tonight, William; you have had trouble enough, and to spare, already.'

William's only answer was to dart to the door and run downstairs. Presently he reappeared, carrying in one hand bread and cheese wrapped up in paper, and in the other a pewter measure full of beer.

'It's the best I could do, sir,' he said apologetically. 'I had to beg this from the landlady.'

'Here's to her good health!' exclaimed the young fellow gaily, taking a long pull at the tankard. 'That tastes better than champagne in my father's house.'

'Won't he be uneasy about you?' ventured William, who, having by this time emptied the coals, was now seated on the inverted basket, looking wistfully at the relish with which the son of the former master was eating his bread and cheese.

'No,' was the decided answer. 'When he hears it pouring cats and dogs he will only hope I am out in the deluge, and say a good drenching will cool my pride.'

'I don't think you're right there,' remarked the man.

'But I am sure I am. My father always hated me, as he hated my mother.'

'Begging your pardon, sir; he was over fond of your mother.'

'If you had heard what he said about her today, you might find reason to alter your opinion. He told me I resembled her in mind as well as body; that I was a coward, a simpleton and a hypocrite.'

'He didn't mean it, sir.'

'He did, every word. He does think I am a coward, because I – I – ' And the young fellow broke into a passion of hysterical tears.

'I don't half like leaving you here alone,' said

William, glancing round the room with a quick trouble in his eyes; 'but I have no place fit to ask you to stop, and I am forced to go myself, because I am night watchman, and must be on at twelve o'clock.'

'I shall be right enough,' was the answer. 'Only I mustn't talk any more of my father. Tell me about yourself, William. How did you manage to get such a big house, and why are you leaving it?'

'The landlord put me in charge, sir; and it was my wife's fancy not to like it.'

'Why did she not like it?'

'She felt desolate alone with the children at night,' answered William, turning away his head; then added, next minute: 'Now, sir, if you think I can do no more for you, I had best be off. Time's getting on. I'll look round tomorrow morning.'

'Good-night,' said the young fellow, stretching out his hand, which the other took as freely and frankly as it was offered. 'What should I have done this evening if I had not chanced to meet you?'

'I don't think there is much chance in the world, Master Graham,' was the quiet answer. 'I do hope you will rest well, and not be the worse for your wetting.'

'No fear of that,' was the rejoinder, and the next minute the young man found himself all alone in the Old House in Vauxhall Walk.

Lying on the settle, with the fire burnt out, and the room in total darkness, Graham Coulton dreamed a curious dream. He thought he awoke from deep slumber to find a log smouldering away upon the hearth, and the mirror at the end of the apartment reflecting fitful gleams of light. He could not understand how it came to pass that, far away as he was from the glass, he was able to see everything in it; but he resigned himself to the difficulty without astonishment, as people generally do in dreams.

Neither did he feel surprised when he beheld the outline of a female figure seated beside the fire, engaged in picking something out of her lap and dropping it with a despairing gesture.

He heard the mellow sound of gold, and knew she was lifting and dropping sovereigns. He turned a little so as to see the person engaged in such a singular and meaningless manner, and found that, where there had been no chair on the previous night, there was a chair now, on which was seated an old, wrinkled hag, her clothes poor and ragged, a mob cap barely covering her scant white hair, her cheeks sunken, her nose hooked, her fingers more like talons than aught else as they dived down into the heap of gold, portions of which they lifted but to scatter mournfully.

'Oh! my lost life,' she moaned, in a voice of the bitterest anguish. 'Oh! my lost life – for one day, for one hour of it again!'

Out of the darkness – out of the corner of the room where the shadows lay deepest – out from the gloom abiding near the door – out from the dreary night, with their sodden feet and the wet dripping from their heads, came the old men and the young children, the worn women and the weary hearts, whose misery that gold might have relieved, but whose wretchedness it mocked.

Round that miser, who once sat gloating as she now sat lamenting, they crowded – all those pale, sad shapes – the aged of days, the infant of hours, the sobbing outcast, honest poverty, repentant vice; but one low cry proceeded from those pale lips – a cry for help she might have given, but which she withheld.

They closed about her, all together, as they had done singly in life; they prayed, they sobbed, they entreated; with haggard eyes the figure regarded the poor she had repulsed, the children against whose cry she had closed her ears, the old people she had suffered to starve and die for want of what would have been the merest trifle to her; then, with a terrible scream, she raised her lean arms above her head, and sank down – down – the gold scattering as it fell out of her lap, and rolling along the floor, till its gleam was lost in the outer darkness beyond.

Then Graham Coulton awoke in good earnest, with the perspiration oozing from every pore, with a fear and an agony upon him such as he had never before felt in all his existence, and with the sound of the heart-rending cry – 'Oh! my lost life' – still ringing in his ears.

Mingled with all, too, there seemed to have been some lesson for him which he had forgotten, that, try as he would, eluded his memory, and which, in the very act of waking, glided away.

He lay for a little thinking about all this, and then,

still heavy with sleep, retraced his way into dreamland once more.

It was natural, perhaps, that, mingling with the strange fantasies which follow in the train of night and darkness, the former vision should recur, and the young man ere long found himself toiling through scene after scene wherein the figure of the woman he had seen seated beside a dying fire held principal place.

He saw her walking slowly across the floor munching a dry crust – she who could have purchased all the luxuries wealth can command; on the hearth, contemplating her, stood a man of commanding presence, dressed in the fashion of long ago. In his eyes there was a dark look of anger, on his lips a curling smile of disgust, and somehow, even in his sleep, the dreamer understood it was the ancestor to the descendant he beheld – that the house put to mean uses in which he lay had never so far descended from its high estate as the woman possessed of so pitiful a soul, contaminated with the most despicable and insidious vice poor humanity knows, for all other vices seem to have connection with the flesh, but the greed of the miser eats into the very soul.

Filthy of person, repulsive to look at, hard of heart as she was, he yet beheld another phantom, which, coming into the room, met her almost on the threshold, taking her by the hand, and pleading, as it seemed, for assistance. He could not hear all that passed, but a word now and then fell upon his ear. Some talk of former days; some mention of a fair young mother – an appeal, as it seemed, to a time when they were tiny brother and sister, and the accursed greed for gold had not divided them. All in vain; the hag only answered him as she had answered the children, and the young girls, and the old people in his former vision. Her heart was as invulnerable to natural affection as it had proved to human sympathy. He begged, as it appeared, for aid to avert some bitter misfortune or terrible disgrace, and adamant might have been found more yielding to his prayer. Then the figure standing on the hearth changed to an angel, which folded its wings mournfully over its face, and the man, with bowed head, slowly left the room.

Even as he did so the scene changed again; it was night once more, and the miser wended her way upstairs. From below, Graham Coulton fancied he watched her toiling wearily from step to step. She had aged strangely since the previous scenes. She moved with difficulty; it seemed the greatest exertion for her to creep from step to step, her skinny hand traversing the balusters with slow and painful deliberateness. Fascinated, the young man's eyes followed the progress of that feeble, decrepit woman. She was solitary in a desolate house, with a deeper blackness than the darkness of night waiting to engulf her.

It seemed to Graham Coulton that after that he lay for a time in a still, dreamless sleep, upon awaking from which he found himself entering a chamber as sordid and unclean in its appointments as the woman of his previous vision had been in her person. The poorest labourer's wife would have gathered more comforts around her than that room contained. A four-poster bedstead without hangings of any kind – a blind drawn up awry – an old carpet covered with dust, and dirt on the floor – a rickety washstand with all the paint worn off it – an ancient mahogany dressing table, and a cracked glass spotted all over – were all the objects he could at first discern, looking at the room through that dim light which often-times obtains in dreams.

By degrees, however, he perceived the outline of someone lying huddled on the bed. Drawing nearer, he found it was that of the person whose dreadful presence seemed to pervade the house. What a terrible sight she looked, with her thin white locks scattered over the pillow, with what were mere remnants of blankets gathered about her shoulders, with her claw-like fingers clutching the clothes, as though even in sleep she was guarding her gold!

An awful and a repulsive spectacle, but not with half the terror in it of that which followed. Even as the young man looked he heard stealthy footsteps on the stairs. Then he saw first one man and then his fellow steal cautiously into the room. Another second, and the pair stood beside the bed, murder in their eyes.

Graham Coulton tried to shout – tried to move, but the deterrent power which exists in dreams only tied his tongue and paralysed his limbs. He could but hear and look, and what he heard and saw was this: aroused suddenly from sleep, the woman started, only to receive a blow from one of the ruffians, whose fellow followed his lead by plunging a knife into her breast.

Then, with a gurgling scream, she fell back on the bed, and at the same moment, with a cry, Graham Coulton again awoke, to thank heaven it was but an illusion.

3

'I hope you slept well, sir.' It was William, who, coming into the hall with the sunlight of a fine bright morning streaming after him, asked this question: 'Had you a good night's rest?'

Graham Coulton laughed, and answered: 'Why, faith, I was somewhat in the case of Paddy, "who could not slape for dhraming". I slept well enough, I suppose, but whether it was in consequence of the row with my dad, or the hard bed, or the cheese – most likely the bread and cheese so late at night – I dreamt all the night long, the most extraordinary dreams. Some old woman kept cropping up, and I saw her murdered.'

'You don't say that, sir?' said William nervously.

'I do, indeed,' was the reply. 'However, that is all gone and past. I have been down in the kitchen and had a good wash, and I am as fresh as a daisy, and as hungry as a hunter; and, oh, William, can you get me any breakfast?'

'Certainly, Master Graham. I have brought round a kettle, and I will make the water boil immediately. I suppose, sir' – this tentatively – 'you'll be going home today?'

'Home!' repeated the young man. 'Decidedly not. I'll never go home again till I return with some medal hung to my coat, or a leg or arm cut off. I've thought it all out, William. I'll go and enlist. There's a talk of war; and, living or dead, my father shall have reason to retract his opinion about my being a coward.'

'I am sure the admiral never thought you anything

of the sort, sir,' said William. 'Why, you have the pluck of ten!'

'Not before him,' answered the young fellow sadly.

'You'll do nothing rash, Master Graham; you won't go 'listing, or aught of that sort, in your anger?'

'If I do not, what is to become of me?' asked the other. 'I cannot dig – to beg I am ashamed. Why, but for you, I should not have had a roof over my head last night.'

'Not much of a roof, I am afraid, sir.'

'Not much of a roof!' repeated the young man. 'Why, who could desire a better? What a capital room this is,' he went on, looking around the apartment, where William was now kindling a fire; 'one might dine twenty people here easily!'

'If you think so well of the place, Master Graham, you might stay here for a while, till you have made up your mind what you are going to do. The landlord won't make any objection, I am very sure.'

'Oh! nonsense; he would want a long rent for a house like this.'

'I dare say; *if he could get it*,' was William's significant answer.

'What do you mean? Won't the place let?'

'No, sir. I did not tell you last night, but there was a murder done here, and people are shy of the house ever since.'

'A murder! What sort of a murder? Who was murdered?'

'A woman, Master Graham – the landlord's sister; she lived here all alone, and was supposed to have money. Whether she had or not, she was found dead from a stab in her breast, and if there ever was any money, it must have been taken at the same time, for

444

none ever was found in the house from that day to this.'

'Was that the reason your wife would not stop here?' asked the young man, leaning against the mantelshelf, and looking thoughtfully down on William.

'Yes, sir. She could not stand it any longer; she got that thin and nervous no one would have believed it possible; she never saw anything, but she said she heard footsteps and voices, and then when she walked through the hall, or up the staircase, someone always seemed to be following her. We put the children to sleep in this big room, and they declared they often saw an old woman sitting by the hearth. Nothing ever came my way,' finished William, with a laugh; 'I was always ready to go to sleep the minute my head touched the pillow.'

'Were not the murderers discovered?' asked Graham Coulton.

'No, sir; the landlord, Miss Tynan's brother, had always lain under the suspicion of it – quite wrongfully, I am very sure – but he will never clear himself now. It was known he came and asked her for help a day or two before the murder, and it was also known he was able within a week or two to weather whatever trouble had been harassing him. Then, you see, the money was never found; and, altogether, people scarce knew what to think.'

'Humph!' ejaculated Graham Coulton, and he took a few turns up and down the apartment. 'Could I go and see this landlord?'

'Surely, sir, if you had a hat,' answered William, with such a serious decorum that the young man burst out laughing.

'That is an obstacle, certainly,' he remarked, 'and I

must make a note do instead. I have a pencil in my pocket, so here goes.'

Within half an hour from the dispatch of that note William was back again with a sovereign; the land-lord's compliments, and he would be much obliged if Mr Coulton could 'step round'.

'You'll do nothing rash, sir,' entreated William.

'Why, man,' answered the young fellow, 'one may as well be picked off by a ghost as a bullet. What is there to be afraid of?'

William only shook his head. He did not think his young master was made of the stuff likely to remain alone in a haunted house and solve the mystery it assuredly contained by dint of his own unassisted endeavours. And yet when Graham Coulton came out of the landlord's house he looked more bright and gay than usual, and walked up the Lambeth Road to the place where William awaited his return, humming an air as he paced along.

'We have settled the matter,' he said. 'And now if the dad wants his son for Christmas, it will trouble him to find him.'

'Don't say that, Master Graham, don't,' entreated the man, with a shiver; 'maybe after all it would have been better if you had never happened to chance upon Vauxhall Walk.'

'Don't croak, William,' answered the young man; 'if it was not the best day's work I ever did for myself I'm a Dutchman.'

During the whole of that forenoon and afternoon, Graham Coulton searched diligently for the missing treasure Mr Tynan assured him had never been dis-covered. Youth is confident and self-opinionated, and this fresh explorer felt satisfied that, though others had failed, he would be successful. On the second floor he found one door locked, but he did not pay much attention to that at the moment, as he believed if there was anything concealed it was more likely to be found in the lower than the upper part of the house. Late into the evening he pursued his researches in the kitchen and cellars and old-fashioned cupboards, of which the basement had an abundance.

It was nearly eleven, when, engaged in poking about amongst the empty bins of a wine cellar as large as a family vault, he suddenly felt a rush of cold air at his back. Moving, his candle was instantly extinguished, and in the very moment of being left in darkness he saw, standing in the doorway, a woman, resembling her who had haunted his dreams overnight.

He rushed with outstretched hands to seize her, but clutched only air. He relit his candle, and closely examined the basement, shutting off communication with the ground floor ere doing so. All in vain. Not a trace could he find of living creature – not a window was open – not a door unbolted.

'It is very odd,' he thought, as, after securely fastening the door at the top of the staircase, he searched the whole upper portion of the house, with the exception of the one room mentioned.

'I must get the key of that tomorrow,' he decided, standing gloomily with his back to the fire and his eyes wandering about the drawing-room, where he had once again taken up his abode.

Even as the thought passed through his mind, he saw standing in the open doorway a woman with white dishevelled hair, clad in mean garments, ragged and dirty. She lifted her hand and shook it at him with a menacing gesture, and then, just as he

447

was darting towards her, a wonderful thing occurred.

From behind the great mirror there glided a second female figure, at the sight of which the first turned and fled, uttering piercing shrieks as the other followed her from storey to storey.

Sick almost with terror, Graham Coulton watched the dreadful pair as they fled upstairs past the locked room to the top of the house.

It was a few minutes before he recovered his self-possession. When he did so, and searched the upper apartments, he found them totally empty.

That night, ere lying down before the fire, he carefully locked and bolted the drawing-room door; before he did more he drew the heavy settle in front of it, so that if the lock were forced no entrance could be effected without considerable noise.

For some time he lay awake, then dropped into a deep sleep, from which he was awakened suddenly by a noise as if of something scuffling stealthily behind the wainscot. He raised himself on his elbow and listened, and, to his consternation, beheld seated at the opposite side of the hearth the same woman he had seen before in his dreams, lamenting over her gold.

The fire was not quite out, and at that moment shot up a last tongue of flame. By the light, transient as it was, he saw that the figure pressed a ghostly finger to its lips, and by the turn of its head and the attitude of its body seemed to be listening.

He listened also – indeed, he was too much frightened to do aught else; more and more distinct grew the sounds which had aroused him, a stealthy rustling coming nearer and nearer – up and up it seemed, behind the wainscot.

'It is rats,' thought the young man, though, indeed, his teeth were almost chattering in his head with fear. But then in a moment he saw what disabused him of that idea – *the gleam of a candle or lamp through a crack in the panelling*. He tried to rise, he strove to shout – all in vain; and, sinking down, remembered nothing more till he awoke to find the grey light of an early morning stealing through one of the shutters he had left partially unclosed.

For hours after his breakfast, which he scarcely touched, long after William had left him at midday, Graham Coulton, having in the morning made a long and close survey of the house, sat thinking before the fire; then, apparently having made up his mind, he put on the hat he had bought, and went out.

When he returned the evening shadows were darkening down, but the pavements were full of people going marketing, for it was Christmas Eve, and all who had money to spend seemed bent on shopping.

It was terribly dreary inside the old house that night. Through the deserted rooms Graham could feel that ghostly semblance was wandering mournfully. When he turned his back he knew she was flitting from the mirror to the fire, from the fire to the mirror; but he was not afraid of her now – he was far more afraid of another matter he had taken in hand that day.

The horror of the silent house grew and grew upon him. He could hear the beating of his own heart in the dead quietude which reigned from garret to cellar.

At last William came; but the young man said nothing to him of what was in his mind. He talked to him cheerfully and hopefully enough – wondered where his father would think he had got to, and hoped

Mr Tynan might send him some Christmas pudding. Then the man said it was time for him to go, and, when Mr Coulton went downstairs to the hall-door, remarked the key was not in it.

'No,' was the answer, 'I took it out today, to oil it.'

'It wanted oiling,' agreed William, 'for it worked terribly stiff.' Having uttered which truism he departed.

Very slowly the young man retraced his way to the drawing-room, where he only paused to lock the door on the outside; then taking off his boots he went up to the top of the house, where, entering the front attic, he waited patiently in darkness and in silence.

It was a long time, or at least it seemed long to him, before he heard the same sound which had aroused him on the previous night – a stealthy rustling – then a rush of cold air – then cautious footsteps – then the quiet opening of a door below.

It did not take as long in action as it has required to tell. In a moment the young man was out on the landing and had closed a portion of the panelling on the wall which stood open; noiselessly he crept back to the attic window, unlatched it, and sprang a rattle, the sound of which echoed far and near through the deserted streets, then rushing down the stairs, he encountered a man who, darting past him, made for the landing above; but perceiving that way of escape closed, fled down again, to find Graham struggling desperately with his companion.

'Give him the knife – come along,' he said savagely; and next instant Graham felt something like a hot iron through his shoulder, and then heard a thud, as one of the men, tripping in his rapid upward flight, fell from the top of the stairs to the bottom.

At the same moment there came a crash, as if the house was falling, and faint, sick and bleeding, young Coulton lay insensible on the threshold of the room where Miss Tynan had been murdered.

When he recovered he was in the dining-room, and a doctor was examining his wound.

Near the door a policeman stiffly kept guard. The hall was full of people; all the misery and vagabondism the streets contain at that hour was crowding in to see what had happened.

Through the midst two men were being conveyed to the station-house: one, with his head dreadfully injured, on a stretcher, the other handcuffed, uttering frightful imprecations as he went.

After a time the house was cleared of the rabble, the police took possession of it, and Mr Tynan was sent for.

'What was that dreadful noise?' asked Graham feebly, now seated on the floor, with his back resting against the wall.

'I don't know. Was there a noise?' said Mr Tynan, humouring his fancy, as he thought.

'Yes, in the drawing-room, I think; the key is in my pocket.'

Still humouring the wounded lad, Mr Tynan took the key and ran upstairs.

When he unlocked the door, what a sight met his eyes! The mirror had fallen – it was lying all over the floor, shivered into a thousand pieces; the console table had been borne down by its weight, and the marble slab was shattered as well. But this was not what claimed his attention. Hundreds, thousands of gold pieces were scattered about, and an aperture behind the glass contained boxes filled with securities and deeds and bonds, the possession of which had cost his sister her life.

*   *   *

'Well, Graham, and what do you want?' asked Admiral Coulton the following evening as his first-born appeared before him, looking somewhat pale but otherwise unchanged.

'I want nothing,' was the answer, 'but to ask your forgiveness. William has told me all the story I never knew before; and, if you let me, I will try to make it up to you for the trouble you have had. I am provided for,' went on the young fellow, with a nervous laugh; 'I have made my fortune since I left you, and another man's fortune as well.'

'I think you are out of your senses,' said the admiral shortly.

'No, sir, I have found them,' was the answer; 'and I mean to strive and make a better thing of my life than I should ever have done had I not gone to the Old House in Vauxhall Walk.'

'Vauxhall Walk! What is the lad talking about?'

'I will tell you, sir, if I may sit down,' was Graham Coulton's answer, and then he told this story.

A Strange Christmas Game

When, through the death of a distant relative, I, John Lester, succeeded to the Martingdale Estate, there could not have been found in the length and breadth of England a happier pair than myself and my only sister Clare.

We were not such utter hypocrites as to affect sorrow for the loss of our kinsman, Paul Lester, a man whom we had never seen, of whom we had heard but little, and that little unfavourable, at whose hands we had never received a single benefit – who was, in short, as great a stranger to us as the then Prime Minister, the Emperor of Russia, or any other human being utterly removed from our extremely humble sphere of life.

His loss was very certainly our gain. His death represented to us not a dreary parting from one long loved and highly honoured but the accession to lands, houses, consideration and wealth by myself – John Lester, Esquire, Martingdale, Bedfordshire, whilom Jack Lester, artist and second-floor lodger at 32 Great Smith Street, Bloomsbury.

Not that Martingdale was much of an estate as county properties go. The Lesters who had succeeded to that domain from time to time during the course of a few hundred years, could by no stretch of courtesy

have been called prudent men. In regard of their
posterity they were, indeed, scarcely honest, for they
parted with manors and farms, with common rights
and advowsons, in a manner at once so baronial and
so unbusinesslike, that Martingdale at length in the
hands of Jeremy Lester, the last resident owner,
melted to a mere little dot in the map of Bedfordshire.

Concerning this Jeremy Lester there was a mystery.
No man could say what had become of him. He was
in the oak parlour at Martingdale one Christmas Eve,
and before the next morning he had disappeared – to
reappear in the flesh no more.

That night, one Mr Warley, a great friend and boon
companion of Jeremy's, had sat playing cards with
him until after twelve o'clock chimed, then he took
leave of his host and rode home under the moonlight.
After that, no person, as far as could be ascertained,
ever saw Jeremy Lester alive.

His ways of life had not been either the most
regular, or the most respectable, and it was not until a
new year had come in, without any tidings of his
whereabouts reaching the house, that his servants
became seriously alarmed concerning his absence.

Then enquiries were set on foot concerning him –
enquiries which grew more urgent as weeks and
months passed by without the slightest clue being
obtained as to his whereabouts. Rewards were offered,
advertisements inserted, but still Jeremy made no sign;
and so in course of time the heir-at-law, Paul Lester,
took possession of the house, and went down to spend
the summer months at Martingdale with his rich wife,
and her four children by a first husband. Paul Lester
was a barrister – an over-worked barrister, who everyone supposed would be glad enough to leave the bar

and settle at Martingdale, where his wife's money and the fortune he had accumulated could not have failed to give him a good standing even among the neighbouring county families; and perhaps it was with such intention that he went down into Bedfordshire.

If this were so, however, he speedily changed his mind, for with the January snows he returned to London, let off the land surrounding the house, shut up the Hall, put in a caretaker, and never troubled himself further about his ancestral seat.

Time went on, and people began to say the house was haunted, that Paul Lester had 'seen something', and so forth – all which stories were duly repeated for our benefit when, forty-one years after the disappearance of Jeremy Lester, Clare and I went down to inspect our inheritance.

I say 'our', because Clare had stuck bravely to me in poverty – grinding poverty – and prosperity was not going to part us now. What was mine was hers, and that she knew, God bless her, without my needing to tell her so.

The transition from rigid economy to comparative wealth was in our case the more delightful, also, because we had not in the least degree anticipated it. We never expected Paul Lester's shoes to come to us, and accordingly it was not upon our consciences that we had ever in our dreariest moods wished him dead.

Had he made a will, no doubt we never should have gone to Martingdale, and I, consequently, never written this story; but, luckily for us, he died intestate, and the Bedfordshire property came to me.

As for the fortune, he had spent it in travelling, and in giving great entertainments at his grand house in

Portman Square. Concerning his effects, Mrs Lester and I came to a very amicable arrangement, and she did me the honour of inviting me to call upon her occasionally, and, as I heard, spoke of me as a very worthy and presentable young man 'for my station', which, of course, coming from so good an authority, was gratifying. Moreover, she asked me if I intended residing at Martingdale, and on my replying in the affirmative, hoped I should like it.

It struck me at the time that there was a certain significance in her tone, and when I went down to Martingdale and heard the absurd stories which were afloat concerning the house being haunted, I felt confident that if Mrs Lester had hoped much, she had feared more.

People said Mr Jeremy 'walked' at Martingdale. He had been seen, it was averred, by poachers, by gamekeepers, by children who had come to use the park as a near cut to school, by lovers who kept their tryst under the elms and beeches.

As for the caretaker and his wife, the third in residence since Jeremy Lester's disappearance, the man gravely shook his head when questioned, while the woman stated that wild horses, or even wealth untold, should not draw her into the red bedroom, nor into the oak parlour, after dark.

'I have heard my mother tell, sir – it was her as followed old Mrs Reynolds, the first caretaker – how there were things went on in these selfsame rooms as might make any Christian's hair stand on end. Such stamping, and swearing, and knocking about on furniture; and then tramp, tramp, up the great staircase and along the corridor and so into the red bedroom, and then bang, and tramp, tramp again.

They do say, sir, Mr Paul Lester met him once, and from that time the oak parlour has never been opened. I never was inside it myself.'

Upon hearing which fact, the first thing I did was to proceed to the oak parlour, open the shutters, and let the August sun stream in upon the haunted chamber. It was an old-fashioned, plainly furnished apartment, with a large table in the centre, a smaller in a recess by the fireplace, chairs ranged against the walls, and a dusty moth-eaten carpet on the floor. There were dogs on the hearth, broken and rusty; there was a brass fender, tarnished and battered; a picture of some sea-fight over the mantelpiece, while another work of art about equal in merit hung between the windows. Altogether, an utterly prosaic and yet not uncheerful apartment, from out of which the ghosts flitted as soon as daylight was let into it, and which I proposed, as soon as I 'felt my feet', to redecorate, refurnish, and convert into a pleasant morning-room. I was still under thirty, but I had learned prudence in that very good school, Necessity; and it was not my intention to spend much money until I had ascertained for certain what were the actual revenues derivable from the lands still belonging to the Martingdale estates, and the charges upon them. In fact, I wanted to know what I was worth before committing myself to any great extravagances, and the place had for so long been neglected that I experienced some difficulty in arriving at the state of my real income.

But in the meanwhile, Clare and I found great enjoyment in exploring every nook and corner of our domain, in turning over the contents of old chests and cupboards, in examining the faces of our ancestors looking down on us from the walls, in walking through the neglected gardens, full of weeds, overgrown with shrubs and birdweed, where the box-wood was eighteen feet high, and the shoots of the rose trees yards long. I have put the place in order since then; there is no grass on the paths, there are no trailing brambles over the ground, the hedges have been cut and trimmed, and the trees pruned and the boxwood clipped. But I often say nowadays that in spite of all my improvements, or rather, in consequence of them, Martingdale does not look one half so pretty as it did in its pristine state of uncivilised picturesqueness.

Although I determined not to commence repairing and decorating the house till better informed concerning the rental of Martingdale, still the state of my finances was so far satisfactory that Clare and I decided on going abroad to take our long-talked-of holiday before the fine weather was past. We could not tell what a year might bring forth, as Clare sagely remarked; it was wise to take our pleasure while we could; and, accordingly, before the end of August arrived we were wandering about the continent, loitering at Rouen, visiting the galleries at Paris, and talking of extending our one month of enjoyment into three. What decided me on this course was the circumstance of our becoming acquainted with an English family who intended wintering in Rome. We met accidentally, but discovering that we were near neighbours in England – in fact that Mr Cronson's property lay close beside Martingdale – the slight acquaintance soon ripened into intimacy, and ere long we were travelling in company.

From the first, Clare did not much like this arrangement. There was 'a little girl' in England she wanted

me to marry, and Mr Cronson had a daughter who
certainly was both handsome and attractive. The little
girl had not despised John Lester, artist, while Miss
Cronson indisputably set her cap at John Lester of
Martingdale, and would have turned away her pretty
face from a poor man's admiring glance – all this I
can see plainly enough now, but I was blind then and
should have proposed for Maybel – that was her
name – before the winter was over, had news not
suddenly arrived of the illness of Mrs Cronson,
senior. In a moment the programme was changed;
our pleasant days of foreign travel were at an end.
The Cronsons packed up and departed, while Clare
and I returned more slowly to England, a little out of
humour, it must be confessed, with each other.

It was the middle of November when we arrived
at Martingdale, and we found the place anything
but romantic or pleasant. The walks were wet and
sodden, the trees were leafless, there were no flowers
save a few late pink roses blooming in the garden.

It had been a wet season, and the place looked
miserable. Clare would not ask Alice down to keep her
company in the winter months, as she had intended;
and for myself, the Cronsons were still absent in
Norfolk, where they meant to spend Christmas with
old Mrs Cronson, now recovered.

Altogether, Martingdale seemed dreary enough,
and the ghost stories we had laughed at while sunshine flooded the rooms became less unreal when we
had nothing but blazing fires and wax candles to
dispel the gloom. They became more real also when
servant after servant left us to seek situations elsewhere; when 'noises' grew frequent in the house;
when we ourselves, Clare and I, with our own ears

heard the tramp, tramp, the banging and the clattering which had been described to us.

My dear reader, you are doubtless free from superstitious fancies. You pooh-pooh the existence of ghosts, and only 'wish you could find a haunted house in which to spend a night', which is all very brave and praiseworthy, but wait till you are left in a dreary, desolate old country mansion, filled with the most unaccountable sounds, without a servant, with no one save an old caretaker and his wife, who, living at the extremest end of the building, heard nothing of the tramp, tramp, bang, bang, going on at all hours of the night.

At first I imagined the noises were produced by some evil-disposed persons who wished, for purposes of their own, to keep the house uninhabited; but by degrees Clare and I came to the conclusion the visitation must be supernatural, and Martingdale by consequence untenantable. Still, being practical people, and unlike our predecessors, not having money to live where and how we liked, we decided to watch and see whether we could trace any human influence in the matter. If not, it was agreed we were to pull down the right wing of the house and the principal staircase.

For nights and nights we sat up till two or three o'clock in the morning, Clare engaged in needlework, I reading, with a revolver lying on the table beside me; but nothing, neither sound nor appearance, rewarded our vigil.

This confirmed my first idea that the sounds were not supernatural; but just to test the matter, I determined on Christmas Eve, the anniversary of Mr Jeremy Lester's disappearance, to keep watch by myself in the red bedchamber. Even to Clare I never mentioned my intention.

About ten, tired out with our previous vigils, we each retired to rest. Somewhat ostentatiously, perhaps, I noisily shut the door of my room, and when I opened it half an hour afterwards, no mouse could have pursued its way along the corridor with greater silence and caution than myself.

Quite in the dark I sat in the red room. For over an hour I might as well have been in my grave for anything I could see in the apartment; but at the end of that time the moon rose and cast strange lights across the floor and upon the wall of the haunted chamber.

Hitherto I had kept my watch opposite the window; now I changed my place to a corner near the door, where I was shaded from observation by the heavy hangings of the bed, and an antique wardrobe.

Still I sat on, but still no sound broke the silence. I was weary with many nights' watching; and tired of my solitary vigil, I dropped at last into a slumber from which I was awakened by hearing the door softly opened.

'John,' said my sister, almost in a whisper; 'John, are you here?'

'Yes, Clare,' I answered; 'but what are you doing up at this hour?'

'Come downstairs,' she replied; 'they are in the oak parlour.'

I did not need any explanation as to whom she meant, but crept downstairs, after her, warned by an uplifted hand of the necessity for silence and caution.

By the door – by the open door of the oak parlour, she paused, and we both looked in.

There was the room we left in darkness overnight,

with a bright wood fire blazing on the hearth, candles on the chimney-piece, the small table pulled out from its accustomed corner, and two men seated beside it, playing at cribbage.

We could see the face of the younger player; it was that of a man of about five-and-twenty, of a man who had lived hard and wickedly; who had wasted his substance and his health; who had been while in the flesh, Jeremy Lester. It would be difficult for me to say how I knew this, how in a moment I identified the features of the player with those of the man who had been missing for forty-one years – forty-one years that very night. He was dressed in the costume of a bygone period; his hair was powdered, and round his wrists there were ruffles of lace.

He looked like one who, having come from some great party, had sat down after his return home to play at cards with an intimate friend. On his little finger there sparkled a ring, in the front of his shirt there gleamed a valuable diamond. There were diamond buckles in his shoes, and, according to the fashion of his time, he wore knee-breeches and silk stockings, which showed off advantageously the shape of a remarkably good leg and ankle.

He sat opposite to the door, but never once lifted his eyes to it. His attention seemed concentrated on the cards.

For a time there was utter silence in the room, broken only by the monotonous counting of the game.

In the doorway we stood, holding our breath, terrified and yet fascinated by the scene which was being acted before us.

The ashes dropped on the hearth softly and like the

snow; we could hear the rustle of the cards as they
were dealt out and fell upon the table: we listened to
the count – fifteen-one, fifteen-two, and so forth –
but there was no other word spoken till at length the
player whose face we could not see, exclaimed, 'I
win; the game is mine.'

Then his opponent took up the cards, sorted them
over negligently in his hand, put them close together,
and flung the whole pack in his guest's face, exclaiming, 'Cheat! Liar! Take that!'

There was a bustle and a confusion – a flinging
over of chairs and fierce gesticulation, and such a
noise of passionate voices mingling that we could not
hear a sentence which was uttered.

All at once, however, Jeremy Lester strode out of
the room in so great a hurry that he almost touched
us where we stood; out of the room, and tramp,
tramp up the staircase, to the red room, whence he
descended in a few minutes with a couple of rapiers
under his arm.

When he re-entered the room he gave, as it seemed
to us, the other man his choice of the weapons,
and then he flung open the window, and after
ceremoniously giving place to his opponent to pass
out first, he walked forth into the night-air, Clare and
I following.

We went through the garden and down a narrow
winding walk to a smooth piece of turf sheltered
from the north by a plantation of young fir trees. It
was a bright moonlit night by this time, and we
could distinctly see Jeremy Lester measuring off the
ground.

'When you say "three",' he said to the man whose
back was still towards us. They had drawn lots for

the ground, and the lot had fallen against Mr Lester. He stood thus with the moonbeams falling full upon him, and a handsomer fellow I would never desire to behold.

'One,' began the other; 'two,' and before our kinsman had the slightest suspicion of his design, he was upon him, and his rapier through Jeremy Lester's breast. At the sight of that cowardly treachery, Clare screamed aloud. In a moment the combatants had disappeared, the moon was obscured behind a cloud, and we were standing in the shadow of the fir plantation, shivering with cold and terror.

But we knew at last what had become of the late owner of Martingdale: that he had fallen, not in fair fight, but foully murdered by a false friend.

When, late on Christmas morning, I awoke, it was to see a white world, to behold the ground and trees and shrubs all laden and covered with snow. There was snow everywhere, such snow as no person could remember having fallen for forty-one years.

'It was on just such a Christmas as this that Mr Jeremy disappeared,' remarked the old sexton to my sister, who had insisted on dragging me through the snow to church, whereupon Clare fainted away and was carried into the vestry, where I made a full confession to the vicar of all we had beheld the previous night.

At first, that worthy individual rather inclined to treat the matter lightly, but when, a fortnight after, the snow melted away and the fir plantation came to be examined, he confessed there might be more things in heaven and earth than his limited philosophy had dreamed of.

In a little clear space just within the plantation,

Jeremy Lester's body was found. We knew it by the ring and the diamond buckles, and the sparkling breast-pin; and Mr Cronson, who in his capacity as magistrate came over to inspect these relics, was visibly perturbed at my narrative.

'Pray, Mr Lester, did you in your dream see the face of – of the gentleman – your kinsman's opponent?'

'No,' I answered, 'he sat and stood with his back to us all the time.'

'There is nothing more, of course, to be done in the matter,' observed Mr Cronson.

'Nothing,' I replied; and there the affair would doubtless have terminated, but that a few days afterwards when we were dining at Cronson Park, Clare all of a sudden dropped the glass of water she was carrying to her lips, and exclaiming, 'Look, John, there he is!' rose from her seat, and with a face as white as the tablecloth, pointed to a portrait hanging on the wall.

'I saw him for an instant when he turned his head towards the door as Jeremy Lester left the room,' she exclaimed; 'that is he.'

Of what followed after this identification I have only the vaguest recollection. Servants rushed hither and thither; Mrs Cronson dropped off her chair into hysterics; the young ladies gathered round their mamma; Mr Cronson, trembling like one in an ague fit, attempted some kind of explanation, while Clare kept praying to be taken away – only to be taken away.

I took her away, not merely from Cronson Park, but from Martingdale. Before we left the latter place, however, I had an interview with Mr Cronson, who said the portrait Clare had identified was that of his wife's father, the last person who saw Jeremy Lester alive.

'He is an old man now,' finished Mr Cronson, 'a man of over eighty, who has confessed everything to me. You won't bring further sorrow and disgrace upon us by making this matter public?'

I promised him I would keep silence, but the story gradually oozed out, and the Cronsons left the country.

My sister never returned to Martingdale; she married and is living in London. Though I assure her there are no strange noises now in my house, she will not visit Bedfordshire, where the 'little girl' she wanted me so long ago to 'think seriously of' is now my wife and the mother of my children.

FITZ JAMES O'BRIEN

What was It?

It is, I confess, with considerable diffidence, that I approach the strange narrative which I am about to relate. The events which I purpose detailing are of so extraordinary a character that I am quite prepared to meet with an unusual amount of incredulity and scorn. I accept all such beforehand. I have, I trust, the literary courage to face unbelief. I have, after mature consideration, resolved to narrate in as simple and straightforward a manner as I can compass some facts that passed under my observation in the month of July last, facts which, in the annals of the mysteries of physical science, are wholly unparalleled.

I live at No. — 26th Street in New York. The house is in some respects a curious one. It has enjoyed for the last two years the reputation of being haunted. It is a large and stately residence, surrounded by what was once a garden but is now only a green enclosure used for bleaching clothes. The dry basin of what has been a fountain, and a few fruit trees, ragged and unpruned, indicate that this spot in past days was a pleasant, shady retreat, filled with fruits and flowers and the sweet murmur of waters.

The house is very spacious. A hall of noble size leads to a large spiral staircase winding through its centre, while the various apartments are of imposing dimensions. It was built some fifteen or twenty years since by Mr A—, the well-known New York merchant, who five years ago threw the commercial world into convulsions by a stupendous bank fraud. Mr A—, as everyone knows, escaped to Europe, and died not long after of a broken heart. Almost immediately after the news of his decease reached this country and was verified, the report spread in 26th Street that No. — was haunted. Legal measures had dispossessed the widow of its former owner, and it was inhabited merely by a caretaker and his wife, placed there by the house agent into whose hands it had passed for the purposes of renting or sale. These people declared that they were troubled with unnatural noises. Doors were opened without any visible agency. The remnants of furniture scattered through the various rooms were, during the night, piled one upon the other by unknown hands. Invisible feet passed up and down the stairs in broad daylight, accompanied by the rustle of unseen silk dresses, and the gliding of viewless hands along the massive balusters. The caretaker and his wife declared they would live there no longer. The house agent laughed, dismissed them, and put others in their place. The noises and supernatural manifestations continued. The neighbourhood caught up the story, and the house remained untenanted for three years. Several persons negotiated for it; but, somehow, always before the bargain was closed they heard the unpleasant rumours and declined to treat any further.

It was in this state of things that my landlady, who at that time kept a boarding-house in Bleecker Street and who wished to move further uptown, conceived the bold idea of renting No. — 26th Street. Happening to have in her house rather a plucky and philosophical set of boarders, she laid her scheme before us, stating candidly everything she had heard respecting the ghostly qualities of the establishment to which she wished to remove us. With the exception of two timid persons – a sea-captain and a returned Californian – who immediately gave notice that they would leave, all of Mrs Moffat's guests declared that they would accompany her in her chivalric incursion into the abode of spirits.

Our removal was effected in the month of May, and we were charmed with our new residence. The portion of 26th Street where our house is situated, between Seventh and Eighth Avenues, is one of the pleasantest localities in New York. The gardens back of the houses, running down nearly to the Hudson, form, in the summertime, a perfect avenue of verdure. The air is pure and invigorating, sweeping, as it does, straight across the river from the Weehawken heights, and even the ragged garden which surrounded the house, although displaying on washing days rather too much clothes-line, still gave us a piece of green-sward to look at, and a cool retreat in the summer evenings, when we smoked our cigars in the dusk and watched the fireflies flashing their dark lanterns in the long grass.

Of course we had no sooner established ourselves at No. — than we began to expect ghosts. We absolutely awaited their advent with eagerness. Our dinner conversation was supernatural. One of the boarders, who had purchased Mrs Crowe's *Night Side of Nature* for his own private delectation, was regarded as a public enemy by the entire household for not having bought twenty copies. The man led a life of supreme wretchedness while he was reading this volume. A system of espionage was established, of which he was the victim. If he incautiously laid the book down for an instant and left the room, it was immediately seized and read aloud in secret places to a select few. I found myself a person of immense importance, it having leaked out that I was tolerably well versed in the history of supernaturalism, and had once written a story the foundation of which was a ghost. If a table or a wainscot panel happened to warp when we were assembled in the large drawing-room, there was an instant silence, and everyone was prepared for an immediate clanking of chains and a spectral form.

After a month of psychological excitement, it was with the utmost dissatisfaction that we were forced to acknowledge that nothing in the remotest degree approaching the supernatural had manifested itself. Once the black butler asseverated that his candle had been blown out by some invisible agency while he was undressing himself for the night; but as I had more than once discovered this coloured gentleman in a condition when one candle must have appeared to him like two, thought it possible that, by going a step further in his potations, he might have reversed this phenomenon, and seen no candle at all where he ought to have beheld one.

Things were in this state when an accident took place so awful and inexplicable in its character that my reason fairly reels at the bare memory of the occurrence. It was the tenth of July. After dinner was over I repaired, with my friend Dr Hammond, to the garden to smoke my evening pipe. Independent of certain mental sympathies which existed between the doctor and myself, we were linked together by a vice. We both smoked opium. We knew each other's secret, and respected it. We enjoyed together that wonderful expansion of thought, that marvellous intensifying of the perceptive faculties, that boundless feeling of existence when we seem to have points of contact with the whole universe – in short, that unimaginable spiritual bliss, which I would not surrender for a throne, and which I hope you, reader, will never never taste.

Those hours of opium happiness which the doctor and I spent together in secret were regulated with a scientific accuracy. We did not blindly smoke the drug of paradise and leave our dreams to chance. While smoking, we carefully steered our conversation through the brightest and calmest channels of thought. We talked of the East, and endeavoured to recall the magical panorama of its glowing scenery. We criticised the most sensuous poets – those who painted life ruddy with health, brimming with passion, happy in the possession of youth and strength and beauty. If we talked of Shakespeare's *Tempest*, we lingered over Ariel, and avoided Caliban. Like the Guebers, we turned our faces to the East, and saw only the sunny side of the world.

This skilful colouring of our train of thought produced in our subsequent visions a corresponding tone. The splendours of Arabian fairyland dyed our dreams. We paced the narrow strip of grass with the tread and port of kings. The song of the *rana arborea*, while he clung to the bark of the ragged plum tree, sounded like the strains of divine musicians. Houses, walls and streets melted like rain clouds, and vistas of unimaginable glory stretched away before us. It was a rapturous companionship. We enjoyed the vast delight more perfectly because, even in our most ecstatic moments, we were conscious of each other's presence. Our pleasures, while individual, were still twin, vibrating and moving in musical accord.

On the evening in question, the tenth of July, the doctor and I drifted into an unusually metaphysical mood. We lit our large meerschaums, filled with fine Turkish tobacco in the core of which burned a little black nut of opium that, like the nut in the fairy tale, held within its narrow limits wonders beyond the reach of kings; we paced to and fro, conversing. A strange perversity dominated the currents of our thought. They would *not* flow through the sun-lit channels into which we strove to divert them. For some unaccountable reason, they constantly diverged into dark and lonesome beds, where a continual gloom brooded. It was in vain that, after our old fashion, we flung ourselves on the shores of the East, and talked of its gay bazaars, of the splendours of the time of Haroun, of harems and golden palaces. Black afreets continually arose from the depths of our talk, and expanded, like the one the fisherman released from the copper vessel, until they blotted everything bright from our vision. Insensibly, we yielded to the occult force that swayed us, and indulged in gloomy speculation. We had talked for some time upon the proneness of the human mind to mysticism and the almost universal love of the terrible, when Hammond suddenly said to me, 'What do you consider to be the greatest element of terror?'

The question puzzled me. That many things were terrible, I knew. Stumbling over a corpse in the dark;

beholding, as I once did, a woman floating down a deep and rapid river, with wildly lifted arms, and awful, upturned face, uttering, as she drifted, shrieks that rent one's heart while we, spectators, stood frozen at a window which overhung the river at a height of sixty feet, unable to make the slightest effort to save her, but dumbly watching her last supreme agony and her disappearance. A shattered wreck, with no life visible, encountered floating listlessly on the ocean, is a terrible object, for it suggests a huge terror, the proportions of which are veiled. But it now struck me, for the first time, that there must be one great and ruling embodiment of fear – a king of terrors, to which all others must succumb. What might it be? To what train of circumstances would it owe its existence?

'I confess, Hammond,' I replied to my friend, 'I never considered the subject before. That there must be one Something more terrible than any other thing, I feel. I cannot attempt, however, even the most vague definition.'

'I am somewhat like you,' he answered. 'I feel my capacity to experience a terror greater than anything yet conceived by the human mind – something combining in fearful and unnatural amalgamation hitherto supposed incompatible elements. The calling of the voices in Brockden Brown's novel of *Wieland* is awful; so is the picture of the Dweller by the Threshold in Bulwer's *Zanoni*; but,' he added, shaking his head gloomily, 'there is something more horrible still than those.'

'Look here, Hammond,' I rejoined, 'let us drop this kind of talk, for heaven's sake! We shall suffer for it, depend on it.'

473

'I don't know what's the matter with me tonight,'
he replied, 'but my brain is running upon all sorts of
weird and awful thoughts. I feel as if I could write a
story like Hoffman, tonight, if I were only master of a
literary style.'

'Well, if we are going to be Hoffmanesque in our
talk, I'm off to bed. Opium and nightmares should
never be brought together. How sultry it is! Good-
night, Hammond.'

'Good-night, Harry. Pleasant dreams to you.'

'To you, gloomy wretch, afreets, ghouls and
enchanters.'

We parted, and each sought his respective chamber.
I undressed quickly and got into bed, taking with me,
according to my usual custom, a book, over which I
generally read myself to sleep. I opened the volume as
soon as I had laid my head upon the pillow, and
instantly flung it to the other side of the room. It was
Goudon's *History of Monsters* – a curious French work,
which I had lately imported from Paris, but which, in
the state of mind I had then reached, was anything
but an agreeable companion. I resolved to go to sleep
at once; so, turning down my gas until nothing but a
little blue point of light glimmered on the top of the
tube, I composed myself to rest.

The room was in total darkness. The atom of gas
that still remained alight did not illuminate a distance
of even three inches round the burner. I desperately
drew my arm across my eyes, as if to shut out even
the darkness, and tried to think of nothing. It was in
vain. The confounded themes touched on by
Hammond in the garden kept obtruding themselves
on my brain. I battled against them. I erected
ramparts of would-be blackness of intellect to keep

them out. They still crowded upon me. While I was lying still as a corpse, hoping that by a perfect physical inaction I should hasten mental repose, an awful incident occurred. A Something dropped, as it seemed, from the ceiling, plumb upon my chest, and the next instant I felt two bony hands encircling my throat, endeavouring to choke me.

I am no coward, and am possessed of considerable physical strength. The suddenness of the attack, instead of stunning me, strung every nerve to its highest tension. My body acted from instinct, before my brain had time to realise the terrors of my position. In an instant I wound two muscular arms around the creature, and squeezed it, with all the strength of despair, against my chest. In a few seconds the bony hands that had fastened on my throat loosened their hold, and I was free to breathe once more. Then commenced a struggle of awful intensity. Immersed in the most profound darkness, totally ignorant of the nature of the Thing by which I was so suddenly attacked, finding my grasp slipping every moment, by reason, it seemed to me, of the entire nakedness of my assailant, bitten with sharp teeth in the shoulder, neck and chest, having every moment to protect my throat against a pair of sinewy, agile hands, which my utmost efforts could not confine – these were a combination of circumstances to combat which required all the strength, skill and courage that I possessed.

At last, after a silent, deadly, exhausting struggle, I got my assailant under by a series of incredible efforts of strength. Once it was pinned, with my knee on what I made out to be its chest, I knew that I was victor. I rested for a moment to breathe. I heard the creature beneath me panting in the darkness, and felt the violent throbbing of a heart. It was apparently as exhausted as I was; that was one comfort. At this moment I remembered that I usually placed under my pillow, before going to bed, a large yellow silk pocket handkerchief. I felt for it instantly; it was there. In a few seconds more I had, after a fashion, pinioned the creature's arms.

I now felt tolerably secure. There was nothing more to be done but to turn up the gas, and, having first seen what my midnight assailant was like, arouse the household. I will confess to being actuated by a certain pride in not giving the alarm before; I wished to make the capture alone and unaided.

Never losing my hold for an instant, I slipped from the bed to the floor, dragging my captive with me. I had but a few steps to make to reach the gas-burner; these I made with the greatest caution, holding the creature in a grip like a vice. At last I got within arm's length of the tiny speck of blue light which told me where the gas-burner lay. Quick as lightning I released my grasp with one hand and let on the full flood of light. Then I turned to look at my captive.

I cannot even attempt to give any definition of my sensations the instant after I turned on the gas. I suppose I must have shrieked with terror, for in less than a minute afterwards my room was crowded with the inmates of the house. I shudder now as I think of that awful moment. *I saw nothing!* Yes; I had one arm firmly clasped round a breathing, panting, corporeal shape, my other hand gripped with all its strength a throat as warm, as apparently fleshy, as my own; and yet, with this living substance in my grasp, with its body pressed against my own, and all in the bright glare of a large jet of gas, I absolutely beheld nothing! Not even an outline – a vapour!

I do not, even at this hour, realise the situation in which I found myself. I cannot recall the astounding incident thoroughly. Imagination in vain tries to compass the awful paradox.

It breathed. I felt its warm breath upon my cheek. It struggled fiercely. It had hands. They clutched me. Its skin was smooth, like my own. There it lay, pressed close up against me, solid as stone – and yet utterly invisible!

I wonder that I did not faint or go mad on the instant. Some wonderful instinct must have sustained me; for, absolutely, in place of loosening my hold on the terrible Enigma, I seemed to gain an additional strength in my moment of horror, and tightened my grasp with such wonderful force that I felt the creature shivering with agony.

Just then Hammond entered my room at the head of the household. As soon as he beheld my face – which, I suppose, must have been an awful sight to look at – he hastened forward, crying, 'Great heaven, Harry! what has happened?'

'Hammond! Hammond!' I cried, 'come here. Oh, this is awful! I have been attacked in bed by something or other, which I have hold of; but I can't see it – I can't see it!'

Hammond, doubtless struck by the unfeigned horror expressed in my countenance, made one or two steps forward with an anxious yet puzzled expression. A very audible titter burst from the remainder of my visitors. This suppressed laughter made me furious. To laugh at a human being in my position! It was the worst species of cruelty. *Now*, I can understand why the appearance of a man struggling violently, as it would seem, with an airy nothing, and calling for assistance against a vision, should have appeared ludicrous. *Then*, so great was my rage against the mocking crowd that had I the power I would have struck them dead where they stood.

'Hammond! Hammond!' I cried again, despairingly, 'for God's sake come to me. I can hold the – the Thing but a short while longer. It is overpowering me. Help me! Help me!'

'Harry,' whispered Hammond, approaching me, 'you have been smoking too much opium.'

'I swear to you, Hammond, that this is no vision,' I answered, in the same low tone. 'Don't you see how it shakes my whole frame with its struggles? If you don't believe me, convince yourself. Feel it – touch it.'

Hammond advanced and laid his hand in the spot I indicated. A wild cry of horror burst from him. He had felt it!

In a moment he had discovered somewhere in my room a long piece of cord, and was the next instant winding it and knotting it about the body of the unseen being that I clasped in my arms.

'Harry,' he said, in a hoarse, agitated voice, for, though he preserved his presence of mind, he was deeply moved, 'Harry, it's all safe now. You may let go, old fellow, if you're tired. The Thing can't move.'

I was utterly exhausted, and I gladly loosed my hold.

Hammond stood holding the ends of the cord that bound the Invisible, twisted round his hand, while before him, self-supporting as it were, he beheld a rope laced and interlaced, and stretching tightly around a vacant space. I never saw a man look so thoroughly stricken with awe. Nevertheless his face expressed all the courage and determination which I knew him to possess. His lips, although white, were set firmly, and one could perceive at a glance that, although stricken with fear, he was not daunted.

The confusion that ensued among the guests of the house who were witnesses of this extraordinary scene between Hammond and myself – who beheld the pantomime of binding this struggling Something – who beheld me almost sinking from physical exhaustion when my task of jailer was over – the confusion and terror that took possession of the bystanders, when they saw all this, was beyond description. The weaker ones fled from the apartment. The few who remained clustered near the door and could not be induced to approach Hammond and his charge. Still incredulity broke out through their terror. They had not the courage to satisfy themselves, and yet they doubted. It was in vain that I begged of some of the men to come near and convince themselves by touch of the existence in that room of a living being which was invisible. They were incredulous, but did not dare to undeceive themselves. How could a solid, living, breathing body be invisible, they asked. My reply was this. I gave a sign to Hammond, and both of us – conquering our fearful repugnance to touch the invisible creature – lifted it from the ground, manacled as it was, and took it to my bed. Its weight was about that of a boy of fourteen.

'Now, my friends,' I said, as Hammond and I held the creature suspended over the bed, 'I can give you self-evident proof that here is a solid, ponderable body, which, nevertheless, you cannot see. Be good enough to watch the surface of the bed attentively.'

I was astonished at my own courage in treating this strange event so calmly; but I had recovered from my first terror and felt a sort of scientific pride in the affair, which dominated every other feeling.

The eyes of the bystanders were immediately fixed on my bed. At a given signal Hammond and I let the creature fall. There was a dull sound of a heavy body alighting on a soft mass. The timbers of the bed creaked. A deep impression marked itself distinctly on the pillow, and on the bed itself. The crowd who witnessed this gave a low cry, and rushed from the room. Hammond and I were left alone with our Mystery.

We remained silent for some time, listening to the low, irregular breathing of the creature on the bed, and watching the rustle of the bedclothes as it impotently struggled to free itself from confinement. Then Hammond spoke. 'Harry, this is awful.'

'Ay, awful.'

'But not unaccountable.'

'Not unaccountable! What do you mean? Such a thing has never occurred since the birth of the world. I know not what to think, Hammond. God grant that I am not mad, and that this is not an insane fantasy!'

'Let us reason a little, Harry. Here is a solid body which we touch, but which we cannot see. The fact is so unusual that it strikes us with terror. Is there no parallel, though, for such a phenomenon? Take a piece of pure glass. It is tangible and transparent. A certain chemical coarseness is all that prevents its being so entirely transparent as to be totally invisible. It is not *theoretically impossible*, mind you, to make a glass which shall not reflect a single ray of light – a glass so pure and homogeneous in its atoms that the rays from the sun will pass through it as they do through the air, refracted but not reflected. We do not see the air, and yet we feel it.'

'That's all very well, Hammond, but these are inanimate substances. Glass does not breathe, air does not breathe. *This* thing has a heart that palpitates – a will that moves it – lungs that respire.'

'You forget the phenomena of which we have so often heard of late,' answered the doctor, gravely. 'At the meetings called "spirit circles", invisible hands have been thrust into the hands of those persons round the table – warm, fleshly hands that seemed to pulsate with mortal life.'

'What? Do you think, then, that this thing is – '

'I don't know what it is,' was the solemn reply; 'but please the gods I will, with your assistance, thoroughly investigate it.'

We watched together, smoking many pipes, all night long, by the bedside of the unearthly being that tossed and panted until it was apparently wearied out. Then we learned by the low, regular breathing that it slept.

The next morning the house was all astir. The boarders congregated on the landing outside my room, and Hammond and I were lions. We had to answer a thousand questions as to the state of our extraordinary prisoner, for as yet not one person in the house except ourselves could be induced to set foot in the apartment.

The creature was awake. This was evidenced by the convulsive manner in which the bedclothes were moved in its efforts to escape. There was something truly terrible in beholding, as it were, those second-hand indications of the terrible writhings and agonised struggles for liberty which themselves were invisible.

Hammond and I had racked our brains during the long night to discover some means by which we might realise the shape and general appearance of the Enigma. As well as we could make out by passing our hands over the creature's form, its outlines and lineaments were human. There was a mouth; a round, smooth head without hair; a nose which was but little elevated above the cheeks; and its hands and feet felt like those of a boy. At first we thought of placing the being on a smooth surface and tracing its outlines with chalk, as shoemakers trace the outline of the foot. This plan was given up as being of no value. Such an outline would give not the slightest idea of its conformation.

A happy thought struck me. We would take a cast of it in plaster of Paris. This would give us the solid figure, and satisfy all our wishes. But how to do it? The movements of the creature would disturb the setting of the plastic covering and distort the mould. Another thought. Why not give it chloroform? It had respiratory organs – that was evident by its breathing. Once it was reduced to a state of insensibility, we could do with it what we would. Dr X— was sent for; and after the worthy physician had recovered from the first shock of amazement, he proceeded to administer the chloroform. Three minutes afterwards we were able to remove the fetters from the creature's body, and a modeller was soon busily engaged in covering the invisible form with the moist clay. In five minutes more we had a mould, and before evening a rough facsimile of the Mystery. It was shaped like a man – distorted, uncouth and horrible, but still a man.

It was small, not over four feet and some inches in height, and its limbs revealed a muscular development that was unparalleled. Its face surpassed in hideousness anything I had ever seen. Gustav Doré, or Callot, or Tony Johannot, never conceived anything so horrible. There is a face in one of the latter's illustrations to *Un Voyage ou il vous plaira* which somewhat approaches the countenance of this creature, but does not equal it. It was the physiognomy of what I should fancy a ghoul might be. It looked as if it was capable of feeding on human flesh.

Having satisfied our curiosity, and bound everyone in the house to secrecy, it became a question what was to be done with our Enigma? It was impossible that we should keep such a horror in our house; it was equally impossible that such an awful being should be let loose upon the world. I confess that I would have gladly voted for the creature's destruction. But who would shoulder the responsibility? Who would undertake the execution of this horrible semblance of a human being? Day after day this question was deliberated gravely. The boarders all left the house. Mrs Moffat was in despair, and threatened Hammond and myself with all sorts of legal penalties if we did not remove the Horror. Our answer was, 'We will go if you like, but we decline taking this creature with us. Remove it yourself if you please. It appeared in your house. On you the responsibility rests.' To this there was, of course, no answer. Mrs Moffat could not obtain for love or money a person who would even approach the Mystery.

The most singular part of the affair was that we were entirely ignorant of what the creature habitually fed on. Everything in the way of nutriment that we could think of was placed before it, but was never touched. It was awful to stand by, day after day, and see the clothes toss, and hear the hard breathing, and know that it was starving.

Ten, twelve days, a fortnight passed, and it still lived. The pulsations of the heart, however, were daily growing fainter, and had now nearly ceased. It was evident that the creature was dying for want of sustenance. While this terrible life-struggle was going on, I felt miserable. I could not sleep. Horrible as the creature was, it was pitiful to think of the pangs it was suffering.

At last it died. Hammond and I found it cold and stiff one morning in the bed. The heart had ceased to beat, the lungs to inspire. We hastened to bury it in the garden. It was a strange funeral, the dropping of that viewless corpse into the damp hole. The cast of its form I gave to Dr X—, who keeps it in his museum on 10th Street.

As I am on the eve of a long journey from which I may not return, I have drawn up this narrative of an event which was the most singular that has ever come to my knowledge.

FITZ-JAMES O'BRIEN

The Pot of Tulips

Twenty-eight years ago I went to spend the summer at an old Dutch villa which then lifted its head from the wild country that, in present days, has been tamed down into a site for a Crystal Palace. Madison Square was then a wilderness of fields and scrub oak, here and there diversified with tall and stately elms. Worthy citizens who could afford two establishments rusticated in the groves that then flourished where ranks of brown-stone porticos now form the land-scape; and the locality of 40th Street, where my summer palace stood, was justly looked upon as at an enterprising distance from the city.

I had had an imperious desire to live in this house ever since I could remember. I had often seen it when a boy, and its cool verandas and quaint garden seemed, whenever I passed, to attract me irresistibly. In after years, when I grew up to man's estate, I was not sorry, therefore, when one summer, fatigued with the labours of my business, I beheld a notice in the papers intimating that it was to be let furnished. I hastened to my dear friend Jaspar Joye, painted the delights of this rural retreat in the most glowing colours, easily obtained his assent to share the enjoyments and the expense with me, and a month afterwards we were taking our ease in this new paradise.

Independent of early associations, other interests attached me to this house. It was somewhat historical, and had given shelter to George Washington on the occasion of one of his visits to the city. Furthermore, I knew the descendants of the family to whom it had originally belonged. Their history was strange and mournful, and it seemed to me as if their individuality was somehow shared by the edifice. It had been built by a Mr Van Koeren, a gentleman of Holland, the younger son of a rich mercantile firm at the Hague, who had emigrated to this country in order to establish a branch of his father's business in New York, which even then gave indications of the prosperity it has since reached with such marvellous rapidity. He had brought with him a fair young Belgian wife; a loving girl, if I may believe her portrait, with soft brown eyes, chestnut hair, and a deep, placid contentment spreading over her fresh and innocent features. Her son, Alain Van Koeren, had her picture – an old miniature in a red-gold frame – as well as that of his father, and in truth, when looking on the two, one could not conceive a greater contrast than must have existed between husband and wife. Mr Van Koeren must have been a man of terrible will and gloomy temperament. His face in the picture is dark and austere, his eyes deep-sunken, and burning as if with a slow, inward fire. The lips are thin and compressed, with much determination of purpose; and his chin, boldly salient, is brimful of power and resolution. When first I saw those two pictures I sighed inwardly and thought, 'Poor child! you must often have sighed for the sunny meadows of Brussels, in the long, gloomy nights spent in the company of that terrible man!'

I was not far wrong, as I afterwards discovered. Mr and Mrs Van Koeren were very unhappy. Jealousy was his monomania, and they had scarcely been married before his girl-wife began to feel the oppression of a gloomy and ceaseless tyranny. Every man under fifty, whose hair was not white and whose form was erect, was an object of suspicion to this Dutch Bluebeard. Not that he was vulgarly jealous. He did not frown at his wife before strangers, or attack her with reproaches in the midst of her festivities. He was too well-bred a man to bare his private woes to the world. But at night, when the guests had departed and the dull light of the quaint old Flemish lamps but half illuminated the nuptial chamber, then it was that with monotonous invective Mr Van Koeren crushed his wife. And Marie, weeping and silent, would sit on the edge of the bed listening to the cold, trenchant irony of her husband, who, pacing up and down the room, would now and then stop in his walk to gaze with his burning eyes upon the pallid face of his victim. Even the evidences that Marie gave of becoming a mother did not check him. He saw in that coming event, which most husbands anticipate with mingled joy and fear, only an approaching incarnation of his dishonour. He watched with a horrible refinement of suspicion for the arrival of that being in whose features he madly believed he should but too surely trace the evidences of his wife's crime.

Whether it was that these ceaseless attacks wore out her strength, or that Providence wished to add another chastening misery to her burden of woe, I dare not speculate; but it is certain that one luckless night Mr Van Koeren learned with fury that he had become a father two months before the allotted time.

During his first paroxysm of rage, on the receipt of intelligence which seemed to confirm all his previous suspicions, it was, I believe, with difficulty that he was prevented from slaying both the innocent causes of his resentment. The caution of his race and the presence of the physicians induced him, however, to put a curb upon his furious will until reflection suggested quite as criminal, if not as dangerous, a vengeance. As soon as his poor wife had recovered from her illness, unnaturally prolonged by the delicacy of constitution induced by previous mental suffering, she was astonished to find, instead of increasing his persecutions, that her husband had changed his tactics and treated her with studied neglect. He rarely spoke to her except on occasions when the decencies of society demanded that he should address her. He avoided her presence, and no longer inhabited the same apartments. He seemed, in short, to strive as much as possible to forget her existence. But if she did not suffer from personal ill-treatment it was because a punishment more acute was in store for her. If Mr Van Koeren had chosen to affect to consider her beneath his vengeance, it was because his hate had taken another direction, and seemed to have derived increased intensity from the alteration. It was upon the unhappy boy, the cause of all this misery, that the father lavished a terrible hatred.

Mr Van Koeren seemed determined that if this child sprang from other loins than his the mournful destiny which he forced upon him should amply avenge his own existence and the infidelity of his mother. While the child was an infant his plan seemed to have been formed. Ignorance and neglect were the two deadly influences with which he sought to assassinate the moral nature of this boy; and his terrible campaign against the virtue of his own son was, as he grew up, carried into execution with the most consummate generalship. He gave him money, but debarred him from education. He allowed him liberty of action, but withheld advice. It was in vain that his mother, who foresaw the frightful consequences of such a training, sought in secret by every means in her power to nullify her husband's attempts. She strove in vain to seduce her son into an ambition to be educated. She beheld with horror all her agonised efforts frustrated, and saw her son and only child becoming, even in his youth, a drunkard and a libertine. In the end it proved too much for her strength; she sickened, and went home to her sunny Belgian plains. There she lingered for a few months in a calm but rapid decay, whose calmness was broken but by the one grief; until one autumn day, when the leaves were falling from the limes, she made a little prayer for her son to the good God, and died. Vain orison! Spendthrift, gamester, libertine and drunkard by turns, Alain Van Koeren's earthly destiny was unchangeable. The father, who should have been his guide, looked on each fresh depravity of his son's with a species of grim delight. Even the death of his wronged wife had no effect upon his fatal purpose. He still permitted the young man to run blindly to destruction by the course into which he himself had led him.

As years rolled by, and Mr Van Koeren himself approached to that time of life when he might soon expect to follow his persecuted wife, he relieved himself of the hateful presence of his son altogether. Even the link of a systematic vengeance, which had hitherto united them, was severed, and Alain was cast adrift without either money or principle. The occasion of this final separation between father and son was the marriage of the latter with a girl of humble, though honest extraction. This was a good excuse for the remorseless Van Koeren, so he availed himself of it by turning his son out of doors.

From that time forth they never met. Alain lived a life of meagre dissipation, and soon died, leaving behind him one child, a daughter. By a coincidence natural enough, Mr Van Koeren's death followed his son's almost immediately. He died as he had lived, sternly. But those who were around his couch in his last moments mentioned some singular facts connected with the manner of his death. A few moments before he expired, he raised himself in the bed, and seemed as if conversing with some person invisible to the spectators. His lips moved as if in speech, and immediately afterwards he sank back, bathed in a flood of tears. 'Wrong! wrong!' he was heard to mutter, feebly; then he implored passionately the forgiveness of someone who, he said, was present. The death struggle ensued almost immediately, and in the midst of his agony he seemed wrestling for speech. All that could be heard, however, were a few broken words. 'I was wrong. My unfounded . . . For God's sake look in . . . You will find . . . ' Having uttered these fragmentary sentences, he seemed to feel that the power of speech had passed away for ever. He fixed his eyes piteously on those around him, and, with a great sigh of grief, expired. I gathered these facts from his granddaughter and Alain's daughter, Alice Van Koeren, who had been summoned by some friend to her grandfather's dying couch when it was too late. It was the first time she had seen him, and then she saw him die.

The results of Mr Van Koeren's death were a nine days' wonder to all the merchants in New York. Beyond a small sum in the bank, and the house in which he lived, which was mortgaged for its full value, Mr Van Koeren had died a pauper! To those who knew him and knew his affairs, this seemed inexplicable. Five or six years before his death he had retired from business with a fortune of several hundred thousand dollars. He had lived quietly since then, was known not to have speculated, and could not have gambled. The question then was where had his wealth vanished to? Search was made in every secretary, in every bureau, for some document which might throw a light on the mysterious disposition that he had made of his property. None was found. Neither will, nor certificates of stock, nor title deeds, nor bank accounts, were anywhere discernible. Enquiries were made at the offices of companies in which Mr Van Koeren was known to be largely interested; he had sold out his stock years ago. Real estate that had been believed to be his was found on investigation to have passed into other hands. There could be no doubt that for some years past Mr Van Koeren had been steadily converting all his property into money, and what he had done with that money no one knew. Alice Van Koeren and her mother, who at the old gentleman's death were at first looked on as millionaires, discovered, when all was over, that they were no better off than before. It was evident that the old man, determined that one whom, though bearing his name, he believed not to be of his blood, should never inherit his wealth or any share of it, had made away with his fortune before his death, a posthumous vengeance which was the only one by which the laws of the State of New York relative to inheritance could be successfully evaded. I took a peculiar interest in the case, and even helped to make some researches for the lost property, not so much, I confess, from a spirit of general philanthropy, as from certain feelings which I experienced toward Alice Van Koeren, the heir to this invisible estate. I had long known both her and her mother, when they were living in honest poverty and earning a scanty subsistence by their own labour; Mrs Van Koeren working as an embroideress, and Alice turning to account, as a preparatory governess, the education which her good mother, spite of her limited means, had bestowed on her.

In a few words, then, I loved Alice Van Koeren, and was determined to make her my wife as soon as my means would allow me to support a fitting establishment. My passion had never been declared. I was content for the time with the secret consciousness of my own love, and the no less grateful certainty that Alice returned it, all unuttered as it was. I had, therefore, a double interest in passing the summer at the old Dutch villa, for I felt it to be connected somehow with Alice, and I could not forget the singular desire to inhabit it which I had so often experienced as a boy.

It was a lovely day in June when Jasper Joye and I took up our abode in our new residence; and as we smoked our cigars on the piazza in the evening we felt for the first time the unalloyed pleasure with which a townsman breathes the pure air of the country.

The house and grounds had a quaint sort of beauty that to me was eminently pleasing. Landscape gardening, in the modern acceptation of the term, was then almost unknown in this country, and the 'laying out' of the garden that surrounded our new home would doubtless have shocked Mr London, the late Mr Downing or Sir Thomas Dick Lauder. It was formal and artificial to the last degree. The beds were cut into long parallelograms, rigid and severe of aspect, and edged with prim rows of stiff dwarf box. The walks, of course, crossed always at right angles, and the laurel and cypress trees that grew here and there were clipped into cones and spheres and rhomboids. It is true that, at the time my friend and I hired the house, years of neglect had restored to this formal garden somewhat of the raggedness of nature. The box edgings were rank and wild. The clipped trees, forgetful of geometric propriety, flourished into unauthorised boughs and rebel offshoots. The walks were green with moss, and the beds of Dutch tulips, which had been planted in the shape of certain gorgeous birds, whose colours were represented by masses of blossoms, each of a single hue, had transgressed their limits, and the purple of a parrot's wings might have been seen running recklessly into the crimson of his head; while, as bulbs, however well-bred, will create other bulbs, the flower-birds of this queer old Dutch garden became in time abominably distorted in shape: flamingoes with humps, golden pheasants with legs preternaturally elongated, macaws afflicted with hydrocephalus, each species of deformity being proportioned to the rapidity with which the roots had spread in some particular direction. Still, this strange mixture of raggedness and formality, this conglomerate of nature and art, had its charms. It was pleasant to watch the struggle, as it were, between the opposing elements, and to see nature triumphing by degrees in every direction.

The house itself was pleasant and commodious. Rooms that, though not lofty, were spacious; wide windows, and cool piazzas extending over the four sides of the building; and a collection of antique carved furniture, some of which, from its elaborateness, might well have come from the chisel of Master Grinling Gibbons. There was a mantelpiece in the dining-room with which I remember being very much struck when first I came to take possession. It was a singular and fantastical piece of carving – a perfect tropical garden, menagerie and aviary in one. Birds, beasts and flowers were sculptured on the wood with exquisite correctness of detail, and painted with the hues of nature. The Dutch taste for colour was here fully gratified. Parrots, love-birds, scarlet lories, blue-faced baboons, crocodiles, passion-flowers, tigers, Egyptian lilies and Brazilian butterflies were all mixed in gorgeous confusion. The artist, whoever he was, must have been an admirable naturalist, for the ease and freedom of his carving were only equalled by the wonderful accuracy with which the different animals were represented. Altogether it was one of those oddities of Dutch conception, whose strangeness was in this instance redeemed by the excellence of the execution.

Such was the establishment that Jasper Joye and myself were to inhabit for the summer months.

'What a strange thing it was,' said Jasper, as we lounged on the piazza together the night of our arrival, 'that old Van Koeren's property should never have turned up!'

'It is a question with some people whether he had any at his death,' I answered.

'Pshaw! everyone knows that he did not or could not have lost that with which he retired from business.'

'It is strange,' said I, thoughtfully; 'yet every possible search has been made for documents that might throw light on the mystery. I have myself sought in every quarter for traces of this lost wealth, but in vain.'

'Perhaps he buried it,' suggested Jasper, laughing; 'if so, we may find it here in a hole one fine morning.'

'I think it much more likely that he destroyed it,' I replied. 'You know he never could be got to believe that Alain Van Koeren was his son, and I believe him quite capable of having flung all his money into the sea in order to prevent those whom he considered not of his blood inheriting it, which they must have done under our laws.'

'I am sorry that Alice did not become an heiress, both for your sake and hers. She is a charming girl.'

Jasper, from whom I concealed nothing, knew of my love. 'As to that,' I answered, 'it is little matter. I shall in a year or two be independent enough to marry, and can afford to let Mr Van Koeren's cherished gold sleep wherever he has concealed it.'

'Well, I'm off to bed,' said Jasper, yawning. 'This country air makes one sleepy early. Be on the lookout for trap-doors and all that sort of thing, old fellow. Who knows but the old chap's dollars will turn up. Good-night!'

'Good-night, Jasper!'

So we parted for the night. He to his room, which lay on the west side of the building; I to mine on the east, situated at the end of a long corridor and exactly opposite to Jasper's.

The night was very still and warm. The clearness with which I heard the song of the katydid and the croak of the bull-frog seemed to make the silence more distinct. The air was dense and breathless, and, although longing to throw wide my windows, I dared not; for, outside, the ominous trumpetings of an army of mosquitoes sounded threateningly.

I tossed on my bed oppressed with the heat; kicked the sheets into every spot where they ought not to be; turned my pillow every two minutes in the hope of finding a cool side; in short, did everything that a man does when he lies awake on a very hot night and cannot open his window.

Suddenly, in the midst of my miseries, and when I had made up my mind to fling open the casement in spite of the legion of mosquitoes that I knew were hungrily waiting outside, I felt a continuous stream of cold air blowing upon my face. Luxurious as the sensation was, I could not help starting as I felt it. Where could this draught come from. The door was closed; so were the windows. It did not come from the direction of the fireplace, and, even if it did, the air without was too still to produce so strong a current. I rose in my bed and gazed round the room, the whole of which, though only lit by a dim twilight, was still sufficiently visible. I thought at first it was a trick of Jasper's, who might have provided himself with a bellows or a long tube; but a careful investigation of the apartment convinced me that no one was present. Besides, I had locked the door, and it was not likely that anyone had been concealed in the room before I entered it. It was exceedingly strange;

but still the draught of cool wind blew on my face and chest, every now and then changing its direction, sometimes on one side, sometimes on the other. I am not constitutionally nervous, and had been too long accustomed to reflect on philosophical subjects to become the prey of fear in the presence of mysterious phenomena. I had devoted much time to the investigation of what are popularly called supernatural matters by those who have not reflected or examined them sufficiently to discover that none of these apparent miracles are supernatural, but all, however singular, directly dependent on certain natural laws. I became speedily convinced, therefore, as I sat up in my bed peering into the dim recesses of my chamber, that this mysterious wind was the effect or forerunner of a supernatural visitation, and I mentally determined to investigate it, as it developed itself, with a philosophical calmness.

'Is anyone in this room?' I asked, as distinctly as I could. No reply; while the cool wind still swept over my cheek. I knew, in the case of Elizabeth Eslinger, who was visited by an apparition while in the Weinsberg jail, and whose singular and apparently authentic experiences were made the subject of a book by Dr Kerner, that the manifestation of the spirit was invariably accompanied by such a breezy sensation as I now experienced. I therefore gathered my will, as it were, into a focus, and endeavoured, as much as lay in my power, to put myself in accord with the disembodied spirit, if such there were, knowing that on such conditions alone would it be enabled to manifest itself to me.

Presently it seemed as if a luminous cloud was gathering in one corner of the room, a sort of dim phosphoric vapour, shadowy and ill-defined. It changed its position frequently, sometimes coming nearer and at others retreating to the farthest end of the room. As it grew intenser and more radiant, I observed a sickening and corpse-like odour diffuse itself through the chamber, and, despite my anxiety to witness this phenomenon undisturbed, I could with difficulty conquer a feeling of faintness which oppressed me.

The luminous cloud now began to grow brighter and brighter as I gazed. The horrible odour of which I have spoken did not cease to oppress me, and gradually I could discover certain lines making themselves visible in the midst of this lambent radiance. These lines took the form of a human figure, a tall man, clothed in a long dressing-robe, with a pale countenance, burning eyes, and a very bold and prominent chin. At a glance I recognised the original of the picture of old Van Koeren that I had seen with Alice. My interest was now aroused to the highest point; I felt that I stood face to face with a spirit, and doubted not that I should learn the fate of the old man's mysteriously concealed wealth.

The spirit presented a very strange appearance. He himself was not luminous, except some tongues of fire that seemed to proceed from the tips of his fingers, but was completely surrounded by a thin gauze of light, so to speak, through which his outlines were visible. His head was bare, and his white hair fell in huge masses around his stern, saturnine face. As he moved on the floor, I distinctly heard a strange crackling sound, such as one hears when a substance has been overcharged with electricity. But the circumstance that seemed to me most incomprehensible connected with the apparition was that Van Koeren held in both hands a curiously painted flowerpot, out of which sprang a number of the most beautiful tulips in full blossom. He seemed very uneasy and agitated, and moved about the room as if in pain, frequently bending over the pot of tulips as if to inhale their odour, then holding it out to me, seemingly in the hope of attracting my attention to it. I was, I confess, very much puzzled. I knew that Mr Van Koeren had in his lifetime devoted much of his leisure to the cultivation of flowers, importing from Holland the most expensive and rarest bulbs; but how this innocent fancy could trouble him after death I could not imagine. I felt assured, however, that some important reason lay at the bottom of this spectral eccentricity, and determined to fathom it if I could.

'What brings you here?' I asked audibly; directing mentally, however, at the same time, the question to the spirit with all the power of my will. He did not seem to hear me, but still kept moving uneasily about, with the crackling noise I have mentioned, and holding the pot of tulips towards me.

'It is evident,' I said to myself, 'that I am not sufficiently in accord with this spirit for him to make himself understood by speech. He has, therefore, recourse to symbols. The pot of tulips is a symbol. But of what?'

Thus reflecting on these things, I continued to gaze upon the spirit. While I was observing him attentively, he approached my bedside by a rapid movement, and laid one hand on my arm. The touch was icy cold, and pained me at the moment. Next morning my arm was swollen, and marked with a round blue spot.

Then, passing to my bedroom-door, the spirit opened it and went out, shutting it behind him. Catching for a moment at the idea that I was the dupe of a trick, I jumped out of bed and ran to the door. It was locked with the key on the inside, and a brass safety-bolt, which lay above the lock, shot safely home. All was as I had left it on going to bed. Yet I declare most solemnly that, as the ghost made his exit, I not only saw the door open, but I saw the corridor outside, and distinctly observed a large picture of William of Orange that hung just opposite to my room. This to me was the most curious portion of the phenomena I had witnessed. Either the door had been opened by the ghost, and the resistance of physical obstacles overcome in some amazing manner, because in this case the bolts must have been replaced when the ghost was outside the door, or he must have had a sufficient magnetic accord with my mind to impress upon it the belief that the door was opened, and also to conjure up in my brain the vision of the corridor and the picture, features that I should have seen if the door had been opened by any ordinary physical agency.

The next morning at breakfast I suppose my manner must have betrayed me, for Jasper said to me, after staring at me for some time, 'Why, Harry Escott, what's the matter with you? You look as if you had seen a ghost!'

'So I have, Jasper.'

Jasper, of course, burst into laughter, and said he'd shave my head and give me a shower-bath.

'Well, you may laugh,' I answered; 'but you shall see it tonight, Jasper.'

He became serious in a moment – I suppose there

was something earnest in my manner that convinced him that my words were not idle – and asked me to explain. I described my interview as accurately as I could.

'How did you know that it was old Van Koeren?' he asked.

'Because I have seen his picture a hundred times with Alice,' I answered, 'and this apparition was as like it as it was possible for a ghost to be like a miniature.'

'You must not think I am laughing at you, Harry,' he continued, 'but I wish you would answer this. We have all heard of ghosts, ghosts of men, women, children, dogs, horses, in fact every living animal; but hang me if ever I heard of the ghost of a flowerpot before.'

'My dear Jasper, you would have heard of such things if you had studied such branches of learning. All the phenomena I witnessed last night are supportable by well-authenticated facts. The cool wind has attended the appearance of more than one ghost, and Baron Reichenbach asserts that his patients, who you know are for the most part sensitive to apparitions, invariably feel this wind when a magnet is brought close to their bodies. With regard to the flowerpot about which you make so merry, it is to me the least wonderful portion of the apparition. When a ghost is unable to find a person of sufficient receptivity, in order to communicate with him by speech it is obliged to have recourse to symbols to express its wishes. These it either creates by some mysterious power out of the surrounding atmosphere, or it impresses, by magnetic force on the mind of the person it visits, the form of the symbol it is anxious to have represented. There is an instance mentioned by Jung Stilling of a student at Brunswick who appeared to a professor of his college with a picture in his hands, which picture had a hole in it that the ghost thrust his head through. For a long time this symbol was a mystery; but the student was persevering, and appeared every night with his head through the picture, until at last it was discovered that, before he died, he had got some painted slides for a magic lantern from a shopkeeper in the town, which had not been paid for at his death; and when the debt had been discharged, he and his picture vanished forevermore. Now here was a symbol distinctly bearing on the question at issue. This poor student could find no better way of expressing his uneasiness at the debt for the painted slides than by thrusting his head through a picture. How he conjured up the picture I cannot pretend to explain, but that it was used as a symbol is evident.'

'Then you think the flowerpot of old Van Koeren is a symbol?'

'Most assuredly; the pot of tulips he held was intended to express that which he could not speak. I think it must have had some reference to his missing property, and it is our business to discover in what manner.'

'Let us go and dig up all the tulip beds,' said Jasper, 'who knows but he may have buried his money in one of them.'

I grieve to say that I assented to Jasper's proposition, and on that eventful day every tulip in that quaint old garden was ruthlessly uprooted. The gorgeous macaws, and ragged parrots, and long-legged pheasants, so cunningly formed by those brilliant flowers, were that day exterminated. Jasper and I had a regular battle amidst this floral preserve, and many a splendid bird fell before our unerring spades. We, however, dug in vain. No secret coffer turned up out of the deep mould of the flowerbeds. We evidently were not on the right scent. Our researches for that day terminated, and Jasper and I waited impatiently for the night.

It was arranged that Jasper should sleep in my room. I had a bed rigged up for him near my own, and I was to have the additional assistance of his senses in the investigation of the phenomena that we so confidently expected to appear.

The night came. We retired to our respective couches, after carefully bolting the doors, and subjecting the entire apartment to the strictest scrutiny, rendering it totally impossible that a secret entrance should exist unknown to us. We then put out the lights, and awaited the apparition.

We did not remain in suspense long. About twenty minutes after we retired to bed, Jasper called out, 'Harry, I feel the cool wind!'

'So do I,' I answered, for at that moment a light breeze seemed to play across my temples.

'Look, look, Harry!' continued Jasper in a tone of painful eagerness, 'I see a light there in the corner!'

It was the phantom. As before, the luminous cloud appeared to gather in the room, growing more and more intense each minute. Presently the dark lines mapped themselves out, as it were, in the midst of this pale, radiant vapour, and there stood Mr Van Koeren, ghastly and mournful as ever, with the pot of tulips in his hands.

'Do you see it?' I asked Jasper.

'My God! yes,' said Jasper, in a low voice. 'How terrible he looks!'

'Can you speak to me, tonight?' I said, addressing the apparition, and again concentrating my will upon my question. 'If so, unburden yourself. We will assist you, if we can.'

There was no reply. The ghost preserved the same sad, impassive countenance; he had heard me not. He seemed in great distress on this occasion, moving up and down, and holding out the pot of tulips imploringly towards me, each motion of his being accompanied by the crackling noise and the corpse-like odour. I felt sorely troubled myself to see this poor spirit torn by an endless grief, so anxious to communicate to me what lay on his soul, and yet debarred by some occult power from the privilege.

'Why, Harry,' cried Jasper after a silence, during which we both watched the motions of the ghost intently, 'why, Harry, my boy, there are two of them!'

Astonished by his words, I looked around, and became immediately aware of the presence of a second luminous cloud, in the midst of which I could distinctly trace the figure of a pale but lovely woman. I needed no second glance to assure me that it was the unfortunate wife of Van Koeren.

'It is his wife, Jasper,' I replied; 'I recognise her, as I have recognised her husband, by the portrait.'

'How sad she looks!' exclaimed Jasper in a low voice.

She did indeed look sad. Her face, pale and mournful, did not, however, seem convulsed with sorrow, as was her husband's. She seemed to be oppressed with a calm grief, and gazed with a look of interest that was painful in its intensity on Van Koeren. It struck me, from his air, that though she saw him he did not see her. His whole attention was concentrated on the pot of tulips, while Mrs Van Koeren, who floated at an elevation of about three feet from the floor, and thus over-topped her husband, seemed equally absorbed in the contemplation of his slightest movement. Occasionally she would turn her eyes on me, as if to call my attention to her com–panion, and then, returning, gaze on him with a sad, womanly, half-eager smile, that to me was inexpressibly mournful.

There was something exceedingly touching in this strange sight; these two spirits so near, yet so distant. The sinful husband torn with grief and weighed down with some terrible secret, and so blinded by the grossness of his being as to be unable to see the wife-angel who was watching over him; while she, forgetting all her wrongs, and attracted to earth by perhaps the same human sympathies, watched from a greater spiritual height, and with a tender interest, the struggles of her suffering spouse.

'By Jove!' exclaimed Jasper, jumping from his bed, 'I know what it means now.'

'What does it mean?' I asked, as eager to know as he was to communicate.

'Well, that flowerpot that the old chap is holding – ' Jasper, I grieve to say, was rather profane.

'Well, what of that flowerpot?'

'Observe the pattern. It has two handles made of red snakes, whose tails twist round the top and form a rim. It contains tulips of three colours, yellow, red, and purple.'

'I see all that as well as you do. Let us have the solution.'

'Well, Harry, my boy! don't you remember that there is just such a flowerpot, tulips, snakes and all, carved on the queer old painted mantelpiece in the dining-room?'

'So there is!' and a gleam of hope shot across my brain, and my heart beat quicker.

'Now, as sure as you are alive, Harry, the old fellow has concealed something important behind that mantelpiece.'

'Jasper, if ever I am Emperor of France, I will make you chief of police; your inductive reasoning is magnificent.'

Actuated by the same impulse, and without another word, we both sprang out of bed and lit a candle. The apparitions, if they remained, were no longer visible in the light. Hastily throwing on some clothes, we rushed downstairs to the dining-room, determined to have the old mantelpiece down without loss of time. We had scarce entered the room when we felt the cool wind blowing on our faces.

'Jasper,' said I, 'they are here!'

'Well,' answered Jasper, 'that only confirms my suspicions that we are on the right track this time. Let us go to work. See! here's the pot of tulips.'

This pot of tulips occupied the centre of the mantelpiece, and served as a nucleus round which all the fantastic animals sculptured elsewhere might be said to gather. It was carved on a species of raised shield, or boss, of wood, that projected some inches beyond the plane of the remainder of the mantelpiece. The pot itself was painted a brick colour. The snakes were of bronze colour, gilt, and the tulips, yellow, red and purple, were painted after nature with the most exquisite accuracy.

For some time Jasper and I tugged away at this projection without any avail. We were convinced that it was a movable panel of some kind, but yet were totally unable to move it. Suddenly it struck me that we had not yet twisted it. I immediately proceeded to apply all my strength, and after a few seconds of vigorous exertion I had the satisfaction of finding it move slowly round. After I had given it half a dozen turns, to my astonishment the long upper panel of the mantelpiece fell out towards us, apparently on concealed hinges, after the manner of the portion of escritoires that is used as a writing-table. Within were several square cavities sunk in the wall, and lined with wood. In one of these was a bundle of papers.

We seized these papers with avidity, and hastily glanced over them. They proved to be documents vouching for property to the amount of several hundred thousand dollars, invested in the name of Mr Van Koeren in a certain firm at Bremen, who, no doubt, thought by this time that the money would remain unclaimed for ever. The desires of these poor troubled spirits were accomplished.

Justice to the child had been given through the instrumentality of the erring father.

The formalities necessary to prove Alice and her mother sole heirs to Mr Van Koeren's estate were briefly gone through, and the poor governess passed suddenly from the task of teaching stupid children to the envied position of a great heiress. I had ample reason afterwards for thinking that her heart did not change with her fortunes.

That Mr Van Koeren became aware of his wife's innocence, just before he died, I have no doubt. How this was manifested I cannot of course say, but I think it highly probably that his poor wife herself was enabled at the critical moment of dissolution, when

the link that binds body and soul together is atten-
uated to the last thread, to put herself in accord with
her unhappy husband. Hence his sudden starting up
in his bed, his apparent conversation with some
invisible being, and his fragmentary disclosures, too
broken, however, to be comprehended.

The question of apparitions has been so often discussed that I feel no inclination to enter here upon
the truth or fallacy of the ghostly theory. I myself
believe in ghosts. Alice my wife believes in them
firmly; and if it suited me to do so I could overwhelm
you with a scientific theory of my own on the subject,
reconciling ghosts and natural phenomena.

THOMAS CROFTON CROKER

The Haunted Cellar

There are few people who have not heard of the Mac
Carthys – one of the real old Irish families, with the
true Milesian blood running in their veins as thick as
buttermilk. Many were the clans of this family in the
south; as the Mac Carthymore – and the Mac Carthy-
reagh – and the Mac Carthy of Muskerry; and all of
them were noted for their hospitality to strangers,
gentle and simple.

But not one of that name, or of any other, exceeded
Justin Mac Carthy, of Ballinacarthy, at putting plenty
to eat and drink upon his table; and there was a right
hearty welcome for everyone who should share it
with him. Many a wine cellar would be ashamed of
the name if that at Ballinacarthy was the proper
pattern for one. Large as that cellar was, it was
crowded with bins of wine, and long rows of pipes,
and hogsheads, and casks, that it would take more
time to count than any sober man could spare in
such a place, with plenty to drink about him, and a
hearty welcome to do so.

There are many, no doubt, who will think that the
butler would have little to complain of in such a house;
and the whole country round would have agreed with
them, if a man could be found to remain as Mr Mac
Carthy's butler for any length of time worth speaking

of; yet not one who had been in his service gave him a bad word.

'We have no fault,' they would say, 'to find with the master, and if he could but get anyone to fetch his wine from the cellar, we might everyone of us have grown grey in the house and have lived quiet and contented enough in his service until the end of our days.'

' 'Tis a queer thing that, surely,' thought young Jack Leary, a lad who had been brought up from a mere child in the stables of Ballinacarthy to assist in taking care of the horses, and had occasionally lent a hand in the butler's pantry: – ' 'Tis a mighty queer thing, surely, that one man after another cannot content himself with the best place in the house of a good master, but that everyone of them must quit, all through the means, as they say, of the wine cellar. If the master, long life to him! would but make me his butler, I warrant never the word more would be heard of grumbling at his bidding to go to the wine cellar.'

Young Leary, accordingly, watched for what he conceived to be a favourable opportunity of presenting himself to the notice of his master.

A few mornings after, Mr Mac Carthy went into his stableyard rather earlier than usual, and called loudly for the groom to saddle his horse, as he intended going out with the hounds. But there was no groom to answer, and young Jack Leary led Rainbow out of the stable.

'Where is William?' enquired Mr Mac Carthy.

'Sir?' said Jack; and Mr Mac Carthy repeated the question.

'Is it William, please your honour?' returned Jack; 'why, then, to tell the truth, he had just *one* drop too much last night.'

'Where did he get it?' said Mr Mac Carthy; 'for since Thomas went away the key of the wine cellar has been in my pocket, and I have been obliged to fetch what was drunk myself.'

'Sorrow a know I know,' said Leary, 'unless the cook might have given him the *least taste* in life of whiskey. But,' continued he, performing a low bow by seizing with his right hand a lock of hair, and pulling down his head by it, while his left leg, which had been put forward, was scraped back against the ground, 'may I make so bold as just to ask your honour one question?'

'Speak out, Jack,' said Mr Mac Carthy.

'Why, then, does your honour want a butler?'

'Can you recommend me one,' returned his master, with the smile of good-humour upon his countenance, 'and one who will not be afraid of going to my wine cellar?'

'Is the wine cellar all the matter?' said young Leary; 'devil a doubt I have of myself then for that.'

'So you mean to offer me your services in the capacity of butler?' said Mr Mac Carthy, with some surprise.

'Exactly so,' answered Leary, now for the first time looking up from the ground.

'Well, I believe you to be a good lad, and have no objection to give you a trial.'

'Long may your honour reign over us, and the Lord spare you to us!' ejaculated Leary, with another national bow, as his master rode off; and he continued for some time to gaze after him with a vacant stare, which slowly and gradually assumed a look of importance.

'Jack Leary,' said he, at length, 'Jack – is it Jack?'

in a tone of wonder; 'faith, 'tis not Jack now, but Mr John, the butler;' and with an air of becoming consequence he strode out of the stableyard towards the kitchen.

It is of little purport to my story, although it may afford an instructive lesson to the reader, to depict the sudden transition of nobody into somebody. Jack's former stable companion, a poor superannuated hound named Bran, who had been accustomed to receive many an affectionate pat on the head, was spurned from him with a kick and an 'Out of the way, sirrah.' Indeed, poor Jack's memory seemed sadly affected by this sudden change of situation. What established the point beyond all doubt was his almost forgetting the pretty face of Peggy, the kitchen wench, whose heart he had assailed but the preceding week by the offer of purchasing a gold ring for the fourth finger of her right hand, and a lusty imprint of good will upon her lips.

When Mr Mac Carthy returned from hunting, he sent for Jack Leary – so he still continued to call his new butler. 'Jack,' said he, 'I believe you are a trustworthy lad, and here are the keys of my cellar. I have asked the gentlemen with whom I hunted today to dine with me, and I hope they may be satisfied at the way in which you will wait on them at table; but, above all, let there be no want of wine after dinner.'

Mr John having a tolerably quick eye for such things, and being naturally a handy lad, spread his cloth accordingly, laid his plates and knives and forks in the same manner be had seen his predecessors in office perform these mysteries, and really, for the first time, got through attendance on dinner very well.

It must not be forgotten, however, that it was at the

house of an Irish country squire, who was entertaining a company of booted and spurred fox-hunters, not very particular about what are considered matters of infinite importance under other circumstances and in other societies.

For instance, few of Mr Mac Carthy's guests (though all excellent and worthy men in their way) cared much whether the punch produced after soup was made of Jamaica or Antigua rum; some even would not have been inclined to question the correctness of good old Irish whiskey; and, with the exception of their liberal host himself, everyone in company preferred the port which Mr Mac Carthy put on his table to the less ardent flavour of claret – a choice rather at variance with modern sentiment.

It was waxing near midnight, when Mr Mac Carthy rung the bell three times. This was a signal for more wine; and Jack proceeded to the cellar to procure a fresh supply, but it must be confessed not without some little hesitation.

The luxury of ice was then unknown in the south of Ireland; but the superiority of cool wine had been acknowledged by all men of sound judgement and true taste.

The grandfather of Mr Mac Carthy, who had built the mansion of Ballinacarthy upon the site of an old castle which had belonged to his ancestors, was fully aware of this important fact; and in the construction of his magnificent wine cellar had availed himself of a deep vault, excavated out of the solid rock in former times as a place of retreat and security. The descent to this vault was by a flight of steep stone stairs, and here and there in the wall were narrow passages – I ought rather to call them crevices; and also certain projections, which cast deep shadows, and looked very frightful when anyone went down the cellar stairs with a single light: indeed, two lights did not much improve the matter, for though the breadth of the shadows became less, the narrow crevices remained as dark and darker than ever.

Summoning up all his resolution, down went the new butler, bearing in his right hand a lantern and the key of the cellar, and in his left a basket, which he considered sufficiently capacious to contain an adequate stock for the remainder of the evening: he arrived at the door without any interruption whatever; but when he put the key, which was of an ancient and clumsy kind – for it was before the days of Bramah's patent – and turned it in the lock, he thought he heard a strange kind of laughing within the cellar, to which some empty bottle that stood upon the floor outside vibrated so violently that they struck against each other: in this he could not be mistaken, although he may have been deceived in the laugh, for the bottles were just at his feet, and he saw them in motion.

Leary paused for a moment, and looked about him with becoming caution. He then boldly seized the handle of the key, and turned it with all his strength in the lock, as if he doubted his own power of doing so; and the door flew open with a most tremendous crash, that if the house had not been built upon the solid rock would have shook it from the foundation.

To recount what the poor fellow saw would be impossible, for he seems not to have known very clearly himself: but what he told the cook the next morning was, that he heard a roaring and bellowing like a mad bull, and that all the pipes and hogsheads

514

and casks in the cellar went rocking backwards and forwards with so much force that he thought everyone would have been staved in, and that he should have been drowned or smothered in wine.

When Leary recovered, he made his way back as well as he could to the dining room, where he found his master and the company very impatient for his return.

'What kept you?' said Mr Mac Carthy in an angry voice; 'and where is the wine ? I rung for it half an hour since.'

'The wine is in the cellar, I hope, sir,' said Jack, trembling violently; 'I hope 'tis not all lost.'

'What do you mean, fool?' exclaimed Mr Mac Carthy in a still more angry tone: 'why did you not fetch some with you?'

Jack looked wildly about him, and only uttered a deep groan.

'Gentlemen,' said Mr Mac Carthy to his guests, 'this is too much. When I next see you to dinner, I hope it will be in another house, for it is impossible I can remain longer in this, where a man has no command over his own wine cellar, and cannot get a butler to do his duty. I have long thought of moving from Ballinacarthy; and I am now determined, with the blessing of God, to leave it tomorrow. But wine shall you have were I to go myself to the cellar for it.' So saying, he rose from table, took the key and lantern from his half-stupified servant, who regarded him with a look of vacancy, and descended the narrow stairs, already described, which led to his cellar.

When he arrived at the door, which he found open, he thought he heard a noise, as if of rats or mice scrambling over the casks, and on advancing perceived a little figure, about six inches in height, seated astride upon the pipe of the oldest port in the place, and bearing a spigot upon his shoulder. Raising the lantern, Mr Mac Carthy contemplated the little fellow with wonder: he wore a red nightcap on his head; before him was a short leather apron, which now, from his attitude, fell rather on one side; and he had stockings of a light blue colour, so long as nearly to cover the entire of his legs; with shoes, having huge silver buckles in them, and with high heels (perhaps out of vanity to make him appear taller). His face was like a withered winter apple; and his nose, which was of a bright crimson colour, about the tip wore a delicate purple bloom, like that of a plum; yet his eyes twinkled 'like those mites of candied dew in money nights – ' and his mouth twitched up at one side with an arch grin.

'Ha, scoundrel!' exclaimed Mr Mac Carthy, 'have I found you at last? disturber of my cellar – what are you doing there?'

'Sure, and master,' returned the little fellow, looking up at him with one eye, and with the other throwing a sly glance towards the spigot on his shoulder, 'a'n't we going to move tomorrow? and sure you would not leave your own little Cluricaune Naggeneen behind you?'

'Oh!' thought Mr Mac Carthy, 'if you are to follow me, master Naggeneen, I don't see much use in quitting Ballinacarthy.' So filling with wine the basket which young Leary in his fright had left behind him, and locking the cellar door, he rejoined his guests.

For some years after Mr Mac Carthy had always to fetch the wine for his table himself, as the little Cluricaune Naggeneen seemed to feel a personal respect towards him. Notwithstanding the labour of these journeys, the worthy lord of Ballinacarthy lived in his paternal mansion to a good round age, and was famous to the last for the excellence of his wine, and conviviality of his company; but at the time of his death, the same conviviality had nearly emptied his wine cellar; and as it was never so well filled again, nor so often visited, the revels of master Naggeneen became less celebrated, and are now only spoken of among the legendary lore of the country. It is even said that the poor little fellow took the declension of the cellar so to heart, that he became negligent and careless of himself, and that he has been sometimes seen going about with hardly a *skreed* to cover him.

JEREMIAH CURTIN

St Martin's Eve

In Iveragh, not very far from the town of Cahirciveen, there lived a farmer named James Shea with his wife and three children, two sons and a daughter. The man was peaceable, honest, and very charitable to the poor, but his wife was hard hearted, never giving even a drink of milk to a needy person. Her younger son was as bad in every way as herself, and whatever the mother did he always agreed with her and was on her side.

This was before the roads and cars were in the Kerry Mountains. The only way of travelling in those days, when a man didn't walk, was to ride sitting on a straw saddle, and the only way to take anything to market was on horseback in creels.

It happened, at any rate, that James Shea was going in the beginning of November to Cork with two firkins of butter, and what troubled him most was the fear that he'd not be home on St Martin's night to do honour to the saint. For never had he let that night pass without drawing blood in honour of the saint. To make sure, he called the elder son and said, 'if I am not at the house on St Martin's night, kill the big sheep that is running with the cows.'

Shea went away to Cork with the butter, but could not be home in time. The elder son went out on St

Martin's eve, when he saw that his father was not coming, and drove the sheep into the house.

'What are you doing, you fool, with that sheep?' asked the mother.

'Sure, I'm going to kill it. Didn't you hear my father tell me that there was never a St Martin's night but he drew blood, and do you want to have the house disgraced?'

At this the mother made sport of him and said: 'Drive out the sheep and I'll give you something else to kill by and by.'

So the boy let the sheep out, thinking the mother would kill a goose.

He sat down and waited for the mother to give him whatever she had to kill. It wasn't long till she came in, bringing a big tomcat they had, and the same cat was in the house nine or ten years.

'Here,' said she, 'you can kill this beast and draw its blood. We'll have it cooked when your father comes home.'

The boy was very angry and spoke up to the mother: 'Sure the house is disgraced for ever,' said he, 'and it will not be easy for you to satisfy my father when he comes.'

He didn't kill the cat, you may be sure; and neither he nor his sister ate a bite of supper, and they were crying and fretting over the disgrace all the evening.

That very night the house caught fire and burned down; nothing was left but the four walls. The mother and younger son were burned to death, but the elder son and his sister escaped by some miracle. They went to a neighbour's house, and were there till the father came on the following evening. When he found the house destroyed and the wife and younger son

519

dead he mourned and lamented. But when the other son told him what the mother did on St Martin's eve, he cried out: 'Ah, it was the wrath of God that fell on my house; if I had stopped at home till after St Martin's night, all would be safe and well with me now.'

James Shea went to the priest on the following morning, and asked would it be good or lucky for him to rebuild the house.

'Indeed,' said the priest, 'there is no harm in putting a roof on the walls and repairing them if you will have Mass celebrated in the house before you go to live in it. If you do that all will be well with you.'

[Shea spoke to the priest because people are opposed to repairing or rebuilding a burnt house, and especially if any person has been burned in it.]

Well, James Shea put a roof on the house, repaired it, and had Mass celebrated inside. That evening as Shea was sitting down to supper what should he see but his wife coming in the door to him. He thought she wasn't dead at all. 'Ah, Mary,' said he, ' 'tis not so bad as they told me. Sure, I thought it is dead you were. Oh, then you are welcome home; come and sit down here; the supper is just ready.'

She didn't answer a word, but looked him straight in the face and walked on to the room at the other end of the house. He jumped up, thinking it's sick the woman was, and followed her to the room to help her. He shut the door after him. As he was not coming back for a long time the son thought at last that he'd go and ask the father why he wasn't eating his supper. When he went into the room he saw no sign of his mother, saw nothing in the place but two legs from the knees down. He screamed out for his sister and she came.

'Oh, merciful God!' screamed the sister.

'Those are my father's legs!' cried the brother, 'and Mary, don't you know the stockings, sure you knitted them yourself, and don't I know the brogues very well?'

They called in the neighbours, and, to the terror of them all, they saw nothing but the two legs and feet of James Shea.

There was a wake over the remains that night, and the next day they buried the two legs. Some people advised the boy and girl never to sleep a night in the house, that their mother's soul was lost, and that was why she came and ate up the father, and she would eat themselves as well.

The two now started to walk the world, not caring much where they were going if only they escaped the mother. They stopped the first night at a farmer's house not far from Killarney. After supper a bed was made down for them by the fire, in the corner, and they lay there. About the middle of the night a great noise was heard outside, and the woman of the house called to her boys and servants to get up and go to the cow-house to know why the cows were striving to kill one another. Her own son rose first. When he and the two servant boys went out they saw the ghost of a woman, and she in chains. She made at them, and wasn't long killing the three.

Not seeing the boys come in, the farmer and his wife rose up, sprinkled holy water around the house, blessed themselves and went out, and there they saw the ghost in blue blazes and chains around her. In a coop outside by himself was a March cock. [A cock hatched in March from a cock and hen hatched in March.]

He flew down from his perch and crowed twelve times. That moment the ghost disappeared.

Now the neighbours were roused, and the news

flew around that the three boys were killed. The brother and sister didn't say a word to anyone, but, rising up early, started on their journey, begging God's protection as they went. They never stopped nor stayed till they came to Rathmore, near Cork, and, going to a farmhouse, the boy asked for lodgings in God's name.

'I will give you lodgings in His name,' said the farmer's wife.

She brought warm water for the two to wash their hands and feet, for they were tired and dusty. After supper a bed was put down for them, and about the same hour as the night before there was a great noise outside.

'Rise up and go out,' said the farmer's wife, 'some of the cows must be untied.'

'I'll not go out at this hour of the night, if they are untied itself,' said the man, 'I'll stay where I am, if they kill one another, for it isn't safe to go out till the cock crows; after cockcrow I'll go out.'

'That's true for you,' said the farmer's wife, 'and, upon my word, before coming to bed, I forget to sprinkle holy water in the room, and to bless myself.'

So taking the bottle hanging near the bed, she sprinkled the water around the room and toward the threshold, and made the sign of the cross. The man didn't go out until cockcrow. The brother and sister went away early, and travelled all day. Coming evening they met a pleasant-looking man who stood before them in the road.

'You seem to be strangers,' said he, 'and where are you going?'

'We are strangers,' said the boy, 'and we don't know where to go.'

'You need go no farther. I know you well, your home is in Iveragh. I am St Martin, sent from the Lord to protect you and your sister. You were going to draw the blood of a sheep in my honour, but your mother and brother made sport of you, and your mother wouldn't let you do what your father told you. You see what has come to them; they are lost for ever, both of them. Your father is saved in heaven, for he was a good man. Your mother will be here soon, and I'll put her in the way that she'll never trouble you again.'

Taking a rod from his bosom and dipping it in a vial of holy water he drew a circle around the brother and sister. Soon they heard their mother coming, and then they saw her with chains on her, and the rattling was terrible, and flames were rising from her. She came to where they stood, and said: 'Bad luck to you both for being the cause of my misery.'

'God forbid that,' said St Martin. 'It isn't they are the cause, but yourself, for you were always bad. You would not honour me, and now you must suffer for it.'

He pulled out a book and began to read, and after he read a few minutes he told her to depart and not be seen in Ireland again till the day of judgement. She rose in the air in flames of fire, and with such a noise that you'd think all the thunders of heaven were roaring and all the houses and walls in the kingdom were tumbling to the ground.

The brother and sister went on their knees and thanked St Martin. He blessed them and told them to rise, and, taking a little tablecloth out of his bosom, he said to the brother: 'Take this cloth with you and keep it in secret. Let no one know that you have it. If you or your sister are in need go to your room, close the door behind you and bolt it. Spread out the cloth then, and plenty of everything to eat and drink will come to you. Keep the cloth with you always; it belongs to both of you. Now go home and live in the house that your father built, and let the priest come and celebrate Monday Mass in it, and live the life that your father lived before you.'

The two came home, and brother and sister lived a good life. They married, and when either was in need that one had the cloth to fall back on, and their grandchildren are living yet in Iveragh. And this is truth, every word of it, and it's often I heard my poor grandmother tell this story, the Almighty God rest her soul, and she was the woman that wouldn't tell a lie. She knew James Shea and his wife very well.

DANIEL CORKERY

The Eyes of the Dead

If he had not put it off for three years John Spillane's
homecoming would have been that of a famous man.
Bonfires would have been lighted on the hilltops of
Rossamara, and the ships passing by, twenty miles
out, would have wondered what they meant.

Three years ago, the *Western Star*, an Atlantic liner,
one night tore her iron plates to pieces against the
cliff-like face of an iceberg, and in less than an hour
sank in the waters. Of the seven hundred and eighty-
nine human souls aboard her one only had been saved,
John Spillane, able seaman, of Rossamara in the
country of Cork. The name of the little fishing village,
his own name, his picture, were in all the papers of
the world, it seemed, not only because he alone had
escaped, but by reason of the manner of that escape.
He had clung to a drift of wreckage, must have lost
consciousness for more than a whole day, floated then
about on the ocean for a second day, for a second
night, and had arrived at the threshold of another
dreadful night when he was rescued. A fog was coming
down on the waters. It frightened him more than the
darkness. He raised a shout. He kept on shouting.
When safe in the arms of his rescuers his breathy,

525

almost inaudible voice was still forcing out some cry which they interpreted as Help! Help!

That was what had struck the imagination of men – the half-insane figure sending his cry over the waste of waters, the fog thickening, and the night falling. Although the whole world had read also of the groping rescue ship, of Spillane's bursts of hysterical laughter, of his inability to tell his story until he had slept eighteen hours on end, what remained in the memory was the lonely figure sending his cry over the sea.

And then, almost before his picture had disappeared from the papers, he had lost himself in the great cities of the States. To Rossamara no word had come from himself, nor for a long time from any acquaintance; but then, when about a year had gone by, his sister or mother as they went up the road to Mass of a Sunday might be stopped and informed in a whispering voice that John had been seen in Chicago, or, it might be, in New York, or Boston, or San Francisco, or indeed anywhere. And from the meagreness of the messages it was known, with only too much certainty, that he had not, in exchanging sea for land, bettered his lot. If once again his people had happened on such empty tidings of him, one knew it by their bowed and stilly attitude in the little church as the light whisper of the Mass rose and fell about them.

When three years had gone by he lifted the latch of his mother's house one October evening and stood awkwardly in the middle of the floor. It was nightfall and not a soul had seen him break down from the ridge and cross the roadway. He had come secretly from the ends of the earth.

And before he was an hour in their midst he rose up impatiently, timidly, and stole into his bed.

'I don't want any light,' he said, and as his mother
left him there in the dark, she heard him yield his
whole being to a sigh of thankfulness. Before that he
had told them he felt tired, a natural thing, since he
had tramped fifteen miles from the railway station in
Skibbereen. But day followed day without his showing
any desire to rise from the bedclothes and go abroad
among the people. He had had enough of the sea, it
seemed; enough too of the great cities of the States.
He was a pity, the neighbours said; and the few of
them who from time to time caught glimpses of him,
reported him as not yet having lost the scared look
that the ocean had left on him. His hair was grey or
nearly grey, they said, and, swept back fiercely from
his forehead, a fashion strange to the place, seemed to
pull his eyes open, to keep them wide open, as he
looked at you. His moustache also was grey, they
said, and his cheeks were grey too, sunken and dark
with shadows. Yet his mother and sister, the only
others in the house, were glad to have him back with
them; at any rate, they said, they knew where he was.

They found nothing wrong with him. Of speech
neither he nor they ever had had the gift; and as day
followed day, and week week, the same few phrases
would carry them through the day and into the silence
of night. In the beginning they had thought it natural
to speak with him about the wreck; soon, however,
they came to know that it was a subject for which he
had no welcome. In the beginning also, they had
thought to rouse him by bringing the neighbour to his
bedside, but such visits instead of cheering him only
left him sunken in silence, almost in despair. The
priest came to see him once in a while, and advise the
mother and sister, Mary her name was, to treat him as

normally as they could, letting on that his useless presence was no affliction to them nor even a burden. In time John Spillane was accepted by all as one of those unseen ones, or seldom-seen ones, who are to be found in every village in the world – the bedridden, the struck-down, the aged – forgotten of all except the few faithful creatures who bring the cup to the bedside of a morning, and open the curtains to let in the sun.

2

In the nearest house, distant a quarter-mile from them, lived Tom Leane. In the old days before John Spillane went to sea, Tom had been his companion, and now of a night-time he would drop in if he had any story worth telling or if, on the day following, he chanced to be going back to Skibbereen, where he might buy the Spillanes such goods as they needed, or sell a pig for them, slipping it in among his own. He was a quiet creature, married, and struggling to bring up the little family that was thickening about him. In the Spillanes' he would, dragging at the pipe, sit on the settle, and quietly gossip with the old woman while Mary moved about on the flags putting the household gear tidy for the night. But all three of them, as they kept up the simple talk, were never unaware of the silent listener in the lower room. Of that room the door was kept open; but no lamp was lighted within it; no lamp indeed was needed, for a shaft of light from the kitchen struck into it showing one or two of the religious pictures on the wall and giving sufficient light to move about in. Sometimes the conversation would drift away from the neighbourly doings, for even to Rossamara tidings from the great world abroad would sometimes come; in the middle of such gossip, however, a sudden thought would strike Tom Leane, and, raising his voice, he would blurt out: 'But sure 'tis foolish for the like of me to be talking about these far-off places, and that man inside after travelling the world, over and thither.' The man inside, however, would give no sign whatever whether their gossip had been wise or foolish. They might hear the bed creak, as if he had turned with impatience at their mention of his very presence.

There had been a spell of stormy weather, it was now the middle of February, and for the last five days at twilight the gale seemed always to set in for a night of it. Although there was scarcely a house around that part of the southwest Irish coast that had not some one of its members, husband or brother or son, living on the sea, sailoring abroad or fishing the home waters or those of the Isle of Man – in no other house was the strain of a spell of disastrous weather so noticeable in the faces of its inmates. The old woman, withdrawn into herself, would handle her beads all day long, her voice every now and then raising itself, in forgetfulness, to a sort of moan not unlike the wind's upon which the younger woman would chide her with a 'Sh! sh!' and bend vigorously upon her work to keep bitterness from her thoughts. At such a time she might enter her brother's room and find him raised on his elbow in the bed, listening to the howling winds, scared it seemed, his eyes fixed and wide open. He would drink the warm milk she had brought him, and hand the vessel back without a word. And in the selfsame attitude she would leave him.

The fifth night instead of growing in loudness and

fierceness the wind died away somewhat. It became fitful, promising the end of the storm; and before long they could distinguish between the continuous groaning and pounding of the sea and the sudden shout the dying tempest would fling among the tree-tops and the rocks. They were thankful to note such signs of relief; the daughter became more active, and the mother put by her beads. In the midst of a sudden sally of the wind's the latch was raised, and Tom Leane gave them greeting. His face was rosy and glowing under his sou'wester; his eyes were sparkling from the sting of the salty gusts. To see him, so sane, so healthy, was to them like a blessing. 'How is it with ye?' he said, cheerily, closing the door to.

'Good, then, good, then,' they answered him, and the mother rose almost as if she would take him by the hand. The reply meant that nothing unforeseen had befallen them. He understood as much. He shook a silent head in the direction of the listener's room, a look of enquiry in his eyes, and this look Mary answered with a sort of hopeless upswing of her face. Things had not improved in the lower room.

The wind died away, more and more; and after some time streamed by with a shrill steady undersong; all through, however, the crashing of the sea on the jagged rocks beneath kept up an unceasing clamour. Tom had a whole budget of news for them. Finny's barn had been stripped of its roof; a window in the chapel had been blown in; and Largy's store of fodder had been shredded in the wind; it littered all the bushes to the east. There were rumours of a wreck somewhere; but it was too soon yet to know what damage the sea had done in its five days' madness. The news he had brought them did not matter; what mattered was his company, the knitting of their half-distraught household once again to humankind. Even when at last he stood up to go, their spirits did not droop, so great had been the restoration.

'We' re finished with it for a while anyhow,' Tom said, rising for home.

'We are, we are; and who knows, it mightn't be after doing all the damage we think.'

He shut the door behind him. The two women had turned towards the fire when they thought they again heard his voice outside. They wondered at the sound; they listened for his footsteps. Still staring at the closed door, once more they heard his voice. This time they were sure. The door reopened, and he backed in, as one does from an unexpected slap of rain in the face. The light struck outwards, and they saw a white face advancing. Some anxiety, some uncertainty, in Tom's attitude as he backed away from that advancing face, invaded them so that they too became afraid. They saw the stranger also hesitating, looking down his own limbs. His clothes were dripping; they were clung in about him. He was bare headed. When he raised his face again, his look was full of apology. His features were large and flat, and grey as a stone. Every now and then a spasm went through them, and they wondered what it meant. His clab of a mouth hung open; his unshaven chin trembled. Tom spoke to him: 'You'd better come in; but 'tis many another house would suit you better than this.'

They heard a husky, scarce-audible voice reply: 'A doghouse would do, or a stable.' Bravely enough he made an effort to smile.

'Oh, 'tisn't that at all. But come in, come in.' He stepped in slowly and heavily, again glancing down his limbs. The water running from his clothes spread in a black pool on the flags. The young woman began to touch him with her finger tips as with some instinctive sympathy, yet could not think, it seemed, what was best to be done. The mother, however, vigorously set the fire-wheel at work, and Tom built up the fire with bog-timber and turf. The stranger meanwhile stood as if half-dazed. At last, as Mary with a candle in her hand stood pulling out dry clothes from a press, he blurted out in the same husky voice, Welsh in accent: 'I think I'm the only one!'

They understood the significance of the words, but it seemed wrong to do so.

'What is it you're saying?' Mary said, but one would not have recognised the voice for hers, it was so toneless. He raised a heavy sailor's hand in an awkward taproom gesture: 'The others, they're gone, all of them.'

The spasm again crossed his homely features, and his hand fell. He bowed his head. A coldness went through them. They stared at him. He might have thought them inhuman. But Mary suddenly pulled herself together, leaping at him almost: 'Sh! Sh!' she said, 'speak low, speak low, low,' and as she spoke, all earnestness, she towed him first in the direction of the fire, and then away from it, haphazardly it seemed. She turned from him and whispered to Tom: 'Look, take him up into the loft, and he can change his clothes. Take these with you, and the candle, the candle.' And she reached him the candle eagerly. Tom led the stranger up the stairs, it was more like a ladder, and the two of them disappeared into the loft. The old woman whispered: 'What was it he said?'

' 'Tis how his ship is sunk.'

'Did he says he was the only one?'

'He said that.'

'Did himself hear him?' She nodded towards her son's room.

'No, didn't you see me pulling him away from it? But he'll hear him now. Isn't it a wonder Tom wouldn't walk easy on the boards!'

No answer from the old woman. She had deliberately seated herself in her accustomed place at the fire, and now moaned out: 'Aren't we in a cruel way, not knowing how he'd take a thing!'

'Am I better tell him there's a poor seaman after coming in on us?'

'Do you hear them above! Do you hear them!'

In the loft the men's feet were loud on the boards. The voice they were half-expecting to hear they then heard break in on the clatter of the boots above: 'Mother! Mother!'

'Yes, child, yes.'

'Who's aloft? Who's going around like that, or is it dreaming I am?'

The sounds from above were certainly like what one hears in a ship. They thought of this, but they also felt something terrible in that voice they had been waiting for: they hardly knew it for the voice of the man they had been listening to for five months.

'Go in and tell him the truth,' the mother whispered. 'Who are we to know what's right to be done? Let God have the doing of it.' She threw her hands in the air.

Mary went in to her brother, and her limbs were weak and cold. The old woman remained seated at the fire, swung round from it, her eyes towards her son's room, fixed, as the head itself was fixed, in the tension of anxiety.

After a few minutes Mary emerged with a strange alertness upon her: 'He's rising! He's getting up! 'Tis his place, he says. He's quite good.' She meant he seemed bright and well. The mother said: 'We'll take no notice of him, only just as if he was always with us.'

'Yes.'

They were glad then to hear the two men in the loft groping for the stair head. The kettle began to splutter in the boil, and Mary busied herself with the table and tea cups.

The sailor came down, all smiles in his ill-fitting, haphazard clothes. He looked so overjoyed one might think he would presently burst into song.

3

'The fire is good,' he said. 'It puts life in one. And the dry clothes too. My word, I'm thankful to you, good people; I'm thankful to you.' He shook hands with them all effusively.

'Sit down now; drink up the tea.'

'I can't figure it out; less than two hours ago, out there . . . ' As he spoke he raised his hand towards the little porthole of a window, looking at them with his eyes staring. 'Don't be thinking of anything, but drink up the hot tea,' Mary said.

He nodded and set to eat with vigour. Yet suddenly he would stop, as if he were ashamed of it, turn half-round and look at them with beaming eyes, look from one to the other and back again; and they affably would nod back at him. 'Excuse me, people,' he would say, 'excuse me.' He had not the gift of speech, and his too-full heart could not declare itself. To make him feel at his ease, Tom Leane sat down away from him, and the women began to find something to do about the room. Then there were only little sounds in the room: the breaking of the eggs, the turning of the fire-wheel, the wind going by. The door of the lower room opened silently, so silently that none of them heard it, and before they were aware, the son of the house, with his clothes flung on loosely, was standing awkwardly in the middle of the floor, looking down on the back of the sailorman bent above the table. 'This is my son,' the mother thought of saying. 'He was after going to bed when you came in.'

The Welshman leaped to his feet, and impulsively, yet without many words, shook John Spillane by the hand, thanking him and all the household. As he seated himself again at the table John made his way silently towards the settle from which, across the room, he could see the sailor as he bent over his meal.

The stranger put the cup away from him, he could take no more; and Tom Leane and the womenfolk tried to keep him in talk, avoiding, as by some mutual understanding, the mention of what he had come through. The eyes of the son of the house were all the time fiercely buried in him. There came a moment's silence in the general chatter, a moment it seemed impossible to fill, and the sailorman swung his chair half-round from the table, a spoon held in his hand lightly: 'I can't figure it out. I can't nohow figure it out. Here I am, fed full like a prize beast; and warm – Oh, but I'm thankful – and all my mates,' with the spoon he was pointing towards the sea – 'white, and cold like dead fish! I can't figure it out.'

To their astonishment a voice travelled across the room from the settle.

'Is it how ye struck?'

'Struck! Three times we struck! We struck last night, about this time last night. And off we went in a puff! Fine, we said. We struck again. 'Twas just coming light. And off again. But when we struck the third time, 'twas like that!' He clapped his hands together; 'She went in matchwood! 'Twas dark. Why, it can't be two hours since!'

'She went to pieces?' the same voice questioned him.

'The *Nan Tidy* went to pieces, sir! No one knew what had happened or where she was. 'Twas too sudden. I found myself clung about a snag of rock. I hugged it.'

He stood up, hoisted as from within.

'Is it you that was on the look-out?'

'Me! We'd all been on the look-out for three days. My word, yes, three days. We were stupefied with it!'

They were looking at him as he spoke, and they saw the shiver again cross his features; the strength and warmth that the food and comfort had given him fell from him, and he became in an instant the half-drowned man who had stepped in to them that night with the clothes sagging about his limbs, ' 'Twas bad, clinging to that rock, with them all gone! 'Twas lonely! Do you know, I was so frightened I couldn't call out.' John Spillane stood up, slowly, as if he too were being hoisted from within.

'Were they looking at you?'

'Who?'

'The rest of them. The eyes of them.'

'No,' the voice had dropped, 'no, I didn't think of that!' The two of them stared as if fascinated by each other.

'You didn't!' It seemed that John Spillane had lost

the purpose of his questioning. His voice was thin and weak; but he was still staring with unmoving, puzzled eyes at the stranger's face. The abashed creature before him suddenly seemed to gain as much eagerness as he had lost: his words were hot with anxiety to express himself adequately: 'But now, isn't it curious, as I sat there, there at that table, I thought somehow they would walk in, that it would be right for them, somehow, to walk in, all of them!'

His words, his eager lowered voice, brought in the darkness outside, its vastness, its terror. They seemed in the midst of an unsubstantial world. They feared that the latch would lift, yet dared not glance at it, lest that should invite the lifting. But it was all one to the son of the house, he appeared to have gone away into some mood of his own; his eyes were glaring, not looking at anything or anyone close at hand. With an instinctive groping for comfort, they all, except him, began to stir, to find some little homely task to do: Mary handled the tea ware, and Tom his pipe, when a rumbling voice, very indistinct, stilled them all again. Words, phrases, began to reach them – that a man's eyes will close and he on the lookout, close in spite of himself, that it wasn't fair, it wasn't fair, it wasn't fair! And lost in his agony, he began to glide through them, explaining, excusing the terror that was in him: 'All round. Staring at me. Blaming me. A sea of them. Far, far! Without a word out of them, only their eyes in the darkness, pale like candles!'

Transfixed, they glared at him, at his round-shouldered sailor's back disappearing again into his den of refuge. They could not hear his voice any more, they were afraid to follow him.

ROSA MULHOLLAND

The Haunted Organist of Hurly Burly

There had been a thunderstorm in the village of Hurly Burly. Every door was shut, every dog in his kennel, every rut and gutter a flowing river after the deluge of rain that had fallen. Up at the great house, a mile from the town, the rooks were calling to one another about the fright they had been in, the fawns in the deer-park were venturing their timid heads from behind the trunks of trees, and the old woman at the gate-lodge had risen from her knees, and was putting back her prayer-book on the shelf. In the garden, July roses, unwieldy with their full-blown richness and saturated with rain, hung their heads heavily to the earth; others, already fallen, lay flat upon their blooming faces on the path, where Bess, Mistress Hurly's maid, would find them, when going on her morning quest for rose-leaves for her lady's potpourri. Ranks of white lilies, just brought to perfection by today's sun, lay dabbled in the mire of flooded mould. Tears ran down the amber cheeks of the plums on the south wall, and not a bee had ventured out of the hives, though the scent of the air was sweet enough to tempt the laziest drone. The sky was still lurid behind the boles of the upland oaks, but the birds had begun to dive in and out of the ivy that wrapped up the home of the Hurlys of Hurly Burly.

This thunderstorm took place more than half a century ago, and we must remember that Mistress Hurly was dressed in the fashion of that time as she crept out from behind the squire's chair, now that the lightning was over, and, with many nervous glances towards the window, sat down before her husband, the tea-urn and the muffins. We can picture her fine lace cap, with its peachy ribbons, the frill on the hem of her cambric gown just touching her ankles, the embroidered clocks on her stockings, the rosettes on her shoes, but not so easily the lilac shade of her mild eyes, the satin skin, which still kept its delicate bloom, though wrinkled with advancing age, and the pale, sweet, puckered mouth, that time and sorrow had made angelic while trying vainly to deface its beauty.

The squire was as rugged as his wife was gentle, his skin as brown as hers was white, his grey hair as bristling as hers was glossed; the years had ploughed his face into ruts and channels; a bluff, choleric, noisy man he had been; but of late a dimness had come on his eyes, a hush on his loud voice, and a check in the spring of his hale step. He looked at his wife often, and very often she looked at him. She was not a tall woman, and he was only a head higher. They were a quaintly well-matched couple, despite their differences. She turned to you with nervous sharpness and revealed her tender voice and eye; he spoke and glanced roughly, but the turn of his head was courteous. Of late they fitted one another better than they had ever done in the heyday of their youthful love. A common sorrow had developed a singular likeness between them. In former years the cry from the wife had been, 'Don't curb my son too much!' and from the husband, 'You ruin the lad with softness.'

But now the idol that had stood between them was removed, and they saw each other better.

The room in which they sat was a pleasant old-fashioned drawing-room, with a general spider-legged character about the fittings; spinnet and guitar in their places, with a great deal of copied music beside them; carpet, tawny wreaths on the pale blue; blue flutings on the walls, and faint gilding on the furniture. A huge urn, crammed with roses, in the open bay-window, through which came delicious airs from the garden, the twittering of birds settling to sleep in the ivy close by, and occasionally the pattering of a flight of raindrops, swept to the ground as a bough bent in the breeze. The urn on the table was ancient silver, and the china rare. There was nothing in the room for luxurious ease of the body, but everything of delicate refinement for the eye.

There was a great hush all over Hurly Burly, except in the neighbourhood of the rooks. Every living thing had suffered from heat for the past month, and now, in common with all Nature, was receiving the boon of refreshed air in silent peace. The mistress and master of Hurly Burly shared the general spirit that was abroad, and were not talkative over their tea.

'Do you know,' said Mistress Hurly, at last, 'when I heard the first of the thunder beginning I thought it was – it was – '

The lady broke down, her lips trembling, and the peachy ribbons of her cap stirring with great agitation.

'Pshaw!' cried the old squire, making his cup suddenly ring upon the saucer, 'we ought to have forgotten that. Nothing has been heard for three months.'

At this moment a rolling sound struck upon the

ears of both. The lady rose from her seat trembling, and folded her hands together, while the tea-urn flooded the tray.

'Nonsense, my love,' said the squire; 'that is the noise of wheels. Who can be arriving?'

'Who, indeed?' murmured the lady, reseating herself in agitation.

Presently pretty Bess of the rose-leaves appeared at the door in a flutter of blue ribbons.

'Please, madam, a lady has arrived, and says she is expected. She asked for her apartment, and I put her into the room that was got ready for Miss Calderwood. And she sends her respects to you, madam, and she'll be down with you presently.'

The squire looked at his wife, and his wife looked at the squire. 'It is some mistake,' murmured madam. 'Some visitor for Calderwood or the Grange. It is very singular.'

Hardly had she spoken when the door again opened and the stranger appeared: a small creature – whether girl or woman it would be hard to say – dressed in a scanty black silk dress, her narrow shoulders covered with a white muslin pelerine. Her hair was swept up to the crown of her head, all but a little fringe which hung over her low forehead within an inch of her brows. Her face was brown and thin, eyes black and long, with blacker settings, mouth large, sweet and melancholy. She was all head, mouth and eyes; her nose and chin were nothing.

This visitor crossed the floor hastily, dropped a courtesy in the middle of the room, and approached the table, saying abruptly, with a soft Italian accent: 'Sir and madam, I am here. I am come to play your organ.'

'The organ!' gasped Mistress Hurly.

'The organ!' stammered the squire.

'Yes, the organ,' said the little stranger lady, playing on the back of a chair with her fingers, as if she felt notes under them. 'It was but last week that the handsome signor, your son, came to my little house, where I have lived teaching music since my English father and my Italian mother and brothers and sisters died and left me so lonely.'

Here the fingers left off drumming, and two great tears were brushed off, one from each eye with each hand, child's fashion. But the next moment the fingers were at work again, as if only while they were moving the tongue could speak.

'The noble signor, your son,' said the little woman, looking trustfully from one to the other of the old couple, while a bright blush shone through her brown skin, 'he often came to see me before that, always in the evening, when the sun was warm and yellow all through my little studio, and the music was swelling my heart, and I could play out grand with all my soul; then he used to come and say, "Hurry, little Lisa, and play better, better still. I have work for you to do by and by." Sometimes he said, "Brava!" and sometimes he said "Eccellentissima!" but one night last week he came to me and said, "It is enough. Will you swear to do my bidding, whatever it may be?" ' Here the black eyes fell. 'And I said, "Yes." And he said, "Now you are my betrothed." And I said, "Yes." And he said, "Pack up your music, little Lisa, and go off to England, to my English father and mother, who have an organ in their house which must be played upon. If they refuse to let you play, tell them I sent you, and they will give you leave. You must play all day, and you must get up in the night and play. You must never tire. You are my betrothed, and you have sworn to do my work." I said, "Shall I see you there, signor?" And he said, "Yes, you shall see me there." I said, "I will keep my vow, Signor." And so, sir and madam, I am come.'

The soft foreign voice left off talking, the fingers left off thrumming on the chair, and the little stranger gazed in dismay at her auditors, both pale with agitation.

'You are deceived. You make a mistake,' said they in one breath.

'Our son,' began Mistress Hurly, but her mouth twitched, her voice broke, and she looked piteously towards her husband.

'Our son,' said the squire, making an effort to conquer the quavering in his voice, 'our son is long dead.'

'Nay, nay,' said the little foreigner. 'If you have thought him dead have good cheer, dear sir and madam. He is alive; he is well, and strong, and handsome. But one, two, three, four, five' (on the fingers) 'days ago he stood by my side.'

'It is some strange mistake, some wonderful co-incidence!' said the mistress and master of Hurly Burly.

'Let us take her to the gallery,' murmured the mother of this son who was thus dead and alive. 'There is yet light to see the pictures. She will not know his portrait.'

The bewildered wife and husband led their strange visitor away to a long gloomy room at the west side of the house, where the faint gleams from the darkening sky still lingered on the portraits of the Hurly family.

'Doubtless he is like this,' said the squire, pointing to a fair-haired young man with a mild face, a brother of his own who had been lost at sea.

But Lisa shook her head, and went softly on tiptoe from one picture to another, peering into each canvas, and always turning away troubled. But at last a shriek of delight startled the shadowy chamber.

'Ah, here he is! See, here he is, the noble signor, the beautiful signor, not half so handsome as he looked five days ago, when talking to poor little Lisa! Dear sir and madam, you are now content. Now take me to the organ, that I may commence to do his bidding at once.'

The mistress of Hurly Burly clung fast to her husband's arm. 'How old are you, girl?' she said faintly.

'Eighteen,' said the visitor impatiently, moving towards the door.

'And my son has been dead for twenty years!' said his mother, and swooned on her husband's breast.

'Order the carriage at once,' said Mistress Hurly, recovering from her swoon; 'I will take her to Margaret Calderwood. Margaret will tell her the story. Margaret will bring her to reason. No, not tomorrow; I cannot bear tomorrow, it is so far away. We must go tonight.'

The little signora thought the old lady mad, but she put on her cloak again obediently, and took her seat beside Mistress Hurly in the Hurly family coach. The moon that looked in at them through the pane as they lumbered along was not whiter than the aged face of the squire's wife, whose dim faded eyes were fixed upon it in doubt and awe too great for tears or words. Lisa, too, from her corner, gloated upon the moon, her black eyes shining with passionate dreams.

A carriage rolled away from the Calderwood door as the Hurly coach drew up at the steps.

Margaret Calderwood had just returned from a dinner-party, and was standing, a splendid figure, at the open door – a tall woman dressed in brown velvet, the diamonds on her bosom glistening in the moonlight that was pouring over the house from eaves to basement. Mistress Hurly fell into her outstretched arms with a groan, and the strong woman carried her aged friend, like a baby, into the house. Little Lisa was overlooked, and sat down contentedly on the threshold to gloat awhile longer on the moon, and to thrum imaginary sonatas on the doorstep.

There were tears and sobs in the moonlit room into which Margaret Calderwood carried her friend. There was a long consultation, and then Margaret, having hushed away the grieving woman into some quiet corner, came forth to look for the little dark-faced stranger, who had arrived, so unwelcome, from beyond the seas, with such wild communication from the dead.

Up the grand staircase of handsome Calderwood the little woman followed the tall one into a large chamber where a lamp burned, showing Lisa, if she cared to see it, that this mansion of Calderwood was fitted with much greater luxury and richness than was that of Hurly Burly. The appointments of this room announced it the sanctum of a woman who depended for the interest of her life upon resources of intellect and taste. Lisa noticed nothing but a morsel of biscuit that was lying on a plate.

'May I have it?' said she eagerly. 'It is so long since I have eaten. I am hungry,'

Margaret Calderwood gazed at her with a sorrowful, motherly look, and, parting the fringing hair on her forehead, kissed her. Lisa, staring at her in wonder, returned the caress with ardour.

Margaret's large fair shoulders, Madonna face and yellow braided hair excited a rapture within her. But when food was brought her, she flew to it and ate.

'It is better than I have ever eaten at home!' she said gratefully. And Margaret Calderwood murmured, 'She is physically healthy, at least.'

'And now, Lisa,' said Margaret Calderwood, 'come and tell me the whole history of the grand signor who sent you to England to play the organ.'

Then Lisa crept in behind a chair, and her eyes began to burn and her fingers to thrum, and she repeated word for word her story as she had told it at Hurly Burly.

When she had finished, Margaret Calderwood began to pace up and down the floor with a very troubled face. Lisa watched her, fascinated, and when she bade her listen to a story which she would relate to her, folded her restless hands together meekly and listened.

'Twenty years ago, Lisa, Mr and Mrs Hurly had a son. He was handsome, like that portrait you saw in the gallery, and he had brilliant talents. He was idolised by his father and mother, and all who knew him felt obliged to love him. I was then a happy girl of twenty. I was an orphan, and Mrs Hurly, who had been my mother's friend, was like a mother to me. I, too, was petted and caressed by all my friends, and I was very wealthy; but I only valued admiration, riches, every good gift that fell to my share, just in proportion as they seemed of worth in the eyes of Lewis Hurly. I was his affianced wife, and I loved him well.

'All the fondness and pride that were lavished on him could not keep him from falling into evil ways, nor from becoming rapidly more and more abandoned to wickedness, till even those who loved him best despaired of seeing his reformation. I prayed him with tears, for my sake, if not for that of his grieving mother, to save himself before it was too late. But to my horror I found that my power was gone, my words did not even move him; he loved me no more. I tried to think that this was some fit of madness that would pass, and still clung to hope. At last his own mother forbade me to see him.'

Here Margaret Calderwood paused, seemingly in bitter thought, but resumed: 'He and a party of his boon companions, named by themselves the "Devil's Club", were in the habit of practising all kinds of unholy pranks in the country. They had midnight carousings on the tombstones in the village graveyard; they carried away helpless old men and children, whom they tortured by making believe to bury them alive; they raised the dead and placed them sitting round the tombstones at a mock feast. On one occasion there was a very sad funeral from the village. The corpse was carried into the church, and prayers were read over the coffin, the chief mourner, the aged father of the dead man, standing weeping by. In the midst of this solemn scene the organ suddenly pealed forth a profane tune, and a number of voices shouted a drinking chorus. A groan of execration burst from the crowd, the clergyman turned pale and closed his book, and the old man, the father of the departed, climbed the altar steps, and, raising his arms above his head, uttered a terrible curse. He cursed Lewis Hurly to all eternity; he cursed the organ he played, that it might be dumb henceforth, except under the fingers that had now profaned it, which, he prayed, might be forced to labour upon it till they stiffened in death. And the curse seemed to work, for the organ stood dumb in the church from that day, except when touched by Lewis Hurly.

'For a bravado he had the organ taken down and conveyed to his father's house, where he had it put up in the chamber where it now stands. It was also for a bravado that he played on it every day. But, by and by, the amount of time which he spent at it daily began to increase rapidly. We wondered long at this whim, as we called it, and his poor mother thanked God that he had set his heart upon an occupation which would keep him out of harm's way. I was the first to suspect that it was not his own will that kept him hammering at the organ so many laborious hours, while his boon companions tried vainly to draw him away. He used to lock himself up in the room with the organ, but one day I hid myself among the curtains, and saw him writhing on his seat, and heard him groaning as he strove to wrench his hands from the keys, to which they flew back like needles to a magnet. It was soon plainly to be seen that he was an involuntary slave to the organ; but whether through a madness that had grown within himself, or by some supernatural doom, having its cause in the old man's curse, we did not dare to say. By and by there came a time when we were wakened out of our sleep at nights by the rolling of the organ. He wrought now night and day. Food and rest were denied him. His face got haggard, his beard grew long, his eyes started from their sockets. His body became wasted, and his cramped fingers like the claws of a bird. He groaned piteously as he stooped over his cruel toil. All save his mother and I were afraid to go near him. She, poor, tender woman, tried to put wine and food between his lips, while the tortured fingers crawled over the keys; but he only gnashed his teeth at her with curses, and she retreated from him in terror, to pray. At last, one dreadful hour, we found him, a ghastly corpse, on the ground before the organ.

'From that hour the organ was dumb to the touch of all human fingers. Many, unwilling to believe the story, made persevering endeavours to draw sound from it, in vain. But when the darkened empty room was locked up and left, we heard as loud as ever the well-known sounds humming and rolling through the walls. Night and day the tones of the organ boomed on as before. It seemed that the doom of the wretched man was not yet fulfilled, although his tortured body had been worn out in the terrible struggle to accomplish it. Even his own mother was afraid to go near the room then. So the time went on, and the curse of this perpetual music was not removed from the house. Servants refused to stay about the place. Visitors shunned it. The squire and his wife left their home for years, and returned; left it, and returned again, to find their ears still tortured and their hearts wrung by the unceasing persecution of terrible sounds. At last, but a few months ago, a holy man was found, who locked himself up in the cursed chamber for many days, praying and wrestling with the demon. After he came forth and went away the sounds ceased, and the organ was heard no more. Since then there has been peace in the house. And now, Lisa, your strange appearance and your strange story convince us that you are a victim of a ruse of the Evil One.

Be warned in time, and place yourself under the protection of God, that you may be saved from the fearful influences that are at work upon you. Come.'

Margaret Calderwood turned to the corner where the stranger sat, as she had supposed, listening intently. Little Lisa was fast asleep, her hands spread before her as if she played an organ in her dreams.

Margaret took the soft brown face to her motherly breast, and kissed the swelling temples, too big with wonder and fancy.

'We will save you from a horrible fate!' she murmured, and carried the girl to bed.

In the morning Lisa was gone. Margaret Calderwood, coming early from her own chamber, went into the girl's room and found the bed empty.

'She is just such a wild thing,' thought Margaret, 'as would rush out at sunrise to hear the larks!' and she went forth to look for her in the meadows, behind the beech hedges and in the home park. Mistress Hurly, from the breakfast-room window, saw Margaret Calderwood, large and fair in her white morning gown, coming down the garden path between the rose bushes, with her fresh draperies dabbled by the dew, and a look of trouble on her calm face. Her quest had been unsuccessful. The little foreigner had vanished.

A second search after breakfast proved also fruitless, and towards evening the two women drove back to Hurly Burly together. There all was panic and distress. The squire sat in his study with the doors shut, and his hands over his ears. The servants, with pale faces, were huddled together in whispering groups. The haunted organ was pealing through the house as of old.

Margaret Calderwood hastened to the fatal chamber, and there, sure enough, was Lisa, perched upon the high seat before the organ, beating the keys with her small hands, her slight figure swaying, and the evening sunshine playing about her weird head. Sweet unearthly music she wrung from the groaning heart of the organ – wild melodies, mounting to rapturous heights and falling to mournful depths. She wandered from Mendelssohn to Mozart, and from Mozart to Beethoven. Margaret stood fascinated awhile by the ravishing beauty of the sounds she heard, but, rousing herself quickly, put her arms round the musician and forced her away from the chamber. Lisa returned next day, however, and was not so easily coaxed from her post again.

Day after day she laboured at the organ, growing paler and thinner and more weird-looking as time went on.

'I work so hard,' she said to Mrs Hurly. 'The signor, your son, is he pleased? Ask him to come and tell me himself if he is pleased.'

Mistress Hurly got ill and took to her bed. The squire swore at the young foreign baggage, and roamed abroad. Margaret Calderwood was the only one who stood by to watch the fate of the little organist. The curse of the organ was upon Lisa; it spoke under her hand, and her hand was its slave.

At last she announced rapturously that she had had a visit from the brave signor, who had commended her industry, and urged her to work yet harder. After that she ceased to hold any communication with the living. Time after time Margaret Calderwood wrapped her arms about the frail thing, and carried her away by force, locking the door of the fatal chamber. But locking the chamber and burying the key were of no avail. The door stood open again, and Lisa was labouring on her perch.

One night, wakened from her sleep by the well-known humming and moaning of the organ, Margaret dressed hurriedly and hastened to the unholy room. Moonlight was pouring down the staircase and passages of Hurly Burly. It shone on the marble bust of the dead Lewis Hurly, that stood in the niche above his mother's sitting-room door. The organ-room was full of it when Margaret pushed open the door and entered – full of the pale-green moonlight from the window, mingled with another light, a dull lurid glare which seemed to centre round a dark shadow, like the figure of a man, standing by the organ, and throwing out in fantastic relief the slight form of Lisa writhing, rather than swaying, back and forth, as if in agony. The sounds that came from the organ were broken and meaningless, as if the hands of the player lagged and stumbled on the keys. Between the intermittent chords, low moaning cries broke from Lisa, and the dark figure bent towards her with menacing gestures. Trembling with the sickness of supernatural fear, yet strong of will, Margaret Calderwood crept forward within the lurid light, and was drawn into its influence. It grew and intensified upon her, it dazzled and blinded her at first; but presently, by a daring effort of will, she raised her eyes and beheld Lisa's face convulsed with torture in the burning glare and bending over her the figure and the features of Lewis Hurly! Smitten with horror, Margaret did not even then lose her presence of mind. She wound her strong arms around the wretched girl and dragged her from her seat and out of the influence

THE HAUNTED ORGANIST OF HURLY BURLY

of the lurid light, which immediately paled away and
vanished. She carried her to her own bed, where Lisa
lay, a wasted wreck, raving about the cruelty of
the pitiless signor who would not see that she was
labouring her best. Her poor cramped hands kept
beating the coverlet, as though she were still at her
agonising task.

Margaret Calderwood bathed her burning temples,
and placed fresh flowers upon her pillow. She opened
the blinds and windows, and let in the sweet morning
air and sunshine, and then, looking up at the newly
awakened sky with its fair promise of hope for the
day, and down at the dewy fields, and afar off at the
dark green woods with the purple mists still hovering
about them, she prayed that a way might be shown
her by which to put an end to this curse. She prayed
for Lisa, and then, thinking that the girl rested
somewhat, stole from the room. She thought that she
had locked the door behind her.

She went downstairs with a pale, resolved face,
and, without consulting anyone, sent to the village for
a bricklayer. Afterwards she sat by Mistress Hurly's
bedside, and explained to her what was to be done.
Presently she went to the door of Lisa's room and,
hearing no sound, thought the girl slept, and stole
away. By and by she went downstairs, and found that
the bricklayer had arrived and already begun his task
of building up the organ-room door. He was a swift
workman, and the chamber was soon sealed safely
with stone and mortar.

Having seen this work finished, Margaret Calderwood went and listened again at Lisa's door; and still
hearing no sound, she returned, and took her seat
at Mrs Hurly's bedside once more. It was towards

evening that she at last entered her room to assure herself of the comfort of Lisa's sleep. But the bed and room were empty. Lisa had disappeared.

Then the search began, upstairs and downstairs, in the garden, in the grounds, in the fields and meadows. No Lisa. Margaret Calderwood ordered the carriage and drove to Calderwood to see if the strange little Will-o'-the-wisp might have made her way there; then to the village, and to many other places in the neighbourhood which it was not possible she could have reached. She made enquiries everywhere; she pondered and puzzled over the matter. In the weak, suffering state that the girl was in, how far could she have crawled?

After two days' search, Margaret returned to Hurly Burly. She was sad and tired, and the evening was chill. She sat over the fire wrapped in her shawl when little Bess came to her, weeping behind her muslin apron.

'If you'd speak to Mistress Hurly about it, please, ma'am,' she said. 'I love her dearly, and it breaks my heart to go away, but the organ haven't done yet, ma'am, and I'm frightened out of my life, so I can't stay.'

'Who has heard the organ, and when?' asked Margaret Calderwood, rising to her feet.

'Please, ma'am, I heard it the night you went away, the night after the door was built up!'

'And not since?'

'No, ma'am,' hesitatingly, 'not since. Hist! hark, ma'am! Is not that like the sound of it now?'

'No,' said Margaret Calderwood; 'it is only the wind.' But pale as death she flew down the stairs and laid her ear to the yet damp mortar of the newly built wall. All was silent. There was no sound but the monotonous sough of the wind in the trees outside. Then Margaret began to dash her soft shoulder against the strong wall, and to pick the mortar away with her white fingers, and to cry out for the bricklayer who had built up the door.

It was midnight, but the bricklayer left his bed in the village, and obeyed the summons to Hurly Burly. The pale woman stood by and watched him undo all his work of three days ago, and the servants gathered about in trembling groups, wondering what was to happen next.

What happened next was this: When an opening was made the man entered the room with a light, Margaret Calderwood and others following. A heap of something dark was lying on the ground at the foot of the organ. Many groans arose in the fatal chamber. Here was little Lisa dead!

When Mistress Hurly was able to move, the squire and his wife went to live in France, where they remained till their death. Hurly Burly was shut up and deserted for many years. Lately it has passed into new hands. The organ has been taken down and banished, and the room is a bedchamber, more luxuriously furnished than any in the house. But no one sleeps in it twice.

Margaret Calderwood was carried to her grave the other day, a very aged woman.

ROSA MULHOLLAND

The Ghost at the Rath

Many may disbelieve this story, yet there are some still living who can remember hearing, when children, of the events which it details, and of the strange sensation which their publicity excited. The tale, in its present form, is copied, by permission, from a memoir written by the chief actor in the romance, and preserved as a sort of heirloom in the family whom it concerns.

In the year —, I, John Thunder, Captain in the — Regiment, having passed many years abroad following my profession, received notice that I had become owner of certain properties which I had never thought to inherit. I set off for my native land, arrived in Dublin, found that my good fortune was real, and at once began to look about me for old friends. The first I met with, quite by accident, was curly-headed Frank O'Brien, who had been at school with me, though I was ten years his senior. He was curly-headed still, and handsome, as he had promised to be, but careworn and poor. During an evening spent at his chambers I drew all his history from him. He was a briefless barrister. As a man he was not more talented than he had been as a boy. Hard work and anxiety had not brought him success, only broken his health and soured his mind. He was in love, and he could not marry. I soon knew all about Mary Leonard, his fiancée, whom he had met at a house in the country somewhere, in which she was governess. They had now been engaged for two years – she active and hopeful, he sick and despondent. From the letters of hers which he showed me, I thought she was worth all the devotion he felt for her. I considered a good deal about what could be done for Frank, but I could not easily hit upon a plan to assist him. For ten chances you have of helping a sharp man, you have not two for a dull one.

In the meantime my friend must regain his health, and a change of air and scene was necessary. I urged him to make a voyage of discovery to the Rath, an old house and park which had come into my possession as portion of my recently acquired estates. I had never been to the place myself but it had once been the residence of Sir Luke Thunder, of generous memory, and I knew that it was furnished, and provided with a caretaker. I pressed him to leave Dublin at once, and promised to follow him as soon as I found it possible to do so.

So Frank went down to the Rath. The place was two hundred miles away; he was a stranger there, and far from well. When the first week came to an end, and I had heard nothing from him, I did not like the silence; when a fortnight had passed, and still not a word to say he was alive, I felt decidedly uncomfortable; and when the third week of his absence arrived at Saturday without bringing me news, I found myself whizzing through a part of the country I had never travelled before, in the same train in which I had seen Frank seated at our parting.

I reached D—, and, shouldering my knapsack,

walked right into the heart of a lovely woody country. Following the directions I had received, I made my way to a lonely road, on which I met not a soul, and which seemed cut out of the heart of a forest, so closely were the trees ranked on either side and so dense was the twilight made by the meeting and intertwining of the thick branches overhead. In these shades I came upon a gate, like a gate run to seed, with tall, thin, brick pillars, brandishing long grasses from their heads, and spotted with a melancholy crust of creeping moss. I jangled a cracked bell, and an old man appeared from the thickets within, stared at me, then admitted me with a rusty key. I breathed freely on hearing that my friend was well and to be seen. I presented a letter to the old man, having a fancy not to avow myself.

I found my friend walking up and down the alleys of a neglected orchard, with the lichened branches tangled above his head, and ripe apples rotting about his feet. His hands were locked behind his back, and his head was set on one side as he listened to the singing of a bird. I never had seen him look so well; yet there was a vacancy about his whole air which I did not like. He did not seem at all surprised to see me, asked had he really not written to me; thought he had; was so comfortable that he had forgotten everything else. He fancied he had only been there about three days; could not imagine how the time had passed. He seemed to talk wildly, and this, coupled with the unusual happy placidity of his manner, confounded me. The place knew him, he told me confidentially; the place belonged to him, or should; the birds sang him this, the very trees bent before him as he passed, the air whispered him that he had been long expected and should be poor no more. Wrestling with my judgement ere it might pronounce him mad, I followed him indoors. The Rath was no ordinary old country-house. The acres around it were so wildly overgrown that it was hard to decide which had been pleasure-ground and where the thickets had begun. The plan of the house was fine, with mullioned windows, and here and there a fleck of stained glass flinging back the challenge of an angry sunset. The vast rooms were full of a dusky glare from the sky as I strolled through them in the twilight. The antique furniture had many a blood-red stain on the abrupt notches of its dark carvings; the dusty mirrors flared back at the windows, while the faded curtains produced streaks of uncertain colour from the depths of their sullen foldings.

Dinner was laid for us in the library, a long wainscoted room, with an enormous fire roaring up the chimney, sending a dancing light over the dingy titles of long unopened books. The old man who had unlocked the gate for me served us at table, and, after drawing the dusty curtains and furnishing us with a plentiful supply of fuel and wine, left us. His clanking hobnailed shoes went echoing away in the distance over the unmatted tiles of the vacant hall till a door closed with a resounding clang very far away, letting us know that we were shut up together for the night in this vast, mouldy, oppressive old house.

I felt as if I could scarcely breathe in it. I could not eat with my usual appetite. The air of the place seemed heavy and tainted. I grew sick and restless. The very wine tasted badly, as if it had been drugged. I had a strange feeling that I had been in the house before, and that something evil had happened to me in it. Yet such could not be the case. What puzzled me most was that I should feel dissatisfied at seeing Frank looking so well and eating so heartily. A little time before I should have been glad to suffer something to see him as he looked now; and yet not quite as he looked now. There was a drowsy contentment about him which I could not understand. He did not talk of his work, or of any wish to return to it. He seemed to have no thought of anything but the delight of hanging about that old house, which had certainly cast a spell over him.

About midnight he seized a light, and proposed retiring to our rooms. 'I have such delightful dreams in this place,' he said. He volunteered, as we issued into the hall, to take me upstairs and show me the upper regions of his paradise. I said, 'Not tonight.' I felt a strange creeping sensation as I looked up the vast black staircase, wide enough for a coach to drive down, and at the heavy darkness bending over it like a curse, while our lamps made drips of light down the first two or three gloomy steps. Our bedrooms were on the ground floor, and stood opposite one another off a passage which led to a garden. Into mine Frank conducted me, and left me for his own.

The uneasy feeling which I have described did not go from me with him, and I felt a restlessness amounting to pain when left alone in my chamber. Efforts had evidently been made to render the room habitable, but there was a something antagonistic to sleep in every angle of its many crooked corners. I kicked chairs out of their prim order along the wall, and banged things about here and there; finally, thinking that a good night's rest was the best cure for an inexplicably disturbed frame of mind, I undressed as quickly as possible, and laid my head on my pillow under a canopy, like the wings of a gigantic bird of prey wheeling above me ready to pounce.

But I could not sleep. The wind grumbled in the chimney, and the boughs swished in the garden outside; and between these noises I thought I heard sounds coming from the interior of the old house, where all should have been still as the dead down in their vaults. I could not make out what these sounds were. Sometimes I thought I heard feet running about, sometimes I could have sworn there were double knocks, tremendous tantarararas at the great hall door. Sometimes I heard the clashing of dishes, the echo of voices calling, and the dragging about of furniture. Whilst I sat up in bed trying to account for these noises, my door suddenly flew open, a bright light streamed in from the passage without, and a powdered servant in an elaborate livery of antique pattern stood holding the handle of the door in his hand, and bowing low to me in the bed.

'Her ladyship, my mistress, desires your presence in the drawing-room, sir.'

This was announced in the measured tone of a well-trained domestic. Then with another bow he retired, the door closed, and I was left in the dark to determine whether I had not suddenly awakened from a tantalising dream. In spite of my very wakeful sensations, I believe I should have endeavoured to convince myself that I had been sleeping, but that I perceived light shining under my door, and through the keyhole, from the passage. I got up, lit my lamp, and dressed myself as hastily as I was able.

I opened my door, and the passage down which a short time before I had almost groped my way, with my lamp blinking in the dense foggy darkness, was now illuminated with a light as bright as gas. I walked along it quickly, looking right and left to see whence the glare proceeded. Arriving at the hall, I found it also blazing with light, and filled with perfume. Groups of choice plants, heavy with blossoms, made it look like a garden. The mosaic floor was strewn with costly mats. Soft colours and gilding shone from the walls, and canvases that had been black gave forth faces of men and women looking brightly from their burnished frames. Servants were running about, the dining-room and drawing-room doors were opening and shutting, and as I looked through each I saw vistas of light and colour, the moving of brilliant crowds, the waving of feathers and glancing of brilliant dresses and uniforms. A festive hum reached me with a drowsy subdued sound, as if I were listening with stuffed ears. Standing aside by an orange tree, I gave up speculating on what this might be, and concentrated all my powers on observation.

Wheels were heard suddenly, and a resounding knock banged at the door till it seemed that the very rooks in the chimneys must be startled out of their nests. The door flew open, a flaming of lanterns was seen outside, and a dazzling lady came up the steps and swept into the hall. When she held up her cloth of silver train, I could see the diamonds that twinkled on her feet. Her bosom was covered with roses, and there was a red light in her eyes like the reflection from a hundred glowing fires. Her black hair went coiling about her head, and couched among the braids lay a jewel not unlike the head of a snake. She was flashing and glowing with gems and flowers. Her beauty and brilliance made me dizzy. Then came faintness in the air, as if her breath had poisoned it. A whirl of storm came in with her and rushed up the staircase like a moan. The plants shuddered and shed their blossoms, and all the lights grew dim a moment, then flared up again.

Now the drawing-room door opened, and a gentleman came out with a young girl learning on his arm. He was a fine-looking, middle-aged gentleman, with a mild countenance.

The girl was a slender creature, with golden hair and a pale face. She was dressed in pure white, with a large ruby like a drop of blood at her throat. They advanced together to receive the lady who had arrived. The gentleman offered his arm to the stranger, and the girl who was displaced for her fell back, and walked behind them with a downcast air. I felt irresistibly impelled to follow them, and passed with them back into the drawing-room. Never had I mixed in a finer, gayer crowd. The costumes were rich and of an old-fashioned pattern. Dancing was going forward with spirit – minuets and country dances. The stately gentleman was evidently the host, and moved among the company, introducing the magnificent lady right and left. He led her to the head of the room presently, and they mixed in the dance. The arrogance of her manner and the fascination of her beauty were wonderful.

I cannot attempt to describe the strange manner in which I was in this company and yet not of it. I seemed to view all I beheld through some fine and subtle medium. I saw clearly, yet I felt that it was not with my ordinary naked eyesight. I can compare it to nothing but looking at a scene through a piece of smoked or coloured glass. And just in the same way (as I have said before) all sounds seemed to reach me as if I were listening with ears imperfectly stuffed. No one present took any notice of me. I spoke to several, and they made no reply – did not even turn their eyes upon me, nor show in any way that they heard me. I planted myself straight in the way of a fine fellow in a general's uniform, but he, swerving neither to right nor left by an inch, kept on his way, as though I were a streak of mist, and left me behind him. Everyone I touched eluded me somehow. Substantial as they all looked, I could not contrive to lay my hand on anything that felt like solid flesh. Two or three times I felt a momentary relief from the oppressive sensations which distracted me, when I firmly believed I saw Frank's head at some distance among the crowd, now in one room and now in another, and again in the conservatory, which was hung with lamps, and filled with people walking about among the flowers. But, whenever I approached, he had vanished. At last I came upon him, sitting by himself on a couch behind a curtain watching the dancers. I laid my hand upon his shoulder. Here was something substantial at last. He did not look up; he seemed aware neither of my touch not my speech. I looked in his staring eyes, and found that he was sound asleep. I could not wake him.

Curiosity would not let me remain by his side. I again mixed with the crowd, and found the stately host still leading about the magnificent lady. No one seemed to notice that the golden-haired girl was sitting weeping in a corner; no one but the beauty in the silver train, who sometimes glanced at her contemptuously. While I watched her distress a group came between me and her, and I wandered into another room, where, as though I had turned from one picture of her to look at another, I beheld her dancing gaily, in the full glee of Sir Roger de Coverley, with a fine-looking youth, who was more plainly dressed than any other person in the room. Never was a better-matched pair to look at. Down the middle they danced, hand in hand, his face full of tenderness, hers beaming with joy, right and left bowing and curtseying, parted and meeting again, smiling and whispering; but over the heads of smaller women there were the fierce eyes of the magnificent beauty scowling at them. Then again the crowd shifted around me and this scene was lost.

For some time I could see no trace of the golden-haired girl in any of the rooms. I looked for her in vain, till at last I caught a glimpse of her standing smiling in a doorway with her finger lifted, beckoning. At whom? Could it be at me? Her eyes were fixed on mine. I hastened into the hall, and caught sight of her white dress passing up the wide black staircase from which I had shrunk some hours earlier. I followed her, she keeping some steps in advance. It was intensely dark, but by the gleaming of her gown I was able to trace her flying figure. Where we went I knew not, up how many stairs, down how many passages, till we arrived at a low-ceilinged large room with sloping roof and queer windows where there was a dim light, like the sanctuary light in a deserted church. Here, when I entered, the golden head was glimmering over something which I presently discerned to be a cradle wrapped round with white curtains, and with a few fresh flowers fastened up on the hood of it, as if to catch a baby's eye. The fair sweet face looked up at me with a glow of pride on it, smiling with happy dimples. The white hands unfolded the curtains, and stripped back the coverlet. Then, suddenly there went a rushing moan all round the weird room, that seemed like a gust of wind forcing in through the crannies, and shaking the jingling old windows in their sockets. The cradle was an empty one. The girl fell back with a look of horror on her pale face that I shall never forget, then, flinging her arms above her head, she dashed from the room.

I followed her as fast as I was able, but the wild white figure was too swift for me. I had lost her before I reached the bottom of the staircase. I searched for her, first in one room, then in another, neither could I see her foe (as I already believed to be), the lady of the silver train. At length I found myself in a small anteroom, where a lamp was expiring on the table. A window was open, close by it the golden-haired girl was lying sobbing in a chair, while the magnificent lady was bending over her, as if soothingly, and offering her something to drink in a goblet. The moon was rising behind the two figures. The shuddering light of the lamp was flickering over the girl's bright head, the rich embossing of the golden cup, the lady's silver robes, and, I thought, the jewelled eyes of the serpent looked out from her bending head. As I watched, the girl raised her face and drank, then suddenly dashed the goblet away, while a cry such as I never heard but once, and shiver to remember, rose to the very roof of the old house, and the clear sharp word '*Poisoned!*' rang and reverberated from hall and chamber in a thousand echoes, like the clash of a peal of bells. The girl dashed herself from the open window, leaving the cry clamouring behind her. I heard the violent opening of doors and running of feet, but I waited for nothing more. Maddened by what I had witnessed, I would have felled the murderess, but she glided unhurt from under my vain blow. I sprang from the window after the wretched white figure. I saw it flying on before me with a speed I could not overtake. I ran till I was dizzy. I called like a madman, and heard the owls croaking back to me. The moon grew huge and bright, the trees grew out before it like the bushy heads of giants, the river lay keen and shining like a long unsheathed sword, couching for deadly work among the rushes. The white figure shimmered and vanished, glittered brightly on before me, shimmered and vanished again, shimmered, staggered, fell, and disappeared into the river. Of what she was, phantom or reality, I thought not at the moment; she had the semblance of a human being going to destruction, and I had the frenzied impulse to save her. I rushed forward with one last effort, struck my foot against the root of a tree, and was dashed to the ground. I remember a crash, momentary pain and confusion; then nothing more.

When my senses returned, the red clouds of the dawn were shining in the river beside me. I arose to my feet, and found that, though much bruised, I was otherwise unhurt. I busied my mind in recalling the strange circumstances which had brought me to that place in the dead of the night. The recollection of all I had witnessed was vividly present to my mind. I took my way slowly to the house, almost expecting to see the marks of wheels and other indications of last night's revel, but the rank grass that covered the gravel was uncrushed, not a blade disturbed, not a stone displaced. I shook one of the drawing-room windows till I shook off the old rusty hasp inside, flung up the creaking sash, and entered. Where were the brilliant draperies and carpets, the soft gilding, the vases teeming with flowers, the thousand sweet odours of the night before? Not a trace of them; no, nor even a ragged cobweb swept away, nor a stiff chair moved an inch from its melancholy place, nor the face of a mirror relieved from one speck of its obscuring dust!

Coming back into the open air, I met the old man from the gate walking up one of the weedy paths. He eyed me meaningly from head to foot, but I gave him good-morrow cheerfully.

'You see I am poking about early,' I said.

'I' faith, sir,' said he, 'an' ye look like a man that had been pokin' about *all night*.'

'How so?' said I.

'Why, ye see, sir,' said he, 'I'm used to 't, an' I can read it in yer face like prent. Some sees one thing an' some another, an' some only feels an' hears. The poor jintleman inside, *he* says nothin', but he has beautyful dhrames. An' for the Lord's sake, sir, take him out o' this, for I've seen him wandherin' about like a ghost himself in the heart of the night, an' him that sound sleepin' that I couldn't wake him!'

* * *

At breakfast I said nothing to Frank of my strange adventures. He had rested well, he said, and boasted of his enchanting dreams. I asked him to describe them, whereupon he grew perplexed and annoyed. He remembered nothing but that his spirit had been delightfully entertained whilst his body reposed.

I now felt a curiosity to go through the old house,

and was not surprised, on pushing open a door at the
end of a remote mouldy passage, to enter the identical
chamber into which I had followed the pale-faced girl
when she beckoned me out of the drawing-room.
There were the low brooding roof and slanting walls,
the short wide latticed windows to which the noonday
sun was trying to pierce through a forest of leaves.
The hangings rotting with age shook like dreary
banners at the opening of the door, and there in the
middle of the room was the cradle; only the curtains
that had been white were blackened with dirt, and
laced and overlaced with cobwebs. I parted the
curtains, bringing down a shower of dust upon the
floor, and saw lying upon the pillow within a child's
tiny shoe and a toy. I need not describe the rest of the
house. It was vast and rambling, and, as far as
furniture and decorations were concerned, the wreck
of grandeur.

Having strange subject for meditation, I walked
alone in the orchard that evening. This orchard sloped
towards the river I have mentioned before. The trees
were old and stunted, and the branches tangled overhead. The ripe apples were rolling in the long
bleached grass. A row of taller trees, sycamores and
chestnuts, straggled along by the river's edge, ferns
and tall weeds grew round and among them, and
between their trunks, and behind the rifts in the
foliage, the water was seen to flow. Walking up and
down one of the paths I alternately faced these trees
and turned my back upon them. Once when coming
towards them I chanced to lift my glance, started,
drew my hands across my eyes, looked again, and
finally stood still, gazing in much astonishment. I saw
distinctly the figure of a lady standing by one of the

trees, bending low towards the grass. Her face was a little turned away, her dress a bluish-white, her mantle a dun-brown colour. She held a spade in her hand, and her foot was upon it, as if she were in the act of digging. I gazed at her for some time, vainly trying to guess who she might be, then I advanced towards her. As I approached, the outlines of her figure broke up and disappeared, and I found that she was only an illusion presented to me by the curious accidental grouping of the lines of two trees which had shaped the space between them into the semblance of the form I have described. A patch of the flowing water had been her robe, a piece of russet moorland her cloak. The spade was an awkward young shoot slanting up from the root of one of the trees. I stepped back and tried to piece her out again bit by bit, but could not succeed. That night I did not feel at all inclined to return to my dismal chamber, and lie awaiting such another summons as I had once received. When Frank bade me good-night, I heaped fresh coals on the fire, took down from the shelves a book, from which I lifted the dust in layers with my penknife, and, dragging an armchair close to the hearth, tried to make myself as comfortable as might be. I am a strong, robust man, very unimaginative, and little troubled with affections of the nerves, but I confess that my feelings were not enviable, sitting thus alone in that queer old house, with last night's strange pantomime still vividly present to my memory. In spite of my efforts at coolness, I was excited by the prospect of what yet might be in store for me before morning. But these feelings passed away as the night wore on, and I nodded asleep over my book.

I was startled by the sound of a brisk light step

walking overhead. Wide awake at once, I sat up and listened. The ceiling was low, but I could not call to mind what room it was that lay above the library in which I sat. Presently I heard the same step upon the stairs, and the loud sharp rustling of a silk dress sweeping against the banisters. The step paused at the library door, and then there was silence. I got up, and with all the courage I could summon seized a light, and opened the door; but there was nothing in the hall but the usual heavy darkness and damp mouldy air. I confess I felt more uncomfortable at that moment than I had done at any time during the preceding night. All the visions that had then appeared to me had produced nothing like the horror of thus feeling a supernatural presence which my eyes were not permitted to behold.

I returned to the library, and passed the night there. Next day I sought for the room above it in which I had heard the footsteps, but could discover no entrance to any such room. Its windows, indeed, I counted from the outside, though they were so overgrown with ivy I could hardly discern them, but in the interior of the house I could find no door to the chamber. I asked Frank about it, but he knew and cared nothing on the subject; I asked the old man at the lodge, and he shook his head.

'Och!' he said, 'don't ask about that room. The door's built up, and flesh and blood have no consarn wid it. It was *her own* room.'

'Whose own?' I asked.

'Ould Lady Thunder's. An' whist, sir, *that's her grave!*'

'What do you mean?' I said. 'Are you out of your mind?'

He laughed queerly, drew nearer, and lowered his voice. 'Nobody has asked about the room these years but yourself,' he said. 'Nobody misses it goin' over the house. My grandfather was an old retainer o' the Thunder family, my father was in the service too, an' I was born myself before the ould lady died. Yon was her room, an' she left her eternal curse on her family if so be they didn't lave her coffin there. *She* wasn't goin' undher the ground to the worms. So there it was left, an' they built up the door. God love ye, sir, an' don't go near it. I wouldn't have told you, only I know ye've seen plenty about already, an' ye have the look o' one that'd be ferretin' things out, savin' yer presence.'

He looked at me knowingly, but I gave him no information, only thanked him for putting me on my guard. I could scarcely credit what he told me about the room, but my curiosity was excited regarding it. I made up my mind that day to try and induce Frank to quit the place on the morrow. I felt more and more convinced that the atmosphere was not healthful for his mind, whatever it might be for his body. The sooner we left the spot the better for us both; but the remaining night which I had to pass there I resolved on devoting to the exploring of the walled-up chamber. What impelled me to this resolve I do not know. The undertaking was not a pleasant one, and I should hardly have ventured on it had I been forced to remain much longer at the Rath. But I knew there was little chance of sleep for me in that house, and I thought I might as well go and seek for my adventures as sit waiting for them to come for me, as I had done the night before. I felt a relish for my enterprise, and expected the night with satisfaction. I did not say anything of my intention either to Frank or the old man at the lodge. I did not want to make a fuss, and have my doings talked of all over the country. I may as well mention here that again, on this evening, when walking in the orchard, I saw the figure of the lady digging between the trees. And again I saw that this figure was an illusive appearance; that the water was her gown, and the moorland her cloak, and a willow in the distance her tresses.

As soon as the night was pretty far advanced, I placed a ladder against the window which was least covered over with the ivy, and mounted it, having provided myself with a dark lantern. The moon rose full behind some trees that stood like a black bank against the horizon, and glimmered on the panes as I ripped away branches and leaves with a knife, and shook the old crazy casement open. The sashes were rotten, and the fastenings easily gave way. I placed my lantern on a bench within, and was soon standing beside it in the chamber. The air was insufferably close and mouldy, and I flung the window open to the widest, and beat the bowering ivy still farther back from about it, so as to let the fresh air of heaven blow into the place. I then took my lantern in hand, and began to look about me.

The room was vast and double; a velvet curtain hung between me and an inner chamber. The darkness was thick and irksome, and the scanty light of my lantern only tantalised me. My eyes fell on some tall spectral-looking candelabra furnished with wax candles, which, though black with age, still bore the marks of having been guttered by a draught that had blown on them fifty years ago. I lighted these; they burned up with a ghastly flickering, and the apartment, with its fittings, was revealed to me. These latter had been

splendid in the days of their freshness: the appointments to be found in the rest of the house were mean
by comparison. The ceiling was painted with fine
allegorical figures, also spaces of the walls between
the dim mirrors and the sumptuous hangings of
crimson velvet, with their tarnished golden tassels
and fringes. The carpet still felt luxurious to the tread,
and the dust could not altogether obliterate the
elaborate fancy of its flowery design. There were
gorgeous cabinets laden with curiosities, wonderfully
carved chairs, rare vases, and antique glasses of every
description, under some of which lay little heaps of
dust which had once no doubt been blooming
flowers. There was a table laden with books of poetry
and science, drawings and drawing materials, which
showed that the occupant of the room had been a
person of mind. There was also a writing-table
scattered over with yellow papers, and a work-table at
a window, on which lay reels, a thimble, and a piece
of what had once been white muslin, but was now
saffron colour, sewn with gold thread, a rusty needle
sticking in it. This and the pen lying on the inkstand,
the paperknife between the leaves of a book, the loose
sketches shaken out by the side of a portfolio, and the
ashes of a fire on the wide mildewed hearth-place, all
suggested that the owner of this retreat had been
snatched from it without warning, and that whoever
had thought proper to build up the doors, had also
thought proper to touch nothing that had belonged
to her.

Having surveyed all these things, I entered the inner
room, which was a bedroom. The furniture of this was
in keeping with that of the other chamber. I saw dimly
a bed enveloped in lace, and a dressing-table fancifully

garnished and draped. Here I espied more candelabra, and going forward to set the lights burning, I stumbled against something. I turned the blaze of my lantern on this something, and started with a sudden thrill of horror. It was a large stone coffin.

I own that I felt very strangely for the next few minutes. When I had recovered from the shock, I set the wax candles burning, and took a better survey of this odd burial-place. A wardrobe stood open, and I saw dresses hanging within. A gown lay upon a chair, as if just thrown off, and a pair of dainty slippers were beside it. The toilet-table looked as if only used yesterday, judging by the litter that covered it: hairbrushes lying this way and that way, essence-bottles with the stoppers out, paint pots uncovered, a ring here, a wreath of artificial flowers there – and, in front of all, the coffin, the tarnished Cupids that bore the mirror between their hands smirking down at it with a grim complacency.

On the corner of this table was a small golden salver, holding a plate of some black mouldered food, an antique decanter filled with wine, a glass, and a phial with some thick black liquid, uncorked. I felt weak and sick with the atmosphere of the place, and I seized the decanter, wiped the dust from it with my handkerchief, tasted, found that the wine was good, and drank a moderate draught. Immediately it was swallowed I felt a horrid giddiness, and sank upon the coffin. A raging pain was in my head and a sense of suffocation in my chest. After a few intolerable moments I felt better, but the heavy air pressed on me stiflingly, and I rushed from this inner room into the larger and outer chamber. Here a blast of cool air revived me, and I saw that the place was changed.

A dozen other candelabra besides those I had lighted were flaming round the walls, the hearth was all ruddy with a blazing fire, everything that had been dim was bright, the lustre had returned to the gilding, the flowers bloomed in the vases. A lady was sitting before the hearth in a low armchair. Her light loose gown swept about her on the carpet, her black hair fell round her to her knees, and into it her hands were thrust as she leaned her forehead upon them, and stared between them into the fire. I had scarcely time to observe her attitude when she turned her head quickly towards me, and I recognised the handsome face of the magnificent lady who had played such a sinister part in the strange scenes that had been enacted before me two nights ago. I saw something dark looming behind her chair, but I thought it was only her shadow thrown backward by the firelight.

She arose and came to meet me, and I recoiled from her. There was something horridly fixed and hollow in her gaze and filmy in the stirring of her garments. The shadow, as she moved, grew more firm and distinct in outline, and followed her like a servant where she went.

She crossed half of the room, then beckoned me, and sat down at the writing-table. The shadow waited beside her, adjusted her paper, placed the ink-bottle near her and the pen between her fingers. I felt impelled to approach her, and to take my place at her left shoulder, so as to be able to see what she might write. The shadow stood motionless at her other hand. As I became accustomed to the shadow's presence he grew more visibly loathsome and hideous. He was quite distinct from the lady, and moved independently of her with long ugly limbs. She hesitated about beginning to write, and he made a wild gesture with his arm, which brought her hand quickly to the paper, and her pen began to move at once. I needed not to bend and scrutinise in order to read. Every words as it was forming flashed before me like a meteor.

'I am the spirit of Madeline, Lady Thunder, who lived and died in this house, and whose coffin stands in yonder room among the vanities in which I delighted. I am constrained to make my confession to you, John Thunder, who are the present owner of the estates of your family.'

Here the hand trembled and stopped writing. But the shadow made a threatening gesture, and the hand fluttered on.

'I was beautiful, poor and ambitious, and when I entered this house first on the night of a ball given by Sir Luke Thunder, I determined to become its mistress. His daughter, Mary Thunder, was the only obstacle in my way. She divined my intention, and stood between me and her father. She was a gentle, delicate girl, and no match for me. I pushed her aside, and became Lady Thunder. After that I hated her, and made her dread me. I had gained the object of my ambition, but I was jealous of the influence possessed by her over her father, and I revenged myself by crushing the joy out of her young life. In this I defeated my own purpose. She eloped with a young man who was devoted to her, though poor and beneath her in station. Her father was indignant at first, and my malice was satisfied; but as time passed on I had no children, and she had a son, soon after whose birth her husband died. Then her father took her back to his heart, and the boy was his idol and heir.'

Again the hand stopped writing, the ghostly head drooped, and the whole figure was convulsed. But the shadow gesticulated fiercely, and, cowering under its menace, the wretched spirit went on: 'I caused the child to be stolen away. I thought I had done it cunningly, but she tracked the crime home to me. She came and accused me of it, and in the desperation of my terror at discovery, I gave her poison to drink. She rushed from me and from the house in frenzy, and in her mortal anguish fell in the river. People thought she had gone mad from grief for her child and committed suicide. I only knew the horrible truth. Sorrow brought an illness upon her father, of which he died. Up to the day of his death he had search made for the child. Believing that it was alive, and must be found, he willed all his property to it, his rightful heir, and to its heirs for ever. I buried the deeds under a tree in the orchard, and forged a will, in which all was bequeathed to me during my lifetime. I enjoyed my state and grandeur till the day of my death, which came upon me miserably, and, after that, my husband's possessions went to a distant relation of his family. Nothing more was heard of the fate of the child who was stolen; but he lived and married, and his daughter now toils for her bread – his daughter, who is the rightful owner of all that is said to belong to you, John Thunder. I tell you this that you may devote yourself to the task of discovering this wronged girl, and giving up to her that which you are unlawfully possessed of. Under the thirteenth tree standing on the brink of the river at the foot of the orchard you will find buried the genuine will of Sir Luke Thunder. When you have found and read it, do justice, as you value your soul. In order that you may know the grandchild of Mary Thunder when you find her, you shall behold her in a vision – '

The last words grew dim before me; the light faded away, and all the place was in darkness, except one spot on the opposite wall. On this spot the light glimmered softly, and against the brightness the outlines of a figure appeared, faintly at first, but, growing firm and distinct, became filled in and rounded at last to the perfect semblance of life. The figure was that of a young girl in a plain black dress, with a bright, happy face and pale gold hair softly banded on her fair forehead. She might have been the twin-sister of the pale-faced girl whom I had seen bending over the cradle two nights ago; but her healthier, gladder and prettier sister. When I had gazed on her some moments, the vision faded away as it had come; the last vestige of the brightness died out upon the wall, and I found myself once more in total darkness. Stunned for a time by the sudden changes, I stood watching for the return of the lights and figures; but in vain. By and by my eyes grew accustomed to the obscurity, and I saw the sky glimmering behind the little window which I had left open. I could soon discern the writing-table beside me, and possessed myself of the slips of loose paper which lay upon it. I then made my way to the window. The first streaks of dawn were in the sky as I descended my ladder, and I thanked God that I breathed the fresh morning air once more, and heard the cheering sound of the cocks crowing.

*   *   *

All thought of acting immediately upon last night's strange revelations, almost all memory of them, was for the time banished from my mind by the unexpected trouble of the next few days. That morning I found an alarming change in Frank. Feeling sure that he was going to be ill, I engaged a lodging in a cottage in the neighbourhood, whither we removed before nightfall, leaving the accursed Rath behind us. Before midnight he was in the delirium of a raging fever.

I thought it right to let his poor little fiancée know his state, and wrote to her, trying to alarm her no more than was necessary. On the evening of the third day after my letter went, I was sitting by Frank's bedside, when an unusual bustle outside aroused my curiosity, and going into the cottage kitchen I saw a figure standing in the firelight which seemed a third appearance of that vision of the pale-faced golden-haired girl which was now thoroughly imprinted on my memory – a third, with all the woe of the first and all the beauty of the second. But this was a living, breathing apparition. She was throwing off her bonnet and shawl, and stood there at home in a moment in her plain black dress. I drew my hand across my eyes to make sure that they did not deceive me. I had beheld so many supernatural visions lately that it seemed as though I could scarcely believe in the reality of anything till I had touched it.

'Oh, sir,' said the visitor, 'I am Mary Leonard, and are you poor Frank's friend? Oh, sir, we are all the world to one another, and I could not let him die without coming to see him!'

And here the poor little traveller burst into tears. I cheered her as well as I could, telling her that Frank would soon, I trusted, be out of all danger. She told me that she had thrown up her situation in order to come and nurse him. I said we had got a more experienced nurse than she could be, and then I gave her to the care of our landlady, a motherly countrywoman. After that I went back to Frank's bedside, nor left it for long till he was convalescent. The fever had swept away all that strangeness in his manner which had afflicted me, and he was quite himself again.

There was a joyful meeting of the lovers. The more I saw of Mary Leonard's bright face the more thoroughly was I convinced that she was the living counterpart of the vision I had seen in the burial chamber. I made enquiries as to her birth, and her father's history, and found that she was indeed the grandchild of that Mary Thunder whose history had been so strangely related to me, and the rightful heiress of all those properties which for a few months only had been mine. Under the tree in the orchard, the thirteenth, and that by which I had seen the lady digging, were found the buried deeds which had been described to me. I made an immediate transfer of property, whereupon some others who thought they had a chance of being my heirs disputed the matter with me and went to law. Thus the affair has gained publicity, and become a nine days' wonder. Many things have been in my favour, however: the proving of Mary's birth and of Sir Luke's will, the identification of Lady Thunder's handwriting on the slips of paper which I had brought from the burial chamber; also other matters which a search in that chamber brought to light. I triumphed, and I now go abroad, leaving Frank and his Mary made happy by the possession of what could only have been a burden to me.

So the manuscript ends. Major Thunder fell in battle a few years after the adventure it relates. Frank O'Brien's grandchildren hear of him with gratitude and awe. The Rath has been long since totally dismantled and left to go to ruin.